She willed herself to sta͏ sky, to fight the emotio͏ and made her want to turn to him, take him into her arms, and apologize. He'd let her down, broken her heart, but somehow she'd failed him, too.

She turned in his direction, the heat in her body turning to ice when she saw the way he was looking at her. She hadn't been imagining anything. His dark eyes flashed as he leaned forward, and she couldn't stop it and didn't want to.

With sudden hunger, his mouth met hers, pressing firmly on her hesitant lips. Quickly, and without thinking, she responded...

A MATCH MADE ON MAIN STREET

Book 2
in the Briar Creek Series

OLIVIA MILES

FOREVER

NEW YORK   BOSTON

Copyright © 2015 by Megan Leavell
Excerpt from *Hope Springs on Main Street* Copyright © 2015 by Megan Leavell

Forever
Hachette Book Group
1290 Avenue of the Americas
New York, NY 10104

www.HachetteBookGroup.com

Printed in the United States of America

First Edition: April 2015
10 9 8 7 6 5 4 3 2 1

OPM

Forever is an imprint of Grand Central Publishing.
The Forever name and logo are trademarks of Hachette Book Group, Inc.

The Hachette Speakers Bureau provides a wide range of authors for speaking events. To find out more, go to www.hachettespeakersbureau.com or call (866) 376-6591.

The publisher is not responsible for websites (or their content) that are not owned by the publisher.

ATTENTION CORPORATIONS AND ORGANIZATIONS:
Most HACHETTE BOOK GROUP books are available
at quantity discounts with bulk purchase for educational,
business, or sales promotional use. For information,
please call or write:

Special Markets Department, Hachette Book Group
1290 Avenue of the Americas, New York, NY 10104
Telephone: 1-800-222-6747 Fax: 1-800-477-5925

For Avery

Acknowledgments

I would like to thank my editor, Michele Bidelspach, for her sharp insight, thoughtful guidance, and encouragement with this book. I couldn't have done it without her. I'd also like to thank my copyeditor, Lori Paximadis, for her remarkable attention to detail; my publicist, Julie Paulauski, for her enthusiastic promotional help; and everyone else at Grand Central Publishing who has had a hand in the creation of my books.

Thank you to my family, husband, and daughter for their love and encouragement. Special thanks as well to authors Natalie Charles and Victoria James for their ongoing support.

To all my friends and family who have cheered me on and celebrated with me on this wonderful journey: thank you.

And to my readers: thank you for spending hours with my characters, writing me heartfelt letters, and allowing me the chance to brighten your day the way you have brightened mine. I'm humbled and forever grateful.

A MATCH
MADE ON
MAIN STREET

CHAPTER 1

A strong friendship is *always* the best foundation for a lasting romantic relationship."

Anna Madison stopped arranging the wild blueberry scones on a ceramic tray and frowned. *Not always*, she thought.

Up until now the chatter from the weekly book club had been nothing but a pleasant buzz, a lively and comfortable backdrop to an otherwise quiet morning in the shop, but now Anna strained her ears over the percolating coffee machine to hear the details of the conversation. Sliding the tray onto the polished wood counter, she narrowed her eyes at the group of women who were gathered around the antique farm table near the big bay window of Main Street Books—or the Annex, as the café extension was called—as they were every Saturday morning since the bookstore had reopened. From her distance behind the counter, she watched them sipping cappuccinos and enjoying fresh pastries, and wondered which of them would be foolish enough to make such a grand statement.

Her gaze fell on Rosemary Hastings, sitting at the head of the table, clutching this month's book club selection, *Sense and Sensibility*, with determined hands. Rosemary's ruby-stained lips were pinched with certainty, her back straight and proud, revealing years of professional dance training, her graying hair pulled back in her famous bun.

"I always told my children to start with a friendship first. If you build on that, true love will follow," she continued sagely. The rest of the group nodded their consent or politely sipped their coffee and tea, knowing better than to voice an opinion to the contrary. "Men and women are never only friends," she went on. "A friendship is just the beginning. It *always* blossoms into something more meaningful."

Oh, now this was too much! "Yeah right," Anna muttered. She shook her head and turned her attention to a basket of ginger-fig muffins, a popular item this morning, she noted with satisfaction as she mentally counted out just seven of the twelve she had brought over fresh from her primary restaurant, Fireside Café, down the road.

"Do you disagree, Anna?"

Well, now she'd done it. Anna glanced up to see Rosemary peering at her sharply from across the room, her head tipped in expectation. She sighed, feeling her shoulders sag slightly as ten pairs of eyes waited for her reply. She knew she should leave it—no good would come from starting an argument with Rosemary—and get on with her ever growing to-do list. Since Main Street Books had reopened, Anna was busier than she could have imagined. The expansion of the bookstore's café was a hit, just as her older sister, Grace, had predicted, and business at Fireside hadn't slowed either. She supposed she should be thrilled that everything was off to a good start—God knew she relied on both establishments to be a success so she could pay off the loan she'd taken out to help reinvent their late father's struggling store—but a business didn't run itself.

"What's that, Rosemary?" Anna's younger sister, Jane, came around the corner, clutching a stack of books to her chest. She glanced at the cover of the one on top and then slipped it into its proper slot in the cookbooks section, which bordered the café.

"Your sister here was disagreeing with my statement that men and women cannot just be friends."

"Sure they can!" Jane smiled. "Look at Luke and Grace. They were friends for years before—"

"Before!" Rosemary raised her finger triumphantly into the air. "They were friends *before* they started dating. But I know my son." She began to wag her finger, oddly enough in Anna's direction rather than Jane's. Anna bit back a sigh and swept the crumbs from the counter into her palm, before dusting her hands off over the trash can. "He didn't want to only be friends with Grace. A pretty girl like that? No, no, *no*. He befriended her as a way of getting to know her. To be close to her." She shrugged smugly. "There's always more to it."

Anna snorted, causing Rosemary's smile to immediately fade. She bristled, glancing around her group with an incredulous look, her blue eyes wide with indignation. At least five of the women ducked their heads, pretending to leaf through the pages of their well-thumbed paperbacks. Anna found herself wishing her mother had decided to join the group, but Saturdays were busy for Kathleen's interior design business. Still, a little backup would be nice, and Jane was much too polite to stand up to the likes of Rosemary Hastings, especially because she now worked for her at the dance studio.

"*Always* is a pretty strong word, Mrs. Hastings. Sometimes friendships do evolve, but sometimes they don't." *And sometimes they shouldn't*, she thought, frowning.

"Well, I'm speaking from personal experience," Rosemary huffed.

"As am I." Anna straightened the baskets of pastries on the counter and untied the strings of her apron. She should have left ten minutes ago, and here she was engaging in an utterly pointless debate.

"Oh?" This bit of news seemed to pique Rosemary's interest.

Refusing to elaborate, Anna handed her apron to Jane, who was taking over the afternoon shift while Grace manned the storefront and register. "Well, it's been lovely, but I'm afraid I have to get to the café. Enjoy your book club, ladies!" She smiled warmly, hoping that would put a gracious end to the conversation, but the expression on Rosemary's face said otherwise.

"Anna Madison, in all the years I have known you, I have never once seen you with a male friend. Romantically or otherwise."

Oh, how little she knew. Anna folded her arms across her chest and looked to Jane for reinforcement, but her sister simply raised her eyebrows and turned back to the coffee machine, adding to Anna's mounting frustration.

"Well, that's not true. I've dated plenty of men." One in particular, but she needn't mention that. Ever. No one in Briar Creek knew about the relationship she'd had in culinary school, and she intended to keep it that way.

"Maybe not recently, but there have been men. Lots and lots of men."

From behind her she heard Jane quickly fumble for the tap. The rush of water did little to drown out her soft laughter. Rosemary, however, was not amused. Her lips pinched as she roamed her gaze over Anna's defensive stance. "You work too hard. A pretty girl like you should be married by now."

A gasp escaped from somewhere deep in her gut. Anna gaped at Rosemary's army of hopeless romantics, now all nervously staring at their open paperbacks as if cramming for a test, and looked around the room for someone, anyone, who would find Rosemary's opinions as appalling as she did. She turned to Jane, who had decided to keep her back firmly to the room, and tossed her hands in the air before slapping them down at her hips. "This is the twenty-first century. I'm a career girl. It happens to suit me perfectly fine."

"Now, calm down," Rosemary ordered. "You clearly misunderstood me."

"Did I?" Anna glanced at her watch, and her pulse kicked with fresh anxiety. Already noon and the lunch crowd was probably in full swing.

"I meant you're all work and no play. You deserve to have a little fun."

All work and no play. Anna could think of one person in this town to whom the exact opposite applied. None other than Rosemary's own nephew, Mark Hastings. Yet somehow she didn't hear Rosemary complaining about his single status.

Not that Mark was ever single, she corrected herself. More like Mark was never committed.

"Last I checked, Briar Creek wasn't exactly crawling with available men," she pointed out, leaning back against a bookshelf. Oh, how her legs ached from standing so much. She hadn't stopped since she climbed out of bed this morning. At four o'clock. A vision of a steaming bath and good glass of Cabernet brought a faint smile to her lips. It was Saturday after all, and it wasn't like she had any other plans for her evening. By the time the dinner crowd trickled out and the receipts were looked over, she could be on the couch and in her flannel pajamas by eleven, easy.

She grimaced. Better to keep that thought to herself.

"Oh, I can think of a few available men around here," Rosemary said cryptically, a sly smile playing on her painted lips.

"Well, that's a few more than I can think of," Anna declared. A familiar pang tightened her chest when she thought of Mark, working just down the street at the diner.

Why was she even thinking about him? She knew his reputation, knew it all too well, and she'd decided long ago to stop hoping one day he'd snap out of it. Mark was a flirt. A gorgeous, irresistible flirt. And a cad. Yes, he was a complete cad. And worse was that he knew it. And he had no intention of doing anything about it, either. So really, this had to stop. Right now.

Anna patted her pockets for her sunglasses and realized they were in her bag. Scolding herself for letting her mind wander down paths that should have been long forgotten, she retraced her steps behind the counter and crouched down to collect her belongings from a cabinet. "Are you going to be all right on your own?" she asked her sister as she stood and gestured with her chin to the increasingly troublesome book club.

Jane gave her a rueful smile. "Don't worry. You're forgetting that Rosemary is my boss for twenty hours a week. If you think this is bad, you haven't seen her at the studio. Trust me, you can never plié low enough for that woman."

Rosemary had a good heart despite her firm exterior, but nevertheless Anna didn't appreciate being on the receiving end of unwanted attention. If anyone deserved to be given the third degree in the romance department, it was Mark.

Mark. There she went again, thinking of the one man she should have put out of her mind years ago. Leave it to Rosemary to stir things up.

From across the room, a murmur arose, followed by what sounded an awful lot like squeals of suppressed glee. Jane's eyes sparked with interest. "Do we want to guess?"

"I don't think I even want to know," Anna groaned, hitching her handbag strap higher on her shoulder. She turned slowly to the group, sensing that Rosemary had one last matter to discuss before she could slip out the door.

"The gals and I have discussed it, and we have an idea." Rosemary paused for dramatic effect. "I am going to find you a man."

"Excuse me?" Anna choked on a burst of laughter, but Rosemary's wide smile did not slip. Her hands remained folded primly on her lap, her back ramrod straight, her gaze locked firmly with Anna's, whose eyes had widened in horror.

"You heard me," she said calmly. "I am going to find you a suitable match."

"Oh... please don't."

"Wait, what about me?" Jane interjected, and at that,

every woman who had previously been pretending to ignore the conversation snapped to attention. It wasn't like Jane to have an outburst. "Why Anna and not me?" she repeated, setting her hands on her hips.

Rosemary did a poor job of disguising her shock. "My dear...Anna's been unattached for her entire life! Why, she must be coming up on thirty by now!"

Anna felt her nails embed deeper into her hip, until she feared she might have poked a hole right through her cotton shirt. Only twenty-eight and she was already earning a reputation as an old maid. This was getting worse and worse. Deciding she would only escalate matters by reacting to the insinuation, she said briskly, "I'm the same age as Kara, Mrs. Hastings. And what about her? Why not set up one of your daughters?"

Rosemary waved her hand through the air. "Kara and Molly don't want me meddling in their personal affairs."

And I do? Anna looked past the café to the pedestal tables artfully arranged with books that dotted the storefront, craning her neck to see if another soul could be seen over the tall wooden stacks, but there was no one in sight. Grace was most likely in the back room, going over the inventory lists or joyfully opening the latest shipment of books and planning a new window display, and that left the two younger Madison sisters to keep things afloat. *And my, what a mess of it they were making.*

"What about me?" Jane said again.

Anna stared at her, trying to mask her bewilderment. For a moment she had thought this was Jane's creative way of diverting Rosemary's fixation, but the conviction in her hazel eyes and the pert little lilt of her nose said otherwise, even though it had been only a matter of months since Jane had filed for divorce. "Don't you think it's a little soon?" Anna asked gently.

"It wasn't too soon for Adam! He got a jump start while we were still married!" Jane retorted with a lift of her chin. Sensing the alarm in Anna's expression, she added, "Oh, please. It's hardly a secret." She looked at Rosemary. "Fair's fair. If you can find someone for Anna, you can find someone for me, too."

"But I don't even want to be set up!" Anna wrapped her arm around Jane's shoulder and announced, "Perfect. Mrs. Hastings, you can call on all these so-called available men in Briar Creek and give them Jane's number."

"Nope." Rosemary made a grand show of shaking her head until her dangling earrings caught on her red cashmere scarf, which was loosely draped around her neck. She winced as she gingerly unhooked it, and frowned as she inspected the snag in the material.

"Jane just told you she needs help getting back out there."

"Oh, I heard," Rosemary mused, dropping her scarf with a sigh of defeat. She smiled at Jane fondly. "And I'm going to help you, my dear. On one condition."

Beside her Jane was beaming, but Anna was no fool when it came to matters of the heart. She had been once, but that was a long time ago. "What's that?" Anna hedged, her chest heavy with dread.

"You have to let me set you up, too, Anna." Rosemary hid her triumphant smile behind the rim of her mug.

"No way—"

"Oh, come on!" Jane begged, elbowing her gently. Anna stared into the pleading eyes of her sister, noting the flicker of disappointment she saw pass through them.

It was the same look that had been there for months now, a lingering sadness behind that brave smile. Jane was the strong one, the supportive one, not the demanding one. Jane was the one who would hand you the last ten bucks in her wallet and then silently go without herself. Jane never asked for anything. And here she was, asking Anna for the one thing she didn't want to give.

She'd spent how many years avoiding the very thing she was being asked to do: date. Dating led to falling in love, and falling in love led to heartbreak. Jane of all people should have learned that lesson by now, but from the hopeful look in her expression, for some reason it appeared she had not. Somehow, having the father of her child and the man who had vowed to love her 'til death repeatedly cheat on her, lie to her, and then leave her had not destroyed her sister's belief in love.

"Fine," Anna said through gritted teeth, ignoring the whoop that went up from the table of women. She was too busy focusing on Jane's grateful smile. It was the happiest she had seen her younger sister in months, possibly more, she realized. She blinked quickly, never wanting to think of Jane hurting that way again. "And with that, I'm really leaving now."

"Go, go!" Rosemary said over the ruckus. "I don't know how you can expect to run that place if you spend all day chatting with us."

Anna took a deep breath, this time forcing herself to remain silent, and turned to leave. Jane grabbed her by the arm. "Thank you," she said.

"You owe me," Anna warned as she slid her sunglasses over her nose. She wound her way through the maze of bookshelves and pushed out into the early spring sunshine, wondering how she could get out of this little promise she had made. There was no time in her life for men or dating or any of that nonsense. There was only time for work. That's how it had to be, and that's how she preferred it. Most of the time.

She lifted her chin, focusing on the sidewalk ahead, on the hours of work that would give her the sense of purpose she craved, when panic stopped her dead in her tracks. There, at the corner of Main Street and Second Avenue, was a gray cloud of smoke. A crowd had gathered opposite the familiar brick storefront, and people along the way had stopped to stare.

A fire truck with sirens blazing whizzed by her, forcing her long blond hair to whip across her face, and it was then that Anna started to run. *Not the café*, she silently begged, *please not the café*. She weaved her way through the shocked onlookers, almost knocking over a small child who was grinning at the trucks rushing by, knowing with each step that her worst nightmare was coming true.

Smoke was billowing out the windows now, and broken glass littered the sidewalk. A team of firefighters was jumping off the truck, clutching a long hose. By the time Anna arrived at the Fireside Café, gasping for breath that felt thick and tight in her lungs, there was so much commotion that she couldn't get a straight answer from anyone. Red lights flashed through the soot that filled the air and caused her to cough. The sheriff was marching forward, barking commands, ordering people to stand back. Firemen stretched their arms wide as they formed a barrier and the mass moved slowly back, gathering Anna into its frantic progression.

She stared at the crowd as she stumbled backward,

searching through the blur of her vision for a familiar face, for someone, anyone, to tell her it was all going to be okay, that it was nothing, just a scare.

"Anna, oh God!" Anna whirled around to face her assistant manager, finding some relief in the sight of her friend. Kara's face was stained with tears.

Panic tightened her chest, forcing her out of her haze. "Is anyone in the building?"

"No. No, I don't think so," Kara muttered, shaking her head. She covered her face with both hands as a loud crash split through the town, eliciting a wave of cries from the crowd.

"Probably just a support beam," a gruff voice called out, and Anna felt her knees begin to buckle. Just a support beam. Just a café. No one was hurt—she was safe, she should focus on that. Yet somehow she couldn't. All she could do was stand there, clutching Kara's arm and watching helplessly as everything she had built for herself, everything she depended on, came crashing down around her. Just like everything did in the end.

The Saturday crowd was bustling in Hastings. Every table was filled and the counter was lined with the regulars, mostly bachelors and widowers looking for good company, strong coffee, and Mark's popular weekend special, the Hastings Scramble, which was about as creative as things got around here, much to Mark's disappointment.

The wait was seven families deep, huddled together near the front door or lining the benches outside the glass window that gave a full view of Main Street's shops. Even Jackson Jones, Briar Creek's mayor, was staring down the man and woman lingering at his favorite table in the corner, clutching coffee mugs, and skimming the newspaper. From across the crowded room, Mark could sense the impatience in his face, but like the mayor or the tired-looking couple with a squirming toddler, no one showed any sign of turning away. If they wanted Saturday brunch, there was only one place in town that delivered, and this was it.

Of course, Mark supposed there was always the Fire-side Café, but that was different—a little trendier, a little less kid-friendly. Or so he'd been told by loyal patrons. Mark had never stepped foot in that establishment and he didn't intend to start now. He and Anna Madison weren't exactly on speaking terms these days, and her restaurant made him uneasy. Even if his mother owned the building, the entire place was just a longstanding reminder of how cruel life could be.

"Refill?" Mark took the pot of premium roast from the burner and held it up to his cousin Luke, another Saturday staple, though Mark had to wonder how much longer that would last. Since Luke and Grace Madison had rekindled their relationship over Christmas, Luke was spending less time shooting pool and meeting for a beer and more time holed up in his luxury log cabin making up for lost time with his high school sweetheart.

"You know you can kick me out at any time," Luke said as Mark topped him off.

Mark spared a wry grin and started a fresh brew, relieved that Luke was sticking around a few minutes longer, even though he hated to admit it. After Luke's wife died two years ago, Luke quietly immersed himself in Mark's life, joining him for dinners and holidays, and any other excuse not to be alone. Mark knew the feeling and was happy to return the favor Luke had paid him all those years ago, when they were just kids and Mark's entire world felt like it had been ripped out from under him. But now Luke had Grace and Mark had…He stiffened. He had what he needed. Himself. His dog. His dreams of something better than this joint. Anything beyond that was trouble.

From across the room Mark heard a plate crash to the floor and a baby wail at a decibel level that caused him to wince. His newest waitress scrambled to the counter, red-faced and frazzled, hissing to the cook through the service window, "Another garden omelet with extra hash browns. And, um, hurry, if you can." She met Mark's gaze and lowered her lashes before ducking back into the throngs, nearly crashing into Jackson Jones, who was finally being seated after his twenty-minute wait.

"Popular spot today," Luke commented, stirring his coffee.

Mark grunted something of a response.

Luke set down the spoon and frowned. "I'd think you'd be pleased with all the foot traffic. It's what you set out to do, after all."

Hardly. Mark tossed a rag over his shoulder and poured himself a coffee, drinking it black. Frustration tightened his gut, and he pushed back the things he really wanted to say. "Maybe I'll mix things up around here. Change the menu."

He was compromising again, selling himself short, and the lack of energy he felt for the idea was evident in his voice. He leaned back against the far counter and stared into his mug, feeling like he was looking into the black hole of his future, and swallowed the last of it.

Hastings was supposed to be a temporary stop, a way to help out his mother and earn a few bucks while he figured things out. It was never supposed to be a long-term plan, yet somehow there didn't seem to be an end date. He'd been thinking about leaving this town for years. At a certain point, he just had to pack his bags and do it. Start fresh. Stop holding on to things that were never meant to be. Leave the past in the past. *Where it belonged.*

"What kind of food would you offer?" Luke asked,

and Mark felt himself getting downright excited, the way he always did when he started brainstorming his plans.

"I was thinking modern American. A fresh twist on classic comfort foods." Only he wasn't thinking of this menu for Hastings. Or for any place in Briar Creek. But Luke didn't need to know that. Not yet, at least.

From the end of the counter, Arnie Schultz coughed and sputtered, "Modern American? Fresh twist on classic comfort food?" He snorted and bit into a greasy strip of bacon, shaking his head with a chuckle. "You getting all fancy on us, Mark? Too good for the diner?"

Mark inwardly cursed. Yep, he never should have said anything. Not until he had the idea off the ground, anyway. If he ever had it off the ground. Ideas cost money, and then there was this place to think about…

"Forget him," Luke said, finishing his coffee. He leaned into his elbows on the counter, meeting Arnie's eye, and jerked his thumb in Mark's direction. "This guy is a certified chef, you know."

Arnie nodded and gulped his orange juice. "And he slings the best hash around. That's the kind of food I like. That's why I'm here seven mornings a week."

"It's just talk, Arnie. Just an idea." *Just a pipe dream.* Mark scrubbed at some spilled syrup on the counter, grumbling to himself.

It was the same internal argument he had every time he started letting his mind run with thoughts of a new place. Thinking about what it could be was one thing, setting things into motion was another. The restaurant business was volatile—you could be hot one month and out of business by the next—he'd seen it with his own father to know how quickly things could turn. Hastings was a steady stream of income. A sure thing. Few things in life were.

He rubbed at his forehead, feeling the onset of a headache. The noise from the room often did it to him, which was why he kept a bottle of aspirin in his back pocket. He pulled it out now and shook one into his palm before bringing it to his mouth and swallowing it dry.

A fire truck roared by at full speed, lights blaring, its horn warning cars to clear Briar Creek's main strip. The group of people waiting outside the diner rose from their benches, and through the glass Mark could see the frantic movement in their hands, the way their gazes all trailed to something in the distance.

Mark jutted his chin to Luke. "That's the second one." He tossed the empty aspirin bottle in the trash and frowned out the window. "Think there's something going on?"

Standing, Luke pulled his wallet from his jacket pocket and peeled off a twenty. "Only one way to find out."

Mark handed a menu to the next customer, who eagerly slid into his cousin's place, and began reciting the daily specials—though he didn't think there was anything particularly special about them—when Luke's voice jarred his attention to the front of the room.

"It's Fireside!" Luke shouted. The squeak of metal chair legs pushing against the well-worn floorboards was the only sound louder than the murmurs and gasps from every customer in the room, who abandoned their eggs and pancakes to run to the window and take in the scene.

A hard knot formed in Mark's stomach. *Anna.*

Tossing down his rag, he stepped around the counter, heading for the door. Even through the mass of people pushing their way to the front of the diner, he could see the anguish in Luke's face and the panic in his eyes. He knew what Luke was thinking, where his mind had gone: Grace.

Luke had already lost his first wife. Mark knew all too well how it felt to fear another loss.

"She's at the bookstore," Mark said firmly, stepping quickly into the role he'd occupied since he was ten, the head of the Hastings family, the provider, the rock, but his mind was spinning, his heart hammering in his chest, and even as he said the words, he was thinking not of Grace, but of her sister. "It's Saturday. Grace is always at Main Street Books on Saturdays." *But Anna never leaves Fireside.* It was her passion, her life. A dark thought took hold when he considered it her possible undoing. Nothing good ever came from that place.

Luke nodded once, but the shadow that darkened his blue eyes told Mark he wasn't convinced. "Kara works at the café on weekends. She covers while Anna's at the bookstore."

Relief was quickly replaced with newfound dread for Luke's sister. Mark pushed open the door. "Come on. No use standing here worrying."

Outside, the air was cloudy with smoke. They hurried the four blocks south, where barricades had been set up around the corner of Main Street and Second Avenue. Firefighters swarmed outside the Fireside Café, ordering people to stay back. Mark spotted Sam Logan, the town sheriff, huddled with a team of men, and caught a glimpse of a bright pink sweater and a sweep of honey blond hair. *Anna.*

As she noticed them approach, she broke away from her conversation with Sam and ran toward Luke, her silky hair swinging behind her, her turquoise eyes lit with tears. Mark stopped walking, feeling his jaw set, the knot in his stomach tighten its grip.

It was better for Luke to take care of this. He was practically a member of the Madison family by now. He and Grace had dated for years growing up; Anna was like a kid sister to him.

To Mark, however, she was so much more. Or she had been. Once.

From a few feet away, Mark watched his cousin embrace Anna, then Kara, and heard the panic in Luke's voice when he managed the single question: "Grace?"

Anna shook her head, managing a trace of a smile. "She's fine. She wasn't here."

"Oh, thank God."

Catching Anna's eye, Mark cleared his throat and took a step forward. "Everyone okay?"

Even now, in the midst of this chaos, with her business burning to ash behind her, she had the nerve to press her lips together and lift her chin, giving him a full view of that perfectly upturned nose. Mark balled his hands at his sides, willing himself not to lose his temper. Briar Creek was a small community, damn it, and he had every right to know if one of his friends or, heaven forbid, another family member had been in that café when the fire broke out. He had a right to know if she was okay. Even if they didn't speak, even if they were both hell-bent on pretending they had never meant anything to each other, she had meant a great deal to him once.

He swept his gaze over her, ignoring the way the air stalled in his lungs as his eyes came to rest on her lips, slightly parted, and her eyes, so clear and blue. It had been a long time since he'd allowed himself to look at her. A long time since she'd let him. He pulled in a breath, checking himself right there.

"No one was injured," Anna said coolly. She slid her eyes back to Luke, dismissing him, and Mark grit his teeth against mounting frustration. It had been more than seven years since they'd broken up, and she was still punishing him for it.

Cursing under his breath, he pulled his phone from his pocket, but Sam Logan appeared beside him, his sheriff badge dusted in soot. "Your mom's on her way. I called her first thing; said she's a good ninety minutes out, visiting a friend. I hope she has insurance."

Mark frowned. His mother had been through hell and back twice in her life. Three times if you counted her husband abandoning her and leaving her with two small boys and a stack of bills that could have tiled the roof of their house. She'd started working at the diner, back when it was run by old Gary Sullivan. The stretch of buildings that spanned Second to Third Avenue along Main Street was the only good thing Mark's father left in his wake, his mother now claimed, but that was only now, once she had tenants to keep it going. It was easy to forget those dark days when his dad's restaurant space sat empty and the financial loss nearly destroyed her.

Nearly killed her, Mark thought angrily.

"What the hell happened?" he asked, surveying the scene. Grease fires could spread fast, but from the looks of it, the damage was extensive.

Sam shook his head. "We can't know for sure just yet—probably electrical. The fire started in the kitchen."

Mark let out a low whistle. "Anything salvaged?"

"Not much," Sam said grimly, and Mark shook his head in disappointment. He glanced at Anna, who was still being comforted by Luke, with Kara standing tearfully at her side, wiping her eyes with a balled-up tissue. It suddenly hit Mark that Anna wasn't shedding a tear. Her usual porcelain complexion was a shade whiter than normal, her blue eyes a bit brighter, but instead of falling to her knees or breaking down in hysterics as some in her position might do, she simply stood there, shell-shocked, listening to Luke's reassuring words.

She was stoic that way. Hardened almost. He'd seen it in her from a distance over the years, admiring it almost, the way she set her mind to building her restaurant and never let a hard day tear her down. From across the crowded church at her father's funeral last spring, he'd seen her stand at her mother's side, her jaw set, her eyes somewhere far away.

He couldn't say he'd be capable of the same himself. Hell, he was still recovering from the loss of his father more than twenty years ago. If you could even call it a loss.

He rolled back on his heels, sucking in a breath as he broke his stare. He and Anna hadn't spoken more than a few stilted words since his final year at culinary school after he'd put an end to their relationship. Even working blocks from each other on Main Street for nearly six years since hadn't broken her down. She was determined to shut him out. To punish him. To remind him every damn day of how much he'd hurt her.

From the end of Main Street he saw Grace and Jane sprinting at full speed, followed by a pack of middle-aged women led by none other than his aunt Rosemary, her oversized crimson scarf flapping in the wind. He stifled a grin, sobering himself. The woman sure could run, even in heels. He supposed it was all those years of self-discipline and dancing.

"What in God's name happened?" she demanded, jerking her head from Luke to Mark as she grabbed Kara, holding her daughter close. Noticing Anna, she extended an arm to bring her into the fold, and Mark's brow furrowed when he saw the way Anna allowed herself to be held, the way she rested her head on Rosemary's small shoulder and let his aunt stroke her hair. He was the one she used to turn to—first as a friend, then as something more.

"We're all okay, Mom," Kara reassured her.

"This is going to *devastate* Sharon." Rosemary released Anna and shook her head, looking up at the site of his father's former restaurant. Tavern on Main. Once again, in a state of disaster. "Does she know yet, Mark?"

"She's on her way." Mark hated to think of his mother's reaction when she saw the site. He shoved his hands in his pockets and squinted at the familiar storefront, which only this morning had been cheerfully dotted with potted red geraniums and sunny marigolds. The large, lead-paned window had been shattered, and shards of glass littered the sidewalk. The little wrought iron tables and chairs Anna kept outside on warmer days had been turned over in the chaos.

Cursed. The place was just cursed. No good ever came from it. Not then. Not now. His mother should have sold the building years ago.

"What am I going to do?" Anna asked to no one in particular.

"You have insurance, don't you?" Grace asked, her

expression lined with worry. Anna nodded, and blinked several times.

"But the bookstore," Anna hissed, and Grace shot a look of panic to Luke. "I relied on my kitchen to do all the baking for the Annex. We only have a counter and limited equipment there. I can't exactly bake scones in a toaster oven!"

Everyone was gathered around Anna now, studying her with concern. Mark glanced around at the Madison sisters, Luke, and the staff from the café, and decided it was time to leave. He wasn't doing any good by standing around, watching the spectacle, and, besides, Anna wouldn't want him here. She'd made that more than clear over the years, never returning so much as a wave from a distance until he'd finally given up, and her stance hadn't wavered with time.

Much as he wished it would.

"We'll just have to think of a short-term solution," Grace said firmly as Mark started to turn away.

"And I have the perfect one," Rosemary declared. Without even looking in Mark's direction, she swung out an arm and grabbed him by the wrist, just before he was out of reach. "You can use the diner's kitchen until you've rebuilt the café. Mark won't mind."

Mark and Anna exchanged frozen looks. He stared at Anna, his jaw set, and willed her to speak first. Out of the corner of his eye he could see his aunt's satisfied smile.

"I..." Anna blinked rapidly and then shifted her gaze to Rosemary. "I don't know what to say."

Rosemary leaned forward and patted Anna's arm. "Of course you don't. You're in shock!" Glancing pointedly at Mark, she continued, "You'll work in Mark's kitchen, and that way you can still keep the bookstore café open. It's a perfect solution."

Anna looked unconvinced, but Grace was thanking Rosemary profusely, and Jane looked nearly weak with relief. "It *is* one less thing to worry about," Anna murmured, and Mark felt his pulse race. She wouldn't—not Anna—in *his* kitchen? After all this time? Alarm bells went off in his head, and they had nothing to do with the flashing blue and red lights that reflected off every shop window.

Rosemary reached down and took one of Anna's hands in her own. "Then it's settled," she said, her voice clear and authoritative, and the flash in her eyes told Mark there was no room for argument.

Like he dared to think there ever was. Even if his aunt were one to back down, he'd have to be the bastard of the century to turn his back on the community now. He'd have to be like his father. And he'd vowed a long time ago not to go down that path.

CHAPTER 3

As if the day wasn't already bad enough, someone had the brilliant idea to take stock of the events at Hastings. Rosemary, Anna realized, hooking an accusatory glance in her direction. Rosemary was full of suggestions today.

The fire had been extinguished more than half an hour earlier, but the trucks still remained, blocking the intersection as heavily booted workers climbed through the rubble, inspecting the scene for a source, shouting out muffled orders she couldn't make out from this distance. Anna kept her back firmly to the Fireside Café. Every time she caught a glimpse of its smashed windows she felt almost sick, and poor Kara's face went pale in alarm. She couldn't afford to indulge her mounting emotions. She had a sixty-thousand-dollar loan hanging over her head from that bookstore expansion, and without the income from the café, there was no way to meet the monthly payments.

It had seemed like such a great investment back in December, when Grace had approached her with the plan to save their father's dusty old bookstore before its lease expired. Her heart had literally sped up as Grace detailed her vision for renting out the neighboring vacant storefront and tearing down the wall, adding an adjacent café where patrons could linger over books and sip coffee. It was exactly what had been missing from Main Street Books all along, and with the foot traffic she was getting at Fireside, it seemed like the time to branch out had never been better.

My, how wrong she had been. Not much more than a month into opening the Annex, and her primary source of income was gone.

"Don't mind the mess," Mark instructed, as the group narrowed down to a single file line and fed into the diner. Anna caught the pity in his soft brown eyes and shifted her gaze in the opposite direction.

It was far too late for him to start giving her any consideration.

This was her first time in Hastings since Mark had taken it over from his mother after he'd graduated culinary school seven years ago, and she surveyed the establishment with impassive interest. Usually she avoided this stretch of Main Street, and even on the few times she drove past the diner, she kept her eyes fixed to the road in front of her, telling herself that she was being a responsible driver—there were kids around, after all—and forcing herself to resist the temptation to sneak a peek into Mark's haven. It would be just her luck that the moment she dared to drift her attention through the windows, Mark would somehow look up and see her car crawling by, and she certainly couldn't have that.

Anna sunk herself into the nearest chair and rested her chin in her hand. Beneath her elbow there was a distinctive feeling of grease on the Formica surface. She slid a plate of congealed eggs to the opposite end of the table, her depression growing.

Mark was working the room, quickly piling plates on his forearm and tucking in chairs with the other. He was alert and in control, and it didn't escape Anna that this was precisely what she always found so appealing about him, what had made her fall for him in the first place. She never could resist that take-charge demeanor. Or that grin.

God help her, what was she going on about? The man was a cad. A shameless, ruthless playboy. He'd more or less admitted it to her face all those years ago, even if his actions had spoken volumes long before he'd had the decency to be direct and cut things off. They'd only been romantically involved for four bliss-filled months, but their connection had been two years in the making. He'd been her friend, her closest friend, and friends, at the very least, weren't supposed to dump you. Yet he had. One day, it was like the light switched off, and he was gone. He stopped calling, started making up excuses not to get together, and then, only then, did he finally sit her down and set her straight. *I can't give you what you're looking for. We're not looking for the same things.*

Damn right they weren't! It only took a week after their breakup for him to take up with another girl. Mark was looking for a flavor of the week, and she was ... Well, she wasn't looking for anyone anymore. The only person you could depend on in life was yourself. When you were in control of your own path, no one could come along and take it out from under you.

At least that's what she had thought until today.

"Mark!" Rosemary settled herself into a chair next to Kara and wrinkled her nose as she pinched a dirty napkin between her thumb and index finger. "Bring these poor girls some coffee. And how about a slice of that fresh lemon meringue pie while you're at it?"

Anna slunk deeper into her chair and skirted her eyes to Mark, whose jaw remained set, his brow pulled tight. He hesitated, seeming to look to her for confirmation, and then gave a tight grin. "Lemon meringue all around."

"Oh, none for me," Rosemary corrected. "Dancer's figure and all." She leaned back and patted her flat stomach.

Jane quietly set down the fork she had just eagerly unfolded from a napkin at the next table. Anna knew that Jane wasn't entirely comfortable slipping into tights and leotards every day to teach her ballet lessons, even if she was probably prettier than ever before. Motherhood brought out a glow in Jane. A sense of purpose. It was because of her daughter, Sophie, that Jane had overcome the struggle of the past year. First losing their father. Then the end of her marriage.

Now this, Anna couldn't help but think. Just when they were all getting on their feet again, excited over the grand reopening of their father's bookstore, everything had to fall apart.

She motioned Jane over to her table, her motivation being purely selfish in that moment. If Jane took the spot that meant Mark couldn't.

Not that he would, of course. Mark avoided her as much as she avoided him. She saw the way his eyes shifted from hers if they happened to pass each other on the sidewalk, the way he had mastered the art of talking to everyone at a party but her. It was a silent agreement that suited them both fine. Even if it did sting.

Sometimes, when she saw him across the crowded bar

on a weekend night, or darted away from his line of vision at the grocery store and then raced to the checkout, often forgoing half the items on her list that hadn't yet made it to her cart, she felt as if it was all in her head, as if they had never known each other at all. Never laughed. Never kissed.

Never created a child together.

Already the dark thoughts she'd tried to keep at bay were stirring inside her, bringing her back to times when she'd felt just as hopeless as she did now—just as alone and lacking a sense of purpose. If she allowed herself to give in to it, she wasn't sure she would ever recover; the only way she'd managed was to keep busy, to move forward, and to work until she was so tired she dropped into bed at night.

"Sam said they managed to control the structural damage," Mark was saying as he delivered the slices of pie.

"Thank God for that," came Rosemary's reply.

"The kitchen was the most affected, but the water damage from the sprinklers will probably take a toll," Anna said, cringing.

"I feel so responsible," Kara cut in. "I was manning the bakery counter. I didn't even know what was happening in the kitchen until it was too late . . ."

"It's not your fault," Anna told her. "It's no one's fault." Still, a part of her wondered if she could have prevented it had she not been lingering at the bookstore, thinking about *Mark*.

Through her blurred vision a ceramic mug appeared before her, steaming with hot coffee. Anna blinked quickly—she'd come too far to unravel now. Emotions didn't suit her, and they served no purpose either. Crying over what was done was pointless. It couldn't bring back what was lost, no matter how much she wished it could.

Straightening her back, she reached for a creamer from the little bowl in the center of the table, added a sprinkle of sugar from the canister, and tapped the teaspoon on the edge of the mug before setting it down on a napkin. She could feel Mark's eyes boring through her as she brought it to her lips. *Not half bad*, she considered, and her expression must have shown it.

She glanced up to find Mark smirking. He folded his muscular forearms across his chest and turned on his heel, his stance a bit straighter than it had been just a moment ago as evidenced by the broad shoulders stretching against the tight green T-shirt. Anna rolled her eyes to the ceiling and sucked in a breath. So help her, she would not let him get the better of her. She would not react to him—she had made that promise to herself years ago.

Mark was nothing to her. Nothing. Even if he had once been everything.

She slid her plate to Jane and said, "Here. I'm not hungry." The truth was she was famished. She hadn't eaten since she'd made a grilled cheese and heirloom tomato sandwich at six o'clock last night and chased it with a double espresso before the dinner rush. About six months ago, they'd expanded the menu at Fireside to accommodate dinner on the weekends, and it had been a wild success. The opening night, she'd been forced to turn people away, and within weeks they were taking reservations. The demand had been enough for her to take the risk and agree to the loan for the renovation of the bookstore. Kara joined the café as the assistant manager, taking over weekend shifts and helping with the extended Friday night dinner hours. She had a desire to learn, and Anna had envisioned putting her in charge of the dessert station, maybe even adding a sous chef, and then increasing their hours to five nights a week, with Mondays and Tuesdays off. Instead...she'd be lucky to have a restaurant at all now.

Her stomach growled, whether from anxiety or hunger, she wasn't sure. She eyed the strange little cat-shaped clock with the wagging tail perched on the top of the cash register and realized it was already ten past three. She had no food in her house since she normally ate at the café, but there was no way she was eating that pie. No matter how delectable it looked.

If experience taught her anything, it was probably equally delicious, too. Mark had always been a rising star in culinary school, and his dishes were inventive. She'd imagined him running some chic and trendy restaurant.

And she'd imagined herself at his side.

Catching herself, she shook her head clear, banishing all images of Mark's former self. She swept her gaze quickly over the room, hoping not to look overtly interested in what she saw. Red vinyl booths edged the far wall, and tables for four were clustered in a haphazard pattern. It looked no different than she remembered it from when she was a kid. She knew it was their family place now, that Mark had stepped in when his mom was first diagnosed with cancer, and again after his graduation from culinary school when she relapsed. Still, Sharon had been well for years, and she couldn't help thinking that Mark could do a heck of a lot better than this.

"How long do you think it will take the insurance adjuster to assess the damage?" Grace asked, her brow pinched with worry.

Everyone began to talk at once, but all Anna could make out was the beat of her heart, pounding in her ears. That *loan*.

They had agreed that Grace would run Main Street Books, and Anna would oversee the Annex by supplying food and covering a few shifts, until things picked up and she could become a silent partner. While Grace had sunk her savings into leasing both storefronts for a year, Anna had been the one with enough security to garner the loan from the bank to oversee the expansion and renovation. In time, Anna was certain that their father's new and improved shop would turn a profit, but it would take a while to cover their costs, and until that happened, she was relying on income from Fireside to meet the monthly payment. Grace knew this, of course. What she didn't know was how little savings Anna had. She'd sunk most of her earnings into bettering her businesses—adding new equipment or a new piece of furniture and, as of late, adding new staff. She had plans to grow Fireside, build it into something that would meet demand, and that didn't come free.

Everything had been going so well, chugging along in line with her plan.

Something inside her panged when she thought of the last time her plans had been yanked out from under her, without warning, without a cushion to catch her fall. Reality was hard. Shame on her for getting too comfortable.

Mark held out a glass of water in an emerald-tinted plastic tumbler. "Drink this." His voice was gruff and commanding, and, though she hated to admit it, she appreciated the fact that someone was taking over, telling her what to do, because right then she didn't have a clue.

She took it from him and brought it to her lips. "Thanks," she managed, catching the sincerity in her tone. From the softened expression in his eyes, he'd caught it, too.

With a quick nod of the head he turned away and began

piling more dirty dishes onto a tray. Anna took another sip from the cup, wishing it was a magical potion, or even a glass of Scotch, instead of tap water.

Sam Logan appeared in the doorway. "The team will be on site for the next few hours. We're taping off the premises and we ask that you don't enter until we've cleared it for safety." He paused, lowering his head slightly before turning to her. "We'll have a full report to you and Sharon Hastings once we've confirmed the source."

The sheriff's phone began to vibrate in his hand, and without a word he connected the call. Anna watched him walk away, feeling a weight of unease settle over her chest. From two tables over, she caught Rosemary watching her sharply.

"Nice young man, that sheriff," she observed. "Handsome, too."

Oh, for crying out loud! Anna balled the napkin in her hand, rubbing it between her fingers until the thin material pulled apart.

She frowned out the window, and her breath caught when she looked over to see Mark watching her carefully, a lock of wavy brown hair spilling over his forehead, his eyes dark as midnight, unwavering in their hold. She held his gaze, waiting to see a hint of a smile, a whisper of the person she had once known and cared for, but any connection they had once shared was gone. He was a stranger now, and maybe she had wanted it that way, willed it that way, even.

But damn it if he wasn't a handsome stranger.

Who was she kidding? Sam—or anyone else in this town for that matter—had nothing compared to Mark. No one did.

CHAPTER 4

Anna accepted a glass of wine from the bartender and took a long, cool sip. "I don't know why I let you talk me into this," she said to her sisters, who were scrutinizing her every move with watchful expressions.

"Feeling sorry for yourself at home won't do you any good," Grace said.

Jane nodded her agreement. "It's better to distract yourself."

Anna took another gulp of wine. Jane had her there.

"Order another," Grace suggested, motioning to Anna's half-empty glass. "Drinks are on me tonight." She waited until Anna had finished her first glass of Chardonnay and a second was being poured before leaning forward and lowering her voice. "I wanted to talk to you about the loan for Main Street Books."

"Don't worry," Anna said with more conviction than she felt. "The loan will be covered. I have some savings." *Some* was the appropriate way of describing the state of her bank account. She had about enough to cover one payment on that loan—two if she stretched. Sharon Hastings had been optimistic when they'd spoken on the phone, saying that Fireside could reopen within three months. Anna wanted to believe her landlord, but that still left her two months to worry about.

"You know if we need any help, Luke will pitch in—"

Anna shook her head firmly. Taking financial help from Luke was not an option. Fireside was hers. She'd dreamed it, created it, built it. All on her own, without Mark. Without anyone.

She'd spent nearly six years since returning to Briar Creek showing Mark how much better her life was without him in it. She'd be damned if she let him see that she couldn't succeed on her own after all.

"Grace, it's fine." Anna took a long sip of her wine, happy that it was chilled. It was always too warm in the pub, but she suspected tonight her body was reacting to the waves of panic that hit her at every turn.

Grace looked unconvinced. "If you're sure..."

"Of course, I'm sure," she said quickly, though she'd never been further from it.

Grace flagged the bartender and ordered another drink for herself. "That was clever of Rosemary to think of sharing the diner's kitchen."

Clever, yes. Anna could think of another word for it, too. She'd been caught off guard, in a state of shock, at her lowest, and her mind was buzzing. She couldn't have formed a clear thought if she'd tried, and she wasn't quick enough to think of an excuse on the spot. Not with Mark's deep-set gaze locked on hers, not when every nerve in her body tingled with the awareness of his proximity.

Anna pressed her fingers to her forehead and closed

her eyes briefly before taking another sip of wine. "That. Well...I'm still wondering if there's another way." She'd been thinking about it all afternoon, when she wasn't busy worrying about finding contractors, dealing with insurance claims, and protecting her loyal staff. And, oh, covering that loan, not to mention her apartment rent and other bills.

"Another way?" Grace frowned. "Is this because of Mark? I know you two have never really gotten along, but he's being nice, Anna. He's offering you the use of his kitchen!"

"I know," Anna sighed, looking away. The room was buzzing, and all around her were groups of people— laughing, smiling, happy people. People who didn't have to wake up tomorrow and face the person who had broken their heart and then stomped all over it.

Alone in a kitchen with Mark, day after day...She couldn't think of anything worse. Or, sadly, anything more desirable.

"I still don't understand why you and Mark don't get along," Jane commented. "When you were younger you got along just fine. I thought you guys were friends at culinary school, too. Is the restaurant business in Briar Creek really that competitive?"

When their friendship took a romantic turn, Anna and Mark had agreed to keep their relationship to themselves, fearing that the bond between their families would only add unnecessary pressure. Later, she was grateful for their decision—it meant she could walk around town without being reminded of what they had once shared. Well, in theory.

Jane was looking at her with interest, and for a brief

moment Anna considered telling her sisters everything. She could just imagine the surprise on their faces when she told them that, actually, she and Mark had gotten along very well at one point in time. Well enough to plan a future together. A future that had never happened.

Her heart was beginning to pound at the memory of their breakup, bringing every painful detail back to the surface. He'd been in her arms one day, flirting with some girl the next, acting like he didn't care, like it was so easy for him to just move on with his life, to forget her, forget the summer they'd shared, the plans they'd put into place to open a restaurant together. Better not to think about it, she'd told herself a long time ago. She couldn't change the past and undo the fatal mistake of trusting the wrong man, but she sure as hell could make certain she never repeated it again.

"I was thinking of trying to do some of the baking at home." As she heard her words, she knew she was being unrealistic, and newfound dread tightened in her chest.

Grace tipped her head. "No offense, Anna, but your kitchen is pretty small. And you only have one oven. The diner has an industrial-sized kitchen."

"Besides, isn't there some health code about stuff like that?" Jane asked.

Of course she couldn't rely solely on her kitchen. A couple dozen muffins, sure, but enough pastries and scones and gourmet sandwiches to feed any loyal customers who might transfer their support to the Annex while Fireside was rebuilt? Impossible.

She groaned inwardly and took another sip of her drink, waiting for its sweet effect to take hold. She could still remember when she opened Fireside Café; this summer would mark its sixth anniversary. She'd built that business from the ground up, pinched and saved for it and worked for nineteen hours a day sometimes to keep it going. Its success had surpassed her wildest hopes, and she knew in time the Annex would, too. Grace was counting on her. Their dad, God rest his soul, was, too.

She'd come too far to let Mark win now. *He's not worth it.*

"You're right," she said breezily. "I don't know what I was thinking. It's just a pain to share a kitchen, especially when it's not your own." *Especially when you're sharing it with your ex.*

She began idly folding a cocktail napkin into the shape of a small sailboat to keep from looking at her sisters. Opening up about Mark was never going to be a good idea. Grace would tell Luke and Luke would tell Mark, and the last thing she needed was for Mark to think she was still licking her wounds. Or that she ever had.

And oh, had she . . .

"Speak of the devil." Jane jutted her chin toward the door. Sure enough, Mark was standing in the doorway, casually combing a hand through his dark brown hair as his date for the evening tap danced around him in heels that were way too high for this slick floor.

Grace craned her neck to get a better look. "He's seeing *her* now?"

Jane nodded while Anna eyed Nicole Johnson, the local preschool teacher, from across the room, feeling a sickness coat her stomach. She couldn't help it; she was jealous. Jealous of a girl who would no doubt be in tears by next weekend, but jealous nonetheless of the joy in her face at this moment.

Mark had that kind of effect on people. She should know.

"Sophie told me that all Miss Johnson can talk about is her new boyfriend," Jane said.

"Well, that's not a very appropriate thing to discuss with a group of four-year-olds." Anna eyed her empty glass and signaled to the bartender for another.

"On the house," he said, tucking a square napkin under a fresh glass of Chardonnay.

Anna shifted in her seat. "Oh. I couldn't...Thanks." She forced a tight smile. She understood. When bad things happened to people, you wanted to do what you could to help, no matter how small the effort, and in Briar Creek, people pulled together in times of need.

Even Mark, she thought, and her stomach rolled over at the thought of walking into that diner tomorrow morning. What would she even say to him? Now, after all these years of practiced silence? She'd be forced to interact, to let a wall down. She'd worked so hard to keep it up.

She let her attention roam back to Mark, knowing she should be used to seeing him with a date by now. Nicole was dressed in a sequined miniskirt, fishnet tights, and a transparent tank top that left little to the imagination. And those shoes! Anna wouldn't be surprised if by the end of the night Mark had to carry her to her front door. She narrowed her eyes at the thought and took another sip of wine.

"A few of the kids have apparently asked if she has a husband," Jane said, "and she's been sure to let them know she does have someone special in her life."

Beside her, Grace snorted. "For about three weeks! Just a few months ago she had her sights set on Luke. Now Mark. Who's next?"

"Exactly. Who's next? It's only a matter of days before

Mark gets bored and forgets all about her," Anna said, surprised at the sharpness in her tone. For a strange second, she felt sorry for Nicole. She was too caught up in Mark's charms to realize his true nature.

Her sisters blinked at her and, after a quick exchange of glances, looked down at their glasses. Anna turned away from the spectacle and went back to folding her napkin—a nervous habit she'd developed from spending too much time in restaurants. Anything to get her mind off the man somewhere in this room, the man who could pretend she didn't even exist, who couldn't even come up to her and say hello, even after what she had been through. Even though they were about to be sharing a kitchen. Even though they'd once shared so much more than that.

"Hello."

She jumped. Her hands, which had just reached for the stem of her wineglass, now tipped it over, and the cool, golden liquid flowed freely over the polished surface of the bar. The bartender quickly grabbed a rag as Anna dabbed at what she could.

Anna stiffened as Mark's hand slid beside hers, helping with the effort. She could feel the heat of his body close to hers, the hard wall of his chest pressed against her back. She heaved a breath. Her heart was pounding. She hadn't been this close to him in—

"Something sweet!" Nicole's high-pitched voice cut through her thoughts, forcing her back to reality. Anna blinked and shifted her gaze to Mark. The air locked in her chest when she saw him watching her, his deep-set eyes locked with hers, his face so close she could skim his lips with her own if she wanted to and God, did she want to. *Badly.*

She swallowed hard and tucked a strand of hair behind her ear, breaking his hold on her. "Thanks," she managed.

"Any time." His gaze lingered, his voice as smooth as the purr of an engine, and Anna felt something inside her uncoil, bringing back all those feelings she had tried so hard to deny. She lingered on his mouth, feeling her stomach twist as she replayed their first kiss. They both had jobs on the Cape that summer, working at one of those seasonal spots on the beach. They'd gone out after their shift ended, just like they had every night that first week there, but that night something was different. The sun was fading, and the sky glowed pink and orange. Waves lapped at their bare feet as they walked along the coast, falling into a natural step—it was always so natural with Mark. She was laughing as he told her about something that had happened that day—some funny conversation with a customer—but instead of joining in, he'd stopped talking, and watched her. The merriment left his eyes, replaced with something far more intense, and suddenly he was kissing her, his lips gently exploring hers, his hand light on her waist at first and then reaching back to draw her close. She hadn't had time to react or hesitate. She knew how he was—that he bounced from girl to girl, never staying with one for long—but somehow none of that mattered. None of it counted.

But they were different. *She* was different. Those girls might come and go, but she was his constant. She was his friend. For two years leading up to that kiss, he'd been her confidant, her ally. He wouldn't sabotage that, she'd told herself. He couldn't.

Her breath caught now, and she gave him a tight smile. His eyes were hooded, studying her closely, but with a lift of his chin, he turned. Just like that, gone again.

"Hey." Luke appeared at the bar, leaning down to give Grace a casual kiss, and something in their understated ease of the gesture made Anna's spirits sink further. She'd told herself over the years that she liked being alone, that it was better that way, safer—and maybe it was. Wasn't anything better than having your heart broken?

But that wasn't the only reason she was alone. She hadn't just lost Mark. She'd also lost that tiny part of him that had grown inside her, the part that could never be replaced. The part she still clung to, even if Mark was long gone.

Luke ordered a beer and brought it to his lips. "Why don't we grab a table?"

Anna stifled a sigh and ordered another drink. She was going to need it more than ever now that Mark was in the room. The pub was thankfully dark, illuminated by flickering votive candles nesting in amber-colored glass. Her eyes darted as she followed her sisters to a table, searching for any hint of those dark waves, that grin that lit dark brown eyes, that deep roar of laughter that brought her back to a time she should have forgotten and emotions she had tried so hard to resist.

He was at the far end of the pub, his elbows splayed on the table as he leaned in to his date. Suddenly he looked up, his gaze lingering ever so swiftly in her direction, before snapping to Luke.

Luke stopped to chat with his cousin, and Anna watched with a heaviness in her chest as he said something to Grace, who nodded in agreement, and then bent down to say something to a person at a neighboring table. Soon chairs were being dragged to Mark's table, and the only one looking more miserable than Anna felt was Nicole.

"You know, I think I'll take a walk," Anna said to Jane, who immediately looked alarmed.

"What? No, please stay, Anna. It will do you good to be around friends right now."

Anna eyed Mark warily. "It's hitting me in waves, Jane. I just—"

Jane gripped her arm and met her gaze. "I know. Believe me; I know what it's like to have something you've poured your entire life into snatched out from under you."

Anna nodded. It was just a business, she told herself. Just a café. She had insurance; it would be built again. It was just money. Jane had lost her family. Her husband. Everything she had imagined her life would always be.

She knew that feeling all too well. More than her sister could ever know.

"I don't mean to sound shallow," she said. Her eyes met Mark's and she quickly looked away as her pulse sped up. "That café was all I had." *Left*, she finished privately. It was all she had left.

"And you'll have it again," Jane told her. "Feeling sorry for yourself won't help."

She was right, and sitting in an empty apartment with only her dark thoughts was the exact behavior Anna had worked so hard to avoid. Deciding there was no way to duck out early, she slid into a chair safely next to Grace.

"Mind moving over there so I can sit next to Grace?" Luke asked.

Anna glanced up at him, horror stricken. Luke stared down at her expectantly, a frown knitting his brow as her hesitation lingered.

"Me?" she asked faintly.

"Just move across," Grace pressed.

Gritting her teeth, Anna complied, refusing to meet Mark's eye as she slid her body to within inches of his. The length of her thigh skimmed his, and her stomach fluttered before she quickly crossed her leg over the other. She reached for her wineglass, frowning at the tremble in her own fingers, and then cursed as she sloshed the contents. Quick to react, Mark grabbed the glass just before it shattered on the table.

"That's twice in one night." Mark laughed easily and set the empty glass upright.

Anna laughed under her breath to hide the embarrassment that flamed her cheeks. "It's been a rough day. I'm not myself."

It was perhaps the most she had spoken to him in years, and certainly the most she had revealed in as long. She'd let him in, even a little, and now she wanted to snatch it all back.

She forced herself to look up, expecting to see a twinkle in his eye, a victorious smirk for having finally broken her down, but his mouth was a straight line, and his deepset eyes were clouded in confusion. His attention rested on her long enough to leave her unsettled, and she looked away, busying herself with the sopping napkins.

Mark leaned back in his chair and signaled a passing waitress. "I'll have another beer. The lady will have another Chardonnay. In a sippy cup, please."

Despite herself, Anna laughed, but something deep within herself broke at the same time. It was Mark, the same old irresistible, irreplaceable Mark. Only Mark could make her smile on a day when her world was crashing down around her. But then, Mark always had that special power to lift her up. And tear her down.

He glanced at her sidelong, his lips curving into that

slow, easy grin that made her stomach uncoil. "You're on a bit of a bad luck streak today. Figured I'd help you out."

"Thanks for that." She stiffened slightly. "Thanks for letting me use your kitchen, too. I'd use my home kitchen, but it's pretty cramped."

Mark shrugged. "Doesn't seem like there's any way around it then."

Anna narrowed her eyes. "I didn't realize it was a problem."

"It's not." Mark turned to Nicole, who was pouting and twisting a blond ringlet around her finger.

"Marky...maybe we should go," she whined, sliding a pointed glance in Anna's direction.

Anna managed something of a smile. "I didn't mean to interrupt your date."

"Oh, this isn't a date," Mark said quickly.

Anna tipped her head, holding Mark's eyes with hers, noticing the way his jaw had tightened. Beside him, Nicole was blinking quickly, but there was a decided quiver to her chin, and she shook slightly when she managed a brave smile.

"You never change," Anna muttered as Nicole excused herself to the bathroom.

"Why should I?" Mark countered.

Anna stared at him flatly, wanting to believe the grin was there to mask the guilt, that he couldn't really be this callous, that the guy who could once make her laugh until her ribs ached and who could take her so tenderly in his arms was a real person under this untouchable façade.

The waitress appeared with their drinks, and Anna took her glass, holding it carefully by the stem. Across the room she noticed Nicole burst out of the bathroom, hiding her face with the side of her hand as she hurried to the front door.

"Your date just left," Anna informed him.

"I told you—"

"She's not your date. Fine. Well, Nicole just left."

Mark said nothing and took sip of his beer. There was a sadness to his profile. An edge that she hadn't seen in a long time. For a brief moment Anna wondered if she was wrong. If he had changed. Then she thought of the poor girl outside the bar, most likely crying into her phone, at the mercy of some girlfriend to give her a ride home, and she scowled.

"You should apologize to her," Anna scolded, realizing the irony of this situation.

"Nothing to apologize for," Mark replied evenly. "She knows where I stand. Can I help it if she wants something more?"

More than he could give.

Anna gave him a withering look and turned back to her sisters, but Mark cut in, "Look, I'm not here to fight, Anna, but I don't like feeling judged."

Ever so slowly, she turned to him, an eyebrow arched. "Judged?"

His eyes roamed her face. "I know you think I'm some kind of jerk."

Anna felt her lips spread into a brittle smile. "You're right. I do."

"I never knew you were such a petty grudge holder, Anna."

"And I never knew you were such heartless ass, Mark." The relief felt from expressing herself quickly turned to anger and a pain so deep, she thought it might break her. How had it all come to this? Harsh, cutting words at the person she'd once loved the most. As much as she wanted to beat on his chest, lash out with all the hurt that brewed just below the surface, a bigger part of her wanted to tell him everything, to make him understand.

Only one person could share her loss, her grief for a baby she had never even met, but only dared to imagine. And he didn't even know.

She could feel her blood rushing in her ears as her heart began to pound. She reached for her glass but her hands were trembling so hard she didn't trust herself, and she tucked them between her legs.

Mark dragged in a breath and brushed a few unruly locks from his forehead. He turned to face her, and Anna felt her temper wilt, only to be replaced with a much more lethal emotion. This was the image she had fought to avoid, the very one she had tried to banish from her mind, her dreams, all of it. Mark with his warm brown eyes and tousled hair, with that slight bump on his nose and that broad, defined chest. Mark who knew every inch of her bare body, all her secrets, all her joys and sorrows.

All except one. He'd never known about the baby. Never given her a chance to tell him. He'd been too busy flirting, having his fun with his latest fling. Cassie. That had been her name. One she'd never forget.

For years she had refused to go there, to allow herself to remember his face, the way his skin felt under her fingers, the way his lips tasted, and the way everything about them, every kiss, every laugh, was so effortless. She'd forced her eyes to drift whenever they came in contact, desperate to fight that tightening in her chest that occurred every time she saw that smile, an attraction she couldn't deny, a love she knew she could never have. She'd look away, bury her mind in other things, and break free the first chance she had. Now she was facing her fear head on, staring straight into the eyes of the man she hadn't properly looked at since he broke her heart, confronting every crushed dream he had ever brought her. And damn it if her gut didn't stir, not with anger or contempt, but with longing.

"Look," Mark said. "We're going to be working in the same kitchen for a few weeks at least. We may as well try to get along."

"You're right," Anna replied, feeling embarrassed over her emotional outburst. She'd done far too good a job at shielding herself to let Mark rattle her now. "The past is in the past. It's better to leave it there."

Beside her, Mark shifted in his chair. "So this is how it's going to be, huh? We're just going to keep on ignoring each other?"

Ideally, Anna thought. "No. I figured I'd come into the kitchen before your breakfast crowd hits. It must get pretty crazy then."

Mark nodded, but his lips pursed with displeasure. "Too busy."

She lifted an eyebrow. "You don't sound happy about that."

Mark peeled the label off his bottle. "I'm just burned out."

Ah. Of course. "Honestly, I'm surprised you've stuck with it as long as you have."

Mark snapped his gaze to her, his eyes flashing in anger. "What's that supposed to mean?"

"I'm just saying that commitment has never been your strong suit."

He opened his mouth as if to say something, and then clamped it shut. "You're right," he surprised her by saying.

Anna leaned back in her chair, at a loss for words. At the other side of the table, Grace and Luke were having an animated conversation with Jane, and Anna could tell from Luke's wide-eyed interest and Jane's grin that she was telling them about Rosemary's newest career as the town matchmaker. On their side, however, silence stretched. Anna watched the light from the candle flicker against the amber glass of the empty beer bottle, wondering what to say. What was even left to say?

"I really do appreciate being able to use the kitchen," she said, softening her tone. She was at his mercy, a place she never imagined she would be, but she needed to heed her own advice and leave the past behind her and focus on the present. She was good at that, throwing herself into work, and her career was more important than ever now. She had to do anything she could to salvage it. Even spend time with Mark. "I'd like to pay you in some way."

"Nah. Don't worry about it." Mark brushed a hand through the air and then returned it to the beer bottle. He tipped it to the left, holding it against the light, seemingly lost in thought.

"Really though," Anna pressed. "I could be in there for months. At least let me do something. It was . . . really kind of you to offer me the space."

He looked at her sidelong, his expression revealing nothing. "It wasn't my idea. But hell, it's the least I can do, all things considered."

Anna felt her lips thin. She reached for her glass, bringing it to her mouth before she said something she would later regret. He was right: It *was* the least he could do for her.

CHAPTER
5

Mark turned his key in the back door of Hastings and flicked on the lights to the kitchen, wincing as the fluorescent glare roused him from his sleepy haze. He blinked and rubbed his forehead and then pulled a bottle of water from the fridge. He could blame the headache on one too many beers, but he knew that wasn't its true source.

He was still reeling from his interaction with Anna last night at the bar, playing the conversation over and over and not getting anywhere. She hated him, that much was clear, and could he really blame her? He'd ruined the good thing they had, just like he screwed up every relationship before and after that. He could pretend he didn't care, hadn't come across like the jerk Anna clearly believed him to be. But deep down, it gnawed at him.

With the exception of Luke, Anna was one of the few people he'd ever let in. He'd let himself get comfortable with her, vulnerable even, and he'd let himself start to trust her. He'd let himself slip—the one thing he'd promised never to do.

He set his jaw. It was better to get out first. Better to be the one in control, not the one left behind.

That's what he'd told himself. Now, though, he wasn't so sure ...

Mark drained the water and tossed the empty bottle in the recycling bin. He pushed through the door to the dining room, which was dark and quiet, the chairs neatly tucked into place. He turned the lock on the front door, even though the diner didn't open for another three hours, and lingered there, searching down the street for any hint of that silky blond hair and those legs that seemed to go on for miles.

Mouth thinning, he turned from the window and went back to the counter, where he started a fresh pot of coffee. He leaned back against the wall, training one eye on the road as he waited for the brew to finish, hating the sense of expectation that pulsed with each tick of the minute hand.

At five sharp, just as the first warm glow of sun was beginning to bloom in the horizon, Anna's face appeared in the window. Mark set his coffee mug on the counter and lifted a hand, waving her in, trying to ignore the kick in his chest. The bell above the door jingled as she entered, and he let his gaze fall over her impassively, his groin tightening at the way her blue T-shirt hugged her small waist, and her jeans clung to the flare of her hips, defining every curve of her slender legs. He'd half hoped the attraction he felt at the bar had just been the dim lighting and whisper of her thigh against his, but now, in the diner's bright, overhead lighting, he knew that was wishful thinking.

He could try to talk himself out of it all he wanted, but it was useless. Anna was under his skin. She'd crawled into his life when he was twenty-one years old, and nearly ten years later, she was still there, even though he'd tried so hard to scratch her out.

She set her leather handbag on the nearest table. "How long have you been here?" She glanced at him, her expression revealing nothing as she reached up and began gathering her long blond hair with her hands, expertly retrieving a hair band from her wrist and securing it in place. Her shirt rode up, just barely an inch, but enough for him to make out the smooth, creamy hint of skin beneath.

Mark cleared his throat and drained his coffee. This was going to be more difficult than he first thought.

"I just got in." He gestured to his mug. "Coffee?"

She smoothed her ponytail and dropped her hands. A hint of a smile passed over her mouth. "I'd love some."

He took his time filling her mug. "Cream and sugar are on the counter. It's not as fancy as the stuff you make."

"It's five in the morning. Anything will do." She ripped the seal off an individually wrapped creamer. Mark cursed to himself, wishing he'd had the foresight to pour some fresh milk into a glass. "Besides, your coffee's pretty good."

Mark lifted a brow. "A compliment? I'll take it."

"Oh, come on, you know you can cook circles around me if you put your mind to it." She grinned over the rim of her mug.

Mark decided to ignore the insinuation that he wasn't living up to his best, but the reminder hit him square in the gut. This wasn't what he had set out to do, and Anna knew it. She alone knew all about the real dreams he had for himself, the ones that involved inventive menus and wine pairings. The ones that involved her.

"I'll walk you around the kitchen," he said, pushing back from the counter.

Anna grabbed her handbag with her free hand and followed him, pausing in the doorway of the large kitchen. Her gaze swept over the room, from the nine-foot stainless steel island to the ten-burner range and then, finally, landed steadily on him. "This will do."

He tried to see the space through her eyes, knowing Fireside had a much bigger kitchen. He'd spent as many weekends there as he could, back when it was Tavern on Main, watching his dad in action, calling out orders and working the pass. It was a big kitchen, bright, with more stations than Anna had certainly ever put to use. It was a restaurant kitchen, fully loaded, and capable of great things. Anna was an exceptional chef, but God, did he hate the fact that she'd taken over that spot. Only one person belonged in that kitchen, and that man was never coming back.

Mark hated even thinking of the place. Hated that it still excited him. That the memory of his father's voice, the clanking of pans, the heat from the stovetops, still made his heart speed up. That the thought of it falling dark, or worse, burned out and covered in soot, made him feel like he'd lost it all over again. Lost his dad all over again.

He forced himself back to the present. "Well, it's a diner. It's functional."

Anna nodded, causing her long, blond ponytail to spill over her slim shoulder. "As I said, it will do."

Mark felt his temper stir but he kept his thoughts to himself. "My crew gets in around seven thirty."

"Just you and me then. Like old times." In any other context, the words might have been flirty, suggestive even, but Anna's eyes were hard and the statement came out more like a bitter observation than a pleasant remark.

He watched her steadily, wanting to say something, anything that would take the hurt away. He set his jaw. There was nothing he could do.

"I've got some prep work to do," Mark said, taking a step back. "Feel free to use the station near the door, if that suits you."

Something in her blue eyes softened. "Thanks."

Mark nodded once and turned on his heel, his mind spinning. He crossed the room with purpose and began gathering eggs and meats from cold storage, doing his best to ignore her presence behind him. Curiosity finally got the better of him, and he glanced ever so slightly to his left, refusing to turn his neck or show the least amount of outward interest, and watched as she hauled cloth grocery sacks into the kitchen and then marched back out again, only to return with more.

He should offer to help, but that would be sending the wrong message. It would imply teamwork, a partnership, and they were merely sharing a space, not joining an effort.

They worked in silence for half an hour, heads bent over their work with fixed determination. He finished chopping the vegetables and set them in stainless steel bowls, covering them with plastic wrap. Across the center island, Anna was mixing dough for scones, her eyebrows pinched in concentration, her mouth set in a serious line. Something about the silence, the way they each covered their tasks, working side by side but independently, brought him back to a happier time, a time he had tried to forget, when he had dared to think his life could be so much more than it now was.

He could still remember waking up and sipping coffee, Anna in one of his old shirts that skimmed the back of her thighs, padding barefoot around him, chopping vegetables while he whisked eggs. So easy. So simple. So perfect.

"Mind if I turn on the radio?" He couldn't take the memories for another second.

Anna looked up at him, seeming briefly startled at the interruption, and brushed a loose wisp of honey-colored hair from her face with the back of her hand. "If you must."

Mark flicked it on. "It's better than standing here in silence."

"I'm not standing here. I'm working."

Mark hesitated. "Is this how it's going to be between us? You're just going to ignore me the way you've done for the last six years since you've been back in Briar Creek?"

"I don't ignore you," Anna replied crisply.

Mark leveled her with a look and to prove her own point, she held his stare. God, she was exasperating. "You avoid me, Anna. You act just polite enough not to let on that we have a history, but you're hardly friendly."

"Well, we're hardly friends."

He waited a beat. "Why can't we be?"

Anna sighed audibly and made a grand show of setting her wooden spoon on the counter. She glared at him, and something within Mark swelled. Damn it if he didn't want to kiss her right then and there, if he didn't want to push aside that kitchen island and grab her by the shoulders and swipe that pinch right off her pretty little mouth. He wanted to shake her up, give her something to get worked up about, ruffle that cool, calculated exterior and see if there was still a hint of the girl he once knew under that determined shell.

She used to laugh. She used to smile and joke.

He grimaced. He supposed he was to blame for stealing that joy from her, even if all he'd ever wanted to do was to protect her—and himself—from this exact situation.

"If it would make things easier, I'd like to pay you for the use of the space, that way we can both be clear this is purely a professional transaction."

He looked at her squarely. "I don't want your money, Anna. I'm doing this to help you."

"I know, I know. Because your aunt asked you to. I know it wasn't your idea," she added bitterly.

He shouldn't have said that last night, and he hadn't intended to—not until she had to go and make that jab about him still running the diner. She'd hit a nerve; voiced his unspoken disappointment.

"If I didn't want you here, I wouldn't have agreed to it." Mark set his hands down on the cool steel worktop that separated their bodies and huffed out a breath. "We used to be friends once, Anna. Good friends."

"The best." Her voice was barely audible. She held his gaze, her expression unreadable until her blue eyes suddenly flashed. "And then you had to go and throw it all away."

"Now that's not fair."

"You're right. It wasn't fair." Anna picked up her spoon and began furiously stirring the thick, sticky dough. She tipped the bowl, emptying its contents on a flour-coated surface and began shaping it into a circle.

"Anna."

She slapped her palm over the top of the dough, patting it flatter.

"Anna." His voice was low and husky, and he watched as she blinked quickly, paused, and then set her mouth in that familiar thin line, her eyes fixed on her work. "I'm sorry I hurt you. I never set out to do that." Relief rolled off his shoulders. He'd held that in for too long.

She snapped her gaze to him, her eyes sharp and accusatory, her cheeks flushed. "Get over yourself, Mark. If you think I'm still sore about the way you dumped me and then took up with another girl two days later, you can relax. I assure you I didn't cry a single tear for you then, and I'm certainly not losing any sleep about it now."

"Well, I just assumed by the way you've ignored me—"

"Last night we established that what we had was meaningless. If it wasn't, you wouldn't have ended it like you did."

He balled a fist at his side. That wasn't true, but she didn't need to know that—it didn't change anything. She had always been looking for more than he could give. She *deserved* more than he could give, but try telling her that. It was his own damn problem that what he could give and what he wanted to give were two very different things. She wanted it all—the restaurant, the relationship. Those two could never go hand in hand. In the end, one always won out.

He looked around the diner, frowning.

Turning back to her, he said, "We were friends, Anna. Best friends. For two years before it became something more. Didn't that friendship mean anything to you?"

Her gaze held his, and for a moment he thought she might smile, she might back down, and they might forget the awkward strain of their past and move forward, falling back on what they had, what they should have kept in the first place. A friendship. Nothing more.

"No." She slammed the dough onto a baking tray and

strode to the oven. She kept her back to him, working at the far counter that lined the wall rather than returning to the island. Mark watched her warily until finally sighing, and giving up. He pulled a sack of potatoes from a cabinet and began peeling them over the sink, frowning with each stroke of the knife. The silent minutes ticked by.

"What's this?"

He looked up to see Anna leaning against the counter, trays of beautifully plump, crumb-topped muffins at her sides, holding a small stack of paper in her hands. His notes. His dreams. Every doodle and idea. Every detail of his plan to finally get out of this damn town and away from all its painful memories.

"Give those to me!" he snapped, tossing the potato and knife into the sink and lurching across the room.

Anna's mouth curled into a mischievous smile as she held the papers out of his reach. He reached for them, but she arched her back and held her arms high. If he stepped any closer, his chest would skim the swell of her breasts— not that he minded, but he had a feeling the interaction would spark a less than desirable reaction from Anna.

She frowned, squinting at the sloppy handwriting from an arm's length distance. "Grilled polenta with seasonal ratatouille. Pan-seared tuna with wasabi mashed potatoes." She looked at him quizzically. "What is this?"

Mark dropped his hands and dragged out a sigh. "It's none of your business. Let me have it." He reached up to grab the papers but she snatched them away before he could get a firm grip.

"Sunday brunch pancake flights. Mascarpone-stuffed French toast with fresh berry purée." She leaned in for a closer look, and he took the opportunity to yank the notes from her hand. "Are you thinking of expanding the menu here or something?"

Mark folded the papers in half and tucked them into his apron pocket before she could tease him about them anymore. He shouldn't have been so careless as to leave them out, but Anna shouldn't have been so nosy as to look at things that weren't hers. They were just lists of random thoughts, ideas he had for a new place when the day dragged on here, when he got tired of slinging hash and started remembering how it felt to be in a crisp white jacket, experimenting with new ingredients and flavors, designing plates that were as visually stunning as they were delicious.

Just a bunch of stupid lists. He wasn't going anywhere, and deep down he knew it. Circumstances had dragged him back to Briar Creek and kept him here. Every time he got ready to leave, another situation crept up and another opportunity was lost. He couldn't focus on his career and take care of his family at the same time. His father had taught him that lesson, the hard way of course.

"I didn't mean to upset you," Anna said, but Mark didn't want to hear it.

"If you're going to use my kitchen, then you have to respect my space."

She lifted her chin. "Fair enough. Then please let me pay you. I'd prefer to pay you."

Mark folded his arms over his chest. Her blue eyes skittered, and he could tell she was lying. She'd never been good at keeping things from him. He knew her too well.

His gut tightened on that thought.

"No. I'm not taking money from you." Even if she had it to give, which he doubted very much that she did, he couldn't take cash from her, no matter how much it could help his effort to make a fresh start. It would feel wrong, callous. Regardless of what she thought of him, he cared about her. Too much.

His gaze drifted lazily over her face, his groin stirring as his attention came to rest on her lips, slightly glossed and parted.

"If you're afraid you won't look like a gentleman by taking the money from me, I can assure you, you needn't worry. I know where you stand in that department."

Mark narrowed his gaze. "This isn't going to work."

"No, it's not." Her eyes blazed, but from somewhere beyond the anger, he thought he detected another emotion. One that looked an awful lot like fear.

They stood so close he could see the faint freckles dusting her nose, count the lashes that rimmed those big blue eyes, saying nothing. He should be relieved, happy that she agreed that this was a stupid idea, but for some reason, he wasn't. He'd spoken more to Anna in the past two days than he had in the nearly seven years since he'd graduated from culinary school, even if almost six of those were spent with her just down the road, in his father's old restaurant. He missed her, damn it, he missed her more than he wanted to admit. He'd told himself it was better this way, that he could only ever let her down, that he was doing the right thing for them both by cutting her out and setting her free. Hell, he'd even told himself that it was better that she'd frozen him out—it made the temptation of rekindling anything they might have once had impossible. She was doing him a favor in that sense. Almost.

"I don't see what else you're going to do if you want to keep the bookstore's café open." He told himself he was thinking of Grace, and by extension Luke, and of how crushed they would be if their plans for Main Street Books didn't succeed. How Luke had helped Grace realize her dreams, how her father, who had overseen the place until the day he died, had helped Luke to realize his. Oh, who was he kidding? He didn't want Anna to go. Not yet. Not like this.

Not again.

He reached into his pocket and pulled out his key ring, plucking the spare free and setting it on the cool steel surface. "We need to set some ground rules."

Anna studied the key and, after a brief hesitation, brought her hand to it. "I'm glad you mentioned that. I have a few rules of my own."

He stared at her in wonder. "Go on."

She stiffened. "You first."

"Ladies first. I insist."

She lifted her chin a notch higher, until she was practically looking down at him despite his five-inch advantage. "No talking about the past."

He shrugged. "Easy enough. Now it's my turn. No rifling through my stuff."

"Fair." She relaxed her shoulders. "And you'll let me pay you back in some way once I'm back on my feet. This is purely a business transaction."

He locked her gaze for a beat, sending a rush of heat coursing through his blood. "Purely," he managed. "Nothing personal about it."

Nothing personal at all.

CHAPTER
6

Anna sat at the old oak farm table in Sharon Hastings's sunny kitchen and sipped her Earl Grey tea. The plate of homemade oatmeal cookies Sharon had set out for her remained untouched. Realizing that the effort had been made especially for her, Anna reached out and took one.

"I baked those fresh this morning," Sharon offered.

Sensing her stare, Anna bit into the cookie and chewed, allowing herself to taste the subtle flavors of butter and cinnamon and a dash of ginger. "Delicious."

"I used to make those for the diner." Sharon gave a dismissive shrug, but a faint blush rose in her cheeks. "They don't compare with what you make at the café. Mark makes some amazing desserts, too. His father would be proud..." Her expression stiffened for one quick moment, and she blinked quickly, forcing a tight smile.

Tavern on Main had been considered one of the best restaurants in Vermont, if not New England, in its prime. Anna had been too young to ever experience it personally, but she remembered her parents often choosing to celebrate their anniversary at Bill Hastings's establishment. From passing by the windows on her bike, Anna recalled the white tablecloths and heavy silverware, the fresh cut flowers centered on each table in cut glass vases. It was a beautiful restaurant, inside and out, and it had been a great success. Until it wasn't.

Mark had never talked about his father's leaving or the closing of Tavern, but his mother hinted at it briefly. Sharon had helped out where she could with the restaurant, and it made sense for her to seek employment where her skills matched after it closed. The diner was the only other establishment in town back then, and Sharon was a natural fit. She was chatty and personable. Like Mark.

Anna knew the place suited him in some ways, but not in all. Unlike Sharon, Mark was a chef. He'd followed in his father's path, and then suddenly ground to a halt.

Anna crammed the rest of the cookie into her mouth so she didn't have to say anything about Mark or her thoughts on his choices. The two women had grown close since Anna began renting out the restaurant space, and despite her initial trepidation about being connected to Mark, however loosely, Anna quickly found herself looking forward to her chats with Sharon, except when the conversation shifted to Mark, of course. As far as she knew, Sharon had no idea that Anna and Mark had ever dated, much less been close friends. Their relationship at school was confined to the campus, and on breaks and holidays in Briar Creek, Sharon seemed to regard Anna as one of the gang—no different than Grace or Kara or any of the others who had run through town since they were knee-high. She'd been in Sharon's home many times over the years since their relationship had turned professional—to drop off a gift around the holidays, or some homemade soup or a casserole when Sharon was going through her chemotherapy treatments. Those days were over, and she'd been in remission for more than five years, thankfully, but Anna still found the purpose of her visit to be under less than ideal circumstances.

Like many things in Briar Creek, Sharon's house had a sense of history and permanence. The gray Colonial with black shutters and a white front door sat at the edge of town near the creek, and aside from stripping old wallpaper and sprucing up some finishes, Sharon had done little to the place over time. The kitchen was large—Mark's father had insisted on it, Sharon had once told her—and it still remained the heart of the home in his absence. Her pride and joy, by evidence, was the original hearth in the breakfast nook, lovingly decorated with silver-plated framed photographs of her two sons.

Anna usually avoided the mantel on her visits, taking a chair that kept her back firmly to it, but today she scanned the photos with a strange sort of interest, the kind she knew she shouldn't indulge. The kind that made her wish for something she shouldn't.

Her eyes lingered on one of Mark when he was just a baby until a familiar sadness pierced her.

"How's Brett these days?" Anna grabbed another cookie while Sharon's expression turned wistful at the mention of her younger son, always a safe subject.

"He's still doing his residency." Sharon grinned, pride shining in her deep brown eyes. "He likes the hospital in Baltimore, but I still hope he'll come back to Briar Creek eventually. It was so nice to have him home for Christmas."

"It must be difficult having him so far away," Anna

commented. She knew how hard it was on her parents when Grace moved to New York and stayed there for five years. Though they never said it, Anna saw the change in her mother now that her older sister was back. A large part of it, Anna knew, was Grace's determination to preserve their father's bookstore—somehow it kept him with them.

Anna's stomach churned at the mere thought of Main Street Books and she helped herself to another cookie, trying to forget about the loan for a few minutes.

Sharon set her tea cup on its saucer. "Well, Mark's here at least. Tell me, how has it been working out for you at the diner? Mark treating you well?"

Anna lowered her eyes, managing a weak smile. The poor woman would pass out if she knew just how Mark had treated her. She swallowed hard, resisting the urge. Sharon had had enough heartache, and Mark was her pride and joy. Probably better to let it stay that way. "Oh, it's going fine…I haven't seen much of Mark this week, actually. I've been working out of my own kitchen."

Sharon regarded her quizzically. "It must take twice as long in your apartment kitchen!"

"Oh…" Anna gave a nervous chuckle. Longer, really. "I haven't been sleeping well, with everything. I've been getting up in the middle of the night, and, well, it's something to keep my mind off everything." It wasn't a lie, she told herself. She wasn't sleeping, and if making tea breads at two or three in the morning helped her work through her anxiety and avoid Mark at the same time, then really, what was wrong with that? *Nothing, nothing at all.*

"You poor girl." Worry creased Sharon's forehead and she reached over and squeezed Anna's hand. "It's all going to work out. The insurance representative came out

Monday and talked with Sam. They've confirmed it was electrical, so we can take steps toward prevention. I'm meeting with a contractor this afternoon to take a look at the kitchen. It was the most damaged, and I'm sure you'd like that rebuilt first."

Anna was nodding quickly. It was all good. It would all be rebuilt. It was the best she could expect from the situation. So why did she feel like she could burst into tears?

Because you're running on four hours of sleep, that's why.

"Have you filed the claim with your insurance?" Sharon inquired.

"I spoke with them on Monday. I don't think there will be any problems."

Sharon released her hand and patted it fondly. "It will all work out. Leaning on friends and family is what's gotten me through the tough times. Just remember you're not in this alone. You've got your sisters and mother. And me. And Mark." She smiled brightly and Anna gritted her teeth into a smile.

"It's very nice of him to let me use his kitchen," she managed, as she stood and brought her cup and saucer to the sink. "I should probably get over to the bookstore, though. Are you sure I can't offer you some muffins? They're in my car. Fresh from the oven."

Sharon waved away her offer as she walked her to the front door. "Don't you worry about me. You just take that hard work and turn a profit with it. Every little bit helps right now."

That it does. Anna sucked in a breath and gave Sharon a hug goodbye before hurrying down the front steps. When she got to her car, she paused with her hand on the door handle and turned back. Sharon was still in the door-way, rubbing her arms to keep warm against the morning chill, her grin encouraging, her wave eager, and Anna held up her hand in return, giving a smile that hurt her heart.

She knew Sharon was being strong for her, decidedly optimistic about their unfortunate circumstance, and for that she didn't want to let her down. Sharon had been a friend to her when her spirits were at their lowest. She'd given Anna a lease on the Tavern's old space when she was fresh out of culinary school, a sign of faith that many wouldn't have in someone of such a young age, and for that Anna had been eternally grateful. She'd worked hard to prove to Sharon that she'd been right to take a chance on her—almost as hard as she'd worked to drive the ache from her chest.

She couldn't let Sharon down now. And she couldn't let Grace down, either. It was only Thursday, but already Anna knew that she was in trouble. Sales at the Annex had been steady, but that type of income wouldn't pay off the loan. Not yet anyway.

She must still have been frowning by the time she arrived at Main Street Books because the second she pushed through the door, Grace's face fell. "Is everything okay?" She pushed in a chair at the children's reading table and straightened a stuffed Peter Rabbit on a bench in the corner.

The addition of the adjacent storefront had improved the bookstore more than Anna could have anticipated. The size of the store was nearly doubled, allowing for more bookshelves and clusters of cozy reading chairs and end tables. The Annex sat at the front of the addi-tion, lined with wall-to-wall windows. Grace and she had argued at first over the decision to remove the entrance directly into the café by replacing the door with a window panel, but Anna was happy she had lost that battle. Now customers were forced to enter through the storefront, where they were met with the beautifully designed display tables boasting all the latest releases, and some of Grace's old favorites. Behind the café section of the store, Grace had added more shelves and another sitting area. The children's area was expanded to include a rug large enough to hold a weekly story hour, and she'd replaced the bright overhead lighting with floor lamps that lent a warm and inviting touch to the room.

Everything in the store felt fresh and welcoming, like their father's spirit was still with them. Anna could sense it every time she entered the store. It was all they had left of him now. Losing it was not an option.

"Is something wrong? How did your meeting with Sharon go?"

Anna glanced at her sister, realizing she had been staring at the old mahogany counter in the middle of the room, remembering their dad standing behind it, his glasses sliding down his nose as he rang up a customer. This store had been his passion, just as Fireside was hers. She knew more than ever how it would have felt for him to lose this place. She didn't want that for him. Not even now.

"Oh, it went well. She's really wonderful." *If only the same could be said for her son.* Anna handed a shopping bag of freshly baked muffins, scones, and pastries to Grace. "Help me carry these into the café, will you?"

"Are you sure you're feeling okay? You look a little pale," Grace hedged after she set the bag down on the bakery counter. She pulled a box from the top of the bag and lifted the lid. "Raspberry muffins. My favorite."

"I'm fine, just tired." Anna scooped some fresh coffee beans into the grinder and pressed the button, hoping the mere smell of coffee would revive her. She felt herself sway ever so slightly to the left. It was no use.

"Maybe you should get some rest..."

"Now isn't exactly the time for sleep."

Grace set the muffins on a tray. "So, how was Mark this morning?"

Anna deposited the fresh grounds into the filter, wishing she could banish the image of those dark, deep-set eyes and that square jaw. "I didn't see him. I worked at home this morning."

Grace stared at her. "In your tiny kitchen? What time did you have to start?"

"Four," Anna fibbed. It had been two. Two in the morning, the same as yesterday and the day before that, and it would continue this way until the kitchen at Fireside was pieced back together. Medical students got by on lack of sleep and still operated on patients; surely she could handle a few dozen baked goods and a handful of sandwiches and salads. She'd learn to adjust. It would take some getting used to, but it would be worth it. Anything was better than another one-on-one session with Mark.

"Damn." Grace's eyes were wide. "If I didn't know better, I might think you were doing this just to avoid Mark."

Anna said nothing. Grace knew she and Mark weren't close, but she didn't know the source. She supposed she could just silence her sister's speculation once and for all, but certain things were better left in the past and Mark was one of them. What they had shouldn't still matter, even if for some reason, it did.

"You two seemed to be getting along pretty well at the pub Saturday night."

Anna turned to her sister, noticing the hopeful gleam that had taken over her bright green eyes, and the realization caused her to burst out laughing. "Don't you go playing matchmaker on me, too."

"Jane told me about Rosemary." Grace grinned and Anna felt her shoulders relax now that they had finally dropped the topic of Mark. The mere mention of him always made her tense. "Are you really going to let her set you up?"

Anna gave a helpless shrug. "I just said it so she would help Jane. Besides, with everything, I can hardly think about dating at a time like this. Surely even Rosemary will understand that."

"Understand what?"

Anna looked up to see Rosemary standing in the arched doorway that separated the bookstore from the café, her hair pulled tight and a long, flowing pink silk scarf wrapped loosely around her neck.

"We're not open until ten, Mrs. Hastings," Anna said, darting her gaze to Grace for assistance.

"Oh, I forgot to tell you. I changed the hours to help drive traffic. Just until Fireside is back up and running." Grace smiled warmly at Rosemary, but Anna felt her stiffen slightly. Rosemary had always terrified Grace, especially since she returned to Briar Creek a few months ago after running off to New York to pursue her writing career. Grace was convinced that Rosemary was still harboring a grudge over her breakup with Luke more than five years ago, even though it was obvious Rosemary was thrilled about their reunion.

Still, Rosemary was an intimidating force, Anna considered, feeling that familiar sense of dread creep into her gut, and something told her that she wasn't going to let this little matchmaking scheme drop.

The door jingled once more, and Jane stepped into the shop, rosy-cheeked and clutching her dance bag. "Everyone's here!" She smiled and helped herself to a mug of fresh coffee. "How did it go with Mark this morning?"

Anna set her jaw as she folded the paper shopping bag and set it in the recycling bin. "I didn't see him."

"I just got off the phone with Sharon, and she told me you and Mark haven't crossed paths at all this week." Rosemary pinched her lips. "She says you've been working in your apartment kitchen, baking in the dead of night!"

Jane's brow furrowed as she scanned Anna's face. "Is this true? Oh, you do look pale, Anna."

Rosemary gave her a disapproving frown and, sighing, turned her attention to Jane. "My dear, I have some wonderful news," she announced as she slid into a slat-back chair near the window and crossed one long leg over the other. "I've set up a date for you this Saturday night."

"What? So soon?" Jane croaked.

"That was fast!" Grace couldn't disguise her grin, and her eyes danced as she slid them to Anna.

Anna noticed the way the color had drained from Jane's face. Who could blame her? She'd married her high school sweetheart. Adam was the only man she'd ever dated. "Maybe Grace could give you some dating tips since you don't have much experience," Anna said.

Jane's cheeks turned red. "I probably have more than you!"

"Oh, you leave that to me," Rosemary said mildly.

"You both will have *plenty* of experience by the time I'm done with you."

Exasperated, Anna started slicing a banana chocolate chip bread she'd made somewhere around three that morning. Though she'd prepped the same number of muffins, scones, chocolate croissants, tea breads, and coffee cakes as she did every day, it wouldn't make up for the loss of revenue from Fireside. Even if people stopped in for a light dinner of a mozzarella, tomato, and basil on ciabatta with a side of mixed greens and toasted lentils, it wouldn't help. The Annex wasn't expected to turn a profit for at least six months, if not a year—not with what they'd sunk into it. Until then, they'd relied on the sure thing. And now, that sure thing was gone. Roped off with yellow police tape. It didn't even have a door anymore.

She rubbed the bridge of her nose. Her head was beginning to pound.

Beside her, Jane had recovered. "I'll go on the date." She did a poor job of masking her smile, but Anna detected a lingering undercurrent of terror in her large hazel eyes.

"Good. Then it's settled." Rosemary gave a satisfied smile. "Meet him at eight sharp at Piccolino's," she added, referring to the only full-service restaurant in Briar Creek, even if Anna did think her food was better.

"Piccolino's..." Jane gulped.

"A word to the wise, Jane," Rosemary continued. "Order one glass of *white* wine and nurse it—nothing says 'kiss me!' like red-stained teeth! And whatever you do, be sure to show off those long dancer's legs, you know, with a miniskirt or something. It's easy to fall into the yoga pants trap when you're married, but this, my dear, is a date, so just make sure you shine!"

Jane's smile withered, and Anna cast her eyes to the ceiling. It was really time to get on with the day.

An idea had come to her after she'd left Sharon's and she was eager to discuss it. "Grace, we don't have a liquor license, so we can't serve, but what are your thoughts on having a bring-your-own-wine night? We could stay open longer, serve a cheese and chocolate flight, and maybe feature a few related books. It might help generate interest."

Grace beamed. "I love it! I'll put together a sign right now."

Anna let out a pent-up breath. She could do this. She'd built a restaurant once before and she could do it again. It was like riding a bike; she just needed a little practice remembering how to get things off the ground.

It had been harder the first time around. Daunting, really. It amazed her she'd only been twenty-two then, brazen and determined, refusing to give in to self-doubt or fear. Mark had stripped away the plans they'd so carefully detailed over the span of two years, leaving her to scramble, pick up the pieces, and assemble them as best she could, all on her own. It was better that way, she'd told herself. No one could take her dream from her again.

Yet somehow, it had still gone up in smoke. Literally.

Shaking the dark thoughts from her head, Anna began gathering her handbag to leave, but Rosemary stopped her. "Now don't run off just yet, Anna. I have something to discuss with you."

Anna paused, cursing to herself. She had hoped Jane's blind date would deflect Rosemary's interest in her own personal life, but the gleam in the woman's eye said otherwise.

"Have you heard of the Sugar Maple Culinary Competition?"

Anna felt the tightness in her expression fade. Cooking contests always interested her—she'd entered one back in school, and had come in second to Mark even though he was a year ahead of her. They were two rising stars; they had places to go. They had imagined Zagat ratings and Michelin stars.

They had imagined a lot of things.

Sensing she now had her attention, Rosemary arched a perfectly plucked brow. She reached into her bag and took out a magazine, open to a marked page, and pressed it flat on the old farm table in front of her. She tapped it proudly with her finger and said, "Have a look for yourself!"

With more hope than she knew she should permit, Anna leaned forward and skimmed the article, and then, feeling her pulse quicken, started over again from the beginning.

"But . . . the contest is in three weeks!"

"So?" Rosemary just stared at her.

"So, my life is crazy right now. I have to deal with the insurance, the contractors, not to mention this place." She swept her arm around the bookstore. "How can I enter this contest? I don't even have a real kitchen!"

"Mark does," Rosemary pointed out.

Aha. Anna let out of a soft chuckle. "Oh, no. No. No way." Noticing the lift of Rosemary's brow, she added, "It wouldn't be fair to take advantage. He's letting me use his kitchen so I can keep the Annex afloat. Not so I can enter some contest."

"First place gets one hundred thousand dollars," Rosemary crooned, and Anna snapped her mouth closed. Rosemary held her gaze, not even blinking, but the merriment that passed through her blue eyes revealed far more than her impassive expression.

Anna swallowed. "One hundred thousand dollars?"

"That's right." Rosemary shifted so she could read the article. "It says right here that entrants must be certified chefs, which you are. Judges will score on three categories: taste, originality, and presentation. Three courses must be presented in the form of an appetizer, entrée, and dessert; each recipe must include Vermont's very own Sugar Maple brand maple syrup, and the winning recipes will be included on the company's packaging for a year. The competition will take place in the grand ballroom at the Cedar Valley Mountain Resort," Rosemary added pointedly. "Such a *luxurious* location."

That it was, and one hundred thousand dollars would pay for the loan, and leave a little extra, too. She might even be able to expand... Secretly she'd always dreamed of having both a café section and a fine dining section at Fireside. Anna's mind began to whir with possibilities until she shook herself free.

"What's the catch?"

"No catch." Rosemary twitched, giving herself away.

Anna narrowed her eyes. "Oh, come on... for that kind of money? There has to be a catch."

"No catch." Rosemary said simply. "The best team wins."

"Team." *Of course.* Anna folded her arms across her chest and leaned back against a table, giving Rosemary a level stare. "And who would I team up with?"

"Well, Mark, of course."

"Of course." Anna shook her head and stood. "Thanks for the suggestion, Rosemary, but I'm not interested."

"Why not?" It was Grace who cried out from behind the bakery counter. "That's a lot of money, Anna!"

Fifty thousand dollars would still cover most of that

loan, at least until she was back on her feet...Wait. Was she actually considering this?

"I probably won't win!" Anna tossed her arms up, feeling frustration mount. "I have to worry about Fireside, and this place, and do the cooking and baking...I can't spend my time on some contest that dozens of other qualified chefs are entering. They've all been preparing for months, no doubt."

"You won't know unless you try," Rosemary insisted.

"No." Anna picked up her bag and started toward the door. Now was the time to stay planted in reality; it was not the time to let her mind float with magical possibilities. She'd been down that road before, letting her head take her to places that would never come to fruition. Then she'd learned the value of good hard work.

She wasn't going to spend her next few weeks whipping up new recipe ideas. She was going to call the insurance provider again, get in touch with some contractors, and hopefully make enough gourmet salads and sandwiches to feed half the town of Briar Creek this afternoon.

After all, the sooner Fireside was rebuilt, the sooner everyone would drop the subject of Mark. The last thing she needed was to spend one more minute with him than she had to, even if Rosemary had found a way to make the possibility even more enticing than it should be.

CHAPTER 7

Jane checked her watch for the tenth time in as many minutes and let out a small whimper. A flutter of butterflies chased through her stomach, heaving it with dread. Why had she agreed to this? A date with a stranger? What would they even talk about? Sophie, the bookstore, ballet, his job?

Oh God, there would be *flirting*. She'd be expected to laugh, to come up with witty and clever comebacks, to seem quick and energetic. Desirable.

She eyed her sweats and T-shirt, now thrown over the edge of her bed along with half the contents of her closet. Anna was right; she didn't date. She didn't know how to date. Her husband had been her first and only boyfriend. He was her world, her life, the only man she'd ever known. She knew what made him laugh, how he liked to be touched and kissed, what he liked to eat, when he liked to eat... She could spot the signs of a grumpy mood hours before it manifested. She could read each expression, however subtle. She could detect the slightest shift in his tone or behavior.

But she hadn't noticed when he'd been lying to her. Somehow she'd managed to miss that.

Sighing, she fastened her earring and smoothed down her skirt, giving herself one last hard look in the mirror. The thought of getting to know another man wasn't just overwhelming, it was downright exhausting. It would be so much easier to slip into her pajamas, curl up on the sofa with a bowl of popcorn, and bury herself in a good movie. Instead, she was hiding in her bedroom in a black skirt that was a little too tight on the hips and a sparkly top of Grace's that left a little too much to the imagination. She was out of her comfort zone, but then, what was comfortable about a first date?

"Oh, you look so beautiful!" Sophie nearly squealed as she came bounding into the room, her brown eyes sparkling.

Jane managed a wan smile as she turned from the mirror. "Thanks, sweetheart."

"Auntie Grace says you have a *hot date* tonight, but won't you be chilly wearing that shirt, Mommy? Your arms are bare!"

Jane muttered under her breath as she rifled through her discarded outfits in search of a lightweight black cardigan. She ran a brush through her shoulder-length hair one more time, wondering if she should pull it back instead, and then decided to leave it down. She was a twenty-five-year-old mother of a four-year-old child, and even though her life experience made her feel older than both of her sisters combined, she knew many women her age were still single, still comfortable wearing slinky tops and strappy heels instead of yoga pants on the school run.

She wasn't a wife anymore. She wasn't going to find a guy by still acting like one. Or dressing like one.

Taking Sophie's hand, she flicked off her bedroom light and took the stairs slowly, barely registering her daughter's excited chatter about all the fun things her aunts had planned for her tonight. Her stomach was twisting into a hard knot, and her heart was starting to pound. She was actually doing this. Going on a date. What was she thinking?

She could hear Grace and Anna discussing the bookstore as she rounded the hall. When she stopped in the entranceway to the kitchen, all conversation ceased.

"Look at you!"

Jane gritted her teeth and wrestled with the waistband of her skirt. "Don't remind me," she told Grace. "I feel conspicuous enough as it is."

"You look great." It was the first smile Anna had offered since the fire nearly a week ago.

"Well, I feel ridiculous. I look like one of Adam's tram—" She stopped herself before the words slipped. She'd promised herself when Adam moved out that she would not badmouth Sophie's father in front of her, but sometimes, when she thought of the way he'd lied, that was a challenge.

"I just wore that top to a birthday party two weeks ago," Grace insisted.

Jane gave her a long look. "Exactly. You wore it to a party. This is a date." *Just saying the word!* "With a man I don't even know." She looked down at the flimsy fabric. "I don't want to look like I'm trying too hard."

"Well, what did you think you would wear?" Anna chuckled and licked the back of a wooden spoon before dropping it in a bowl. She carried a pan of brownies to the oven and set the timer. "Your usual mom jeans or perhaps that uptight pink twinset you had on last week for the PTA conference?"

Grace began to laugh, but Jane felt her cheeks flame. "I don't wear mom jeans!" That twinset was uptight, yes. But the jeans? "Those jeans are new, I'll have you know. I thought they were . . . cool." Cool. Did people even say *cool* anymore? She'd spent too much time in the house with Sophie over the years, or at the park. She'd lost touch. With the world. With fashion. With herself.

Her sisters exchanged a look. "Jane," Grace said, softening her tone. "You look wonderful; trust me. You look like every other girl your age. Young, carefree, stylish. Just go out and enjoy yourself. You could use a night on the town, and you never know, you might really like him."

She had a point. Jane fingered the thin cardigan that was draped over her arm. "I think I'll wear the cardigan there, and then if I decide I like the guy, I'll take it off."

Grace sighed. "If that will make you more comfortable."

"What do you know about this guy anyway?" Anna asked. She hoisted Sophie onto a counter stool and gave her the same wooden spoon she'd just licked. Catching Jane's disapproval, she said, "What? We're family."

Jane couldn't help but smile. That they were, and thank God for it. "I don't know much. His name is Brian and Rosemary said he works at the Forest Ridge Hospital. She's one of his patients."

"A doctor!" Grace waggled her eyebrows, and Jane felt her spirits lift.

"I guess it's just one dinner," she mumbled, barely able to suppress a pleased smile.

"Perhaps the first of many," Anna said brightly. "Don't hurry home on our account. We've got everything covered."

Jane eyed Sophie warily. Her cheeks were painted in chocolate batter, and her eyes were already turning glassy from the sugar intake. "Maybe I should stay home."

"Don't be ridiculous! Besides, what would you tell Rosemary?"

Grace had her there. Jane shook her head, feeling angry with herself for even asking for this date in the first place, and wiped the brownie mix from Sophie's face with a paper towel before quickly planting a kiss on her cheek.

"Behave," she instructed, as she grabbed her keys from the hook near the door.

"Oh, of course she will," Grace assured her.

Jane paused with her hand on the knob. "I wasn't talking to Sophie."

Before she wimped out, she unlocked her car, slipped inside, and pulled out of the driveway. By the time she'd reached the end of her street, she was feeling downright liberated, and the butterflies were starting to feel more excited than nervous in nature. As she pulled into Piccolino's parking lot, however, she felt as if she could be sick at any moment. She sat in her car, her eye trained on the door, watching each man who walked up its cobblestone steps with unwavering scrutiny, wondering if one of them was her date. Brian was said to be in his early thirties, with brown hair and glasses. Jane liked glasses on men; Adam had worn his only at night, and by the end of their marriage, he was rolling in so late she never saw him wear them.

Already this date had potential. And a doctor, a doctor who wore glasses, couldn't be so bad, could he?

Jane laughed at herself. It wasn't like the man was going to bite. The worst that could happen was that he didn't like her. Didn't find her funny or witty, didn't smile at her attempt at humor. Didn't kiss her goodnight.

But did she even want him to kiss her goodnight? She hadn't thought of that—kissing another man. She hadn't kissed anyone other than Adam since she was a teenager, and it wasn't like she'd had much practice before him. She didn't even know how to kiss, not really. Well, she knew how to kiss Adam, but generally speaking...*Oh, God.*

She pressed a hand to her stomach. She was getting ahead of herself. She hadn't even seen the guy yet. She'd know if she wanted him to kiss her once she met him. And if she didn't...She'd tell him she didn't kiss on the first date. Perfect.

Jane lurched open the car door and shrugged on her cardigan, feeling Grace's disapproving frown from half-way across town. A light drizzle had started, and she hurried across the concrete parking lot and up the winding cobblestone stairs to the arched oak door of the brick building that housed Piccolino's.

Inside, the restaurant was loud and lively, the waiting area crowded with couples. Darting her gaze swiftly over the room and not seeing anyone who matched Brian's description, Jane inched away from the door just as a cool gush of spring air floated into the room.

She turned, bracing herself for the arrival of her date, but the buzz of the room around her fell silent when she came face-to-face with her husband.

Soon-to-be-*ex*-husband, she scolded herself.

"Adam!" Her gaze drifted immediately to his left, where Kristy stood, shaking out an umbrella. It was one of the few times Jane had been so close to her; usually when she picked up Sophie after one of Adam's appointed nights, Kristy stood back in the kitchen instead of coming into the hall to greet her. Now, up close to the other woman—her husband's mistress, her replacement—she couldn't stop staring. Kristy's long blond hair was pulled back in a loose ponytail that looked effortlessly chic; it would only look sloppy if Jane attempted the style. She wore tight jeans and stilettos, with a gray patterned silk top that Jane had eyed in a window on Main Street just last week.

"Hello, Jane," Adam said.

Without so much as a smile in Jane's direction, Kristy set her hand on Adam's arm. "I think our table's ready, honey."

Jane felt her breath still as she watched the exchange. She stared into the eyes of the man who was, for all intents and purposes, still her husband—still a part of their little family unit—and felt something within her begin to crack.

The heartache came in waves. At first, when she had discovered Adam was cheating on her, she denied the truth, but as he grew increasingly distant and she felt him slip away, the realization chipped away at her heart, until she was barely holding it together for their daughter's sake, or for her mother and sisters, who needed her in the wake of her father's sudden death last spring. When Adam finally admitted the truth and moved out just before Christmas, she felt an odd mix of relief, but it wasn't until later, in the middle of the night when she woke alone to an empty and quiet house, that she knew the relief wasn't that he was gone and never coming back. It was that the pain was finally over—that it had reached its limit—and she didn't have to worry about holding herself together anymore. She just had to focus on healing, and moving forward.

And that's why she was here, wasn't it? She was getting on with her life. She was going on a date. In the same restaurant as her husband and his girlfriend.

Jane watched as he walked away, weaving his way through the tables, his fingers placed intimately on the small of Kristy's back as he guided their path through the crowded restaurant, and the hollowness in her chest began to fill with anger as the distance between them grew larger. He hadn't even asked about Sophie! Kristy was laughing as he pulled out her chair, and Jane caught the grin on Adam's face as he sat down beside her, already deep in conversation as he casually picked up the menu and scanned it. It was as if she didn't exist. As if she wasn't standing in this room. As if the nearly six years of their marriage had never happened, never mattered. She wasn't even an old friend. She was just forgotten.

Blinking back tears, Jane headed for the bar, deciding it would be a safer place to wait than here in the open, exposed and raw. She took a seat behind a large arrangement of sunflowers and, remembering Rosemary's advice, ordered a white wine, without bothering to specify anything more, and then accepted it with a shaking hand, waiting for her pulse to steady.

She eyed the door, almost willing it to open, imagining the look on Adam's face when she strolled through the dining area, a handsome doctor at her side, her cardigan officially off. She was just getting to the part in the fantasy where Adam's face would turn ruddy, the way it did when he was especially angry, and where Kristy noticed his reaction and tossed down her napkin with a *harrumph* and stormed out of the establishment when her phone rang.

She glanced at the caller display. "Rosemary?"

"Are you already at the restaurant?"

Jane frowned. "Yes."

There was a pause on the other end of the line. "I didn't think to give Brian your number, but he just called me. Something came up with a patient. He has to reschedule."

Panic tightened her chest. Adam would see her leave. Alone. Minutes after he had arrived. The bastard would probably assume she'd fled on account of him.

Jane quickly ended the call and popped the phone back into her bag. She slid the unfinished glass of wine away, slapped a generous tip on the sleek mahogany bar, and forced herself to stand up. Lifting her chin, she marched back to the door, aware of Adam's presence behind her, somewhere in the bustling crowd of tables.

Her cheeks burned as she pushed through the bar area. She kept her eyes forward, locked on the door, hoping he might think she was just popping into the bathroom, or ducking outside to make a call and check on Sophie. Judging from the way he eagerly leaned into Kristy, she highly doubted his daughter was forefront in his mind.

Adam has reclaimed his life, choosing to continue on without her in it. He was back in the game, out to dinner at the end of a long hard week, looking good and sipping wine, laughing and carefree. While she...she had three loads of laundry to do...of yoga pants and *mom jeans*.

Outside dusk had fallen. The rain came down in a steady drip, splashing against the stone stairs and making her path slippery. She clung to the rail, cursing her decision to wear these shoes Grace had insisted she borrow, and hurried to the car, not even caring that her hair was sopping by the time she slid inside. She was safe. She was free. And she was utterly alone.

Hot tears mixed with rain wet her face, and she fumbled in the glove compartment for a tissue—she always kept some on hand because that's what she did. She was responsible. She was a mother. But she wasn't a wife. Not really.

Her husband was inside that very room, eating dinner with another woman. And her date had stood her up.

She'd told herself she didn't even want to go on the date, that she'd rather sit at home, eat ice cream, and maybe watch a late movie. That wasn't true.

She wanted to feel alive. She wanted to get out there, feel special and pretty like Kristy and the dozens of other girls whose laughter had filled that room.

But the sad fact of the matter was that she wasn't sure anyone could ever make her feel that way. Not like Adam had. Once.

CHAPTER 8

Anna stared at the television screen and realized she hadn't retained anything that had transpired in the last half hour. It wasn't exactly riveting stuff, unless you were a four-year-old girl and could call a princess cartoon edge-of-your-seat material, but still she'd hoped to be able to sink into the couch, eat a couple double chocolate fudge brownies, and forget about her troubles for just one night.

So much for that.

Sophie giggled at something in the movie, and Anna looked over, feeling a familiar range of emotions. It was hard to look at her niece sometimes and not wonder what her own child would have looked like. Would her child have had her own blue eyes and blond hair, or Mark's darker coloring? She'd always pictured a boy, but sometimes, around Sophie, she thought of the little girl she might have had, and all the things they would have done together. She imagined teaching her child to bake cookies, ride a bike, pump her legs on the swings. In each of her fantasies, she was alone, but she'd never stopped to ask herself the tough question. What would Mark have said if she'd told him about the baby? Would he have wanted it?

Sophie giggled again and Anna smiled sadly.

Grace set her plate on the end table. "Have you given any more thought to that contest?" Anna groaned and turned to her sister, who feigned surprise at her expression. "It seemed like a good idea to me."

"There's a lot that would need to go into it," Anna countered. "Brainstorming ideas, testing recipes..." *Spending more time with Mark...* An image of that boyish grin popped up and she reached for another brownie, hoping the sweet taste of fudge would override that other pesky temptation. She chewed miserably. Nope.

Anna wiped the corner of her mouth with a napkin and took a long, cool sip of water. Yep. Still there. Even six days later, the heat of last Sunday morning in Mark's kitchen still lingered. All the more reason to stay away, she decided, but her heart sunk with fresh dread when she caught the time on the clock above the mantel and realized she would have to get up in only five and a half hours if she wanted to get everything made in her single oven before the Annex opened at...nine! Just to add a little more stress, Grace had to go and open early; Anna knew her head was in the right place, but if she had any idea...

"I just can't stop thinking about that prize money," Grace pressed. "Think of what you could do with it!"

Anna forced the rest of the brownie into her mouth so she wouldn't shout out the awful truth. She knew exactly what she would do with that prize money—if she entered the contest.

"It's almost eight. Jane should be well into her date by

now." Anna perked up at the thought. "I wonder how it's going."

An opening and closing of the door to the garage answered that question. Grace turned to her, frowning, her green eyes asking a hundred questions that matched Anna's own confusion.

"Mommy's home!" Sophie sprang from the couch and dashed out of the room.

Mommy. It was a name Anna had never been called, and now probably never would.

Anna slowly followed Grace into the kitchen, where Sophie was chatting excitedly. "We had brownies—*four each*, but I wasn't supposed to tell—and I got chocolate milk, too. Aunt Grace said it's sometimes okay to eat dessert before dinner, especially if you're feeling sad. Did you know Auntie Anna was sad? Are you going to have a pizza party with us?"

Jane looked up, her expression frozen somewhere between bemusement and confusion, and set her handbag on the counter with a sigh. "I'd love to have a pizza party. Did you by any chance save a brownie for me?"

Sophie blinked guiltily and then cried, "Anna ate the last one! She gobbled it all up."

Anna raised a hand, offering a wry grin. "Guilty as charged. I can make another batch, though. We hadn't expected you so soon."

Jane shook her head. "Don't bother; pizza will be fine. First, I'm going to change into something more comfortable." Her smile didn't quite meet her eyes as she took Sophie's hand and disappeared into the hall.

By the time she reemerged in sweats and an old cotton T-shirt, the pizza had arrived and a bottle of wine was uncorked and ready. Jane smiled and laughed as she helped Sophie cut a corner slice, but her eyes were red, and Anna thought she detected a noticeable quiver in her hands.

They ate and talked as if nothing was amiss, and both Grace and Anna knew better than to pry in front of Sophie. When the last of the meal was polished, and Sophie began rubbing her eyes, Jane called it a night.

"She wants to be alone," Grace observed as they stepped onto the stoop a few minutes later.

"That's what has me worried," Anna agreed. The rain had stopped, and the spring air smelled sweet. Somewhere in the darkness, crickets croaked, and a breeze rustled through the new leaves. Anna shivered and rubbed her bare arms, wishing she'd worn a sweater. "Something tells me there's a lot more below the surface."

I should know. No one would ever know the secrets she harbored, the heartache she'd experienced. She kept it bottled up in a neat little package, her own private pain. Somehow it was easier that way; somehow letting it out there, sharing the hurt, would only give it power, make the entire situation impossible to tuck away again. To forget.

"Something tells me Jane will land on her feet," Grace said. "She has Sophie, at least."

There was that pang again.

Anna pushed the hurt aside and waved as she walked to her own car, hating the thought of going home to her dark, empty apartment. Grace had found a good guy, a guy she'd no doubt be meeting tonight. Even though she and Luke had drifted apart for more than five years, somehow, in spite of it all, they'd found a way back to each other. The same wouldn't be true of Jane and Adam, though. Or her and Mark.

Deciding that was just about enough thinking about Mark for one night, Anna flicked on her headlights and pulled out of the driveway, humming to the radio as she steered through the winding residential streets. The houses sat serenely back from the road, a soft glow illuminating a handful of windows, most of which were filled with families, young parents who were probably tucking their children into bed, looking forward to a quiet evening after a long hard day.

Mark hadn't seemed to want a family. She didn't know for certain; they'd never gotten that far. But judging from his behavior, he wasn't looking to settle down. Not with her. Not with anyone. Maybe it was easier that way.

Frowning, she took a sharp right at Mountain Road and slammed on her brakes as something dodged in front of her car. She gasped, heart pounding, and stared at the golden retriever who now stood at the edge of the road. It blinked into the glow from the headlights and then lowered its head before slowly walking away.

Shifting the gear into park, Anna quickly unhooked her seat belt and climbed out of the car, careful not to make a noise that would scare the poor creature away. The dog stopped walking and stared at her as she took a step forward, and then another, willing him not to run. The woods were deep and dark; if she made a mistake, she might never grab him. She stepped on a twig, wincing as it snapped, and hurried forward. Her breath escaped her when her fingers took hold of the nylon collar. She had him.

"There you go," she said, crouching down to inspect the tag. The dog was friendly and didn't resist her touch as she stroked his back. "Let me just see your tag. Hold still, buddy."

She bent down closer, trying to make out the carved letters and numbers on the set of metal tags. "Scout, huh? That's a good, solid name." She grinned and flipped the tag over, but her relief quickly turned to alarm when she saw the contact information.

So much for avoiding Mark for the rest of the week.

Scout insisted on sitting in the front seat, even though she had let him into the back, and more than once he had tried to climb into her lap—while she was turning. When that failed, he pawed at her hands, causing her to accidentally honk the horn, which in turn elicited a watchful yelp. Right in her ear.

Finally she had no choice but to allow his head on her knee, and she idly stroked his soft fur as she pulled off the road and began the slow ascent to Mark's house. Gravel crunched under her tires as she slowed to a stop in front of the renovated cabin. Anna stared into the windows, at the warm glow of the rooms beyond, wondering if Mark had heard her approach.

Cursing under her breath, she flicked off the engine and climbed out—a tricky feat as Scout pounced with excitement, nearly knocking her over as he jumped from the car and ran to the front door. His head arched back as he gave two loud barks, announcing his arrival.

Anna couldn't help but grin, but trepidation quickened her pulse as she hesitated near the base of the front porch that wrapped around the house. The door swung open, and Mark stood in the shadows of the porch light, barefoot and holding a beer. She raked her gaze over his well-worn jeans, and the white cotton shirt that clung to his broad chest, resenting the way her stomach tightened with longing.

The crickets were louder in this rural stretch, and fireflies flickered in the darkness. It was too quiet, too remote for Anna's liking, making her all too aware that they were alone.

"How's my boy?" Mark asked good-naturedly. He squatted and Scout jumped up, licking his face while Mark grinned and gave him a good rub.

"I found him over on Mountain Road." Anna's voice cut through the night air. She shifted on her feet, darting her eyes to Mark as he rolled back on his heels and stood.

Confusion creased his features, pulling at his brow, and he frowned down at Scout. "You wandered off, little guy?"

Oh, for God's sake. "He was a solid mile from here."

Mark had the nerve to look perplexed. He glanced from her to Scout. "Huh."

"He could have been hurt," she snapped. "It's dark out there. There's no telling what's in those woods."

He gave her a lazy grin; one that might have once made her go all warm and tingly. "Well, lucky for us, you came along."

"Seems you're about as careless with pets as you are with women." She glared at him, feeling the rise and fall of her chest as her heart pounded against her rib cage. Possibly she'd overstepped, but she didn't care. Scout was a sweet dog. She hated to see him meet the same fate she had.

Mark's jaw tensed, and in the dim light she saw his stance change. Through lowered brows, he speared her with a look. "The latch on the fence is loose. I was inside for all of fifteen minutes looking for the right tools to fix it. I even propped the gate with some firewood to make sure it stayed closed. Check for yourself if you don't believe me."

She pushed aside her shame. "Sorry."

He held her gaze for a beat, and his features relaxed. "You were protecting my dog. I can't fault you for that."

Anna looked fondly at Scout, who stood by Mark's side, tail wagging, staring at her with big, soft eyes. She climbed the stairs, ignoring Mark's watchful gaze, and crouched to stroke the dog's smooth honey hair. He really was a sweet thing.

"He tried to sit on my lap while I was driving." She smiled, giving Scout's regal head a pat.

Mark took a sip of his beer and leaned against the doorjamb. "Probably my fault. He's spoiled."

Anna glanced up into those deep brown eyes and felt her breath catch at their intensity. Even now, after everything, Mark still had a way of looking at her that made all rational thought cease to exist. "No harm in that," she said. She uncurled her knees and stood, shifting the weight on her feet under Mark's penetrating stare. He was relaxed as he lifted the bottle to his mouth once more and then held it out for her. She shook her head at the offer, watched how a simple shrug could pronounce the curves of his biceps, the span of his shoulders. She inched backward. "I didn't know you had a dog. He wasn't at your Christmas party."

Something in his gaze flickered. Awareness, perhaps, of the strange irony of their situation. They'd coexisted in virtual silence for years, but Briar Creek was small, and people talked. If you didn't want gossip—and neither of them did—then you had to go along with the flow, keep up pretenses. Attend Mark's annual bash.

She hated to admit how much she planned for that party each year. How much she dared to hope that he might come up to her, say something. But what? An apology would be a starter, but after that...Deep down she knew nothing could make up for their history.

Mark held the beer bottle by its neck, letting it hang at his side. "Seems you don't really know much about me at all anymore." He was watching her. Goading her, if she didn't know better. Whatever it was, he was enjoying this entirely too much. "Sort of sad, isn't it?"

"Very," she said, her tone clipped and definitive. She scuffed the toe of her shoe along the worn floorboards of the porch. It was very, very sad.

"I kept thinking one day you'd come around, start liking me again." His mouth tipped into that slow, easy grin and her heart skipped a beat. Damn him. He had no right. No right at all to be digging this up, to resurrect something they'd once had.

He folded his arms across his sculpted chest, pronouncing the thick biceps that used to hold her close. She knew how he felt—his arms, his skin, the heat of his body next to hers, the wave of his hair threading through her fingertips. She inhaled sharply, allowing herself one good hard look, for memory's sake, nothing more. So the man radiated sex. So what? He knew it, and judging from the easy way he stood, watching her impassively, not seeming to feel the least bit awkward in her company, he liked it that way. For good measure, he reached up and scratched at his rib cage, causing the hem of his T-shirt to pull up and reveal a washboard stomach, taut and smooth. Oh, Lordy.

She looked away, across the dark sky, and then let her gaze fall on Scout, who had rolled up in a ball at the edge of the porch. His peaceful snores broke the silence. "You always did like dogs," she murmured, remembering the way he'd light up when they passed one on the street or in the park, usually stopping to give them a friendly pat, or compliment them to the owner.

From the corner of her gaze, she saw Mark shrug. "I didn't think it would be fair to get one, with my schedule and all. Seemed selfish in a way."

Anna narrowed her eyes. Since when did Mark think about being selfish?

"Some things in life choose you, though, you know." His stare bored through hers, locking the air in her chest, leaving every nerve ending on high alert. "Scout came to me about two months ago," Mark told her. "I was walking by a shelter in Forest Ridge and there he was. A runaway, but he's still a pup. Still has a wandering spirit."

Anna pressed her lips together; all prior tingling screeched to a halt. Seemed they were a perfect match then. Mark never could sit still. He always had his eye on the next best thing. The next best someone.

"Well, I'm happy he's home." She took a step backward, then another, giving a tight smile by way of a good-bye, when Mark called out to her.

"Wait."

She turned, her chest pounding with an emotion she didn't want to feel. Something that felt an awful lot like hope. Or excitement. "Yes?"

He was close, too close, determined if she didn't know better. But for what? To have his say, to make her talk, to make up for his laundry list of sins? His breath was heavy, his eyes steady, drifting ever so slightly to her lips. He wouldn't—he couldn't. She didn't move. Didn't breathe.

Just waited. "You could come in if you want, have a drink. It's the least I can do for returning my dog."

Anna shook her head, even though her toes tingled to move forward, to follow Mark into his house, and close the door behind them. "It was no problem. Consider us even. Now we've helped each other."

Mark hesitated, and she allowed herself one last, long look. Yep, still gorgeous. But still an ass, she reminded herself. "You know you're welcome to use my kitchen, Anna—"

Now why'd he have to go and be nice? She waved a hand through the air. "Don't worry about it. I've been getting a lot done at home." Her tone sounded forced. It was probably close to nine now. She'd be lucky to get four hours of sleep tonight.

Mark didn't look convinced. "Well, you have the key. I...don't mind the company."

Anna felt her cheeks flush, and she was grateful for the darkness. "You know what they say about too many cooks in the kitchen." She hesitated, rooted to the spot by the depth of that gaze. "I should go."

She turned before she did something stupid, clutching her keys until they pressed into her palm. She was already halfway to the car when she heard his voice, low and husky. "Good night, Anna."

She started to turn, half wishing she had accepted that drink and hating the part of herself that did.

"Good night. And good night, Scout."

At the sound of his name, Scout's eyes sprung open. Tail wagging, he bounded down the stairs and jumped up on her, the weight of him pushing her back against the car with a loud whoop of surprise.

"Sorry about that." Mark looked tense. "Scout. Scout! Come here, boy." He hurried to her, lunging for Scout's collar, and set his hand lightly on her waist. "You okay?"

She couldn't move. She swallowed hard, and a shiver ripped down her spine despite the way her skin warmed under his touch. Just as quickly it was gone. She shoved her hands into her pockets, nodding quickly.

"Don't worry about it. He was just thanking me."

"He likes you. But then, you were always easy to like." There was that lopsided grin again. Yep, definitely time to go. With a small pang of regret, Anna climbed into her car and watched as Scout jovially ran up the stairs, making sure Mark had a firm hold of his collar before she started the engine.

They stood on the porch, watching her until their reflection in her rearview mirror faded into the darkness and her tires hit the main road. The image of those dark, penetrating eyes, and that hint of regret in Mark's tone stirred up unwelcome emotions. Feelings that had no right being there but ones she still couldn't shake.

A man with a dog as likeable as Scout couldn't be all that bad. In theory. Like Mark, Scout was playful and charming, and completely irresistible. But unlike Mark, he was loyal and dependable.

Those were traits he must have learned from his previous owner.

CHAPTER 9

The alarm clock buzzed at four thirty but Mark was already awake. He set his coffee on the counter and wound through the house, Scout's paws treading softly behind him. It was the normal routine, no different than any other day, but he couldn't shake the restless feeling that had kept him from sleep.

He sighed, looking around the empty bedroom. It was a man's room with sparse bedding and furniture, just like this entire house was a man's house, empty and functional, probably in need of a woman's touch. Oh, he knew he liked to joke with Luke, comment on the various shaped soaps, throw pillows, or printed hand towels that filled his cousin's place, first from his wife, and now, after her passing, from Grace, but a part of it gnawed at him. Living alone was getting old.

He looked down at Scout, managing a grin. At least he had him.

Showering and dressing quickly, he took Scout on a brief walk through the trail in the woods that bordered the back of his lot and then drove into town, drumming his fingers against the leather steering wheel to the beat of the music. He kept the windows down, inhaling the cool morning breeze, but still, coffee was in order. It had been a long night, filled with thoughts he didn't want to acknowledge, with feelings that had no place coming to the surface, and the day was just beginning. He'd tried to forget Anna. At times he'd even thought he'd succeeded. Yet all it took was the sight of her standing at the edge of his porch, petting his dog, giving him that watchful stare, and he knew he was kidding himself.

She'd been special, and that's why he'd run, farther and faster than he had with all the others. That day all those years ago on the beach when he kissed her, he'd wanted to think that he could do this. That for once, he could commit to someone, trust in them to do the same. They'd been inseparable those two years in culinary school, and they'd grown up together, too. But the closer they got, the more a part of him was already pulling away—from her, and from every plan they were setting in motion.

They had a vision: a big, gleaming restaurant with local ingredients, innovative recipes, and just the right combination of style and comfort. He often wondered if it would have been a success, or if he would have met the same fate as his father . . . bankrupt and dejected, with nothing else to do but run from the mess he'd created. He'd avoided that path. Rejected the mere possibility. Rejected the person who could make it all come true.

She'd wanted too much. A restaurant. A relationship. He'd wanted both, too. But he couldn't risk one over the other. In the end he would have hurt her more, just like good ol' Dad had all those years ago. Tavern on Main was his baby, and when that was gone, well ... so was he.

Now, however, just the thought of flipping a pancake or scrambling an egg made him feel tired. He had to get out of here, move on to something better. So what was stopping him now? Money. But after that? His mom was better. Luke was out of his rut. He could focus on business without having to worry about it consuming him, or letting someone down. No one needed him. He was free. Just how he liked it, right?

This time, he'd take the risk. And hope to hell he didn't make the wrong decision.

The problem was that a little part of him was beginning to think he already had.

Hastings was dark when he arrived, and Mark felt a twinge of sadness that another morning would pass without Anna's arrival. How she managed to prepare all that food in her home kitchen escaped him, but the mere thought of it made him angry—at himself, at her. She was stubborn, and she didn't back down. The part of him that wasn't driven crazy by this was left admiring her for it. Even more than he already did.

He shouldn't have gotten so defensive last week when she found those notes. He should have just let her stay, enjoyed the fact that they were speaking again, rather than pushing her away.

But then, wasn't that what he did best?

He worked in silence for more than an hour, greeted the staff as they trailed in, and then turned the sign on the door. The coffee was percolating behind the counter, and he was just pouring himself an extra mug, trying to drum up some energy for the weekend rush, when the bell jingled, announcing the first customer.

He smiled in surprise at the sight of his aunt Rosemary.

"Good day to you," she said, taking a seat at the counter and flipping over a mug that had been resting on its saucer.

Mark took his cue and reached for the coffeepot. "Don't usually see you in here this early." *More like ever at all*, he corrected himself.

"A dancer's figure is hard to maintain at my age," she explained, and then helped herself to a liberal dose of sugar. She blew on the coffee and took a sip. "I was up early, and so I thought I'd stop in."

Mark nodded, knowing better than to pry. Rosemary was here for a reason. In time she'd let it be known. He handed her a menu. "Hungry?"

"Oh...I'll have some wheat toast. No butter. And a side of strawberries, but only if they're fresh." She hesitated as her eyes slid to the menu on the wall. "You know, on second thought, make that a number six."

Mark grinned. "Two eggs with bacon, biscuits, and a side of hash coming up. Did you still want the strawberries?"

Her blue eyes were wide in alarm. "Well, you don't need to shout it! Yes, I'll still have the berries. But only if—"

"Only if they're fresh. I know, I know." Mark clipped a ticket to the top of the service window. All that training, all those dreams, and he was running a place where people questioned the produce.

Rosemary waited until her meal was served before broaching the real reason she had stopped in. She finished telling him about his cousin Molly's graduate school roommate and her hopes that Kara had finally figured out what she wanted to do in life, and then fell into silence, preparing herself for whatever was coming next. Mark leaned back against the counter, crossing his arms over his chest as he settled in for her explanation. His mouth twitched in amusement as he watched her bristle, clearly having an inner struggle, and then push her plate away.

"This was absolutely delicious," she announced. "So good, in fact, that I think you could, and maybe should, be doing more with your talents."

Mark didn't bother pointing out that he hadn't cooked the meal. "Oh? And what would that be?"

His pulse kicked as he thought of Anna, the notes she had found. Had she mentioned something to Rosemary in passing? He stopped himself—*Luke*. Even though he considered Luke to be nearly as much a brother as Brett, Rosemary could easily draw information out of him when she set her mind to it. He shouldn't have said anything the other morning. Next thing he knew, his mother would be knocking on his door, asking if he had anything he wanted to share. It was just the problem with this town— everyone knew everything about you. Well, almost every-thing, he thought, his mind trailing to Anna. There were still a few secrets.

"Well, the Sugar Maple Culinary Competition, of course!"

Mark frowned. "Excuse me?"

Rosemary could barely conceal her excitement. "It's a new contest for professional chefs. First prize wins a hun-dred thousand dollars."

Mark leaned in. "That's a lot of money." Enough to break ground on a permanent place. Enough to get on with life once and for all.

"Indeed. You prepare three courses, each with the Sugar Maple brand's maple syrup. The winning recipes will be featured on the back of the product and the winning team will be spotlighted by the Vermont tourist bureau."

"A team." He speared her with a look. "And let me guess, you thought I should team up with Anna."

"Well, it seemed the obvious choice," she said airily. "Although, I suppose there's that guy over at Piccolino's or perhaps one of the chefs here..."

Mark wasn't buying it. Piccolino's was stale and unimaginative. It still hit a nerve that it had survived for twenty-three years while Tavern on Main had tanked. "You know that Frank over at Piccolino's is a giant ass. His food isn't even good; it's just the best in town for white tablecloth service. And Vince here isn't a certified chef; he's a line cook. So that leaves Anna."

Rosemary jutted her chin. "What's wrong with that?"

Nothing and everything all at once. "I don't think she'll go for it," he settled on.

Rosemary considered his response as she fished for her wallet, but Mark held up a hand. She demurred and patted her mouth one last time before setting down her napkin and hopping off the stool. "I must run. Rehearsals for the spring recital start today."

"Break a leg," Mark said, and Rosemary whipped around.

"Break a leg is for actors, not dancers." She looked around, fist ready to knock on wood, but the entire joint consisted of metal, Formica, and vinyl.

Mark gritted his teeth, thinking of the restaurant he'd envisioned. Polished wood tables, lit by a single pillar candle. Wide plank bamboo floors in a warm stain. Beamed ceilings against ivory walls, and heavy velvet drapes in burnt orange. He could picture the gleaming bar with top-shelf liquor, the wine cellar just to the side, and a cluster of club chairs around a crackling fireplace. The kitchen would be sleek, with a manager at each station, buzzing and electric, just like his dad's had once been.

He stopped himself right there.

Fifty thousand dollars would go far to support his plan. It would be enough to get it off the ground. To get him out of this town. To give him another chance at reclaiming the dream he'd somehow let slip away. Or thrown away, if he was being honest with himself.

"Hey, Aunt Rosemary," he called just before she slipped out the door.

She turned, a knowing smile playing at her lips. "Yes?"

"When's the contest?"

"Two weeks from Saturday," she said. "And you have to register by this coming Saturday."

He pulled in a breath. Just shy of three weeks, then. It would be a struggle, but it wouldn't be impossible. "Thanks."

"My *pleasure*," she said, hurrying out the door.

Mark mulled the idea as he stepped back into the kitchen, daring to briefly skim his notes and plans before stuffing the papers into a drawer in his office, where no one would find them. He was still thinking about Rosemary's suggestion when he cut out of the diner just after noon, having somehow survived the Sunday brunch crowd without a broken plate, screaming baby, or tripping waitress.

Winning that contest wouldn't just set him up for the

new restaurant; teaming up with Anna would force her to spend time with him, interact with him, hell, even speak with him. It might be just the chance he needed to make things right between them. But would she go along with it? Even now, when she was struggling, she was still resisting his help. She was stubborn, but she'd have to be a fool to turn down an opportunity like this.

Mark paused at the corner of Second Avenue and looked across to the charred storefront of the Fireside Café. If he tried hard enough he could almost see the old sign—Tavern on Main—and the red awning above the door. The owner just before Anna had removed it. Mark must have been eleven at the time, maybe twelve, and when he rode his bike through town and saw that it was missing, it was like a punch straight to the gut, a bitter, unbearable reminder that it wasn't his father's restaurant anymore, and that it never would be again, that his father really wasn't coming home. Bill Hastings had left that place just like he'd left his wife and two sons. Without a look back. Not once in all these years.

He hated that the realization still hurt. Now, twenty years later.

Fireside had been an appropriate choice of name, Mark thought grimly, letting his gaze skim the now boarded-up windows and door. He wasn't sure what had possessed Anna to take over the space to begin with, knowing the connection it had to his family. Even though he was grateful for the rent money his mom collected, a part of him wanted the place to stay empty. It was his dad's place, no one else's. If he couldn't make it work, why should anyone else think they could?

The police tape was gone, but a makeshift fence had

been erected to keep people away from the structure. His mother had told him they'd start rebuilding soon, beginning with the kitchen, and he supposed Anna might have survived this setback if she didn't have the bookstore to think about. Even without a kitchen at the Annex, the loan on that expansion must have been hefty. Half of the prize money would certainly go a long way for her, too.

He stuffed his hands into his pockets and turned toward the town square. The Briar Creek farmers market kicked off its season today, and already crowds had gathered on the green. Mark wandered over to an artisan cheese stand and sampled sharp, salty cheddar from a local dairy farm and creamy herbed goat cheese. He wove his way through the various stands, stopping to load his bag with fresh produce, then spotted Anna across the green.

Her back was to him, but he'd recognize that long, honey blond hair anywhere. And that rear. Telling himself it was just attraction, nothing more, he lingered on her curves a while longer, enjoying the way her jeans defined every contour of her hips and thighs. She was laughing as she carefully placed a bundle of greens into her straw bag, and Mark grinned. It was good to see her like that. Carefree. Happy. It was the way he liked to remember her.

Mark watched as she roamed to the next stand, the crowds making it hard for him to keep her in his line of vision. He pulled in a sigh and narrowed his gaze. He had a decision to make, and time wasn't on his side. The contest was just over two weeks away, and there was only one match for him when it came to heating up that kitchen. It might take some convincing, but he would bet that Anna had just as much motivation to enter and win as he did.

They needed each other, whether she liked it or not. Time to remind her of that.

He gripped his bags and put one foot in front of the other, taking long strides until he caught up with her. "Hello there."

He grinned as she turned to face him, ignoring the fact that the pleasant smile that curved her mouth fell when she locked his gaze. She hesitated, finally breaking his stare, and glanced to the left, as if for escape.

"I see old Mr. Beckett talked you into the ever delicious asparagus," he said affably.

She managed something of a grin, and then quickly checked herself. "I thought I'd make an asparagus tart with Gruyère."

Mark liked hearing her talk like this. Back in culinary school, it was one of their favorite pastimes; he could sit and listen to her brainstorm ideas for new recipes, watching her eyes come alive while she spoke, and he'd chase her into a test kitchen, or the cramped little space in the back of her student apartment, and they'd cook, for hours, talking about food, about life, sometimes not talking at all…

"How about you?" she asked, tipping her head into his bag to discover a bundle of asparagus. "Ah, and here I thought you had gotten away clean. I'll buy it off you if you want."

It was the first gesture she'd made to him in years, aside from returning Scout, of course, but that was sort of obligatory. They locked eyes for a beat, and he finally said, "No, that's okay. I have some plans of my own."

"Oh?"

His gut stirred at the way her lips pursed to form that

single syllable. "Yeah, I thought I'd roast it, maybe toss in a few capers and a soy balsamic reduction." Not that he'd offer that up as a special at the diner—he could just hear Arnie Schultz grumbling now. Lately, he saved his real time in the kitchen for personal use, like some secret guilty pleasure.

"Interesting." Anna turned to inspect a bucket of eggs. She plucked one from the top and considered it before setting it back. "Although I shouldn't be surprised. You were always coming up with great menu ideas for—" She stopped herself and looked away.

They'd never settled on a name for their place, and in a way, he was glad they hadn't. The plan had never been finalized. It didn't have a true identity.

In theory, that should make it easier to forget.

He tried not to think about all it entailed, all the hours of planning that had gone into their big, shared plans. From the success she'd had with Fireside Café, he hadn't considered that she ever thought about their other ideas. Now, seeing the downward curve of her mouth, he started wondering if he had been wrong about that, too.

Mark swallowed hard. "My mom tells me they're finishing the demolition today," he said, eager to change the subject.

"Hopefully the rebuilding will start soon after. I'd love to be back in business before the height of summer," Anna added. He followed her to the next stand, where she selected two pints of wild strawberries.

"Things going well with the bookstore?" he asked casually. He stuffed his hands into his pockets, falling into step beside her, daring to glance at her sidelong.

His heart zinged at her simple beauty. Her creamy

complexion was free of makeup, and her cheeks and lips were stained with a natural blush. Her turquoise eyes were rimmed with black lashes that fluttered when she blinked or dropped her gaze, just as she did now. He'd hit a nerve.

Just as quickly, she jutted her chin. That proud, stoic profile he'd come to recognize—and resent—replacing the softer side, the Anna he'd once known. The Anna he'd loved.

He gritted his teeth. Better not to think about that anymore. He'd made his decisions. Made them for the best.

More and more, though, he struggled to convince himself of that.

"Oh, fine, just fine. It's really working out just as we'd hoped," she said, referring of course to Grace, whose idea it had been all along to expand the original bookstore in an effort to revive it and generate more business. So far it did seem to be working, but Mark questioned how much could be earned off pastries, coffees, and the occasional gourmet sandwich. Fireside was one thing—that place was booming. A new place, however...Those start-up costs couldn't be cheap.

The loss of their father hadn't been easy for any of the Madison girls, and their mother, Kathleen, had only just started to pick herself up again with the help of Grace's return. The bookstore renovation kept the sisters bonded and their father's memory alive. He'd stopped in a few times, despite Anna's chilly greeting, and he'd seen the work they'd put into the place. It was impressive—cozy and inviting and still true to the original. It would be a shame to let it go now.

"Well," Mark said, stopping at the base of the white gazebo where several people had stopped to gather on its steps for an impromptu lunch of fresh bread, cheese, and fruit. "I was hoping to find Frank. Have you seen him around here?"

Anna's brow furrowed with suspicion. "Frank Piccolino?" When he nodded, her tone turned wary. "Why?"

He gave a small shrug, not bothering to mask his grin. He was enjoying this far too much to try to deny it, and she was responding to him just as he had hoped. He knew women—how to read them, how to woo them—and of all the girls who had flitted in and out of his life, Anna was the one he knew best. A few doubts, a hint of a possible missed opportunity, and a few little reminders about her current financial state should be just the trick. "Oh, I just wanted to talk to him about a business venture."

Her brow pinched tighter. "I thought you didn't like Frank."

"People can change." His pulse kicked up a notch as their eyes met and a flicker of awareness passed through her blue irises. He wasn't talking about Frank, and she knew it.

She blinked, breaking the spell. "I tend to think most people are who they are. At the end of the day, you just fall back on old behaviors."

He locked her eyes. "I'd like to think it's never too late."

Her lips pinched tight for one telling second and she pulled in a breath, huffing, "Well, I haven't seen Frank. Perhaps you should try him at the restaurant in a few hours."

He had no intention of doing any such thing, but he wasn't about to tell her that. "Nah, I'll just give him a call. What I have to discuss can't exactly wait."

She tried to look casual as they wandered to the next

stand, but she chewed on her bottom lip—something she only did when she was working through something. "You thinking of joining forces with the competition?" Her low laugh sounded forced.

"Something like that." He moved his eyes over her inquisitive face. Here it went. "I was actually looking for a teammate for the Sugar Maple Culinary Competition."

She groaned. "Not you, too." She shook her head, her pretty lips pursing. "Rosemary mentioned it to me the other day."

Mark stopped walking. So she already knew about it then. Just what was his aunt up to?

He shrugged it off. He'd deal with that later. "It sounds like fun, doesn't it? And the prize..." He let out a long whistle.

Anna stalked to the next stand, and he quickened his pace to keep up with her. "The prize money is definitely appealing, but I don't plan on entering."

Somehow he found this hard to believe. "I would think you'd be eager to compete, especially now with everything that's happened."

She sighed, shaking her head. "The timing is bad. I can't possibly focus on something like a contest when I have a hundred other things to deal with right now." Her tone was brusque, but she couldn't meet his eye.

"Here I thought you'd be stiff competition. Maybe I stand a fighting chance after all. People sure do like Frank's cooking..."

"Well, good luck with that. I worked for Frank Piccolino the summer after my freshman year if you recall, and he's a control freak and an egomaniac. Besides, you can cook circles around him."

True, all true, which was why Mark would never even consider teaming up with the man. The few times he'd deigned to eat at Piccolino's out of social obligation, he'd seen Frank, red-faced and ill-tempered, shouting out commands as his staff scurried around him, heads bent.

Time to soften the approach. "Well, I don't really see any other options if I want to enter."

Her hand hesitated above a bunch of kale. Recovering quickly, she ran her tongue over her bottom lip and said firmly, "Nope, it's probably your only option."

"Although I suppose he could already be entered with his sous chef," Mark mused, watching Anna carefully as he casually shelled out cash for a brick of aged Gruyère.

"Perhaps," Anna said airily. She tucked a loose strand of hair behind her ear, revealing the perfect slope of her neck. "You won't know until you ask."

"That's exactly what I was thinking." He took a step backward, immensely enjoying the bewildered expression that fell over her pretty face. "I should probably get going. Lots to do today. People to see…"

Her lips parted for one telling second before pinching tight again. "Good luck," she said.

"Thanks." Mark grinned. Something told him he wasn't going to need it.

By this time tomorrow, he'd have a partner for the contest. But it sure as hell wouldn't be Frank Piccolino.

CHAPTER
10

Okay, so fifty thousand dollars was a lot of money. And yes, it was enough to pay off the loan she'd taken for the Annex, more or less. But was it enough to make her work side by side with Mark, for hours on end, for the next two and a half weeks?

No. You couldn't put a price on that kind of temptation. Or destruction. She'd rather work with that inflated head Frank Piccolino, barking out orders at the pass, red-faced and puffy in his starched apron, than team up with Mark. The thought had occurred to her...but then she might end up competing against Mark, and if she was being honest with herself, she wasn't sure she could beat him. Mark was talented. Too talented to be whisking pancake batter seven days a week. Sharon had taken over the diner out of necessity, not passion. Anna never could understand why her son clung to Hastings instead of doing all the things he'd set out to do.

Was Mark really entering the contest with Frank Piccolino? Anna frowned. It didn't matter. Not in the least. She wasn't going to enter—with or against Mark was beside the point. She had a restaurant to rebuild, staff to worry about, and a loan hanging over her head. As much as the prize money could solve her problems, it would create a dozen more if she sacrificed her current problems for a fictional one.

Anna blew a loose strand of hair from her forehead and finished scooping dough onto a cookie sheet. The egg timer on the counter rang, letting her know it was time to remove the lemon and blueberry tea cake. Anna grabbed a potholder from the butcher block that centered her island, managing to knock the canister of flour to the floor in the process. Fine white powder dusted the hardwood, and Anna resisted the urge to burst into tears right then and there. The entire kitchen looked like it had exploded. Her limited counter space was covered in mixing bowls and sugar canisters, and the small kitchen table was lined with the cooling racks. She'd run out of space and had to set a few on chairs, and now, in her rush to get the tea cake from the oven before her effort was wasted, she tripped on a chair leg, sending a dozen double chocolate chunk cookies scattering across the floor.

Anna flung open the oven. Sure enough, the surface of the bread was tinged and dark. Overbaked.

She set the pan on the stovetop, beside the stacks of other baking pans that weren't filling her small sink, and contemplated it. She could glaze the top, but it wouldn't matter. She'd messed up; she'd have to redo it. If there was one thing she'd decided early into running Fireside, it was that presenting the highest quality food every day was the best way to stay successful.

She couldn't let herself down. Or her customers.

Or her family.

The doorbell rang and Anna jumped. She checked her watch—*Shoot*. She'd told Kara to stop by at eight and it was already five after. She was running late, and she still had to clean up, load the car, and stop by the Annex before they met with Sharon.

"Sorry," she said, flinging open the door. "I lost track of time." Any suspicions she had that she looked as frazzled as she felt were confirmed by her friend's expression.

"Don't worry about it." Kara hesitantly entered the front hall. "Do you need any help?"

Anna mentally went through her to-do list. "Would you mind popping the oatmeal cookies into the oven and setting the timer for twelve minutes? I need to take a quick shower."

She noticed Kara's eyes widen as she stared past her into the kitchen.

"Never mind the mess," Anna said quickly. "I'll take care of it all later."

A pristine kitchen was top priority at Fireside, and she could only imagine what the current condition of her counters and floors said about her state of mind. She flinched as she stood back and followed her friend's gaze to the open canisters of sugar, the half-peeled sticks of butter, and the carton of eggs filled with empty shells. The flour bag was still resting on its side. At least ten baking sheets were stuck in the sink or set on top of sticky mixing bowls. It was a mess. A complete disaster. Just like her life.

"You know I would have been happy to come over and help you with all this," Kara said. She walked into the kitchen and popped the cookies into the oven. After setting the timer, she pulled a broom and dustpan from the closet and began sweeping the flour.

Anna paused in the doorway, not sure how to reply. "With everything that's happened, it didn't seem fair. You work for Fireside. All this is for the Annex."

Kara stopped sweeping. "Anna. You're my friend. That's what friends do. It's not about me being your employee."

Anna gave a small smile. "Thanks, Kara."

She ducked into the bathroom, feeling guilty. Usually a hot shower made everything feel a little brighter, but as she came back into the kitchen in a fresh T-shirt and a cotton skirt, she felt just as grim. Even the sight of the much improved kitchen did little to perk her up. If anything, it made matters worse.

Kara was her friend, but she was also her employee. And she couldn't pay her a dime. How could she break that news to her? She'd paid everyone through the month, but she couldn't do anything to keep them on beyond that, much as she wished she could.

"I feel bad that we haven't talked much this week," Anna said as they finished loading the last of the bags into the car. She slipped into her seat and fastened her seat belt.

"Don't worry about it. I know you've been busy, and my mom and Aunt Sharon have kept me in the loop."

"No wonder you weren't surprised that I was using my own kitchen instead of the diner."

Kara looked at her strangely. "Is Mark really that bad?"

Anna grew quiet. "I know he's your cousin." For that reason, friend or not, Kara had never been told about their relationship. For all anyone knew, she and Mark just didn't click like the other folks in town did. "It's just... I don't know. Just college stuff." *Not exactly a lie...*

"That's not what I think."

They'd arrived in town quickly, and she pulled into a spot in front of Main Street Books. "Oh no?" she asked lightly.

Beside her, Kara grinned. "Nope. I've been thinking about it, and I think there's a bigger underlying reason for why you and Mark don't get along anymore."

Anna switched off the ignition and jumped out of the car. She began grabbing the shopping bags full of boxed pastries and muffins and met Kara on the sidewalk. The shield of her sunglasses prevented her friend from seeing the panic in her eyes. If Kara knew, then Rosemary would know, and Luke would know, and Grace . . . and then Mark would know how much he hurt her. And she couldn't have that. Ever.

"I think that you and Mark are too alike for your own good." Kara's blue eyes danced as she folded her arms across her chest.

"Oh." Anna felt her shoulders drop with relief. "Ha. Maybe." She popped the trunk and retrieved the last of the bags.

"You're both stubborn to a fault." Catching her stare, Kara said, "Sorry, Anna. I love you both, but it's true. And you're both running restaurants on Main Street."

"You think it's some competition thing?" *Oh, if she only knew.*

"Could be." Kara shrugged. "I just think you'd probably be best of friends if you gave each other a chance."

Anna's lips thinned. Kara's perception was painfully accurate, but then, who better to notice such a thing than someone so close to both of them? For two years he'd been her best friend, until he had to go and blow it.

"Well," she said, "I'll give it some thought."

Kara gathered up a few more bags and closed the door with her hip. "Was it always this way? In culinary school?"

Anna sighed. She tried not to speak about that time period in her life, and she'd mastered the skill of turning the conversation whenever it was mentioned. It saddened her, knowing how much her father had encouraged her to go, how proud he had been of her success there, to know that she, like him, was following his passion. Now, she couldn't even think of those four years without feeling a twinge of sickness.

"Oh, you know. It was a big school. Mark was a year ahead of me..." Anna frowned. Kara hadn't brought any of this up in years. Why start now?

"Look. There he is now!" Kara waved over Anna's shoulder, grinning broadly.

Anna whipped her head around reflexively, her mouth firming at the sight of Mark strolling lazily toward them. God help her if he didn't look better than usual. His dark brown hair was tousled and, from the looks of it, hadn't met a brush that morning. A white T-shirt skimmed his khakis at the waist, hugging every inch of that chiseled torso.

She quickly turned back and began fumbling for the handles of the bags, hoping to dart into the haven of Main Street Books without an exchange.

Too late. Mark stopped beside them, and from the way his Birkenstock-covered feet were planted at her side, he didn't show any signs of going on his way. She slid her eye to him, hating the way her traitorous pulse skipped at the sight of that grin, which was positively wicked. His brown eyes tore through hers, forcing her to blink.

"Lovely morning today," Mark said evenly, his eyes

never straying from hers. He stuffed his hands into his pockets and jutted his chin to the bags of baked goods. "I can see you've been busy, Anna."

Anna stifled a sigh. She really wasn't in the mood for Mark's banter this morning, even if the boyish gleam in his eyes made her heart roll over.

"Very," she said. "And I have lots more to do, so if you don't mind…" She started to walk away but he stopped her.

"Don't leave on my account." His grin never faltered, and Anna felt her eyes narrow.

"You may find this hard to believe, Mark, but not everything I do is because of you."

He gave a shrug. "So you're just baking scones all night for fun instead of using my kitchen for a couple hours?"

She opened her mouth and then closed it.

Kara, whose brow had begun to twitch as she followed the conversation like a spectator at a tennis match, offered, "Mark, have you seen your mother? We're supposed to meet her at Fireside but we're running a bit late."

Mark slid his eyes to Anna and cocked a brow. "Running late? Since when are you—Ah. All those early mornings, I suppose." He grinned a little wider.

Kara cleared her throat. "If you see your mom can you let her know we'll be right over?"

Mark held Anna's gaze for another beat and then slowly pulled his attention to his cousin. "Sure. I'll swing by the café on my way back to Hastings. Stop by after your meeting if you want to go over—"

"Oh." Kara seemed to stiffen. "I'm meeting my mom at the studio after the meeting, so…I'll call you."

Anna frowned in suspicion as a pink flush crept up Kara's cheeks. Kara grabbed the bags from Anna's hand

and, with a murmured excuse Anna couldn't make out, dashed to the door of Main Street Books and slipped inside, leaving Anna to turn helplessly back to the one man she couldn't seem to get away from these days.

He shouldn't be standing here like this, staring at her, but he couldn't bring himself to turn away either. A sudden sadness shadowed her blue eyes, a wariness that he'd so often detected over the years, when he dared to steal a glance at her.

He shouldn't have teased her. He should have just come along, said hello, offered to help carry the bags. But that would have been too...serious. Too real. Too risky.

It was easier to keep her at arm's length, even if sometimes all he wanted to do was reach out and take her by the hand, pull her close, and kiss that frown off her pretty mouth.

"I didn't mean to rile you up," Mark said, giving her a half smile.

The space between her brows pinched. "It's fine." She reached down to grab the handles of the two remaining bags. "I should really get inside."

Mark pulled his hands from his pockets and leaned forward. "Let me."

"Mark." Her voice was urgent, and he knew this was about much more than some bakery bags. His gut tightened when he saw the pain in her expression. "Please. I know you offered to help me, and I appreciate it, but I think we can both agree that it's best for us to keep our distance."

"Is that really what you want?" He held her eyes, looking for an answer he wasn't sure he should be hoping to hear. They should keep their distance; that's what he always told himself. Now he wasn't so sure. He'd let her go once before, and he'd regretted it every damn day since.

"I think it's best," Anna said after a measured silence.

"That's not what I asked."

"Mark." Her tone was impatient, but her eyes had gone flat.

He stepped back, holding a hand in the air, suddenly feeling the need to run, to put not just emotional, but physical distance between them, and this need...this all-consuming need he felt to do just the opposite.

"Hey, don't worry about it. You're busy, and I still have to track down Frank." He waited a beat, hoping for a reaction, but all he met was that distant frown. "I'll let you go."

Let you go. Wasn't that what he did best? She'd been his friend—the closest he'd ever had other than Luke—and he'd shut her off, let her down, turned her away without another glance back. Every time his mind wandered back to her, he forced it away, taking company with whatever girl wanted attention, women who could never worm their way into his heart, who could never reach him, or touch him. Or hurt him.

He waited until she had disappeared behind the red door of Main Street Books before hurrying the eight blocks back to Hastings. The crowd was thin, but it would pick up again around lunch hour, and for once Mark wished there was a line outside, babies wailing, and frazzled waitresses bumping into each other. Chaos would take his mind off Anna. It would drown out the voices in his head that kept pulling him back to her, even now, after all these years. It wouldn't, however, solve his problem about the competition. What if Anna didn't come around?

Did she really hate him enough to lose out on the possibility of fifty thousand dollars, now, when she needed it most? He'd called her bluff, and she wasn't biting. And there was no way in hell he was going to partner with Frank Piccolino, no matter how sweet that cash would be.

He stopped right there. Maybe Anna felt just as firm in her stance against him.

"Well, there you are!" His mother's smile pulled him out of his darkening mood and he snapped back to the present, grateful for the distraction.

"Hi there!" He smiled warmly, and leaned in to give her a hug. Even now, when she'd been in remission for more than five years, he still clung a little tighter, held on a little longer, just in case. "I just ran into Kara," he said, consciously avoiding all thoughts of Anna as he stepped around the counter. "She asked me to tell you she's running a few minutes late."

"I'm glad to hear it, actually. I was hoping to share a cup of coffee with you before the meeting." Sharon settled her bill on the table, but Mark quickly handed the money back to her.

"You know you don't need to pay for anything here. You own it, after all."

"Yes, but you're the one working here now; it only seems fair." Sharon shrugged and glanced around the room. "The place looks great, Mark."

"Eh." Mark tried to muster up some enthusiasm and failed. He grabbed a mug and filled it with coffee, then took a long swig. Hastings didn't look any different today than yesterday, or last year, but he wasn't going to argue. His mother loved this place for some reason. She saw it as a beacon, and for her, perhaps it was. The pay had been steady when she'd needed it, and looking back she had to have been lonely. Locals gathered in the diner, making friendly conversation—people cared, but they didn't get close. For a while, that suited Mark fine. Now...

He rubbed the back of his neck. He was starting to sweat. Now wasn't the time to be thinking about getting close. Now was the time to be thinking of pulling back. If he ever wanted that restaurant, that was.

"Sometimes I miss working here," Sharon mused. Catching his eye, she gave a shy smile and waved her hand through the air. "What am I saying? There's no one better to run it than you."

Mark nodded and finished his coffee. That's what he told himself, what he tried to believe. When his mother was diagnosed with cancer his senior year of high school, he vowed to stay by her side, do whatever it took to help out. He'd driven her to all her doctor's appointments in Forest Ridge and ordered her to take time off. Working at the diner made sense. He'd practically grown up here, and food was... Well, try as he might to deny it, food was in his blood. By the time he'd arrived at culinary school at age twenty, he'd seen his time at Hastings as nothing but good training. He hadn't expected to return to this place any more than he'd expected the cancer to come back.

But then, when was he ever able to count on anything turning out the way he'd hoped?

CHAPTER 11

Standing in the middle of Fireside, in the dim lighting that filtered through the tarps that covered the windows, Anna felt her stomach roil with dread. She knew it would be bad—she'd braced herself—but the reality hadn't really hit her until this moment. It was gone. Just gone. And what remained was destroyed. The wood floorboards were discolored; the walls, stained. Those few things that hadn't been directly touched by the fire or smoke had been too damaged by the sprinklers to bother keeping.

She couldn't even walk into that kitchen.

"This looks even worse than I feared!" Kara murmured.

Anna felt her mouth thin as she followed her friend's gaze to the space that had once housed the beautiful glass bakery counter. It, along with the dozens of polished tables and chairs, had been destroyed, and all that remained of Fireside's cozy dining space was the fireplace itself, made of indestructible brick. Anna let her attention stop there, remembering the thrill she'd experienced when she first set eyes on it. She'd imagined club chairs in a semicircle, the flames crackling, and piano music streaming softly through speakers.

If she tried hard enough, she could picture it not just as it had been, but possibly even better—with a café area near the counter, overflowing with fresh breads and trays of pastries, and a separate dining area to the side, maybe even a hostess stand...

She opened her eyes quickly and steadied herself. Better came with a price tag. The best she could hope for right now was to have things up and running by July. The summer was always a busy time on Main Street: There were weekly festivals in the town square, and people tended to linger, enjoying the warm weather that was so precious in their northern climate, often going out of their way to come in to town and relax at a sidewalk table or enjoy an ice cream from the local parlor.

Anna took a deep breath and wandered toward the kitchen—or what had been the kitchen—and then turned away with a frown. She just couldn't do it. The last time she was in there, she was in her element, moving on autopilot, working hard and loving every minute of it, thriving in the one place where nothing could touch her and no memories seeped in. There was no point in facing the obvious or wishing for things to be different than they were.

Something she should keep in mind more often, she thought, forcing her thoughts from Mark and everything that might have been.

"When do you think it will reopen?" Kara asked.

"I think the best we can hope for is early summer." Being here now, though, her statement felt optimistic. She couldn't imagine the labor it would take to get this place cleaned up and set right again, much less the cost. Insurance would help, of course, but it had taken months, even years, to find some of the little elements that had made this place her own. It almost felt less daunting to choose a new location and start over, but she had a lease agreement she intended to honor, with clauses to deal with this sort of tragedy. She just had to trust and believe . . . and be patient.

She sighed and put her back to the kitchen just as Sharon was coming through the door—or rather, the tarp that had been hung in its place.

"So you've come to have a look then." She gave a small smile. "It's probably just as bad as you imagined. It only gets better from here."

Anna bravely nodded her head and blinked. "I wish I were as resilient as you," she admitted through a watery smile.

"Who says you aren't?" Sharon retorted, and Anna felt her heart skip a beat. If only Sharon knew. "Besides, I wasn't always this way."

Anna pulled in a breath. Of course Sharon wasn't always this way—but life had thrown her a curveball, and then another, and what choice did she have? Anna could still remember hearing rumors around town after Mark's father left. The restaurant was in the red, and Sharon didn't have the skills to keep the place running or the means to hire someone to take over. She'd been one step away from filing bankruptcy, but thanks to Luke's father—Bill Hastings's brother—it didn't have to come to that. He'd handled the debts, worked out a payment plan with the creditors. Sharon started working at the diner, and eventually she found a tenant to fill the old Tavern on Main space. It was touch and go for a while, but eventually it all worked out.

Just like things had worked out for Anna for a while.

Fireside had been her happy ending. Her second chance. Now look at it!

"I'll just be happy when all is set right," Sharon continued. "These old buildings have given me a lot of grief over the years, but they're the only investment I have other than the diner and my home. When it's going well, it's keeping me going." She sighed. "I suppose you heard the stationery store next door broke their lease?"

Anna perked up. "No, I hadn't heard," she said, trying to keep the interest from her tone when it was such an obvious setback for Sharon. It was utterly pointless to carry on with these thoughts of expansion. She'd already taken on more than she could handle with the bookstore. She was in debt. She didn't know how she was going to cover that loan until Fireside was reopened. Now was not the time to dig herself deeper.

Still, she couldn't stop herself from wondering when the opportunity would present itself again. While the contractors were here, they could easily knock down that wall...Oh, what was she thinking? This was nonsense. She didn't have the money. Period.

"The noise and chaos was too disruptive, apparently," Sharon explained. "They're relocating to that empty space on Chestnut, just across the town square."

"Do you have another tenant lined up?" Anna asked, and to her great relief, Sharon shook her head.

"I can't imagine anyone being interested now, with the scaffolding and construction." She gave a small shrug. "I'll worry about it once this place is taken care of. I'm sure I won't have any trouble finding someone in the summer."

"I'm sure you won't have any trouble at all," Anna agreed. Already her mind was beginning to travel to places it shouldn't. She pictured an arched doorway, opening into the main dining space, a lounge just off to the side. The bakery counter could be tightened, to give more space, and cleared out at night to display their dessert offerings. There was another fireplace in the stationery store—one Shea O'Riley used solely for decoration—that could anchor the other half of the restaurant, where clusters of their most private tables could be focused.

Her heart was beginning to pound with excitement, until her gaze came into focus again, and instantly that familiar weight returned.

"We'll have a crew here in the morning," Sharon was saying. "If you need anything, please don't hesitate to call me or stop by."

"Thank you, Sharon. And Kara—" She shook her head as Sharon took her leave. "I know this situation has left you out of a job. I'll be paying you all through the month as I promised but that's the best I can do. I . . . I understand if you need to find something else."

She winced at the thought of it. The staff at Fireside had become like a second family to her over the years, and she didn't see them as her employees so much as a team. This job meant a lot to Kara. It had taken her a long time to figure out what she wanted to do, and when she'd come to Anna and told her she might want to do some of the baking, Anna had been thrilled. In time, she'd thought Kara might even become her pastry chef, while she oversaw the dinner course.

Even though the fire hadn't been anyone's fault, she couldn't help feeling like she'd let Kara down.

Kara's gaze dropped to the floor as she hesitated, and Anna's stomach turned with dread. Here it came . . . "I did accept another job, actually. It's just temporary," she rushed to assure her.

Anna nodded, and a lump formed in her throat. "Of course," she managed, forcing a smile she didn't feel. "I'm happy for you. Where is it?"

Kara grimaced. "Hastings. Mark needed a new waitress. I guess the newest girl kept dropping things."

Of course. Anna's head was bobbing up and down, her eyes wide and unblinking. She willed herself to stop, but it was no use. Kara—ever faithful, loyal, and dependable Kara—was going to work for the enemy.

In fairness, she was a Hastings herself, and Mark was her cousin. Still.

"I hope you're not upset," Kara hedged.

"Of course not. And as you said, it's temporary, so…" Her face had grown hot.

Kara nodded eagerly. "Exactly. Just to get me through. I really don't want to help my mother in that dance studio ever again, and well, a girl's gotta pay her bills." She gave a tense laugh.

Tell me about it, Anna thought gloomily.

"We'll still see each other!" Kara brightened. "I have the evening shift, since Mark covers the counter in the mornings. And you won't have to worry about paying me for the month either, now that I have a new—" She stopped just shy of the word.

"I'm happy for you," Anna forced herself to say. "And I'm relieved, honestly. You can't imagine how worried I've been about everyone that works here. It's one less thing to stress about."

Kara tipped her head. "Feel like grabbing a coffee? It might cheer us up and get our mind off things for a bit."

Anna gave an even smile. Her entire body had gone numb, but her mind was free and clear. "Mind if we take a rain check? I have some things to attend to."

The girls left the building and waved each other off at the corner. In the clear light of day, Anna could see the relief in her friend's eyes, wishing she could feel the same.

So Mark was poaching her staff, was he? Well, she'd just see about that.

Mark was in his office off the kitchen when she stormed in exactly six and a half minutes later. His startled expression quickly turned to a bemused grin as she hovered in the doorway, and Anna felt her temper stir.

"I hear you hired Kara."

He gave a noncommittal shrug and leaned back in his chair, folding his hands behind his head. "She needed a job. I needed a waitress. Seemed perfect."

"Perfect for you," she accused. "You know she's my assistant manager."

"She's also my cousin. Besides, she'll go back to Fireside when it reopens," Mark added mildly, but Anna was too angry to feel any reassurance in his words. "We both know the restaurant industry is extremely transitory. I feel like I'm replacing a waitress every six weeks." He paused, noting her scowl, and met her frown. "What? You're not mad, are you?"

"Damn straight I'm mad."

His look was incredulous. "I would have thought you'd be pleased. I'm helping you out."

No, he was helping Kara out. She knew she should be relieved that Kara had another source of income, and she was, but a part of her couldn't help but feel betrayed. "I told you. I don't need help," she hissed.

"Oh no? Seems to me you need a lot of help. You're just too stubborn to take it from me." He arched a brow and tipped his chair back deeper. Anna tensed. She always hated when he did that, relying on the two back legs to hold him up, balancing precariously with his knee against the desk. She felt on edge, out of sorts, and this wasn't helping. Her nails pressed into her palms.

"I'm not too stubborn—Oh, will you just...*Put* the chair down!" She lowered her tone, feeling a flush rush up her cheeks. "Please."

He flashed her a wicked grin but did as he was told. "Better?"

She waited a beat. "Thank you."

Mark stood, slowly uncurling himself to full height, and Anna watched warily as he arched his back and indulged in a long stretch, spreading his arms wide before dropping them at his sides. She bit on the inside of her lip, hating every inch of his perfectly sculpted body as he gave a sigh of content, and tossed her a lazy grin. He was good-looking—too good-looking—and worse was that he knew it. He had an effect on women, one he counted on, but God help her if she'd let him see it. She'd made a point of acting immune to him, even if her insides uncoiled at the mere glimpse of that smile and her heart beat a little faster when she sensed his proximity.

He came around the desk and took a step closer, and Anna cursed herself for having closed the door behind her. Now they were alone. In his space. On his turf.

If there was one thing she loathed more than Mark himself, it was not being in control. Of her life. Of her emotions. Of the way every nerve ending was tingling, aching to be touched, standing at attention as he inched closer. His effect on her was too powerful. It always had been, and she was beginning to wonder if it always would be.

"It's nice to know you care so much about my well-being." He was close, too close. Close enough for her to see his pupils, often lost in the depths of those dark chocolate eyes. She tried to look away, but something told her he wouldn't let her. He was challenging her, damn it, testing her to see if she would break. And she wouldn't. Not for Mark. She'd done that once, but not again.

"Get over yourself," she said, taking a step back. Still, he didn't move. She took another step, until her tailbone hit the door handle. She reached behind her and grabbed hold of it to steady herself.

"Now, you were saying?" His eyebrow cocked devilishly, and the corners of his lips twitched. She lingered on his mouth, so full and pink and perfectly manly, and hissed in a sharp breath.

"I was saying—" Was it just her, or had he leaned forward? His face was close, his voice low and husky when he spoke, and in the confines of the small room, which was really no more than a cramped and cluttered utility closet, she could feel the heat of his skin, smell the musk on his clothes.

It smelled like Mark.

She blinked heavily, finding escape for just a brief, simple moment behind the curtain of her lids, and then pulled herself up to full height. "Did you talk to Frank Piccolino?" she blurted, and instantly wished she had just kept her mouth shut. It was just idle curiosity, but the sudden kick in her chest as she waited for him to reply told her it was actually much more than that.

His eyes narrowed as he pulled back. He gave a non-committal shrug. "Yeah. Why do you ask?"

"Just wondering," she replied with what she hoped was a breezy tone. She pretended to look for something in the bag hooked to her shoulder. She'd never been good at hiding her emotions. She would have lost her shirt and then some playing poker. Yet, somehow, all these years, she had managed to carefully construct a cool façade around Mark. And then it all slipped. All that work, all that effort, for nothing. Look at her—blushing, having heat flashes, barely able to maintain eye contact.

They were too close to the kitchen, that was all. This room, if you could even call it that, was like a sweat locker. Anyone would be having a physiological meltdown in here. Especially if they were trapped with Mark and that mischievous grin.

Get a hold of yourself!

"Yesterday you seemed so intent on finding him," she continued. She made a grand show of retrieving her sunglasses case and flipping it open. "I just wondered if it all worked out."

"Nah," Mark said, and Anna's fingers stilled mid-task. She recovered by unfolding the small microfiber cloth and carefully rubbing each lens—an act, she freely admitted to herself, typically reserved for the hem of her shirt. "It's not a fit."

"Is he not entering then?" she inquired.

"No, he's entering with his sous chef."

Anna nodded sagely. Of course. A guy like Frank Piccolino liked to be in charge, liked to work the pass and have a last say on every plate before it hit the table. Mark would never stand for that.

She narrowed her eyes as realization took hold. Of course he wouldn't.

"You didn't really ask him, did you?" She dropped the sunglasses and case into her bag and set her hands on her hips. "This was all some ploy to see if I'd bite."

Oh, she could swat that victorious smirk right off that handsome face. Mark was back in his chair now, leaning back so far it set her teeth on edge. He set his head in his hands and tossed her a boyish grin. "So did it work?"

She nailed him with a hard look. "No."

"Aw, come on, Anna!" Mark tipped the chair forward, the weight of it hitting the linoleum with a thud. "We used to be a good team once."

"*Once* being the operative word," she said hastily. "Then you decided to fly solo." She fumbled in her bag for her glasses, again. She was leaving this time, really she was. She reached for the door handle, turning it quickly and yanking it open.

A blaring radio and hot steam greeted her. A cook was plating fries, and another was flipping burgers, sizzling in their own fat. She turned slowly, back to Mark, finding a frown where only a moment ago that smirk had rested. He looked weary somehow, and dare she say unhappy. It was a side of himself he rarely let show.

Her resolve softened. "Why do you want to enter?"

He looked up, his lids heavy. "Because I think I can win."

The answer was satisfactory, but she knew there was more. There had to be. "That list. Those recipes I found the other day. Were those for the contest?"

He shook his head. "No. That was for something else. Just some ideas."

She understood. He wanted more than this. Hell, he

deserved more than this. He was capable. He was driven. So why was he still here, years later? Why was this diner, of all the things in the world, the one thing Mark had been capable of committing to?

"Well, I don't have time," she restated, turning to leave. "I'm sure you'll find someone."

She heard his chair grind against the floor. His voice was rough, firm. "I want *you*."

She paused, her back to him, her chest heaving with each breath. He didn't mean it—not like that—but still, she clung to his words, spoken from his lips, the very same that had kissed her, traced circles over her skin and lit a fire in her that had long since died.

Even as she turned to face him, she was screaming at herself to forget it, to turn and run, to never look back. "If we don't win, I'm in a bigger mess than ever."

His eyes flickered. "Who says we won't win? You know how we connect in a kitchen."

Her heart skipped a beat. Oh, she knew all right.

She gave him a long look over the bridge of her nose. "That was a long time ago. Besides, you saw how it went last week with me being here. We barely made it through one morning."

"You mentioned wanting to pay me for the kitchen time. If you paid me, would you use the kitchen?"

She only needed to think about the way her home kitchen looked this morning to answer that question. If it was even turf, she could bear it for a few weeks. Even if she wasn't sure her heart could survive it. "Maybe."

"Enter the contest with me, then," he challenged. "I need a teammate. You need a kitchen."

Anna hesitated. He made a good argument. "We haven't

cooked together in a long time, Mark. I'm not sure our styles even match."

"Let me cook you one meal. You be the judge. If it's good, we team up. If not . . . then I know I tried."

Her mind trailed to the potential expansion space for Fireside and circled back to the Annex. She could imagine no greater rush than walking into the bank with a check and walking out a free woman. "Okay."

His brow shot up. "Okay? So yes?"

You're going to regret this, Anna Madison. She gave a tight smile. "Yes."

"Tonight at eight? My place?"

"Okay," she heard herself say. It was just dinner. A meeting. Not a date. Definitely not a date.

"I'm looking forward to it," Mark said as she turned to go.

Her heart somersaulted. She was looking forward to it, too. More than she should.

She nodded, just once, and left on shaking legs, doing her damndest to fight the smile in her heart and the bounce in her step that led her all the way to Main Street Books.

CHAPTER 12

Scout lifted his head from the polished wood floorboards and sniffed the air, rich with scents of butter and garlic. His big brown eyes blinked sadly, his nose twitching one last time, before he finally rolled over and rested on his paw.

Well, wasn't he a sight. Mark set the knife on the cutting board and pulled the lid on the dog treat jar, grinning as Scout leapt to his feet. He knew he should instruct Scout to sit or stay to earn the biscuit, just like he should really train him not to jump on people, sniff at them, or sit on laps, but he couldn't bring himself to do it. Scout was easy to love, and unlike humans, his devotion was unconditional.

The smells and sounds of the kitchen were coming alive, and Mark glanced at the clock on the far wall. He was used to running on a tight schedule, but even for himself, this was pushing it. He wanted to impress her—why, he didn't know. Maybe to make up for lost time. Maybe to show her he wasn't as bad as she thought he was. Maybe to prove that he could still cook.

Mark pushed through the last block of bittersweet chocolate with the serrated knife and slid the chunks into a stainless steel bowl, feeling the expectation of a guest's impending arrival.

He ate just about every meal when he wasn't at the diner, Luke's, or his mother's in front of the television, usually with a pizza box resting open on the coffee table. The voices gave him company, at least until Scout had come along—and whether Anna believed it or not, he preferred to spend his nights like that than with Nicole Johnson or one of the other girls in town he'd taken out a few times here and there.

Nicole. He knew she was upset—she'd left a tearful message for him that night after the bar letting him know in no uncertain terms that they were through. He hadn't really thought there was anything to officially call to an end—they'd only gone on a few dinner dates, nothing more than that—but if it made her feel better to tell him off, he supposed it came with the territory. He'd told her, and everyone before her, exactly what he was and was not looking for, just so things didn't get messy. But they always did, anyway.

There was only one person he'd dared to take seriously, and that was Anna. Before her, he'd told himself he'd never get close. After...well, sometimes it was easier to forget what he was missing when he wasn't alone, even if only for a night.

Scout jumped to his feet, tail wagging at the sound of a car door closing. Mark added the mussels to the pot, slid the scallops into the oven, and set a timer just as the doorbell rang at eight sharp.

"You're here," he said, as he opened the door. Loose

blond tendrils slipped over her forehead, cascading to her shoulders. Her white, peasant-style blouse was loose and simple, and as it caught the evening breeze, it rippled against her curves invitingly, giving him a glimpse of what he'd once had, and lost.

"Shouldn't I be?" she quipped with the faintest trace of a smile. As she brushed past him into the house, he caught a whiff of her scent—she still used that coconut shampoo. "Aw, there you are, sweet boy," she said, bending over to give Scout a proper greeting.

Mark's groin stirred as his gaze roamed over the curves of her rear, to the taut firmness of her thighs in those jeans. He startled as she suddenly stood and whirled to face him, her eyebrow cocking as her electric blue eyes narrowed in suspicion.

"It smells good in here," she commented. She looked past the living room, where a sliver of the kitchen could be seen through the arched doorway.

"Can I get you a glass of wine?"

She hesitated, but only briefly. "What does Chef recommend? White or red?"

Chef. It had been a long time since anyone had called him that, and the impact of the word hit him hard, reminding him of a time lived and lost, of a dream yet to be had. He swallowed hard, ignoring the twisting of his stomach, and forced a casual grin. "White it is then."

"What's on the menu?"

"Uh-uh." He wagged his finger, his grin widening as he led her into the kitchen, where the smells of sautéed onions and spices kicked up a notch. "It's a surprise."

He crouched to inspect the wine cooler through its glass door, selecting the best of his collection. He filled two glasses and handed her one. "A toast," he said, clinking her glass. "To the Sugar Maple Culinary Competition. And to one hundred thousand dollars."

"Don't you think you're getting a little ahead of yourself?" Anna brought the glass to her lips and took a sip. "What can I do to help?"

"Your part comes in for dessert. I thought we might see how well we still work together."

She seemed to frown at this. "I didn't realize this was an interview."

"It's a two-way street, baby," he said, leaning both hands on the counter. "A prize like this is a lot of money. I need to know you're in it to win it."

"Of course I am!" she scoffed, but her expression wilted when he arched a brow. Her shoulders dropped slightly as she set her glass on the counter. "Look, if I decide to enter—and I'm not sure I will yet—then I'm going to give it my all. Have you ever known me to not throw myself into something entirely?"

He didn't need to consider the question. Fireside was living proof. "No," he replied, his jaw setting when he considered where he fit into that grand statement. She'd given her heart to him, and look what he'd done with it.

He went to the stove and peered through the glass lid covering the pot of mussels, shaking it one last time, just to make sure all the shells were open before flicking off the gas.

"Frankly," she continued, "I have some reservations about your commitment. How do I know you won't bail on me if we agree to team up?"

He tightened his grip on the large slotted spoon he plucked from the canister. Of course she had to go there, and really, could he blame her? Ending their relationship, when all he really wanted to do was stay in it forever, had been the hardest thing he'd ever done. She couldn't see that. Not then. Not now. He'd been mean about it, dodging her calls, then hanging around Cassie, a random girl from his pastry class, making sure Anna saw it, too, and knew that it was over, that he wasn't the man for her. Judging from the way she'd ignored him ever since he'd sat her down and told her it was over—their relationship, their friendship, even their dreams of a restaurant—she'd gotten the message.

He gave her a hard look over his shoulder. "That would be pretty damn stupid, wouldn't it?"

It would be stupid all right, about as stupid as it had been to ever think he and Anna could have opened a restaurant together. He'd loved her, and he couldn't keep his feelings at bay, couldn't keep it platonic. He'd given in, kissed her, pursued her, told himself it would be different this time, that what they shared was real, a love that had two years of friendship backing it up, a common goal, a shared passion. He'd told himself they could have it all, even when he knew deep down that was bull. Tavern on Main was proof of that—his father had sunk everything into that place, and the stress of the business took a toll on his marriage, until eventually the relationship was over, and so was the restaurant. Mark couldn't risk coming out with nothing, so how, in the end, had he ended up in the exact position he'd tried to avoid?

Cursing under his breath, Mark began transferring the mussels to their bowls, double checking that each had opened, and tossing the few that hadn't into the bin. The room went silent as he finished preparing the starter, the tension in his shoulders slowly working itself out in the comfort of the task, the simple enjoyment he derived from each step. He diced the butter and stirred it into the white wine broth, letting the flavors fuse together before he added the fresh tarragon.

His dad had taught him this recipe on a slow night at Tavern on Main. Mark must have been about nine at the time, and he'd eagerly listened as his father walked him through the steps, letting him assist. "You're going to make a fine chef one of these days," he'd said, grinning, setting his heavy hand on Mark's shoulder.

What would his father think of him now? Would he be proud that he'd done as he'd set out to do, followed in his footsteps by going to culinary school? Or would he see him like half the town did these days—just some regular Joe behind the counter at the diner, serving up coffee, good for a few laughs.

Mark frowned. He'd never know.

With a heavy heart, Mark poured the mixture over the mussels, leaving a generous pool at the bottom. Finally, he pulled garlic toasts from the top oven and tucked two slices each into the bowls.

"Have a seat. Please," he added, his gaze skirting to the table and the unlit candles. His stomach tightened at his folly—and how close he had come to overstepping. This wasn't a date. He wasn't wooing Anna, wasn't wining and dining her into bed the way he did with half the other women who floated through his door. She was too smart for that—too burned.

Besides, that's not what he wanted from her. Anna wasn't a short-term fling. Anna was the real deal. And that was just the problem.

"Go ahead and start." He pivoted and walked back to the oven to check on the main course, and then grabbed the neck of the wine bottle.

Anna was hunched over the bowl, turning over each mussel with the help of her spoon, and her face flushed with guilt when he appeared at her side.

He sunk into his chair. "Making sure I wasn't poisoning you?"

She let out a small laugh that sent his mind into a tailspin; it had been too long since he'd heard that sound. He'd forgotten it somehow, its melodic sweetness, but its memory came flooding back, reminding him of happier times.

"Force of habit," she said, picking up her fork and spearing the mussel. He watched as she brought it to her mouth and chewed slowly, no doubt analyzing the precision of his seasoning.

Mark hesitated before he tucked into his dish, anxiety greeting him like an old friend, and then decided to hell with it. If it was bad, she'd certainly let him know. He couldn't resist the grin that tugged at his mouth if he'd tried. Any worry of oversalting faded with that first bite. It tasted exactly the way it had all those years back, in that kitchen at Tavern—now Fireside. If he closed his eyes, he could almost picture his father's expectant grin, waiting for Mark's assessment of the dish. "Not bad, huh?" he'd said. *Not bad at all.*

"What do you think?" he asked, chasing down another bite with the cool, dry wine.

"I think..." She paused, and wiped her mouth with the corner of her napkin before returning it to her lap. Her eyes were soft when they met his, and her lashes fluttered as she sucked in a small breath. "I think you could do a hell of a lot better than Hastings." A flush of pink spread over her cheeks and her long fingers graced the base of her glass. "Sorry. I know it's your mother's place."

He knew he should be mad, insulted really—but she was right. And she knew it. He set down his fork. "Don't apologize. You're right."

Her blue gaze shifted to his. "Then why do it? Why the diner?"

He knew he could make up some lame excuse, switch the topic, but he didn't want to. It had always been easy to talk to Anna—too easy, at times—and he missed the bond they'd once shared. Sometimes, when a particularly crappy thing had happened at work, something industry related, something Luke wouldn't get and his mom shouldn't be burdened with, he'd talk aloud on the drive home, and the person he imagined he was talking to was Anna. She always had the right thing to say, and when she didn't, she just had a way of looking at him, those soft eyes patient and understanding, her response always spot on. Encouraging when he needed a kick in the pants, empathetic when he needed commiseration. She was the perfect teammate. Always on his side.

"You know that I helped out there after high school, when my mom was first diagnosed." He took a long sip of wine, hating to remember those days, the fear of not knowing what would happen, if she'd ever get better. He was drifting then, and he wasn't sure what he wanted to do with himself. It was his mother who had told him to follow his heart, to apply to culinary school. He'd worried he'd betray her somehow by doing it. Now look at what he'd done with the opportunity.

"It made sense to pitch in again after my mom's relapse. I guess you could say my reasons for sticking with it aren't enough anymore. I want to feel excited again." He drained the rest of his glass, briefly meeting her gaze. "Maybe I've just fallen out of love with it."

Her eyes flashed as her lips drew tight, and all at once the softer side of Anna he'd known and loved so much was replaced with that tough, hard, unbreakable shell he'd seen so many times over the past few years. "Seems to be a theme of yours."

The timer for the oven went off and Mark clenched a fist around his napkin, hesitating before he tossed it on his chair in exasperation. He strode to the broiler, hating the rigid way she sat, the distance in her face, and pulled the pan from the grates. The scallops were perfectly cooked—he could tell by the caramelized crust on each one—but his appetite for them was lost.

"Do you really want to talk about this right now?" he demanded as he returned to the table.

"No," she said coolly.

"Well, I do," he blurted, surprising even himself.

Anna's stunned expression had paled, darkening her eyes as she locked his gaze. "There's nothing to discuss," she snapped. "We dated, you dumped me, it's over."

"It wasn't that simple."

"Oh yes, it was." Her eyes turned on him. Hard. "It's what you do, Mark. You use girls, and you spit them out. You move on to the next."

"That's really how you see me." It was more of a statement than a question—an affirmation of his worst fears.

He didn't want be seen as that man—a man like his father, a man who turned his back on the people who counted on him, the people he was supposed to love. He could still remember the hurt in his mother's eyes when she told him and his brother that their dad wasn't coming home. She'd tried to be brave and strong for them, but he heard those tears that carried her long through the night. He saw the way her eyes sparked with each ring of the phone for months after he'd left, never to be heard from again.

Anna shrugged, her lips turning downward. "I was just the fool who fell for your charm." She shook her head, giving an unhappy chuckle under her breath. "I thought... I thought maybe I was different."

Mark hated the hurt he saw in her eyes. He'd seen it before, that first week back at school his fourth year after he and Anna had spent their summer break on the beach, working in local kitchens all day and climbing into bed together each night. The season had come to an end, and he'd known that their relationship would, too. It was moving too quickly, he was starting to feel anxious, restless at night as he set his head on the pillow next to hers, watching the steady rise and fall of her breath as she slept.

He'd come back to school a week early, knowing what he had to do, telling himself the next time he saw her he'd be over her, but that look on her face when he sat her down and told her it was over, the smile he'd loved that faded for the final time, and the confusion that clouded her eyes cut him like a knife.

It would have been so much easier to carry on, as they were, forever, but what really lasted forever? And if it didn't? He couldn't bear it.

"You *were* different," Mark insisted. When she didn't react, his stomach constricted. "I was young then, Anna. I was... scared."

That got her attention. Her brow pulled in confusion as she met his tormented gaze.

"Scared?" She stared at him. "Please."

"It's true, Anna."

"And what were you so afraid of, hmm?" Her eyes were sharp as steel. "Being tied down to one person? Losing your freedom?"

"Anna—"

"I know your drill, Mark. I was just too stupid to see it back then, but I know how you work. You like the thrill of the chase." She shook her head. "This was a mistake."

He was on his feet before she was out of arm's reach. He reached out and grabbed hold of her wrist, forcing her to face him, finding more anger in those eyes than he could bear.

"Let go of me," she hissed through gritted teeth.

He tightened his hold. Her wrist felt so small in his hand, he feared he might hurt her, but he couldn't let her go. Not yet. "Not until you've heard me out."

She brought herself up to full height. "You have nothing to say to me that I don't already know."

Oh, but she was wrong about that. He watched her eyelashes flutter, her pupils grow large as the distance between them closed, and her pretty pink mouth worry itself, torn between a scowl and another biting retort.

"I was scared, Anna. Scared of the way I felt." He felt her body relax. "Scared of what would happen if it didn't work out."

"So it made sense to end it first, then?"

He dropped her arm. "Something like that."

He expected her to back away, to turn and leave, but she didn't move. "You broke my heart, Mark." Her voice cracked on the word and she dropped her gaze. Her lashes fluttered quickly as she blinked.

He gritted his teeth against the pain of her words. "I know."

"You didn't have to be so brutal about it."

Ah, but he did. It was the only way to make sure he stayed away, that he wasn't tempted to go back to her. Because he never could resist Anna. From the moment she arrived at the school, all grown up and prettier than ever, he was under her spell—caught up in her laughter and her warmth, in that fierce determination.

"We should have just stayed friends," he said firmly. Sometimes, when he saw her around town, through a window or across a street, chatting with one of her sisters, setting flowers on a bistro table outside Fireside, or just walking by herself down Main Street, pausing to study shop windows, he had to physically restrain himself from catching up with her, telling her about something crazy that had happened at the diner, or worse, all those years ago, about how worried he was for his mother—his only parent, who was fighting for her life for the second time in six years. How he couldn't sleep because he was so filled with worry and instead stayed up long into the nights, watching movie after movie until slumber simply found him.

She was his person, the one he could confide in, take comfort in. She was so close. She was right there. And he couldn't tell her anything.

And he had no one to blame but himself.

Anna nodded slowly. "Maybe we should have."

"I cared about you, Anna." He'd never told her he'd loved her—not out loud. He didn't trust the feelings he had. What was love? Did it even exist? It sure as hell wasn't guaranteed to last.

Silence stretched and he knew they were each remembering what they'd shared. Mark pulled in a breath. "We both know we can win this contest if we set aside our differences."

She sighed, dropping her gaze to the floor. "I don't know, Mark."

"Let's not let our past stand in the way of the future. Let's enter the damn contest, Anna." When she didn't reply immediately, he said with more force, "I'll tell you what—you enter the contest with me, and after that, you never have to speak to me again."

"It is just two and a half weeks." She looked up at him, and his heart raced as their eyes locked.

"It's going to be a lot of late nights," he warned.

She shrugged. "I'm used to running on little sleep."

He suppressed a smile. "Can we shake on it?"

Pursing her lips, Anna shifted the weight on her feet and ever so slowly brought her hand up to his. He wrapped his fingers over hers, feeling the faint tick of her pulse in her wrist, the smooth, warm lines of her bones. She felt small, fragile almost, and shame bit at him when he thought of how badly he'd hurt her.

It wasn't a mistake he intended to repeat. He'd make it up to her somehow, and it would start with winning this contest.

"Welcome to the team, Chef," he murmured, lazily dropping his gaze to her lips. It was the closest he had been to her in years, but it felt as if no time had passed at all.

He leaned in, just a fraction of an inch, his lips parting as the lids of his eyes fell. She was looking up at him, blinking almost in question, but she hadn't pulled back, hadn't pushed him away. He hesitated, feeling the heat of her body, sensing the rise and fall of her breath, the questions in those big blue eyes. Abruptly, he pulled back, just like he had all those years ago. He had to be the one to stop this.

He was no good for her. She knew it all those years ago, but she couldn't let him go. She believed in him, saw him for more than he was, for the man he wanted to be— the man he was when he was with her. Not the man he really was.

He couldn't give her what she wanted. Not then. Not now. And the only way to stop hurting her was to never lose sight of that, no matter how tempting it would be to just give in to the feelings that somehow grew stronger each day.

He'd almost kissed her. She'd seen that look, the slight parting of his lips, felt their bodies inch closer, and closer still, until there was only once choice: give in or run.

Thank *God* she'd had the sense to resist him, even if her body was still prickling by the near miss. They'd established rules in the kitchen last week—ones she hadn't stuck around long enough to keep—and they'd have to do so again, even if some were unspoken, or rules only for herself. Rule number one: She would not fall for Mark again. Two: She would most certainly not let him kiss her. Three: She would stop wishing he would.

The whistling teakettle forced her from that thought, and she hurried to the stove, grabbing a potholder along the way to lift the kettle from its burner. Flicking off the gas, she called over her shoulder, "Tea's ready!"

Her mother came around the corner, her eyes bright and alert, with a healthy flush dusting her cheeks. She stopped to catch her breath at the counter before pulling some mugs from the cabinet. "I finally finished unloading the last of those fabric bolts. My goodness, that was a workout, but at least I won't have to feel guilty about taking a second helping of that pasta, Anna. It was delicious."

"You should really let one of us help with that," Jane scolded from her perch at the kitchen island.

"Nonsense," Kathleen huffed. "The exercise is good for me. I haven't felt this good in a long time."

It was true, Anna reflected. The past year had been hard on all of them, and each sister had handled the loss of their father in their own private way. His sudden heart attack had come without warning, leaving them to process their grief slowly, in a state of near disbelief. It wasn't until last Christmas that Kathleen began to take steps toward a recovery. Having Grace move back home for now kept her company, and reopening her interior design business was keeping her busy.

Grace came into the room and helped herself to a mug. "Did we decide what we're having for dessert?"

Anna hesitated. While it was customary to have a full meal on the nights they all gathered together in their childhood home, tonight she was forced to break routine, and worse—explain why. "I have to cut out a bit early tonight, I'm afraid. Too much work to be done."

Grace took the seat next to Jane. "For Fireside or the Annex?"

Anna stirred honey into her tea slowly, waiting for it to melt from her spoon. "Both, you could say. I . . ." Oh, here it went. She braced herself. "I decided to enter that Sugar Maple Culinary Competition."

"That's fabulous!" Grace cried. Her face suddenly fell with realization. "Wait—are you entering with Mark?"

"Kara's picking up some baking skills, but she's not

a professional chef. So yes, Mark. I don't see any other option," Anna was sure to add, even if only to remind herself. She'd mailed another loan payment that day, and watched her bank account dwindle to an alarmingly low number.

"Well, that's great, sweetie." Kathleen smiled. "I know you and Mark have never been the best of friends, but it's just a cooking contest. It's not like you have to marry the guy."

Anna hid behind a sip of her tea, her pulse finally steadying when Jane added, "I'm afraid I won't be able to stay for dessert either."

"Another hot date?" Grace wiggled her eyebrows.

"No." Jane's face flushed a deep pink. "And I'll have you know I don't appreciate you using that term around Sophie. Last night I heard her getting her dolls ready for their hot date. They were going to Piccolino's!"

Anna snorted and joined Grace's laughter, but Jane's eyes flashed. "It was just so humiliating. She apparently brought it up when she was with Adam. I can only imagine what he thinks."

"I hope he's jealous," Grace blurted. Catching Jane's lack of amusement, she cried, "Oh, come on now, Jane. It's good that you're putting yourself out there again; it's a lot easier to just close yourself off."

Anna backed away from the island. This entire conversation was hitting a nerve.

Jane sighed audibly. "I saw them the other night. Adam and Kristy. They were at the restaurant while I was waiting for my date."

Grace glanced at Anna. "Did they see you?"

"Oh, they saw me all right. They saw me get stood up.

All dressed up for nothing. I've never felt so out of place." Her voice cracked on the last word, and Anna extended her arm around her sister's shoulder, giving it a tight squeeze.

"Adam doesn't deserve you."

Jane lowered her eyes. "I know."

"Do you want him back?" Grace hedged.

"No, I don't. At least, I don't think so."

"Of course you don't," Grace said, and Anna nodded her agreement, hating the part of herself that for years had silently wished Mark would have a change of heart.

She looked into Jane's soft hazel eyes, frowning at the hurt she saw pass through them. "Why would you want to be with someone who doesn't deserve you?"

Why, Anna? Why?

Jane shook her head, a small smile parting her lips. "You're right! You're right."

Of course she was right. And she'd be best to heed her own advice, wouldn't she? Anna tossed her spoon in the sink, but her pulse skittered when she caught the time on the clock above the oven. It was almost time to meet him.

"Are you going to let Rosemary match you up again?" Grace wrapped her fingers around her steaming mug.

"Maybe I'll let her give Anna a try instead." Jane grinned.

"What? No!" Anna's face heated. "No way, Jane. I told you and Rosemary straight up that I was only going along with this so she would set you up. If you're backing out now, so am I."

Jane shook her head. "I'm not giving up. I want to move on. Today at the studio Rosemary mentioned another guy she had in mind for me. I think I'll give it one more try."

"It doesn't sound like you're off the hook yet though, Anna," their mother cut in. "I've known Rosemary Hastings most of my life. When she sets her mind to something, she doesn't back down, and it seems to me that she intends to find you a match."

Anna tossed her arms up and let them fall back at her sides. "Why me? Why not Jane? Why not one of her one daughters?"

Kathleen stopped folding napkins. "Maybe it's because she already has someone in mind for you," she said, giving a conspiratorial wink.

Dread knotted Anna's stomach. That was exactly what she was afraid of.

They'd agreed to meet at Mark's house. His kitchen was bigger, and it made sense, but secretly Anna was relieved not to have him in her home. If he came over, it would never be the same. Each room would carry the stain of his memory, bear the weight of his absence.

His grin was broad and genuine when he met her at the door, Scout standing happily at his side, tail wagging, eager to jump up and lick her face in greeting. Mark grabbed a tennis ball and chucked it across the living room, and Anna laughed as Scout ran for it.

"The fence hasn't been repaired yet," Mark explained. He tipped his head toward the kitchen. "Ready to start?"

As ready as she'd ever be. Anna managed a tight nod and followed him through the hallway, permitting only the briefest indulgence when she caught a trace of his familiar scent.

Inside, the kitchen had been scrubbed and polished, and a stack of cutting boards had been set on the big center island. Mark handed her an apron and tied one around his waist, accentuating his broad torso and the taut muscles under his sage green T-shirt.

"Have you eaten?" he asked, and Anna felt her cheeks flame at the memory of the night before. The mussels had been delicious—the white wine broth had been perfectly flavored with garlic and shallots and a hint of tarragon. She vaguely remembered seeing scallops, set on a bed of baby vegetables, but the meal had gone cold by the time they'd called a truce, and by then, her appetite, for food at least, had dissipated.

"I just came from my mother's house. We try to have dinner together once a week."

"That's one thing we have in common besides food. We're certainly loyal to our families. It's probably why we both wanted to keep things to ourselves all those years ago. You don't get much privacy around here." He set his hands on his hips and looked at her. His eyes were dark and tense, but the faintest hint of a smile played at his lips. Butterflies chased through her stomach, and she set a hand there to steady herself.

They needed to get to work. Fast. The sooner she was busy and occupied, the easier it would be to focus on the task and not the painfully attractive man standing next to her who was dead set on bringing up the past every chance he had. Each glance she stole caused a tingle to rip down her spine, her heart to hammer, and her mind to spin. She wished he would stop looking at her like that. It was making her nervous.

She pulled an elastic band from her wrist and combed her hair from her face with her fingers before securing it tightly.

"I wish you wouldn't do that." His voice was low, instantly bringing her back to long, lazy nights in bed, his breath in her ear.

She snapped her gaze to him. "Why?" Mark had always liked her hair down. He'd comb his fingers through the tendrils, releasing the tangles.

His eyes were steady and dark and she willed him to look away, but he didn't. She could feel her heart begin to pound, her chest rise and fall as she waited for him to respond.

Finally, he said, "It doesn't matter."

No, she told herself firmly, *it certainly doesn't*.

"I guess we should brainstorm recipes first," he said, clearing his throat. "Got any ideas?"

She forced her attention back to his question. She'd stayed up late last night flipping through her favorite cookbooks, even experimenting a little in her kitchen. There was no way she was going to get any sleep with the memory of Mark's face so close to hers swimming to the surface of her mind every time she closed her eyes. She'd only just found slumber when she was promptly awoken by the ringing of her alarm clock at two. She supposed she could have slept in for another couple of hours and gone into the diner, but despite their agreement, she couldn't face him. Not yet.

"I was thinking we might use butternut squash. The color would really pop, and the maple syrup would bring out its sweetness."

Mark mulled the idea. "I like that. What else?"

"Well." She realized she was enjoying this. "Salmon might be nice for the main course."

Her gaze subconsciously dropped to his chest, each

muscle defined through the thin material of his shirt. She let her eyes roam lower, to the hands that had once touched every inch of her body. Oh, they were nice hands.

Get a grip, Anna.

"I also had an idea for salmon," Mark said.

Anna realized she was still staring at his hands, and felt her cheeks flame as she looked up at him. Amusement danced in his eyes. "Should we try a few dishes and do a tasting?" she managed, patting her tight bun and then folding her arms across her chest.

"Might be a good way to narrow it down," Mark agreed. Then, with a rueful grin, he added, "Shame you already ate."

"Oh, well…I only like to take a bite of each dish during a tasting anyway."

Mirth flickered in those chocolate brown eyes. "Uh-huh. Sure."

"What?" she cried, but she was grinning, too. "If you're referring to Chef Luciano's class, I'll have you know I hadn't eaten anything that day. I was practically ready to faint."

"Sure," Mark bantered, and Anna swatted him with a nearby towel. To both her surprise and horror, his grin widened and he snatched it from her hand before snapping it back at her rear.

To her utter disappointment in herself, she let out a squeal.

Her body went rigid as a hot flush spread over her face. She stared at the grooves in the cutting board, horrified. "I was famished that day. And I didn't know better. It was my first week at school. There was an entire buffet of food; I thought it was for the taking."

Mark chuckled as he gathered ingredients and began scooping seeds from a squash. "I just remember watching the vein in Chef Luciano's neck pulse as you just filled up your plate and ate, none the wiser."

"It was delicious!" she insisted, laughing at the memory. She hadn't remembered Mark being there that day, but he must have been. It was one of her first classes and everything was a blur. They'd slipped into their friendship so easily, it was hard to pinpoint when it all began.

But it wasn't difficult to know when it ended.

Anna tensed and reached for an onion. "Young and dumb."

"Not dumb. Just young." Their eyes locked. "God you were cute." Mark's voice was low, his grin suggestive, and the spark in his eyes downright lethal.

She sucked in a breath. "Yeah, well, I didn't get a very good grade in that class. Now I understand why." She turned back to the worktop. It really was time to get to work.

Deciding to start with a glaze for the salmon, she reached for the maple syrup at the exact moment Mark did; the surprise of the contact sent an electric shock up her arm. Mark paused, letting the contact linger, and for the briefest of seconds his finger skimmed her own before he pulled his hand away. "Go ahead," he said gruffly.

"Thanks."

After a beat, Mark asked, "Should we make a double portion, just in case you get any notions?"

"Ha." Anna shook her head, but her smile fell when she noticed Mark's serious expression. He was watching her, studying her, as if working up the courage to tell her something. *Please, Mark*, she silently pleaded. No talking about the past. That had been rule number one. But then, when did Mark ever follow the rules?

Mark shifted to the stove, and she used the opportunity to steal a glimpse of his wide back, his broad shoulders pulling at the confines of his shirt. Abruptly, he turned to her, and she looked away quickly.

"Try this," he said, cupping his palm under a wooden spoon.

Anna hesitated, and quietly opened her mouth. Mark slid the spoon to her lips, briefly meeting her eyes. Her stomach turned over as Mark lifted his hand to her cheek and brushed the pad of his thumb over it. A tingle ripped down her spine at his touch and from the way his eyes lazily shifted back to hers and stayed there, she knew he sensed it, too.

He brought the thumb to his lips, licking off a bit of sauce.

"That's really good," she said, pulling back.

"I feel like it's still missing something..."

Mark was still standing next to her, his heat lingering too close for comfort. Her eyes never left her station. "What about a dash of mustard?"

"Good idea!" Mark finally moved away, and Anna let her shoulders relax. "We made a good team, didn't we?" he asked a few seconds later, just when her pulse had finally steadied.

She didn't breathe. Finally, she managed, "We did."

He opened his mouth as if to say something and then stopped. Every nerve ending in her body was on edge, waiting to hear those unspoken words. Disappointment pulled at her—the deflation reminding her of all those days and nights she'd spent with him. Back then, he could do no wrong. She could spend hours listening to him laugh, watching him cook, eating his food, curling up into those thick, strong arms and setting her head against the warm plane of his chest, feeling the soft rise and fall of his breath. She felt a physical ache every time he was out of her presence, a yearning for him, a need to have him close as often as possible.

For the next hour they worked together in silence, following the rules they had set in place that first day she'd come into the diner. Just because she was here, in his home, with soft music playing somewhere in the distance and the cozy presence of Scout on the floor at their feet, didn't make this any different. This was professional, not personal. Mark seemed to grasp that.

It was about damn time that she did, too.

CHAPTER 14

Oh, what a difference a week made.

Jane casually unbuttoned her cardigan and turned to hang it on the back of her chair. Her date's eyes dropped ever so slightly to the sheer material of the blouse she'd yet again borrowed from Grace, and she felt a heat flush her cheeks at the attention, however wanted.

She had to hand it to Rosemary. Jason Fitzpatrick was everything she'd built him up to be and more. He was an assistant district attorney in Burlington; he volunteered at an animal shelter and had two rescue dogs of his own, which he clearly doted on; he visited his mother in Massachusetts on the last Sunday of each month, always bringing her favorite flowers and a fresh dessert from a local bakery. He had no children, yet, but judging from his standing on the board at the children's hospital, Jane decided this was a positive indication of his priorities and life goals. He was also divorced, though they'd chosen not to dwell on that subject.

The waitress appeared at their table and Jason placed

the order in impeccable French. "I hope you don't mind that I took the liberty. I can never resist the opportunity to practice," he said with a wink.

"I took French in high school." Jane grinned apologetically. "I'm afraid I don't remember very much of it."

"I lived abroad for a few years before law school, working my way through France and Spain. I speak Spanish, too," Jason added, fighting off a grin.

Jane's pulse fluttered. Gorgeous, smart, and he spoke two Romance languages. Could he be more perfect?

The soft sounds of a piano began to trickle into the dining room and Jane glanced into the lounge area, where couples had gathered around a baby grand near the window. Feeling Jason's eyes on her, she pulled her attention back, flustered at the intensity of his piercing blue gaze.

"Do you play?" he asked, gesturing to the piano.

"I wish," she said ruefully. "My mother was forever trying to get us to practice, but I was the youngest of three girls and I think she lost the battle by the time it came to me. I'd like my daughter to learn, though."

His brow furrowed ever so slightly. "You have a daughter?"

"Sophie." Jane beamed. "She's four."

"I knew about the divorce, but Rosemary never mentioned you had a child." The line between his eyebrows deepened.

Jane felt her heart sink. Why would Rosemary not have mentioned her daughter? Taking a sip of her wine, she asked, "How do you know Rosemary again?"

"Her daughter Molly is in grad school with my younger sister." He signaled to a passing waitress. "I'll take another Scotch. Single malt."

Jane eyed the crusty baguette in the middle of the table, feeling tense as the silence stretched. "Maybe I'll just run to the powder room for a minute," she said, already starting to stand.

She wove her way through the tables to the back of the restaurant and all but flung herself through the bathroom door. Okay, so maybe he wasn't perfect, after all, but he was pretty damn close. He was trilingual. He volunteered. He was gorgeous. Really, she was just being overly critical. She was looking for problems where they didn't exist—looking for a flaw, for a reason to end this and go home. And then what? Would she honestly feel better curled up in flannel pajamas in a big lonely bed?

Her lips pinched as she studied her reflection in the gilded mirror. It was the best she'd looked in a long time, with the exception of last Saturday—but that night she'd still been wearing her old lady cardigan, the one that made her look like she was joining a convent, Grace had said, not going out on a *hot date*.

Hot date. Yes, she was on a hot date, damn it, and she was going to enjoy herself.

She chuckled under her breath, forcing the last of her nerves from her system. She was overthinking this. It wasn't like she was going to marry the man...Her hand began to tremble as she leaned into the mirror and touched up her lipstick, and she quickly tossed it back in her clutch. She wasn't going to think about marriage now. Not with Adam. Not with Jason. Not with anyone.

Tonight she was a young, single girl in a beautiful—if slightly revealing—lacy top, in a fancy restaurant, dining with one of the most handsome men she had ever seen in her life. Even if he did seem to like to drink. And even if he did have a funny look on his face when she mentioned Sophie.

Well. She wasn't going to think about that either. She was being overly sensitive. One glass of Scotch and a little jolt that she had a child were to be expected, right?

Jane smoothed her hair and then flattened her blouse at her hips. With one last check in the mirror over her shoulder, she lifted her chin and pulled open the door. Her heels tapped along the polished wooden floorboards as she retraced her way to the table, and her heart warmed at the sight of that clean-shaven face, the designer charcoal suit, and the navy silk tie that offset the electric hue of his irises.

Jason sipped his Scotch, barely noticing her as she slid into her seat. Jane opened her mouth to break the silence, but the waitress reappeared at that moment with their starter salad. And another Scotch. *How long had she been in the restroom?*

"So." The polite smile froze on Jane's face, and the first onset of anxiety hit her as Jason's lids fell lower. He clutched the glass in his hand at a precarious angle, and she reached out to right it before the amber liquid could spill all over the untouched baguette.

Oh, why not? she thought, reaching for the baguette, and tore off a large chunk. She slathered it in butter with quick, determined strokes, seething. She couldn't even meet Jason's eyes as she bit into the bread and chewed. It was nearly as good as Anna's, but not quite. Either way, she decided then and there that she may as well enjoy the meal.

"So how long have you been divorced?" she inquired, deciding to latch onto the most obvious topic. She'd been carefully instructed by Rosemary not to mention such a painful subject, but considering Jason was chasing his wine with a third glass of liquor, rules didn't seem to apply anymore. She tore off another piece of bread, more liberal with the butter this time.

"Oh." Jason pulled in a sigh and ran a hand over his jaw. "About four years."

Jane tried to hide her surprise. She stopped chewing momentarily, thinking of uttering the same words so many years from now. Alone for four years. Sophie would be nearly nine by then; any hope of another child would seem lost. She'd loved growing up with two sisters, and she'd wanted the same for her daughter. Now, that seemed like a slim possibility. The losses just kept coming. One after the next.

She swallowed the bread too early, and sputtered. Tears prickled her eyes as she patted her chest and fumbled for the glass of water. Across from her, Jason only slightly perked up.

"Sorry," Jane managed when she'd recovered. "Down the wrong pipe."

When he said nothing, she refilled her wine from the bottle in the center. She'd always thought a gentleman might be the one to make this gesture, but it didn't seem she was dining with one tonight.

Not that Adam was really a gentleman, she reminded herself. *Not in the end.*

"So four years?" Jane shook her head. "Divorce isn't an easy process, I'm finding."

"Tell me about it," Jason spat. He leaned eagerly across the table, his eyes glinting with anger. "She took my house, the car, and she would have probably taken the kids if we'd had any, which, fortunately, we didn't."

Jane was aware that her eyes had grown wide. "Thank goodness for that," she muttered.

She inhaled with relief as the waitress delivered their entrées. *A little food might be just what he needs*, Jane thought, forcing herself to focus on the positive. It had all been so promising when he picked her up tonight— she'd immediately shed that cardigan—and she *had* gone against Rosemary's prudent advice and mentioned the divorce, which was *clearly* a touchy subject indeed. She herself was hardly free of sometimes venomous thoughts about Adam after all...

She returned her gaze to Jason as the waitress moved to the next table, and her lips thinned at the sight of his slumped posture, the tousled hair, and the lazy drift of his gaze.

Okay, so the guy was drunk.

"I'm sorry I mentioned your divorce."

"Oh, I'm over it," Jason said, taking a hearty bite of his steak.

Jane lowered her eyes to her food. She'd focus on the artful display. The delicate cream sauce that Anna would be sure to grill her about later. That must be rosemary in there, but Jane would never be able to decipher the other herbs. "Yes, well, it's not easy to mend a broken heart," she admitted.

He snorted. "The only broken heart was hers. What's that saying?" He leaned into his elbow on the table and twirled his fork in the air. "Hell hath no fury..."

Jane gave him a long look. "Like a woman scorned?"

Jason gave a thin smile and pointed the fork in her direction. "*Scorned* is a very good word for her. I made one little mistake, just one time, and she's never let me forget it."

One little mistake. Jane could surmise what that would be.

She plucked her cardigan from the back of her chair and quickly shrugged it on, buttoning it to the very top. Her heart was pounding when she considered her options, knowing what she must do. Setting her napkin on her half-eaten dinner, she said calmly, "It's been a really interesting evening, Jason, but I'm afraid I'm going to have to call it a night."

Panic filled his expression as she grabbed her bag and pushed back her chair, and for a moment, Jane wavered. He was a lawyer, after all, and a handsome one. He spoke three languages and he was an Ivy League grad. So he had too much to drink—maybe he was nervous!

But no, she thought. *No*. He was a cheater. And that was one thing she could never look past.

"But—dinner! And...dessert! If you don't like the food, then at least stay for a drink. I thought we could have a little fun at my place after this."

Jane blinked. "Thank you, but no. I have a daughter to get home to."

He was on his feet now, his hand on her arm, and she lowered her gaze to it. He had the sense to heed the silent warning, even in his current state. "Aw, damn. Rosemary's going to make my life a living hell for this."

Jane couldn't help but smile. It was the most approachable thing he'd said all evening.

"At least let me give you a ride home," he insisted.

"No," Jane said sharply, pulling back. "I'll find my way."

She turned on her heel and quickened her pace to the door, pausing only to tell the waitress to cut him off or take his keys, and then pushed through the doors into the cool spring air. She hesitated with the phone in her hands, wondering who she should call. Her mother was watching Sophie, who would certainly be asleep by now, so that left Grace or Anna.

Grace was probably with Luke. Besides, she would probably be far too disappointed for Jane that the evening hadn't gone well. Anna, on the other hand, didn't seem to bother with romantic entanglements. Jane could learn a lot from that sister.

Anna answered on the third ring and told her she'd be there in twenty minutes. Instantly feeling better, Jane noticed a coffee shop at the corner and stepped inside. She ordered a tea and sat near the window, eagerly watching for her sister's car. When it finally pulled to a stop just shy of twenty-five minutes later, she couldn't slide in fast enough.

"Another bust?" Anna asked.

"I had to tell the waitress to take his keys." Jane met Anna's wide-eyed stare and they both burst into a fit of laughter.

"You don't seem disappointed," Anna mused, glancing in the rearview mirror as she pulled her car from the curb, then turned onto the road that led back toward Briar Creek.

"No," Jane sighed. She stared out the window, as the shops and restaurants were replaced with a dark and seemingly endless forest. "He wasn't looking to settle down. Maybe he wasn't even capable of it. It's better to know that up front, so you don't end up surprised later."

Anna nodded. "Nothing worse than a man finally showing you his true colors when it's too late."

Jane frowned. The edge in her sister's tone seemed much too personal to be about Adam's betrayal.

"I hope I didn't interrupt your evening," Jane said casually, noticing that Anna was dressed in her designer jeans and favorite blue top. There was a telltale smudge of gloss on her lips.

"Oh, I was just finishing up with Mark. Tweaking recipes for the contest..." She glanced at Jane and gave a quick shrug.

"I see," Jane said, smiling to herself. She'd love for Anna to win the contest; it would be just the trick to get over the setback of the fire. She dropped her head back against the seat. "Is he still waiting for you then?"

"What? Oh no...no." Anna had started to drum her pointer finger on the steering wheel: a nervous tic.

Jane narrowed her eyes. There had always been something weird between Anna and Mark. They'd been friendly enough growing up given their three-year age difference, but then after they both returned to Briar Creek from culinary school they could barely even be in the same room. Anna had never said a word on the subject, but she didn't need to now. Her body language said everything.

Something was up between Anna and Mark. And it went deeper than running competing restaurants on Main Street.

"So things are going well then?" Jane slanted a glance at Anna, whose eyes were fixed on the road as they came into town.

"Oh, better than I expected, really. I hate to jinx things, but I think we stand a chance at winning." She smiled. "That would be...a huge relief."

"Are you still nervous about the loan?"

Anna pulled to a stop at a red light and tucked her

hands under her thighs. "If I'm being honest, a bit, but please don't tell Grace. She'll just tell Luke and...I'd rather handle this myself. Grace and I are only now getting back on good terms. You know things were strained for us after she moved away."

"I know." Jane frowned as the light switched back to green. Anna had always resented Grace for moving to New York and not being there when their father died. Main Street Books was in sight now, and as they passed by it, she felt a physical ache for her father, remembering how much that old place meant to him. "Dad would be so proud of you. You know that, don't you?"

Anna smiled sadly. "He'd be proud of all of us."

Jane studied her sister's stoic profile. "I wish I had money to lend you to help with everything, but you know I don't."

"Oh, Jane! That was never even a consideration. You have enough on your plate without worrying about this." Anna lifted her chin. "I'll get through it. Once the café reopens everything will be just fine."

Jane's frown deepened at the hesitancy in her sister's voice. It wasn't like her to be so unsure of herself.

"So," Anna said, sliding her a grin. "You ready for another date?"

"Nope." Jane shook her head firmly. "This was it. I'm telling Rosemary I'm done."

"You sure?"

Jane gave her sister a pleading look. "I don't think I'm ready to date. The thought of having my heart broken again..." She remembered who she was talking to and checked herself. "Sorry. I must sound ridiculous to you."

Anna stared pensively ahead. "I think I understand

better than you know." She turned up the radio dial, shutting down any chance of the conversation continuing.

Jane studied her sister for a long moment, letting her words resonate, thinking back on the change she'd seen in her after she'd graduated from school, and then again this past week.

Yes, Anna might just understand her better than she thought, but not because Anna was good about avoiding romantic entanglements, but because, like Jane, she might be silently dealing with her very own.

CHAPTER
15

Mark was in his office when Anna finished transferring the last of the croissants from the cooling rack. She'd worked slowly, purposefully stalling so she could casually leave without any awkwardness, or perhaps dragging out the moment until she had to depart, but now she was left with the dilemma of knocking on his door specifically to say goodbye, or just leaving without a word.

The latter was unfortunately not an option, even if a clean break was exactly what she needed. She hadn't wanted to come to Hastings this morning, even if she was able to accomplish all her baking for the Annex in a little more than two hours. The contest was now exactly two weeks away, and if they were going to work on their entry tonight, it would be better to discuss that now rather than pop in later or God forbid pick up the phone.

She loaded the last of the boxes into the trunk of her car, which she'd parked just beside Mark's black SUV in the alley behind the diner, and then reentered through the kitchen door. She could still make out the soft lull of his voice as she neared his half-open office door, but as she was just about to lean in and knock, Mark appeared in the doorframe.

"You startled me," she said, covering her embarrassment with a smile.

She'd tried not to let herself look his way while they were in the kitchen, each separately preparing for their day, but now she couldn't avoid it. His nut brown hair was tousled as if he had been dragging his hands through it, and his deep espresso eyes were warm and alive. A day's worth of stubble had collected on his chin, framing his square jaw. Her eyes rested firmly on his mouth, just as they had the night before, first in his kitchen while they'd again tested recipes and then all through the night, while she'd tossed and turned in search of sleep that never came.

Mark, on the other hand, seemed to have not had trouble in the sleep department. He looked well rested and energized, while her left eye was starting to twitch with fatigue. *Figures*, Anna thought bitterly. Nothing touched Mark, nothing rattled him, and nothing kept him awake. He was untouchable—a trait she'd aspired to and achieved once. Look at her now; only a matter of a week into letting her wall down, and she was already feeling raw and exposed.

She wouldn't let him in again. She couldn't.

"Were you waiting for me?"

If you counted standing around in the kitchen waiting for him to get off the phone as waiting, then guilty as charged. "I'm heading over to the bookstore," she informed him.

His eyes never strayed. "Will I see you later?"

She ran through her calendar. She was covering the counter at the Annex until noon, and her meeting with Sharon would last until one. After that, she had hoped to visit the furniture store where she'd first purchased the seating for Fireside—she'd have to charge anything she bought with the plan to pay it off when the check from the insurance company cleared.

"Does seven work for you?"

"It's a date." Mark tossed her a lopsided grin that made her stomach roll over. She knew what he meant by it, but the part of her that liked his word choice entirely too much made her feel anxious. She had to get through this damn contest and get back to her own kitchen once and for all.

She waved goodbye and turned on her heel before she could linger on the definition of his lips a second longer, and her heart thrummed with each step she took toward the back door, feeling Mark's eyes on her back.

It wasn't personal, she reminded herself firmly as she pushed through the door without another glance back. With Mark, it was never, ever personal.

Rosemary was already seated at the long farmhouse table near the window of the Annex when Anna came in with a high stack of pastry boxes. Spread on the table was this week's book club selection, but Rosemary's attention was on anything but the paperback in front of her. Jane stood at the head of the table, fury reddening her face, as Rosemary pursed her lips and batted her eyelashes, her hands folded calmly in her lap.

"Everything okay this morning?" Anna asked. She set the boxes on the counter and began quickly plating the triple berry muffins. She should have been here at least ten minutes ago, and instead she'd stood around the diner waiting for one last exchange with Mark. *Pathetic.*

A rush of anger fueled her as she took the last muffin

from the box and popped the top on another. It was just like the day he broke up with her.

They'd agreed to meet but he'd kept her waiting, and fool that she was, she'd stood outside his class while he'd chatted with another girl, that long-legged brunette named Cassie, not even bothering to look in her direction through the open door, even though he had to have known she was there. He'd been distant for a week, but that was the moment she first knew for certain that his feelings for her, like those before her, had cooled.

She'd studied him sidelong the entire walk to a nearby coffee shop—he'd been quieter than he'd been in the two years they'd grown close, the laughter and ease had faded, and he didn't reach for her hand the way he had those glorious four months when they couldn't take their hands off each other. She asked if something was wrong, hoping it was her imagination, even if deep down she knew—this was Mark. She'd seen him brush off girl after girl before their friendship had turned romantic. She'd rolled her eyes as she'd watched him across campus, kissing some pretty classmate, knowing that within a few weeks he'd break up with her. His dating life was a revolving door, but she... she was his constant friend. She'd expected more from him, but she'd wanted more than he could give.

If she dared to think of that day—and she'd worked hard not to—she could still feel the weight of it square in her chest. The realization that she'd been played. That he never loved her, never would, and that she'd fed into his charms, and the fantasy he'd created, of how life might have been.

For all three of them.

She'd gone home that day and studied the pregnancy test stick over and over. Each time she got the same result:

positive. Her life with Mark was still moving forward some-how, even if he had already left her without a glance back.

"I was just telling Rosemary about my date last night," Jane told Anna, without looking back. She stared stonily at Rosemary, who casually inspected her nails.

"So he had a little too much to drink," she replied airily.

"He had two glasses of wine and three Scotches. Before the meal was even served."

Anna hid a smile as Rosemary's eyes went wide. Recovering her fluster, she waved a hand dismissively. "Worse things have happened."

"Like cheating on your wife?" Jane set her hands on her hips. "He also doesn't seem particularly fond of children."

"I didn't know he cheated on his wife," Rosemary murmured, frowning. "Who told you this?"

"He did, more or less. After about his fifth drink, it all just slipped out." Jane gave an unhappy laugh.

Rosemary tutted. "He seemed like such a *nice* young man."

Jane nodded. "He seemed that way at first, but in the end, he wasn't."

Anna tied her apron at the waist, pulling the strings tight. "Isn't that usually the case? Things start out so promising, and then...then they really show you what they were all about." The difference with her, though, was that she knew Mark's pattern.

She set the last basket of croissants on the counter and was just about to start on the coffee when she caught Rosemary's expression. Even Jane had turned ever so slightly to face her, one eyebrow cocked in question.

"Sounds like you're speaking from firsthand experience," Rosemary commented.

Anna's fingers began to tremble as she scooped Kona beans into the grinder, remembering the brush of Mark's hand on her own, the way they'd worked side by side in the kitchen last night, the way she had started watching the clock and then reluctantly left to fetch Jane, not wanting their time together to end anytime soon.

Something about him felt different. There was something hesitant about him, something less cocky. Something more…genuine. She smiled when she thought of the way he doted on Scout, even if he spoiled the poor dog rotten. Maybe he wasn't as cold-hearted as she'd come to believe…

Nonsense! Just two weeks ago he was cavorting with her niece's preschool teacher. Who was next?

Not her. Definitely, certainly, not her.

She jammed her finger on the pulse button, watching the coffee beans whirl and whiz until the pieces chipped and broke off, and all she was left with were the fragments. Just like Mark had done to her heart.

Anna set the coffee to brew and looked across the room at Rosemary. "You've set Jane up on two dates. I think it's my turn now." Her tone was clear and determined, and she felt her resolve tighten. She would go out on a date—it was about damn time.

She'd expected Rosemary to be ecstatic, but the woman sat rooted in her chair, her blue eyes wide with something close to alarm. Anna stood expectantly, waiting for her to say something.

"*Well.*" Rosemary pinched her lips. "I assumed you were too busy. What with the fire, and now the contest… Can Mark really spare you right now? This contest is only two weeks away; you must be spending nearly every spare minute together!"

Anna tipped her head. It wasn't like Rosemary to back down on one of her own suggestions. "I can make time," she said brazenly. Just saying the words aloud gave her conviction.

"If you're sure..." Rosemary frowned and set her hands in her lap. "I just...it's just that I know how great it would be for the two of you to win this contest. I wouldn't have mentioned it if I didn't think it was...exactly what you both needed. I hate to interfere now."

Interfere? Since when did Rosemary Hastings worry about interfering?

The door chimed and from behind the tall stacks of books, Anna spotted a few of the book club women arriving for their weekly meeting. She counted out the mugs, making sure enough were clean, and stood at attention near the register, waiting to take their orders. The book club was a nice little perk to Saturday's profit, and several of the women stopped in throughout the week as well, often bringing other friends. Many had enjoyed the bring-your-own-wine night; Anna would have loved to have been there, but Grace understood why she'd missed it. They were a team—with Grace covering Main Street Books and Anna holding up her end with the food and now the contest—and she liked it this way. Too many years of silence had passed between the sisters, and Anna still felt sorry for the time they had lost.

She and Grace were different, and they were still coming to terms with that. Grace had fled town when she and Luke broke up, whereas Anna could never give up Briar Creek, no matter what Mark had done to her.

Anna poured three coffees and made two cappuccinos, taking a moment to add a little heart shape with the foam.

Back when the Fireside Café was getting off the ground, she'd worn many hats; that was years ago, but still she could nearly work the machine with her eyes closed.

She'd nearly forgotten how far she'd come. Now she had a manager, a barista, a dishwasher, two waitresses, and part-time staff to watch the bakery counter when she was busy in the kitchen. To think she used to manage all that by herself!

But then, what other choice did she have?

She plated a vanilla bean scone and handed it to Jane, who brought it over to the table. The women had all begun to chatter noisily, but several stopped to compliment her on the food. She never tired of a pleasant remark from a satisfied customer—it reminded her why she stuck with this. Why she was still fighting to keep her passion alive. Why she was even daring to dream bigger.

Fifty thousand dollars. In two weeks it could be hers. And then, if the space next door to Fireside was still free...

She sucked in a breath. She shouldn't get ahead of herself. Not when reality could be so harsh.

"So, will you do it, Rosemary?" She folded her arms across her chest and waited.

Rosemary regarded her through her suspicious eyes, but finally smiled. "Of course. And come to think of it, I know just the man, too."

Anna felt her pulse kick with instant regret. "Oh?"

"Yes," Rosemary said with a lift of her chin. "This date will do the trick, my dear. I'm quite sure by the end you'll begin to realize exactly what—or should I say who—has been missing from your life all along."

CHAPTER
16

Mark flicked to the last page of one of the dozen cooking magazines he subscribed to and set it on the glass coffee table with a sigh. It was Wednesday, Vince was covering the diner for the rest of the afternoon, and like so many quiet days that seemed to go on forever, Mark found himself wondering what the hell he was doing with his life.

At his feet, Scout was snoring softly, and Mark reached down to lay a hand on his soft fur, finding something soothing in the comfort of the dog's body under his hand. He wasn't alone anymore, and he liked it that way—more than he dared to admit.

Regret gnawed at him when he thought of how many years he'd spent holed up in an empty house, occasionally opening the door to the random girl or friend, but always shutting it firmly behind them on the way out. He'd told himself he was happy that way, that he liked his space, that he didn't want the complications that came with letting someone in and sharing…anything. It was better to control his world, to choose who came in and who went out, to know that in his carefully chosen orbit, there was no room for disappointment or heartache.

No room for surprises.

"Don't know what I'd do without you, buddy," he murmured, giving Scout a light pat on the back.

The dog lifted his head from his paws and turned to him with big brown eyes. Since Scout had slipped through the gate, Mark had secured the fence and taken extra care in keeping the latch closed at all times. He was too ticked at Anna's negative assumption to give her the satisfaction, but the truth was that he was scared to the bone when she told him Scout had wandered all the way down to Mountain Road, in the dark, and that he had been none the wiser. The thought of losing the one good thing that had come his way in years left him rattled, stirring up all those feelings of self-doubt he'd tried to bury over the years. It would have been his damn fault if something had happened to the pup, just like Anna had accused.

She'd been right. He was careless. A few nights ago with Scout. Years ago with her.

For two years she was his closest friend. Then he had to bring it to the next level. Ruin everything they'd shared.

He should have known better than to take that risk. With Anna. With anyone.

Mark stood, stretching his back, which had begun to ache more and more from so many hours on his feet, reminding him that he wasn't young anymore—as if the sight of all his friends with babies wasn't enough. Deciding some fresh air would be good for his mood, he took Scout's leash from the hook near the back door and attached it to his hunter green collar. Handing over a treat, he stuffed a few more into his pocket and stepped outside. They took the driveway to the road and followed it for a mile south. By Mark's calculations Luke should be home from work now; a chat with his cousin was just the thing he needed to remind him of the family he had in his life, not the one who had chosen not to be a part of it.

He'd been thinking about his dad too much these days. It happened every time he started making plans for himself, daring to open the kind of restaurant he envisioned. He could see it all, lively and bustling, and then just as quickly the image would be replaced with the dark and dead Tavern on Main.

If his father's restaurant hadn't failed, would he have stuck around? Mark's parents had often fought over that place, especially toward the end. It started with the time and attention Bill gave the business, and then turned to shouting matches over money. Sometimes Mark hated that restaurant—wished it would go away. But what he didn't know was that Tavern on Main was the best of his father, and when it was gone, he was, too.

Luke's black Range Rover was in his driveway, and he opened the door before Mark and Scout made it to the top of the stairs. "Perfect timing," Luke grinned. "I was going to call you later. Beer?"

Mark nodded. "Thanks."

He unhooked Scout's leash and handed him another biscuit, which Scout eagerly accepted and then took to the living room to enjoy. Mark winced as he watched the dog jump onto one of the soft leather sofas Luke had centered around the large stone hearth. "Sorry about that."

Luke just grinned. "Don't worry about it; you know I like dogs. I'm hoping Grace and I will get one of our own soon." He popped the cap off two beers and handed him one.

"You seem to be in good spirits today," Mark commented, eyeing his cousin steadily. "Normally, you'd jump on the opportunity to jab me about Scout's lack of training."

Luke just shrugged, but his grin widened. "I'm going to propose to Grace."

The beer remained halfway to Mark's mouth. "But... I mean...I assumed you might ask her to move in first."

"It's been good for her to stay with her mom these past few months. They both needed that time together, especially with Ray's passing."

Mark nodded slowly and took a long sip from his bottle. He didn't taste a thing. "It just seems so soon."

Luke frowned. "I thought you'd be happy for me."

What the hell had gotten into him? No one knew better than Mark how much Grace meant to Luke. When she'd come back to town over Christmas, he'd been the one who encouraged Luke to see if something was still there between them. He should be thrilled that his cousin was marrying his first love. Instead, that stomach-churning feeling he'd been fighting off and on for years was hitting full force, knocking every rule he'd ever made for himself upside down.

He pushed back the unwanted emotions. "Of course I'm happy. Just shocked, that's all. Jeez, man, congratulations!" He thumped Luke on the back and then brought the beer to his mouth, feeling the cool, foamy liquid trace its way down his throat.

Luke was getting married, and not for the first time. After the pain of losing his first wife, he was finally getting a second chance at happiness, with the girl he'd been crazy about since they were just kids. He'd been down. He'd been crushed. First by Grace when she'd broken his heart, then by Helen's death. Somehow, despite it all, he was willing to try again. Willing to let Grace in. Willing to believe this time it would be different.

Willing to accept the risks if it wasn't.

Mark gritted his teeth. All week he'd been pushing aside this pesky attraction to Anna, telling himself it was the friend he was missing, nothing more. She was a pretty girl, so what? But he couldn't deny the part of him that wondered...could there be a second chance for him and Anna *if* he wanted there to be?

Luke reached into his pocket and pulled out a box, setting it on the counter with a determined smack. Mark's eyes widened on it, the reality of the commitment setting in. When had he ever shown such a leap of faith?

He looked into the living room, where Scout had moved over to the large floor-to-ceiling windows, basking in the late afternoon sun. A dog was one thing. A person...a person could leave you. Hell, even Scout had nearly wandered away.

Luke flipped the lid and Mark let out a low whistle, leaning in closer for a better look at the solitaire diamond on a thin platinum band. "When are you going to do it?"

"Tomorrow," Luke said. He tapped his finger against the counter, his stare fixed on the box, his jaw set with resolve. He suddenly looked nervous as hell. "Think she'll like it?"

Mark grinned, resisting the urge to joke with Luke's sudden uncertainty. There had been enough of that. "She'll love it."

Luke slipped the box into a drawer. "I've already

talked to Kathleen, and we're going to have an engagement party this Friday at the Madisons' house. She's planning everything for it, along with my mother."

Mark's mind spun at how quickly this was happening.

"Another thing," Luke said, leaning against the counter.

Mark shifted the weight on his feet, fighting the growing restlessness. It was one thing when Luke had married
Helen—Mark hadn't cared much about it then, other than
to be happy for his cousin. The years of loneliness hadn't
set in yet; plenty of friends were still single. Not anymore.
After Helen died, Luke had fallen back into bachelorhood,
and his bachelor status made Mark feel more normal, less
unfocused. Less alone.

Had he really assumed it would continue like that forever? A little part of him maybe had. Instead, Luke had
found love again. He was moving forward with his life.

While Mark…Well, Mark was left behind. Even
though he'd promised himself never to be in this position
again, it couldn't be avoided.

"I know you've already been there for me once, but I
can't think of anyone else I'd rather have stand at my side.
You were the one who got me out of my rut after losing
Helen. You helped me start living again. So what do you
say, will you be my best man?"

"Of course!" Mark gritted his teeth harder, hoping his
smile wouldn't waver. He clinked his beer to Luke's and
knocked it back, waiting for his racing pulse to slow, wondering what it would take to banish this feeling that had
suddenly consumed him. Normally when he got like this,
he hit the bar, chatted up a friendly girl, and took his mind
off his troubles. A little fun, a little flirting, and he had his
fix. More and more, though, it wasn't enough. It left him

feeling more empty, more alone, and more filled with an aching reminder of what was missing.

By Friday morning, it was official. Luke and Grace were engaged. Anna announced it breathlessly within minutes of arriving at the diner, but Luke had already called Mark late the night before to tell him Grace had accepted.

As if there were ever any doubt.

"I'm the best man. Again." Mark gave a half-hearted grin as Anna pushed up her sleeves and began measuring flour.

"That's quite an honor." She caught his eyes, and his gut tightened at the clarity of her blue gaze. "I'm not sure if I'll be the maid of honor. Even though I'm the middle sister, Grace and Jane always had a special bond. Or she might ask Ivy Birch. They've been friends since they were children."

Mark nodded thoughtfully. He supposed he'd have the same dilemma if he ever made it to the altar. He loved his brother, but he was closer to Luke than Brett in many ways. Being the oldest, he'd had to look out for his mother and brother after his father cut town—it was a strain Luke understood firsthand when his own father passed away a few months later. Those types of bonds were unspoken and deep.

His brow furrowed as he peeled an onion. What the hell was he even thinking about this for? He was never getting married. He knew firsthand that marriage didn't last. In the end, someone always left. One way or another…

His mind trailed to his mother and his heart began to wrench like it did every time he thought of her lying in bed, thin and pale, with that patterned scarf around her head. She shouldn't have been alone then—and she wasn't, because he'd made damn sure of it. He'd put two years of his life on hold, deferring college until she was in remission, working in the diner to keep it going. He'd done it again by coming back here after culinary school, vowing that he'd do what he had to, just so long as she got better.

A wave of guilt washed over him when he thought of the way he'd been thinking about his father again recently, remembering the way it felt to work side by side in Tavern's clamoring kitchen. The man had treated his mother like dirt, leaving her with two young sons and no money, not bothering to check in or be there for her when she was staring death in the face. What kind of son did that make him?

His frown deepened as he hacked at the onion.

"You all must be relieved. I know Luke went through a dark period after Helen died. It was tough for him to be alone like that," Anna said, as if reading his thoughts.

That it was. Luke had suffered. Greatly. He deserved this happiness. *Everyone does.*

"Luke and Grace were meant to find their way back to each other. I'm glad it worked out for them." He chopped the onion over and over until it was more of a mince than the course chop he had intended. *Damn it.* He slid it to the side and plucked another from the bowl.

"It makes me feel optimistic," Anna said. "If they found their way back to each other, then there's hope for us all, right?"

They locked eyes. Anna blinked slowly, the black lashes that rimmed those turquoise blue irises fluttering. In the heat of the kitchen, her cheeks glowed with pink nearly as rosy as her mouth.

His gut stirred with desire, tightening with longing he wasn't sure he could resist. But even if he dared to try, stepped outside his comfort zone and reached for her, would she let him back in? He wasn't so sure of it. They'd come a long way in recent weeks, further than he'd thought they ever could, but that didn't mean she'd forgiven him. And it didn't mean he was ready for anything more.

Her lips curved into a smile and her eyes disappeared behind those lashes as she returned to her task. He watched her for a second longer, fighting the weight in his chest. She could be his friend again maybe, and maybe that could be enough this time. It had meant something once—enough for him to take the leap, to think it would be enough to last, to give him the guarantee he needed.

Instead, it had only scared him more than ever.

"Guess we'll have to take tonight off from recipe testing for the engagement party," he said. The disappointment that gnawed at him quickly disappeared when he imagined Anna in some sexy little number. "Hard to believe the contest is a week away. Maybe we can get an early start on the recipes tomorrow to make up the time."

Anna hesitated. "Mind if we meet a little later, actually? Is nine too late?"

His smile faltered, but he hid his surprise with a low laugh. "You got some hot date or something?"

He'd meant it as a joke, but the blush that colored her cheeks hit him square in the gut. She didn't look at him as she muttered, "Something like that."

His hands were on autopilot, scoring the flesh of another onion. The blade worked in even strokes, but his mind was spinning. "Anyone I know?"

Anna sprinkled her work surface with flour before

transferring the dough from its bowl. "Perhaps." She glanced up at him. "Your aunt is playing matchmaker. She has someone in mind."

Rosemary loved to meddle. She was forever hinting that he needed the love of a good woman, and that he couldn't hold out forever.

"Well." He forced a tight smile. "Lucky guy."

Anna's hands froze on the dough she'd been working for a split second, but he didn't regret his words. Let her take from them what she would—let her spear him with a hard look, rattle off a caustic remark. Let her say all the things he felt. Let her voice his worst fears.

Yes, this guy was lucky, damn it. Yes, this guy would be smart enough to treat her better than he had. Was he a hypocrite to want the very same thing he dreaded?

"You know, why don't we just skip tomorrow night?" His voice was sharper than he intended, and she snapped her gaze to him, confusion knitting her fine brow. Or perhaps—he pressed his mouth firmly—perhaps it was hurt. He cracked an egg for a quiche. "We've been tweaking these recipes all week. A couple nights off might be just what we need to take a step back and reassess."

Oh, he'd be reassessing all right. And getting a firm grip. Come Sunday at this time, he'd have a clear head on his shoulders, the one he'd boasted—with the exception of that one little hiccup that last summer of school—since the day his dad had walked out, never to return.

Anna set the scones in the oven and set the timer. "If you think that's best."

He ignored the hint of sadness in her tone. "Yeah," he said, cracking another egg, and another. He whisked in some salt and pepper, a splash of heavy cream. "We've been working hard. A break will be good." A break was always the answer. When things got too tense, too serious, the best thing was a little distance.

He finished the quiche in silence and slid it into one of the ovens. From the corner of his eye, he could see Anna watching him from her position at the center counter, each step of her task seeming slower and more deliberate than usual.

"I've got some paperwork to go through," he said brusquely, motioning to his office just off the back of the kitchen.

He bolted through the door, closing it firmly behind him, and threw himself into his chair. Anna was going on a date, and his aunt was the one behind it all. It felt like a betrayal, like some sick, twisted irony, even though Rosemary of course didn't know. She couldn't. As far as he knew, Anna had never told anyone what had happened between them that summer and neither had he. By the time they'd returned to Briar Creek after each of their graduations, it was over, and he surely would have had an earful if Anna had let anything slip. That time had been theirs, their secret, their haven, and when it was gone...

Anna changed. She hardened. She didn't share, and she didn't let people get close. And now, after all these years, the walls were finally coming down. She was letting him back in, and he had a sinking feeling it was because only now, after all this time, the thing he'd feared the most had happened. She was over him.

CHAPTER 17

Anna could honestly say that Grace had never looked prettier. Standing near the hearth in a black sweetheart-neck cocktail dress, she glowed brighter than the ring on her finger as she stared up at Luke and gently kissed him, eliciting a chorus of cheers from the crowd that had gathered in the Madison home.

Anna chased the lump from her throat with a sip of champagne. She was getting swept up in the beauty of the affair, in her sister's contagious smile, and, maybe, in the twinge of sadness that their father couldn't be with them tonight.

"Dad would have loved this," she said wistfully to Jane, who stood with her at the back of the living room.

Jane tipped her head into a strained smile. "He's here right now. You know he wouldn't miss this."

Anna blinked quickly. Luke had been like a son to their father, and Grace was his golden girl. He'd been so proud of the books she'd had published, but Anna knew deep down this was what he wanted most for her. To love and to be loved.

It's what he wanted for them all.

"As much as I miss him, I'm glad he wasn't here to see how I ended up," Jane said with a frown.

"You'll find love again, Jane. Just give it time." Anna paused at her words, wishing she could take her own advice and knowing she couldn't. She was already dreading her date tomorrow night. What had she been thinking, asking Rosemary to set her up? She didn't want to put her heart out there any more than she wanted to share a future with anyone. She was good on her own. Things had been okay for the past few years; these last few weeks had just been a setback. Before long, she'd be back into her routine, busy, and happy. Well, almost happy.

Jane glanced around the room and took another sip from her champagne flute. "Well, there's no one of interest here tonight. I feel a little embarrassed admitting I'd sort of hoped there would be."

Anna returned her wry smile. "Briar Creek is rather limited when it comes to romantic options."

"Not for some." Jane jutted her chin and Anna turned to follow her gaze, wishing she hadn't when she locked eyes with Mark standing in the arched entrance to the front hall.

She hadn't seen him come in, even though her eyes had darted the room for the better part of Luke's toast, but there he stood, tall and dark with his hair tousled, reminding her of the way he looked when he hovered over her, bare chested and warm on the cool wet sand, his lips parting for a kiss. His eyes were deep and hooded, in contrast with the easy grin he wore, and on his arm was none other than Nicole Johnson, giggling and flushed.

Anna's eyes narrowed as she turned away. Her heart was pounding so loudly she was sure Jane could hear it, and her hand trembled as she brought the glass to her lips, gulping the last of her drink.

It took a special kind of fool to fall for the same trick twice, and yet she had. She knew it now, by the ache in her chest—she'd fallen. Hard and fast, and against her better judgment, just like she had all those years ago. She had been charmed by that grin, so slick and self-assured; warmed by that laughter, so rich and elusive; and seduced by the depths of those eyes, so dark and unreadable. He'd put her at ease, showed her kindness she had long forgotten, and reminded her of how easy it was to just be with him. She'd made herself believe she was over him, that she was ready to move on, that someone else could elicit that heat only he seemed capable of unleashing.

She was wrong. Wrong, wrong, wrong. Her gut knew it, but her heart had won out.

"Is the food in the dining room?" she asked, even though she knew full well that it was. She'd personally prepared each bacon-wrapped date, crab cake, and goat cheese tartlet. She may as well enjoy them, though something told her, as she edged out of the living room and farther from Mark, that even the taste of her Gruyère-stuffed puffed pastry couldn't lift her spirits now.

Rosemary was already at the dining table, helping herself to a wedge of the mushroom-stuffed Brie en croute. "My, isn't this impressive, Anna. Is this on your menu at Fireside?"

Anna nodded. "It's part of our weekend dinner menu."

Rosemary brought a smoked salmon and herbed cream cheese canapé to her lips. The flutter of her lashes forced a reluctant smile from Anna. "Have you ever considered adding more dinner shifts?" she inquired, snatching another canapé from the platter.

She surveyed the spread impassively, finding herself unable to make a decision. "I have," she confessed, adding a roasted vegetable empanada to her plate. "I was waiting until things settled down with the Annex first. Then with the fire…"

"Well, no better time to kick off your full dinner service than with your grand reopening," Rosemary said.

Wouldn't that be nice? As Anna had suspected, no one had expressed interest in the former stationery shop yet. It was just there for the taking, and oh, how she wanted it.

"Thinking of expanding your services, are you?"

Anna spun around to see Mark standing behind her. His grin split his face, but his eyes were a notch darker than usual.

She pursed her lips and turned her head, adjusting the strap on the aubergine-colored dress she'd found in the back of her closet.

"Mark, have you seen this? Anna did it all." Rosemary beamed, letting her gaze roam over the table. "But then, I suppose you're already fully aware of all of Anna's merits."

"She certainly is a wonderful chef." Mark's hand grazed her fingers as he reached for a plate, sending a shiver down her spine. She sidestepped, hoping to gain distance, but Rosemary inched forward, just enough to block her path.

"I must get the recipe for this olive bread, Anna," she said.

Anna nodded politely and darted her eyes over the room. Jane was helping Sophie select a pink-glazed petit four from the tiered dessert tray. No matter how relentlessly Anna's gaze bore into her, she didn't detect it, and finally, Anna gave up.

"So, Aunt Rosemary," Mark said as he turned to join their group. Anna gritted her teeth, feeling mocked and angered. There was a decided glint in his eyes. A smirk curled that full mouth. He was goading her, baiting her, and he was enjoying it, too. "I hear you've found a match for Anna."

Heat burned her cheeks as she glared at him, but if he noticed he didn't react. He crammed a mini quiche into his mouth and chewed, daring to tip his head in consideration when he'd finished.

The bastard.

"Oh, I most certainly have." Rosemary gave a knowing smile. "I know *just* the man for her."

Anna cast a withering glance at Mark to find his jaw had set. He stopped chewing a parmesan breadstick for a beat and then resumed. "Well, good. You'll make some lucky fellow really happy one day."

"Indeed she will!" With that, Rosemary grabbed one last tartlet from a tray, turned on her heel, and walked through the arched doorway to Anna's mother, who was chatting with a few neighbors in the front hall.

Anna could feel the blood coursing through her veins. Mark's eyes sparked with challenge, but his mouth was a grim line. "I see Nicole's a glutton for punishment," she offered, hastily adding more food to her plate.

Mark shrugged. "I think she's having fun."

"Someone ought to tell her to enjoy it while it lasts," she mused, giving him her full attention.

"I'd like to think you did," Mark replied tersely. He tipped his chin, his voice low and husky as he insisted, "We had our share of fun, right, Anna?"

Anna felt someone's eyes on her and glanced over to

see Rosemary watching them with interest from across the room. She forced a pleasant smile, despite the fury fueling each breath. The last thing she needed was for Rosemary Hastings to put two and two together and start speculating. She'd pester and prod until the truth spilled out and then...The last thing Anna wanted was to make her love life—or lack thereof—a family affair.

Besides, there was nothing left to discuss, was there?

"I don't see any point in hashing out our past, Mark. We've both moved on. Some of us sooner than others," she hissed through the permanent grin she wore.

The party was buzzing around them, lively conversation interrupted by waves of laughter. This was her sister's engagement party. She would have a good time if it killed her. Mark had spoiled enough for her; she wouldn't let him taint this night, too.

Mark opened his mouth to say something but she stopped him before he had the chance. "If you don't mind, I wanted to talk to Kara a bit before the night gets away from us. Give Nicole my regards. And my condolences."

She grinned wider, blinking away her mounting emotion, careful not to let it show in her face, as she merged through the crowd, stopping to mingle, to even laugh, and to pretend like nothing in the world was wrong.

Tonight was a happy night for their family. Her own disappointments had no place in this room.

Or in her heart.

Jane peered across the room, realization beginning to unfold at the interaction between her sister and Mark. From a distance, Anna seemed perfectly fine, smiling and laughing with this friend or that, but Jane had seen the way she'd stiffened when Mark walked in with Nicole Johnson. She couldn't get away from the pair fast enough, whereas Mark, it seemed, had other ideas in mind. Not only had he followed her into the dining room, but now, after what appeared to be a brief and tense exchange despite their false cheer, his gaze lingered on Anna, minutes after she had wandered away from him, without a glance back.

"Mommy. Mommy!"

Jane ignored the tugging at her skirt and craned her neck, just in time to see Nicole saunter over and take Mark by the arm, forcefully pulling his attention away from Anna, who was now chatting animatedly with Kara in the corner of the living room.

"Mommy, can I have another cookie?"

"Sure. Sure." She righted herself, and looked sharply at Sophie, who was grinning ear to ear. She hadn't been paying attention, and now she'd promised too much. "What? No. I'm sorry; you've had enough sugar for one night."

"Aw, but it's a special night," Sophie pointed out.

Jane hid her grin. "One more, but that's it."

Sophie's eyes lit up and she ran over to the dessert table and carefully selected a cookie from the abundant selection. Jane watched as she took a small bite of the cookie, smiled, and then twirled around in the new pink dress Jane had bought her especially for the party. Grace had asked Sophie to be her flower girl, and it was a role Sophie was already taking very seriously. Jane figured tonight might be a good practice run for attending an adult event, and as she watched Sophie take hands with the son of one of Luke's friends, she felt her heart grow heavy.

It might be an adult party, but Sophie was falling into step easier than she could say she was.

Pulling her silk wrap tighter around her shoulders, Jane glanced around the room, trying hard not to frown. All around her it seemed people were paired off, talking to other couples. She knew she could go over and sit with Anna and Kara, or chat with Luke's youngest sister, Molly, who had driven in for the weekend to attend the party, but she wasn't feeling up for it just yet. It was the first social event she had been to without Adam, and his absence was more prominent than she had expected.

Jane checked to make sure Sophie wasn't up to trouble and then ducked out into the hall, happy for a chance to escape on her own for just a few seconds. As part of her mother's recent design changes, she had removed most of the family photos that had hung in the downstairs of the house, choosing instead to pepper the bookshelves in the study with black-and-white candids. Along the sweeping staircase leading to the second floor, however, she had carefully assembled a collage of their best photos, most professionally taken over the years. Jane took the first step, smiling at her parents' wedding photo housed in a silver frame. They were so young. So much life was still ahead of them—so much left to be discovered.

It was the same way she'd felt when she married Adam. It was a sense of security, a feeling of knowing that they were in this together, that at the end of the day, they would always come home to each other. That they'd never have to be alone.

And look at her now.

Jane took a sip of her wine and climbed higher, gliding her hand along the smooth, polished banister, soaking in the memories that had unfolded under this roof. There was Grace as a baby, then Anna, then Jane. And Sophie.

She paused, frowning, when she noticed the frame that had once held her own wedding photo now boasted a picture of Grace and Luke, taken this past New Year's Eve, right after they got back together.

Her pulse sped up, and she steadied herself on the railing. Of course her wedding picture would be taken down. She was going through a divorce. Yet, somehow, imagining her mother going through the premeditated act of removing the frame, replacing the photo, and then rehanging it was just too much.

Her marriage was over. Not just in her head. Not just on paper. Everyone else had accepted it. It was about time she did too.

"Psst!"

Jane startled, grateful for a reason to pull herself from darkening thoughts, and turned to see Rosemary standing at the base of the stairs.

"I was hoping to steal you away for a few minutes," she said, hoisting her long black taffeta skirt as she began to ascend the stairs. "I have to reapply my lipstick. Come with me."

Jane didn't bother mentioning that Rosemary was wearing enough lipstick to last her through the night and straight through to morning, and instead took relief in the company and the excuse to slip upstairs for a few stolen minutes. She brought Rosemary into her old bedroom, relaxing at the sight of the purple canopy and ruffled curtains—Kathleen may have transformed the lower level of the home into a design showcase, but the upstairs remained firmly rooted in the past, and Jane was grateful for that.

Unlike her current house, this was a room she had

never shared with Adam. It wasn't full of his ghosts, tainted by his memories. It was just hers.

She sat down on the floral bedspread while Rosemary fished through her beaded evening bag, finally finding her lipstick. "Now, Jane, I know you weren't very pleased with me about the last date I set you up on, but I do hope you'll let me try again."

Jane let out a weary sigh. "Oh, Rosemary. I think I'm stepping back from the dating world for now."

"But you can't!" Rosemary's blue eyes were wide with panic, but she composed herself when she met Jane's shocked expression in the mirror. She busied herself by plucking the silver cap off her tube of lipstick and turning the bottom until the signature red emerged from the top. "The thing is, Jane, if you don't let me set you up, then Anna will have no reason to let me help her."

Jane tipped her head. "I thought you were setting her up with someone tomorrow night."

Rosemary stopped applying her lipstick, doing a poor job of hiding her smile. "Oh, I am, yes." She glanced at her reflection from a few more angles and then popped the cap back on the tube. Turning, she leaned back on the dresser and fixed Jane with a look. "After tomorrow night, I'm afraid Anna might not agree to be set up again."

Jane wasn't following. "You made it sound like you knew just the man for Anna."

"Oh I do." Rosemary gave a mysterious smile. "I absolutely do. It just might take some…*convincing*, though."

Jane considered this. Knowing Anna, Rosemary had a point. "I really don't want to go on any more dates," she sighed, shaking her head.

Rosemary pressed her mouth together in overt disappointment. "Just one more date, Jane. It doesn't have to be right away. If Anna knows I'm still fixing you up, then as part of our bargain, she has to let me help set her up, too."

Jane groaned, but the pleading look in Rosemary's expression made her pause. "You really want to match Anna."

"I do." Rosemary folded her hands in front of her. "I wouldn't insist if I didn't have a . . . vested interest."

"Fine," Jane said on a breath.

"Thank you, my dear. I promise you won't regret this. And you never know," she added, wiggling her eyebrows suggestively. "You might just fall in love with the next guy I set you up with."

"Ha." Based on her track record, she wouldn't count on it. Jane flicked off the light switch and led Rosemary back down the hall, trying to muster up more enthusiasm for the party going on below. It wouldn't be fair of her to let her own feelings shine through tonight. This was Grace's night. Eventually it might be Anna's night. At some point, Jane had to make peace with being alone.

She'd had her time, her moment in that white dress with the flowers and the smiles. Her sisters had been at her side then. Now it was her turn to do the same for them.

And it started with continuing on with this silly matchmaking scheme. Who knew, maybe Rosemary was right. Maybe she would fall in love with the next guy she went on a date with—and maybe, if Rosemary was right about her hunch, Anna would, too.

What the heck was Rosemary thinking?

Anna replayed that thought over and over and over. It started with the moment she first came face-to-face with the fair-haired and slightly hunchbacked Simon, who greeted her with earnest eyes and a smile that made the room stop. She tried not to let her gaze linger on the retainer, even when he pulled it free of his teeth and set it on a bread plate right next to his water glass. She told herself Rosemary must have had a reason for choosing Simon specifically; after all, he had made his feelings for Anna known over the years, and he stopped in to the café five mornings a week, making sure to linger near the counter, grinning slyly as he slowly stirred creamer into his to-go cup.

Despite his overt interest in her, they had nothing in common, but even this didn't seem to deter his pursuit. She'd tried to hide her shock when he handed her the sad bouquet of red carnations and then escorted her proudly to her chair, right in the center of Piccolino's, for all of Briar

Creek to see. She kept the conversation neutral, purposefully chatting about old classmates and school memories, but as he began listing his food allergies, then informed her he was a strict vegan and politely asked her if she planned to go to a real college someday, Anna decided that Rosemary had officially lost her marbles.

"Where do you see yourself in five years?"

What was this? An interview? "Oh, running Fireside, I suppose." She didn't mention that she saw it doubled in size, with a full dinner service seven nights a week, and a handful of sous chefs helping her in the kitchen. The image brought a faint smile to her lips, despite how disastrously the evening was going, or how lonely the prospect of her future was if she stopped to think about it.

"What about kids?" Simon pressed, and Anna nearly choked on her water.

She set the glass down. This was getting a little too personal for a first date, but seeing that Simon had known her forever and had asked her to dance at every school event since the fifth grade, she couldn't exactly say they were strangers.

"What about them?" she asked, trying to sound casual.

"Do you want to have children?"

Anna froze. "No," she said simply.

Simon paused for a moment. "No?"

"That's right. No." She reached for her water glass again, noticing the way her hand shook. She couldn't expect him to understand, and she certainly wasn't going to tell him her reasoning. She'd had her child and now it was gone. Nothing could bring her baby back; nothing would ever replace it. The thought of having another... it was too much. It wouldn't bring back what she had lost.

And it wouldn't be Mark's. She would have no way of knowing what their baby might have looked like, and no amount of searching the face of another child would make that image any clearer than it was now.

She had nothing to hold on to. Not even a picture. But she wasn't ready to let go.

She scooped the rest of her tiramisu from its dish. It was a sloppy effort, lacking richness of flavor. Frank should have added a bit more mascarpone, and she questioned the strength of the espresso he'd used to soak the ladyfingers, but she wouldn't be saying anything. She'd worked for Frank Piccolino her first summer out of culinary school, and she could still recall with vivid clarity his reaction after she'd merely suggested they add more cream to the vodka sauce. Frank had an ego; he considered himself the best chef in town.

She hoped to kick his butt in the contest.

"I should probably get going, Simon," she said, breaking the silence. "I have more work to do tonight."

He nodded, and after settling the bill, they walked to the car in silence. *Maybe I've officially turned him away*, she considered, but the thought did little to perk her up. Most men would want children, a family, a future. There really was no hope for her.

But now, as Simon's lips curled and a flash of his metal retainer reflected off the parking lot lamp, Anna felt the first true prickle of panic.

God help her, he was going to try to kiss her.

She inched closer to the car, forcing a tight smile. "I really need to get to bed. Four o'clock rolls around pretty quickly!"

"I thought you said you had to work tonight," Simon said.

Anna gave a nervous laugh. "Oh, did I? See? I'm so tired I nearly forgot. Chef's hours and all that."

"It's Saturday night," Simon insisted. "Why don't we take a stroll through the town square?"

Anna darted her eyes to the left, where the dimly lit gazebo sat in the center of the park. On the other side of the square, she could see the darkened storefront of Fireside, and a few blocks to the north, the faint glow of lights at Hastings farther up Main Street. Mark was probably with Nicole Johnson right this very moment, doing God knows what with her, while she was standing in the parking lot of Piccolino's with the local pharmacist, who happened to have had a crush on her since she was in the second grade.

Oh, Rosemary.

"I'll see you around, Simon." She flashed him an easy grin, and quickly unlocked the car. "Thanks again for dinner. It was fun catching up!"

Simon's frown deepened, and she scrambled into the car before he got any notions. "Maybe we can try it again sometime," he called out.

"Maybe," she said, waving.

She pulled out of the parking lot. Honestly, what had Rosemary been thinking? Simon had asked her out a dozen times in high school, and she'd had to turn him down every time, lest she lead him on. Now she feared she'd done just that.

Anna tutted under her breath as she rounded the town square, slowing her pace as she crept down Main Street, which was dark and quiet at this time of night aside from the pub at the end of the strip.

She stopped the car at the corner of Second Avenue and unlocked her seat belt. The glow of the lampposts lit the new large paned window at the front of the café, hidden behind scaffolding. She rounded the building slowly, peering through the windows and into the darkness, trying to see inside. Progress was being made; that was something. The new front window looked exactly like the old. That was reassuring. She worried about her kitchen, though. Even though it would be just as functional, if not more so than the original, she liked the comfort of her ways. She knew which drawers stuck and how to set the timer on the ovens without even looking at the screen. She could move swiftly through the room without even stopping for consideration.

Change was good, she reminded herself. Some change.

A rustling caught her attention and she turned, jumping at what she saw.

"Mark." She gasped when she saw him sitting on the bench at the corner of the sidewalk. He was in the shadows, under the shade of a big oak tree that lined the street, and even in the dusk she could see the lines in his face, the fatigue in his eyes. "What are you doing here?"

He leaned forward, resting his elbows on his knees, and speared her with a look that caused her breath to catch. After everything they had been through and all that he had done to her, her body still reacted to him all on its own.

"I was just thinking," he finally said. He heaved a sigh that rolled through his broad shoulders and paused, tenting his fingers. "Just thinking about...Tavern on Main. My dad's place."

She nodded slowly, not quite knowing what to say. He rarely opened up about his father, and she'd gathered it was not something he wanted to discuss. It was a sensitive subject, Anna understood, even if a little part of her wished he had felt he could confide in her.

There was a long pause. "Well, I was going to check on the progress in the kitchen." Jingling her keys, she stepped toward the tarp covering the door, but Mark straightened with sudden interest.

He leaned back against the bench. "I thought you had a date tonight."

Oh, that. Anna mentally rolled her eyes when she thought of the glee he'd take in learning that Simon had finally gotten his way after all these years.

"I did," she said breezily, shifting under the heat of his gaze. She wished he would stop looking at her like that. Like he was enjoying this. Like he saw right through her. Like he knew things hadn't gone well. Or as planned.

When did they ever?

His eyebrow cocked. "Over so soon?"

She hadn't even looked at her watch, but something told her it was barely eight thirty. Any chance she had of passing her so-called date off as a success would be in vain.

"I have a lot going on right now, and I have to be up at four o'clock."

Mark nodded slowly, doing a poor job of suppressing his grin. "Who was he?"

"Oh…" She could hardly say he was no one Mark knew. It wasn't true, and in a town this small, he was bound to find out. "It was just… Simon."

Mark hooted in laughter, clapping his hands together with boyish glee, while Anna felt her anger stir.

"How's that for an obvious selection?" Mark continued. "And here I thought Aunt Rosemary was going to hand select you some mysterious stranger."

That makes two of us, Anna thought bitterly. "Well, now you know."

Mark spread his arms wide on the back of the bench and grinned. "Where'd he take you? Piccolino's?" He caught her eye and chuckled. "Of course."

"It was informative, actually," she said, edging closer. "I made a point of stopping in to see Frank." As an excuse to break away from the table for ten minutes, but Mark didn't need to know that part. "He's entering the contest, but I don't think we have anything to worry about there."

"We have a fair shot at this," Mark replied. "I wouldn't have partnered with you if I didn't think so."

She stiffened. Of course that's why he wanted to partner with her. Because she was a sure bet. Not because... *Nonsense.*

Motioning to her car, she said, "I should get home. I have to get to the kitchen early tomorrow, and later I'm meeting with your mom to go through some more of the plans with the contractor." She started to go but his voice stopped her.

"Do you ever wonder..." He paused, shoving his hands into the pockets of his chinos as he stood. "Do you ever think about how things might have been if we'd opened that place we always talked about?"

Her throat locked up as she held his gaze, feeling in that moment like he could see straight through to her soul, unlock every private thought she'd ever experienced, every tear she'd ever shed. There was no point in denying the truth.

"Sometimes."

If he'd stuck to the plan, if he'd stayed the course, then they could have had so much more than their restaurant. They might have had their child, too.

She gripped her keys tighter in her hand, pressing the jagged edges into her palm, wanting to feel a pain deeper than the one in her heart. Losing Mark had been terrible, but losing their baby had been so much worse.

And it all could have been avoided.

She didn't want to hear his words, his weak apologies. It didn't make a difference now. She just wanted to win this contest, get back into her own kitchen, and get the hell away from him.

"We could have put Piccolino's out of business." Mark grinned, but Anna didn't find any of this amusing.

She glared at him. "It was your choice. You were the one who had to throw it all away. I was invested. I was committed."

Mark closed his eyes. "I know you were."

Was that regret she sensed in his expression? His eyes were flat, his jaw tense, and all at once she had an urge to ask for the answers she had never received, to know exactly why he had tossed her aside, given up their dreams for something bigger for what . . . a diner?

"Well, it all worked out fine for me. I love Fireside." She wouldn't go there, not now, not ever. She didn't want to hear how it could have been. To know for sure that life could have been different. That Mark regretted his actions that cost her much more than some restaurant. It was too late for regrets.

He dragged a hand through his hair, his expression turning pensive as he stared up at the building. "I still can't believe you chose to take over my father's old place. Of all the locations, Anna."

His tone succeeded in silencing her. She stared at him, aghast, knowing there was truth in his words; she could see the pain in his eyes. It was the most emotion he'd ever revealed about his father, and she hated to see him like this, beaten down and rejected, so far from the smug guy who strutted into the bar with his latest fling. For a moment, she almost missed the swagger, even the damn smirk, if it meant she didn't have to see the hurt in those deep brown eyes.

He'd been her friend once, and despite everything that had passed between them, every injury he'd caused her, a part of her still cared, damn it. Cared enough to not want to see him like this, hunched over, his jaw tense, his eyes far away.

"I know how much your dad meant to you, Mark. I hope you know that I wasn't trying to take this from you. You'd been back at Hastings for a year; I was just trying to move on with my life. There was nowhere else in town. What other choice did you leave me?"

Mark stepped toward her. "I shouldn't have done what I did all those years ago, Anna. I—I should have handled it differently. I thought I was doing the right thing by letting you go. You have to know that."

She turned away. "I want to believe that."

"You have to know how much you meant to me, Anna. You were one of the closest friends I'd ever had before we starting dating."

"I know," she said quietly. She stood at his side, feeling the heat from his body in contrast with the cool night air, sensing the musk of his aftershave, the awareness of his presence. A wave of emotion rolled through her when she thought of how much time had passed and how much had been lost along the way. Not just a plan for a restaurant, not just a dream of a future, but a friend. A good friend. A great one, really.

The best.

Now she stood in front of the rubble, the pieces of the life she had tried to build for herself, all on her own.

"You know where we went wrong, don't you?" She slid him a sad smile. "We should have just stayed friends."

"I thought that, too. Sometimes I still do. But I know that wasn't possible." His eyes locked with hers and her heart skipped a beat. "We had something, Anna. More than a friendship. More than an attraction. We had a connection. We still do."

"Please," she scoffed. "You have a connection with half the women in the state of Vermont. You showed up to my family's home last night, to my sister's engagement party, with your latest fling."

His eyes sparked. "Says the woman coming back from a date tonight."

Her heart skipped a beat. "If I didn't know better, I'd say you sound jealous."

"And what if I were?" His gaze rested on her mouth. He was suddenly close. Too close.

She took a step backward. "I'd say it wouldn't matter."

But it did matter. A lot.

"Do you know how often I've watched you across a crowded room, or from a few blocks down the street? It's taken everything in me not to shout out your name."

She blinked back the tears that threatened to spill. He was telling her everything she had wanted to hear, words she had never thought would ever be voiced, thoughts she'd never dreamed he would share, but it wasn't enough. It didn't change the past. It didn't change a damn thing.

"What about Nicole?" she pressed.

He shook his head. "We've just gone out a few times. She's not looking for anything serious."

"And you are?" Anna gave him a withering smile.

He looked her straight in the eye, finally breaking the distance between their bodies. "I don't know what I'm looking for, Anna."

She gritted her teeth. "Of course not," she said bitterly, angry at herself for thinking for one fleeting, glorious moment that he did. She wrapped her arms around herself as a breeze tore down the street.

"I don't know what I'm looking for, Anna," he said again, and something in the insistence in his tone made her stand to attention. "I just know that when I was with you, I was happy, and I haven't felt that way since."

She stared at him, forcing herself to stay strong, to focus on the pain. The hurt. The loss. "You dumped me, Mark."

"Please don't use that word."

"Why not? It fits, doesn't it? You tossed me aside, chucked all our plans. Left me alone to deal with the fallout."

He looked at her sharply. "What fallout?"

Her breath caught. She'd said too much.

"What do you mean, Anna?"

"Nothing." She shook her head forcefully, backing up. Her heart was hammering, and the chill was gone, replaced with a rush of heat that flooded her face. *"Nothing."*

She could tell by his expression that he didn't believe her, and she didn't trust herself to keep her secret to herself right now.

"I should really go," she said.

He showed no signs of turning to leave, or saying anything at all. He looked lost, like a shadow of the man she'd seen at the party last night, gloating as he did the rounds with Nicole Johnson on his arm.

She opened her mouth to speak, to ask him what was really wrong, where his head was, why he was staring through the rubble of this old place like he was staring into a grave. It was her loss to bear, but from the pain that furrowed his brow, she wasn't so sure anymore.

She stopped herself. Letting Mark in would only lead to more disappointment. She'd gotten a taste of that last night. It was time to start moving forward once and for all. She'd opened Fireside to show him she could do it. That she didn't need him. But she'd rebuild it for herself. Anna turned and walked away without a word.

CHAPTER
19

So, Anna was avoiding him again, was she? Mark heaved a weary sigh and hung his apron on the hook near the back kitchen wall. Another Sunday brunch was rolling to a close, and the day was wide open, but despite the usual thrill he took in the opportunity to kick back on a warm spring day, Mark couldn't deny the twinge of disappointment he felt over Anna's absence this morning.

Ridiculous. Now was the time to be moving forward, not slipping backward. He was better off without the temptation of her presence; the mere fact that he'd spent the better half of the last few hours glancing up every time the door jingled was proof of that. If you didn't get close, you didn't get let down. So why was he suddenly feeling like all he wanted to do was get close to Anna, and not just physically?

Mark grabbed his keys and called over his shoulder to Vince, "I'm heading out. Call if you need me."

It didn't take long to walk the few blocks down Main to Second Avenue. He paused outside the building, listening for voices. Hearing nothing, he pushed aside the tarp that covered the old doorframe and entered the building.

The room was cleared out, the floor stripped, and more tarps hung near the back, separating the kitchen. The walls had been knocked down, but the great stone hearth remained to his right, just as it had been all those years ago, the last time he'd been here, on his tenth birthday.

His mother had worn her best dress, and even Brett, only eight at the time, had used his best table manners. Mark had watched in awe as one beautiful and vibrantly colored dish after another was brought to the tables around him. He'd ordered a steak, ate every last bit of it, and still managed to fit in the chocolate lava cake his father sent out for dessert.

That day was bitter juxtaposition to the way his life was permanently altered only a few short months later.

Gritting his teeth, Mark turned back to the door. He shouldn't have come in here. There were too many hard memories. Too many bad feelings.

"Mark? I thought that was you." He glanced up to see his mother coming in through the kitchen, smiling in surprise.

Mark fought to release the tightness in his expression. "I saw your car out front. Thought I'd say hello."

"I was just seeing how the kitchen was coming along. They've made great progress. Did you want to see?"

Mark stiffened. "Nah, that's okay." He rolled back on his heels, letting his gaze float over the room once more.

Sharon did the same. "It's weird to see it like this, isn't it?" she mused, catching his eye.

Mark rubbed his jaw. Damn straight it was weird. And depressing as hell. Deciding to dodge any mention of his father or Tavern on Main, he said, "I suppose."

"Anna really transformed the place. You should stop in sometime, check out the competition," his mother joked.

Mark nodded thoughtfully. "Guess I didn't see a reason to ever come in here." He'd meant it twofold, but his mother couldn't know about his feelings for Anna. She just knew the main reason—that it stirred up too many memories of his father—and the hurt that sparked in her eyes made Mark regret his words.

He was being self-indulgent, and he'd promised himself a long time ago that when it came to his family, he'd never put himself first the way his father had done.

"This place wasn't always about hard times," Sharon said quietly. "I can still remember when your father opened it." She paused before adding, almost to herself, "That was a happy day."

Mark hesitated. His mother never spoke of the past. A part of him yearned to ask for details of a time when his dad's restaurant was the source of hope and excitement, not bitterness and stress, to go back to the memory that lit her eyes and left a sad smile on her lips, but just as quickly, anger set it.

"I don't know how you can stand to come in here. Why you held on to it at all."

Sharon looked startled. After a pause she said, "It was a smart business decision."

Mark knew she was right. After his father split, leaving them so deep in debt that Sharon had been forced to take a mortgage on their home and start working at a diner for minimum wage, the rental income from the building was their only hope of long-term security, even if it was a short-term problem at first.

"This place is a part of my life, I guess you could say." Sharon shrugged. "The good times and the bad."

"I don't remember many good times in this place," Mark said, forcing out the image of the three of them sitting by the hearth, his mother looking so young and radiant in her red dress, her brown hair pulled back to show off the earrings she wore only for special occasions.

"If Dad had never owned the place, if the restaurant wasn't his life, then things might have been different." Mark scowled.

"Then you might never have become a chef," Sharon pointed out.

Mark balled a fist at his side. "No. That has nothing to do with him." But it did. For years he'd struggled with his decision to follow in his father's path, the one that had ended in their family's destruction, but the one that had given him the only memories of his father he would ever have. His father was always busy, always putting Tavern first, working long hours and missing Little League games and holidays. None of it mattered to Mark back then, though. Their time in the kitchen, working together, testing new recipes and tasting new foods, meant more than any school event.

He stared past his mother and into the kitchen. He couldn't stand the thought of walking in there, finding it empty, finding another person overseeing the stations, reminding him that his dad was gone, and that all those moments together, right there, a mere thirty feet away, were over.

"So, how are things coming along for the contest?" Sharon asked, her smile bringing him back to the present. She'd always been a master of focusing on the positive things in life. He supposed with all she'd gone through, she didn't have much choice.

Mark gave a small shrug. "Only six days to go. We're giving it the best shot we have. Hope it's enough." And God, did he. It was his only chance to move forward, to step out of this limbo, to put all these ghosts behind him and do what he'd set out to do once and for all.

"Well, I hope you both win. It's been a tough year for Anna, first with losing her father and then this place..." Sharon tutted. "I know how it feels to lose everything all at once."

Mark frowned. It saddened him when his mother talked like this, reminding him of the struggle, of the pain his father had brought on her, on so many levels.

"I'm sure she'll land on her feet," he replied, realizing how much he wished it to be true. He'd knocked Anna down, disappointed her, stolen a dream from her, and she'd had to pick up the pieces he left in his wake.

She'd done a hell of a job of it, though. This café was the trendiest spot in town.

"Oh, I'm sure she will," Sharon sighed and walked over to the fireplace. He wondered if she was sharing the same memory he had every time he looked at it. Turning to face him, her brown eyes suddenly looked a notch brighter than usual. "My, look at this old place. Fireside was such a success; I'm sure it will be again in no time. It's been the most secure tenant we've ever had in the space...Just the kind of place the town needed, really."

Mark considered this, knowing his mother had a point, even if both of them were probably wondering how life might have been if Tavern had met the same response from the town. It had its glory, but then it all went south.

He felt his body tense. Maybe it was the sawdust, or the faint smell of fresh paint from the kitchen, but he suddenly felt like he was suffocating, and he couldn't breathe. Memories were choking him, sucking the life out of him, pulling him back to a time and place he'd rather forget, of a life that had been a façade, a family that had never stood a chance in hell. "I should probably go. You coming?"

"Anna's on her way over, so I'll wait for a bit." Sharon bent down and picked up a nail from the floor.

Mark rubbed the back of his neck, resenting the way his stomach roiled at the thought of seeing Anna again. They hadn't left on happy terms the night before, and her absence this morning left him unsettled. He shouldn't have brought Nicole to the party, but he knew why he'd done it. To see if Anna cared. And from the looks of it, she did.

He wasn't sure how he felt about that now.

He crossed the room, deeper into this box of memories, and gave his mother a quick hug before turning on his heel and striding purposefully to the door, not daring to absorb his periphery as he bolted into the warm sunshine, right into Anna.

"Mark?" Anna's sharp blue eyes were more blinding than the afternoon sun. She darted her gaze from the restaurant to him and back again. "Were you looking for me?"

He jammed his hands in his pockets, trying to fight the rush of desire that heated his blood as he raked his gaze over the tight gray T-shirt that scooped well below her fragile collarbone, revealing a hint of her soft breasts, and cinched her tight waist. He forced his eyes back to hers. "I was just talking to my mom."

"You never came in before—"

"Well, you wouldn't have wanted me to." The tone was

sharper than he'd intended, revealing more pain than he knew existed, and he regretted the flash of surprise that passed over her expression. He rolled back on his heels, blowing out a breath. "It looks good."

A brittle laugh cut the silence. "No. It doesn't. The kitchen should be up and running soon, at least." She let her shoulders fall as she inspected the scaffolding that covered the brick storefront. "I tell myself it will look better than ever in no time, but it's hard to believe that some days. I don't like coming by here. Maybe that sounds silly."

"It doesn't sound silly at all." His voice was low, gruff, and he felt his pulse lurch as their eyes met once more. For a moment, she softened, and he thought he saw a flicker of understanding pass through her turquoise irises. Just as quickly she sniffed, and straightened her back. "I missed you at the diner this morning," he said.

She darted her eyes. "I couldn't sleep last night. It made sense to just get started in my own kitchen."

He wondered if that was all there was to it. "We leave for Cedar Valley on Friday. Are we practicing tonight?"

"Of course," she retorted, but he sensed a hesitation. "We need all the practice we can get if we're going to stand a shot at this thing."

"You nervous?

She let out a breath. "Very. It would...well, it would make everything a lot easier to have that kind of prize money."

"It sure would," Mark said, rolling back on his heels. Fifty thousand dollars. He could practically feel it in his hands. The freedom it would buy.

Anna was looking at him with interest. "You know,

you never told me. What do you plan to do with the prize money if you win?"

His attention snapped back to the present. "I haven't really thought about that yet," he lied.

She arched an eyebrow. "Really?"

He shrugged, refusing to give in the way she expected. He wasn't like her or Luke or any of the other people he knew who could make a plan and stick to it. He couldn't depend on the outcome the way they could; he had to reserve a space for setback.

"I've got some debts to pay off," he said vaguely, even though it wasn't true. "Maybe I'll take a vacation, spruce up the diner."

She looked unconvinced, but said nothing more on the matter. Sighing, she shrugged. "Well, I guess it doesn't matter. What you do with your life really isn't any of my business."

He opened his mouth to protest, but it was too late. Anna was already distracted, looking over his shoulder at something in the distance, and from the look on her face, she wasn't happy at what she saw.

"Oh, there you two are!"

Rosemary bustled down the sidewalk, her long, paisley printed skirt flowing behind her. Anna glanced desperately across the street, wishing she could dart away, but it was too late now. They'd been spotted.

"Brainstorming ideas for the contest, hmm?" Rosemary's cheeks were flushed as she glanced from Anna to Mark. "I'm sure Cedar Valley is just breathtaking in the spring, what with the flowers, the birds...the bees." She winked.

Mark shot Anna a glance and she bit back a smile. She didn't want to share any private jokes, didn't want to feel a special bond. What they'd shared was over, and she needed to remember that.

"Only a few more days now!" Rosemary continued eagerly.

A few more days, and then it would all be over. Her kitchen at Fireside would be at least functional by then, the contest would be over, and her time with Mark would come to an end.

She ignored the tightness in her stomach and kept her eyes trained on Rosemary, who was blinking in expectation. This contest did mean a lot to the poor woman, though God knew why. Anna frowned when she realized that she'd be letting Rosemary down in addition to everyone else, even though no one other than Jane had an inkling of her financial mess.

It was all so damn frustrating! Entering and winning was her only hope, because she was desperate. Yes, desperate. She'd have to be to have agreed to spend this much time with her ex.

"You must be working so hard on your recipes. Late nights, I imagine…" Rosemary's blue eyes glistened in the sun.

"Too many," Anna replied. Her face grew hot as she felt Mark's and his aunt's eyes turn on her.

"Oh, well…maybe you should mix it up a bit. Have a little fun in the kitchen," Rosemary suggested.

"I don't have time for fun. Or games," Anna added, glancing at Mark. "Now, if you'll excuse me, I need to meet with Sharon. A contractor's stopping by soon and we need to go over some changes to the plans."

"You're really eager to get back to work there, aren't you?" Mark asked.

Anna gave him a level stare. "More than you know."

She turned on her heel, but a sudden yelp made her jump. She turned, her eyes widening when she saw Rosemary hunched forward.

Anna dropped her bag and hurried over to them on the sidewalk. "Rosemary?" She placed a hand on the woman's arm. "Are you okay?"

"It's just . . . this heat!"

Anna regarded her quizzically. "Heat?" A cool breeze rustled the leaves in the oak trees lining Main Street. "You're worrying me, Rosemary."

Mark frowned in concern. "Let's have you sit down on a bench, Aunt Rosemary. Anna, can you run and grab some water from next door?"

"What?" Rosemary asked sharply. Then, catching their shocked expressions, said hurriedly, "No, no. Don't leave, Anna. Stay right here with me. And Mark."

Anna glanced up the street. "Oh, but—"

Rosemary groaned, and Mark and Anna froze. "I . . . think I might faint. My head . . ."

"Let's get you over to this bench," Mark ordered, and Anna helped, arranging Rosemary gingerly onto a shaded bench. "I'll go get the water."

"No. No. Just stay . . . here. With me. For a few minutes. Both of you."

Anna and Mark exchanged glances and finally, shrugging, did as they were told. Anna inched forward, hoping to sit on the far left, but Rosemary pushed herself all the way to the end, leaving Anna no choice but to sandwich herself in the middle. A strange smile passed over

Rosemary's painted lips as Mark settled onto the bench, so close to Anna that she could feel the heat of his body on hers, and the steady rise and fall of his breath through his chest.

Her chest tightened and she pushed away from him, but Rosemary didn't budge.

"A little more space, dear," she said, and Anna, sighing, inched closer to Mark. "A little more. There."

Anna gritted her teeth, steeling herself against the desire that coursed through her blood. "Why don't I get that water?" she suggested, but Rosemary smacked a hand on her knee.

"No. Just stay. It's only a dizzy spell. It will pass in no time." She smiled wanly and leaned back on the bench, glancing sidelong at Anna's arm, which was unfortunately resting on Mark's upper thigh. "Now, isn't this cozy?"

Cozy. Anna's mind whirred, but her body was doing all the talking. Every shift of his body, every breath that he took brought her back to a time and place she needed to forget. For months after they'd parted, she could still remember the feel of his touch, the way his body felt next to hers, the natural ease of his kiss. It had taken years to banish that memory, and now, thanks to Rosemary's suspicious behavior, it was all flooding back.

Anna plunked into one of the old chenille club chairs near the window of Main Street Books, watching as Grace rang up a customer. Grace handed over the brown paper bag stamped with their newly designed logo and glanced at her ring finger. The cushion-cut diamond on a thin platinum band was stunning, and even from across the room, Anna caught its sparkle.

"Have you and Luke discussed a date?" she asked, determined to steer the topic of conversation away from herself. She didn't need Grace inquiring into the state of her bad mood or the causes behind it. The contest was only two days away. She should be happy. She should be nervous, even. Instead, all she felt was sadness. Come next week, she and Mark would go back to the way things were—the way things had to be, she told herself firmly.

"Oh." A mysterious smile swept over Grace's face. Her eyes went to the ring again. "We were thinking a fall wedding might be nice. It doesn't leave much room for planning, but we've lost enough time."

Anna tried not to let her sister's last comment sink in. "Is Ivy doing the flowers?" she inquired.

Grace nodded. "She'll be in the wedding too, of course, along with you and Jane, and Kara and Molly."

And Mark, she thought.

There was no getting around it, not in a town this small, not when her sister was marrying into Mark's family.

"Are you taking his name?"

Until now, she hadn't considered it. Her sister was going to be Grace Hastings. Once she had thought she might be Anna Hastings. Oh, what a silly girl she had been.

"I think so," Grace said, giving another dreamy sigh. "It feels a little weird to think about not being a Madison anymore. It's just one more connection I'll lose to Dad."

"He loved Luke like his own son." Anna gave her sister a sad smile. "And you have this place. You have Dad's legacy."

"I can't imagine what I would have done if we'd lost this place," Grace agreed, and Anna felt a ripple of panic roll through her stomach. Nearly a month had passed since the fire, and the next loan payment was due in a couple of weeks. She'd be able to cover it—barely—but the next... She blew out a shaky breath.

"You know, it's funny," Grace said as she came around the polished wood counter and began dusting a bookshelf. "I never understood why Mark chose to take over the diner instead of opening a restaurant in his father's old space."

Anna inspected her fingernails, deciding to get a manicure before the weekend's events, if time permitted, and waited for the subject to drop. She knew damn well that Mark hadn't set out to run a diner—not at first, at least—

but Grace didn't need to know that. It would just lead to a series of questions Anna would rather not answer. Ever.

She pushed herself off the chair and smoothed her skirt. The Annex was empty, and on the counter sat at least a quarter of the food she'd brought over that morning. It was already five—the chances of anyone stopping in for more than a hot tea after dinner were slim. At best, they might sell a cookie or two. She'd prepared more than they typically sold in a burst of optimism, hoping that more offerings would entice customers, but now she felt the sting of reality that she might be forced to ask for Luke's help, to admit she had tried and failed.

"Well, I should probably head over to Mark's to work on our contest entry." The words were spoken with such nervous energy that she was sure Grace would notice, but instead her sister's green eyes sparked.

"Good luck. I don't know how I'll sleep tomorrow night; I'll be so nervous for Saturday!"

Anna kept quiet. That made two of them. "I think I'll stop by the dance studio first. Rosemary works Thursday, right?"

Grace set down her dust rag. "Don't be too hard on her about your date with Simon," she warned.

Anna gave her a long look. "Grace, she set me up with the one man in town she knew I would have absolutely no interest in."

Well, not the only one, she thought to herself.

"She probably forgot!"

"You don't believe that any more than I do."

"You're right," Grace said quietly, giving a small smile. "Just . . . go easy on her. I'm sure her intentions were in the right place."

Oh, they most certainly were, if Anna knew Rosemary.

Rosemary did mean well—it was why she had suggested the contest after all—but when it came to her love life, Anna could do without Rosemary's help. Judging from the strange pleasure she'd taken in her so-called fainting spell yesterday, Anna was beginning to think Rosemary had her sights set on Mark for the next date. And there was no way she could allow that to happen.

She pulled the door and a jingle of bells sent her off, but her spirits deflated the moment her feet hit the pavement. She hated keeping the truth from her sister, but worrying her didn't seem fair either. Grace had finally found her happy ending after so many years apart from Luke. Who was Anna to ruin this time for her now, when Grace finally had everything she'd always wanted? It could only lead to more strain between them, when they were finally behaving like sisters again.

She wouldn't say a word about the loan. Not until after the contest. And hopefully by then, she wouldn't need to.

Anna took her time meandering down Main Street, stopping to glance in shop windows and peer into the pub, which was already crowded even though the sun hadn't yet ducked behind the mountains. The sky had turned pink, and clouds swirled in shades of lavender, drumming up images of cotton candy and all sorts of confections Anna had so enjoyed making in her pastry classes back in school.

The studio was four blocks east of Main Street, on the first floor of an old red barn. Rosemary had transformed the space, putting in walls of mirrors, a state-of-the-art sound system, and dressing rooms that were every little girl's paradise with pink walls, crystal chandeliers, and purple velvet–covered benches tucked into white vanities.

Anna pushed through one of the double glass doors

and entered the lobby, which was closed off from the main studio by a one-way window. Inside, she saw Jane shuffling about in her ballet slippers, her pale pink leg warmers pulled to the knee, tidying up what appeared to be a mounting pile of fluffy tutus.

Ducking through the partially open door to the studio, Anna called, "Need a hand?"

Jane tossed her a grateful smile and brushed a strand of hair from her forehead. "I'm just finishing up for the day. Feel free to come in, but remove your shoes first."

"Is Rosemary here?" Anna looked around the studio.

"She might be in her office," Jane volunteered.

"Good. I wanted to talk to her about this matchmaking scheme."

"Oh?" Jane looked away, bending down to stuff the tutus into a wicker basket at the end of the barre.

"You know she set me up with Simon last weekend, right?" Anna bent to help Jane return a pile of classical music CDs to their holders.

Jane laughed. "Grace told me. I take it you didn't have a good time?"

"If you call defending my choice of career—or lack thereof—a nice time, then yes, it was wonderful. About as enjoyable as staring at Simon's retainer, which served as a centerpiece for most of the meal."

Jane's hazel eyes grew large. "He didn't!"

"Oh, yes," Anna said. "He did." •

Jane clapped a hand to her mouth, but it did little to muffle her roar of laughter. "Oh, come on, Anna," she said, when she'd calmed down. "You have to admit it's funny."

"You don't see me laughing about your recent date with Mr. Wonderful," Anna reminded her.

"Fair enough," Jane said. "But this is Simon we're talking about. Remember the time he stole a pair of gold earrings from his mother's jewelry box and gave them to you as a gift?"

"For Valentine's Day." Anna had to laugh at the memory. "I came home and showed Mom and she demanded I return them. I didn't even have my ears pierced."

"He always had a thing for you," Jane said ruefully.

"Yes, but that doesn't mean we're a good match."

"What's this about a good match?" Rosemary stood in the open doorway, wearing a black leotard and matching chiffon skirt that skimmed her knees. She strode into the room, still in her well-worn ballet slippers, and paused with her hand on the barre. An expectant expression took over her fine features, and Anna felt herself begin to waver.

But no. *No.* Rosemary had insinuated she chose her date with Simon for a reason, and Anna wanted to know just what that reason was.

"How are you feeling today, Rosemary?" Anna began.

Rosemary turned to her, her face folded in confusion. "Just fine, of course!"

Anna frowned. "So no more…fainting scares?"

Rosemary seemed to blanch. "Oh. No. No, mercifully, no." Her eyes shifted to the mirror. "It was so sweet of you and Mark to sit with me."

"Yes, well, it's good that you had such a quick recovery," Anna said, recalling the way after half an hour of being pressed against Mark's warm body, feeling the cords of his muscles under the thin material of his T-shirt, and every bit of willpower she had left turn to jelly. Rosemary had claimed she was feeling better, and with a bright smile, all but bounced off, waving off their concern. "It was the least

I could do, since you've helped me out so much recently. And about that…Jane and I were just talking about our recent dates." She squared her shoulders. "I don't think we need your help in the romance department anymore."

Rosemary ever so slowly lifted a brow and turned to the mirror to tuck a loose strand of hair into her bun. "No?"

"No," Anna said firmly. She had expected Rosemary to argue, but her lack of outward reaction was far more disconcerting. "I know I asked you to set me up, but I'm sticking with my original decision. I don't need any help."

"Don't you?" Rosemary tipped her head to the side, admiring her reflection from another angle, catching Anna's eye in the mirror. "Remember, Anna, we had a deal."

"And that deal is over. Jane told you that she didn't want to be set up anymore. I was there when she said it. That means I'm off the hook, too."

Rosemary's blue gaze shifted to Jane, who stayed engrossed in the task of removing her slippers and placing them in the canvas bag she brought with her to work. "Oh, but you see, Anna, Jane's had a change of heart. Go on, Jane; tell her."

Anna snapped her attention to Jane, whose cheeks had turned pink with a guilty flush. "Jane?" she demanded. "Is this true?"

Jane gave a small shrug, barely meeting her eye. "You know what they say…three's a charm."

Anna waited a beat before speaking again, for fear she might lose her temper. "So you've asked Rosemary to match you up again?"

Jane skirted her gaze to Rosemary, whose lips had pursed into a pleased pinch. "That's right, Anna," Rosemary said. "And you know what that means."

She did. All too well. "Rosemary, I'm sorry, but no. I don't have time for dating, not now." Not...ever.

Rosemary tutted. "Nonsense. Everyone needs love."

"Not me," Anna insisted, folding her arms across her chest. "Besides, you told me that you had a perfect guy in mind for my date. You said by the end of it, I would know exactly the man I was looking for."

Rosemary gave a knowing smile. "And did you?"

"Well, I knew exactly what kind of man I wasn't looking for!"

Rosemary's smile broadened. "That's half the battle."

Anna's mouth fell open but no sound escaped. Jane sat on the floor, still unwilling to meet her eye, but Anna knew better than to say anything to her. Her sister wanted to find love, and she couldn't fault her for wanting such a thing.

Even if it was more trouble than it was worth.

CHAPTER
21

Anna lived at the north edge of town, a few miles from her restaurant, on the second floor of a two-flat that bordered Willow Park. Even though Mark had never been invited over, Briar Creek was small, and his cousin Kara lived a few houses down the road, closer to Cedar Lake. More than once he'd seen Anna outside her building, planting tulips or collecting her mail, and each time he'd have to fight the kick in his chest, the urge to pull over and call out to her.

He dropped off the paycheck Kara had left behind that day and cut the engine in front of the green-and-white house set behind a row of hydrangea bushes. They had arranged to meet at his place at seven, but it would just be a repeat of last night, and this morning, and every other interaction since last weekend. Chilly silences, brittle conversation. Missed opportunities.

Time to change that.

His mind made up, he climbed out of the car and took the stairs two at a time. A wreath hung on the door to her unit, oddly welcoming him into a place he'd never been invited. His fist hovered over it, finally falling hard on its oak surface.

Before he had time to reflect, there was a turning of the latch, and the door swung open. Surprise lifted the corners of Anna's mouth into something that bordered on a pleasant smile.

"I was just getting ready to meet you. Did we…" She hesitated, her hand still clutching the doorknob, as she tipped her head in confusion. "Weren't we meeting at your house?"

Mark nodded once, and his groin tightened as his gaze shifted over her body. She was barefoot, in a knee-length cotton skirt and a pale blue tank top that cinched her waist and dipped at the swell of her breasts, revealing the faintest hint of what lay beneath the soft cotton. Honey blond hair skimmed her shoulders, reflecting off the golden sunset filtering through the window at the back of her apartment.

He swallowed hard and forced himself to focus on the inquisitive spark of her turquoise gaze. "I was in the area. I had to drop something off to Kara. Thought I'd see if you were home." He rubbed his chin and shifted the weight on his feet, wondering just what the hell had gotten into him. Talking to women came easily to him—too easily, Anna might say—and yet here he stood, feeling downright nervous.

After a long pause, Anna opened the door wider. "I don't mind using my kitchen tonight, if you don't mind the small quarters."

Mark glanced around the front hall, and the rooms that spiraled off from it. The kitchen was at the back, basking in the golden glow of the fading sun. To the left was the living room, cozy and clean, with a white couch and chairs, and an area rug in a floral pattern. Soft green curtains hung from the tall windows, and lamps dotted the room.

He imagined Anna curled up against one of the colorful throw pillows. He imagined himself next to her. It was a dangerous image, but a tempting one nonetheless.

"Shall we?" she asked, turning abruptly to move into the kitchen. He followed her, his eyes sweeping the rooms, imagining her living here all these years. He spotted the little stuffed bird he'd won for her at a carnival one of those last weekends at the Cape—when everything was so painfully perfect his senses were on high alert, twitchy and panicked, waiting for it all to come crashing down.

"You kept it." He pointed to the small toy tucked on the windowsill of her bedroom. It was no bigger than the palm of his hand. Somehow his memory had distorted it, making it bigger.

"I was saving it for—" She stopped herself, lowering her eyes. "Yes. I kept it."

"Good. I had to chuck about a hundred ping-pong balls into that bucket to finally earn that thing."

"Yes, well. We should probably start cooking," she said. She reached out and closed the bedroom door. "I've been thinking more about whether to use soy or mustard for the maple glaze on the salmon and I still think that mustard is best. I went shopping this afternoon, so I have everything on hand."

She continued to ramble about the food as she took the items from the cloth shopping bags that consumed nearly all of her counter. She hadn't been exaggerating; the space was tight, especially for a chef, but it hadn't stopped her from treating it like a proper kitchen. It seemed that every gadget she owned lined the counters or shelves under the butcher block that centered the room, above which an array of stainless steel pots hung from a rack. Stools were pulled up to the oiled wood surface, and a pedestal table was wedged into the corner.

"I told you it was small," Anna said, catching his eye.

She walked over to the counter, casually leaning a hip against it as she held out an apron, but cooking was the last thing on his mind right now. Their time together was running out, and he wanted to be sure once the contest was over, this brief break in the silence wouldn't be, too.

His gaze traveled over her smooth curves, down to her silky bare legs, half hidden under that knee-length skirt. His fingers itched to trace their way up her calves and higher, to push away the floral cotton material and explore the deepest part of her, to feel her heat.

He rubbed the back of his neck, feeling the knots under his fingertips. "Mind if I grab some water?"

She was watching him warily. "Would wine be better?"

He grinned. "Much." He pulled out a bar stool while she retrieved a bottle of Pinot Grigio from the fully stocked and perfectly organized refrigerator and handed it to him. "Corkscrew's in the drawer behind you."

Mark found the corkscrew and let his gaze drift back to her as she brought two glasses down from a cabinet, his eyes resting on the flare of her hips as she lifted her arm high, arching her back in her reach.

He filled their glasses and clinked his with hers before tossing his head back, letting the cool liquid chase back the heat that lit a fire within him.

"You ready for tomorrow?" Anna came around the butcher block and slid into the stool next to his, and even with the faint aroma of fresh herbs lining the windowsill in porcelain pots, he could make out that whiff of coconut shampoo. God, he loved that smell. He remembered the way it teased him all those years, whetting his appetite for something so much greater than the friendship they shared. After the last night they spent together, her scent had lingered on his pillow for days, until he finally forced himself to wash it, to rid himself of the memory of her touch, of the temptation to want something he could never have.

Along another windowsill were groups of photos, most of them of Grace and Jane, but the one his gaze lingered on was of Anna and her father, taken on what must have been her graduation day from the culinary academy, a year after his own.

"He looks proud," Mark commented.

Anna stared sadly at the photo. "He was the one who encouraged me to go to culinary school. He wanted all us girls to follow our passion, the way he did with the bookstore." She looked down at the floor. "I hate the thought of letting him down."

Mark frowned. "You won't let him down."

"I'm not so sure about that." Anna's face grew pink. "You know, growing up, Grace was always sort of my father's favorite."

"Oh, now—"

Anna held up a hand. "No, it's okay. It's true. They both loved books, and Grace could spend hours in that store... I knew I could never compete with that. Instead, I found another way to stand out—through food. I started helping my mom with dinner and experimenting with new recipes, and oh, I loved making everything look pretty. I guess I just wanted to hold on to that forever. Family dinners." She grinned. "Sounds corny, I know."

"I think about my dad sometimes." There it was. It was always so easy to talk to Anna. Too easy, at times. He wasn't here to get close to her. He was just here to make her understand, once and for all. He'd never meant to hurt her. If anything, he'd tried to protect her from more hurt down the road.

"He would have been proud of you, too." Anna offered a smile of encouragement.

Mark wished he could believe that. "Maybe," he said, thinking of his father walking into Hastings, seeing his son behind the Formica counter, refilling coffee with a towel slung over his shoulder. He grimaced.

"Are you kidding me? Mark, you were the top of your class. Everyone talked about you and all the great things you would do."

Mark shook off the compliment. "All the great things I would do. Like run a diner."

Anna frowned. "I shouldn't have said anything about that the other day; I'm sorry. Your mom took it over. I understand. It's a family place."

"I thought I'd run Hastings until she was better—*if* she got better," he corrected himself, feeling a sharp pang tighten his chest. "I never planned to stick with it for as long as I have."

"Is that why you didn't want to pursue our restaurant? Is that why you ended—" She stopped herself. "Is that why you haven't done something else?"

Wasn't that the million-dollar question? "I saw what

happened to my dad's restaurant, how it affected my parents' marriage and eventually drove him out of town. I guess I've enjoyed the stability of Hastings."

"The restaurant business can be volatile," Anna said.

"Someone should have told my dad that," he remarked.

"Do you . . . do you ever think about reconnecting?"

"No," he said, and then stopped himself. "That's not true. Sometimes I do, I guess. Not that I'd know where to find him."

Anna tipped her head. "I'm sorry, Mark. I shouldn't have pressed."

"It's okay, really. When I was younger, I thought about him a lot, but as I got older, I guess I just tried to put him out of my mind instead. Lately, though . . ."

"I guess that explains why you were sitting outside Fireside the other night." Anna gave a small smile. "Does your mom ever talk about him?"

"Nope. After he left, she tried to keep her feelings to herself. I used to hear her crying, down the hall, late at night." He paused. "She really loved him, even after all he put her through."

A shadow came over Anna's face, and shame gripped him. He knew Anna had loved him, though they'd never spoken their feelings aloud. He'd felt it in the glow of her eyes, in the sweetness of her kiss, in the slump of her shoulders that awful day. So many times he wanted to say it, and he had, once, when she was sound asleep and he knew she wouldn't hear him. The words had slipped out, without planning, and then his chest had begun to pound. Less than two weeks later, he ended it. Abruptly. Swiftly. Doing what he had to do. Striking first.

"My dad worked most evenings, but in the morning,

he was usually home. I remember waking up every day, for months, thinking maybe he'd come back. I'd run down the stairs as fast I could, hoping to see him sitting at that kitchen table. His place was always empty." Often, not wanting to believe the harsh facts, he'd open the garage, his heart sinking when he saw the vacant spot where the blue sedan once sat.

Anna reached out a hand and set it on his arm, and he resisted the part of him that wanted to pull it back. To end this conversation and keep her away. To bury his feelings along with the past. He looked at her, suddenly feeling tired, worn out and old, and full of regrets he couldn't shake. It could have been them sitting here, side by side after a long, busy day at their restaurant, sipping wine and laughing about some order gone wrong, before crawling into bed, ready to do it all over tomorrow.

He remembered the way it felt to slide into bed beside her, to reach for her under the cool cotton sheets, to feel the heat of her skin on his, to hear her moan his name in his ear. Each morning he would wake, hours before her, sometimes before the sun had even risen, and he'd watch the room turn gray with light, listening to her steady breath. She seemed so peaceful, so pure and free of sorrow and pain. She took life in stride, and she loved with all her heart—things he could never do. He'd watch her until she began to stir, wondering how the hell he could ever sleep alone again, and panic would set in.

She told him stories, long into the night, about things she did with Grace and Jane, funny stories that made him laugh. He listened, happy for the chance not to have to talk about his past, his need to distance himself as great as his desire to be close. He wanted to know her. Every inch of her skin, every part of her soul. But he wanted to run, too. The closer he got, the more he worried, about the future, their plans, the thought of a struggling restaurant and bills and blame and arguments and hurt until there was nothing left between them.

His gaze traveled from his arm to her lips, moist and parted, and his groin stirred with arousal, and an urge to kiss her, taste her sweetness, breathe her air. Just once more.

"I don't usually talk about him," he said, clearing his throat.

"He had a big impact on your life," Anna said.

Mark nodded. More than she knew. Anna grazed her thumb over his skin, and an electric current zipped up his arm. She pulled her hand free, letting it fall, and tucked a strand of hair behind her ear.

"It's natural to want to connect with your dad, even when he's no longer a part of your life. I think that's why Grace wanted to keep Main Street Books alive. I know it's why I wanted to invest in the expansion."

There was that flush again, staining her cheeks a vibrant pink that offset the bright turquoise of her irises.

"That bookstore meant a lot to your father," Mark said.

Anna drew pensive for a moment, using the silence to take a sip of her wine. "That's what has me so worried," she muttered.

Mark leaned in, catching a whiff of her sweet scent as he did. He closed his eyes briefly, trying to capture the single sense. When he looked up, Anna was staring at him, her gaze steady. He could lean in, just another inch, remember what it felt like to kiss her mouth, to feel her soft curves pressed against him.

He pulled himself back into the stool instead. He was here to find her friendship again. Nothing more. "The bookstore's doing fine now; I see people in there all the time. It's never looked so great."

Anna sighed through a small smile. "It does, yes. But...that's not what has me worried. I took out a loan to match Grace's investment. She's covering rent and the bookstore renovation; I'm covering well...everything else. For now. It was all going to be fine. More than fine. And then—"

"The fire."

She nodded. "The fire."

"How bad is it?"

She met his stare. "Bad."

He let out a low whistle. It was exactly the kind of situation that made Hastings so appealing. The place was paid up; they owned it outright. A new venture, of any kind, could never offer the same security. One day it could be booming, the next...

"Does Grace know?"

"No," she said quickly, "and I don't intend to tell her."

He leaned into his elbow. "So what's your plan, then?"

She looked at him quizzically. "I intend to win this contest!"

He burst out laughing, hearing his own foolish desires in her preposterous statement. Until now, winning had been a vague notion, not something he was banking on, but hearing her say it aloud, a desire to not only compete but to win made him suddenly believe it was possible. That anything was possible.

"I do intend to win!" Anna cried, but even she couldn't stop from laughing. The sound rolled through the room and pulled at his heart, filling holes he didn't even know were there.

He didn't realize he'd stopped laughing until she did. The air went still, punctured only by the sound of his heart beating in his chest, and he knew he couldn't hold back any longer. Without thinking or daring to consider the consequences, he leaned into her. Her eyes flashed with surprise, her lashes fluttering quickly as he slid off his stool and closed the distance between them.

A gasp of surprise escaped her throat as he brought his lips to hers and his hands came around her waist, pulling her close to his chest until he felt her body relax on each kiss. He sensed her hesitation, but he couldn't pull back, not when her lips were on his, her sweet taste filling his senses. She parted her mouth, and he pulled her closer, feeling the soft swell of her breasts against his chest. His groin pooled with warmth as her thighs rubbed against his. He pressed his palms deeper into her back, and lower, resisting the urge to explore her hips, knowing if he did he wouldn't be able to stop. And he should stop—he should. But . . . he couldn't.

He kissed her, as if for the first time, tasting the forbidden fruit, knowing it was wrong, wrong, wrong, even thought it felt so damn right. He tore his lips from hers, letting his mouth roam her neck, burying himself in her hair, that coconut-scented hair, and breathed into her ear, wondering if she would run, if she'd push him back, tell him to go.

He pulled back, watching the way her eyes searched his. He should say something, explain himself, but there was nothing to say.

Anna's cheeks were dotted with pink as she picked

up a knife and pulled the vegetables from the basket. His gaze lingered her on a few moments more, watching the way she expertly chopped and diced, the way they'd been instructed in school, fingers tucked.

"Anna." His voice was low and husky.

He should tell her it was a mistake, that it couldn't happen again. That he wanted to be friends, to make her understand once and for all that it was all they ever should have been.

"We should get to work," she said abruptly, and he hated the slight quiver in her voice. "We still have a lot to do and we leave for Cedar Valley tomorrow afternoon."

They'd be at the lodge for two nights; he'd have time to talk to her then. For now, she was right. It was time to get to work, put all personal matters aside, and focus on winning this contest. And getting what they wanted at long last.

Eighteen hours later, Anna stood on the front stoop of her apartment building, feeling even more nervous than she had last night when they tasted their recipes for the final time, the heat of that kiss still lingering in her mouth, on her lips, confusing her palate nearly as much as her judgment.

Her stomach twisted a little tighter. She told herself it was the stress from the contest tomorrow, and everything riding on it, but something told her it had a lot more to do with Mark's kiss than perfecting their maple glaze for the salmon. She'd avoided the diner again this morning, baking quick breads and scones and preparing cookie dough that Grace could pop into the oven tomorrow and Sunday. She'd kept busy, baking and cleaning and packing, but try as she might, Mark was never far from her thoughts.

She brushed a finger idly over her lips. After all these years, she'd never forgotten what it felt like to kiss Mark . . . and now she didn't stand a chance of forgetting. Even though that was exactly what she should do. Forget their past. Forget the kiss. Forget Mark.

Just tell him it was a mistake. A casual slip. Whatever it had been, it couldn't be repeated. She knew Mark, and what he was capable of—it was attraction, nothing more. They'd spent too much time together these past few weeks, fallen back on old habits.

Her heart skipped as a car rounded the bend at the edge of the road, but her shoulders relaxed when she recognized the vehicle. Rosemary's car was unmistakable: cranberry red and fit for two; she loved to drive the sports car with its top down in warm weather. The sun shone bright, and Rosemary had wrapped a leopard-print silk headscarf over her hair. Her oversized sunglasses shielded her face, and she plucked them off the second she rolled to a stop.

"I thought I'd come to see you off!" Rosemary sprang up the tulip-lined path with quick, graceful movements, her blue eyes glittering. "Is Mark picking you up?"

Anna nodded and pressed a hand to her stomach, feeling the hard knot beneath its surface. "Yep."

"Oh, good!" Rosemary clapped her hands, beaming, and then seemed to freeze. "I mean, you wouldn't want to be late."

"I'm sure we'll get there on time. The drive isn't too long." Anna glanced anxiously down the street. "He should be here any minute."

"Oh, well, don't let me *interrupt* anything." Rosemary wiggled her eyebrows and stared at her, and Anna tipped her head in confusion. She knew Rosemary was excited about this contest, but she still couldn't understand why. Grace, she could understand, or even Jane, who had a hint of the financial pressure Anna was under.

Anna dismissed her suspicion. Mark was Rosemary's nephew; she probably wanted the best for him.

Rosemary thrust a gift bag at her. "What's this?" Anna asked in surprise.

"Oh..." Rosemary shifted her eyes. "Just a little something to *mark* the occasion."

"You didn't have to get me anything!" Anna grinned, and reached through the hot pink tissue paper to retrieve the present. Rosemary began taking great interest in a potted geranium on the top of the porch banister.

"Knowing you, I'm sure you have all your ingredients lined up and ready. You never know, though. This *might* come in handy..." She tore a dead leaf from the plant.

"Oh, well, this was so thoughtful of—" Anna stared down at the bottle in dismay, frowning as she read the label. "Massage oil?"

"Is it?" Rosemary leaned forward and inspected the label. "So it is. And here I thought it was cooking oil. Oh dear."

"That's okay." Anna gave a half smile and tucked it into the paper bag. She wasn't sure what was going on with Mark, but if Rosemary thought she could step in and help things along, she didn't know her nephew very well. Mark did as he pleased when it came to matters of the heart.

Anna frowned, feeling her stomach tighten with unease. "It's the thought that counts. Thank you."

She reached for the door handle, but Rosemary stopped her before she could turn the knob.

"Where are you going?" Rosemary's voice pitched in alarm.

"I'll bring it inside."

"Oh, no. You don't have time for that!" Rosemary snatched the bag from her hand and pulled the plastic bottle free. "Mark will be here any minute, and you don't

want to keep him waiting. Especially if there's traffic..."
She jammed the bottle into Anna's handbag.

Anna glanced down as Rosemary's determined hand
wedged the massage oil securely into place. Just under her
armpit, the cap read KISS SAFE.

Oh, for crying out loud!

"There's Mark now!" Rosemary trilled and turned to
wave down the street. Sure enough, Mark's black SUV sat
at the stop sign. Anna's heart began to beat a little faster.

Rosemary flashed her a look, giving her the once-over.
"Is that what you're wearing?"

Anna looked down. There was a cocktail reception
planned for this evening, but there would be time to
change once they arrived. Jeans and a tank top seemed fit-
ting for the occasion, because that's what a ninety-minute
car ride with Mark was: an occasion. An event she never
in her wildest nightmares could have imagined she'd be
doing. Though, perhaps, if she was honest, it had been one
of her wildest dreams.

"Yes," she replied firmly.

"Well, it will have to do," Rosemary replied with a
sigh. "It's just that you have such pretty legs. A shame to
hide them..."

Anna opened her mouth to reply, but Mark was already
out of the car, strolling up the path, his hands crammed
into the pockets of his khakis, darting his eyes from Rosemary to Anna.

Her breath caught, remembering the way it felt to hold
him last night, to fold herself against that chest, feel the
heat of his breath on her mouth, her neck. She licked her
bottom lip and bit down hard. She couldn't think this way,
not with the contest tomorrow. Not...ever.

"Perfect timing, Mark," Rosemary said, hurrying to meet him. She gave her nephew a quick peck on the cheek. "I came to see you two off, but let's not linger. Anna has her bags all packed and ready." She glanced at Anna, seeming to send her a message with her widening eyes.

Mark met her eyes and for a moment they exchanged a secret smile. Her heart skipped a beat on impact, and every argument she'd had with herself, every speech she'd firmly recited in the mirror that morning, was gone with the quirk of his mouth.

"Don't worry, Aunt Rosemary. Cedar Valley's only sixty-five miles from here. We'll be there long before sunset."

"Oh, Cedar Valley. Such a stunning resort, don't you think?" Rosemary turned wistful. "Be sure to enjoy the scenery. Maybe take a stroll through the village, enjoy a glass of wine on the veranda..."

"I think we'll be fairly busy," Mark said affably.

Rosemary's brow furrowed. "Now, Mark. Anna's been through a lot these past few weeks. I'm counting on you to show her a good time."

Mark chuckled, a slow deep rumble that stole Anna's breath. "Oh, I intend to."

Rosemary's eyes sprang open, and her red-painted lips formed a little *o* of surprise. "Well, good!" she said when she'd collected herself. "Very good indeed!"

Clasping her hands to her chest once more, she darted to her car, glancing back several times, her eyes flashing.

"Sorry about that," Mark said, turning to the porch. He slipped Anna a bashful grin. "She's pretty excited about this contest."

"I just hope we don't let her down," Anna said, frowning. A flutter of nerves rushed through her stomach at the mere mention of the contest. This time tomorrow, they'd be tying on aprons. The day had arrived, and she suddenly felt unprepared and worried. If they didn't win...She pressed a hand to her stomach to settle herself.

Mark walked up the stairs, and she bent quickly to grab hold of her luggage handle, determined to avoid eye contact wherever she could.

"Let me," he said lightly, reaching out to slide his hand next to hers. A jolt ran up her arm, and her pulse began to race; she dropped the bags quickly. A flash of alarm sparked Mark's dark eyes, but his grin widened.

"Thank you," she said tightly. *Get a grip, Anna. It's just Mark. So you kissed. You've done it before. He kisses all the girls...It's who he is.*

But was that who he was now? She wasn't so sure anymore. She'd stayed up long into the night thinking of what Mark had told her, the way he was haunted by the abandonment of his father, the way he'd clung to hope for something that he probably knew deep down would never happen.

Mark tipped his head toward the car. "Ready?"

Anna nodded, not trusting herself to speak, and followed him down the porch, where he loaded her two bags into the trunk and slammed it shut. She let herself into the passenger seat, quickly fastening her seat belt and hugging her handbag to her chest. The KISS SAFE label stared back at her, and she furiously shoved it deeper into her bag. The last thing she needed was Mark getting any ideas or thinking that last night had meant anything to her. Because it hadn't. It...couldn't.

"So," he said, after he'd done a three-point turn and began driving back toward town. He glanced at her sidelong, causing her pulse to skip. "Nervous?"

Anna startled. Was it that obvious?

She turned her attention to the view ahead. "A little, I guess. How about you?"

"I'm a wreck." Mark grinned, and Anna felt her nerves subside a little.

"I think we have a strong entry," Anna said decidedly.

"We do," Mark agreed, accelerating as they reached a main road. He lazily drooped one wrist over the top of the steering wheel, sipping a thermos of what smelled like coffee with the other. She hated when he did that. It reminded her how reckless he could be.

Catching her disapproving glare, Mark casually said, "I'm happy to share."

"No, thank you. I don't drink coffee after noon. I get headaches."

Mark chuckled under his breath and slowly took another sip. "You have a lot of rules."

"No," Anna said, feeling her defenses prickle. "I just have a certain way of doing things. I know what works for me and I know what doesn't."

"Where does that leave us?" His hooded gaze bore through hers, forcing her pulse to race for the length of a red light. Anna wrapped a hand tighter around her handbag straps, feeling every muscle in her body tense. They'd only been in the car for all of five minutes, and if it kept going like this, she'd be shaking by the time they arrived at the resort. She couldn't deal with this—with him—not now at least. She needed to think. She needed to focus. And she needed to win this damn contest.

"Planning on following your rule to ignore me for another six years?" He laughed again, and she felt her shoulders relax. They'd cleared that bump, but it had sparked a new wave of questions. So far Mark hadn't mentioned the kiss—not that she'd expected him to. But he raised a good point: Was there a place in her life for Mark going forward? And was that what he really even wanted? The contractors were working hard on Fireside, and it was scheduled to be partially operable by next week. After this weekend they wouldn't have to spend time together. Unless they wanted to . . .

"I'll get back to you on that after the contest," she said lightly. Living in silence had started to feel natural, easy. Now . . . it was all a mess. Were they supposed to be friends, or casual acquaintances? She wasn't sure how she could stand it, pretending that everything was fine, when it wasn't. It couldn't be. Not when he didn't know what they'd shared and lost. The magnitude of it hit her again, as it often did when she dared to think of their past, and she looked out the window, at the pine trees that hugged the winding road.

"You know, between you and me, I have more than one goal this weekend," Mark said after a few minutes.

Anna blinked. "Oh?" she asked weakly. It had been one kiss. Surely he hadn't intended to take it further.

"Personally, I'm rather looking forward to the opportunity to stick it to Frank Piccolino."

Anna frowned. "Frank? But why?"

Mark finally set his thermos back in the cup holder and brought his hand to the wheel. Anna heaved a breath and relaxed back against her seat. They were approaching the highway, and the mountain view in the distance held her attention. Nearly.

"Because Frank Piccolino is the reason my father's restaurant failed."

Anna stared at him. "Hothead Frank?"

"Yes." He gripped the steering wheel tightly, his eyes trained on the road.

Anna took the moment to let her gaze linger on his profile, on the strong Roman nose and the thick brow that capped his deep-set eyes. His blue and gray rugby shirt was rolled at the sleeves, revealing muscular forearms and strong hands. She lingered on them, remembering the way the way those fingers traced her body, exploring every curve, every crevice, every place she'd kept hidden since. She closed her eyes and turned away.

"Tavern on Main was the only real restaurant in Briar Creek for a long time, other than the diner, of course," Mark continued. "It was considered the place to go. Good service, good food, great atmosphere. It was a success. For a while," he added, his tone turning somber.

Anna tried to remember when Piccolino's had first opened. She was young, too young to really pay attention to those things. Her family didn't go out to dinner much, and her parents certainly didn't bring three girls to upscale restaurants. She was sad to admit she had never even been to Mark's father's restaurant, but Sharon had shown her photographs in an album she kept in a cabinet in her living room. She always smiled fondly at the pictures, perhaps with a hint of sadness in her eyes, but it was clear she had happy memories of the place and of Mark's father, despite how everything had ended between them.

Anna knew the feeling.

She bit down on her thumbnail and then quickly snatched her hand back, remembering the manicure she'd squeezed in that morning. Working with her hands so much, she usually didn't bother, but tonight's party was on her mind almost as much as the contest tomorrow. Would they go together, or just mingle independently? See, this is where it was better to live in silence. Then she wouldn't have to worry about how to interact.

Mark took another sip of his coffee and set it back in place. "When Piccolino's opened, competition started. Frank was offering a similar dining experience, but for a slightly lower price. I remember my mother arguing with my dad to change things, to give the customers what they wanted."

"And he wouldn't?"

Mark shook his head, his lips thinning. "He was stubborn. He wanted to cook his way. Wanted to run that restaurant for himself. In the end it cost him everything."

Anna knew exactly what he meant by everything. He meant himself. Their family.

"Your mom's told me some of the details of . . . the closing," she said delicately.

She saw Mark's gaze narrow. "He got into debt, and instead of doing what he needed to do to get himself out of it, he put his pride first." He shook his head. "Stubborn."

Dread coated her stomach. The mountains ahead were growing nearer. Soon they'd reach the resort, and their fate would be sealed. She hadn't dared to think of what would happen if they didn't win the contest. She was barely treading water, and without some assistance she would never be able to make the next payment on that loan.

"Everything okay?" Mark glanced at her.

"What? Oh, yeah. I was just thinking that it's easy to get in over your head and not realize it until it's too late."

"Are you referring to the bookstore?" he asked.

Anna watched the trees go by. She was thinking about the store, of course. But she was also thinking about him.

The sky had turned gray by the time they arrived at Cedar Valley Resort, nestled at the base of Cedar Mountain. Mark shook his thermos, frowning at its light weight, and set it back in the holder. The drive, though short, had made him tired, and far too much of it had been spent in silence.

He knew Anna was probably waiting for him to mention the kiss, but he was hoping to avoid that subject for a bit, or at least until he knew better how to react to it. He'd kissed her, touched her, felt her lips on his, and damn if he didn't want to do it again.

He'd opened up to her. Revealed things to her he'd never told anyone—not his mother or brother, not even Luke. Years ago he'd promised himself not to let anyone get close. It gave them power. Power to turn on you, reject you, let you down.

Anna, he knew, had never done any of those things. All she'd ever been was herself. Her sweet, honest self. She'd trusted him, even when he couldn't trust her.

He stole a look, noticing the way her honey blond hair fell over her face like a curtain, closing her off from him. He tightened his grip on the wheel and returned his eyes to the road as they drove through Cedar Valley Village, past the quaint shops and restaurants, and finally rounded the drive to the large resort, where a valet signaled for them to pull over.

Mark let out a low whistle. "Nice place."

Anna was smiling as she leaned forward in her seat, eagerly craning her neck to stare through the windshield.

"When Grace and Jane and I were younger, we thought this was a real castle."

Mark laughed, feeling the tension roll off him. "You've stayed here, then?"

"No, we only came skiing for the day, but I always thought it would be the perfect weekend getaway. It's just so...romantic." Her smile turned wistful and Mark couldn't resist grinning.

Sure enough, her eyes sprang open, that pretty smile fell to an abrupt frown, and a flush of pink crawled up her neck and landed squarely on her cheeks.

"I just meant in general. Not today. Just...you know what I mean." Her eyes darted to the window.

"Don't worry. I know," Mark said easily, and before she could react, he popped his seat belt and opened the door. They were dancing around each other, feeling the strain of the kiss; the prickle of it hung between them. Another boundary, another divider.

But he wouldn't take it back.

It was cooler in the mountains, and the air felt fresher somehow, with a faint scent of pine. He looked up at the mountain, towering high above him, wondering what the weekend had in store for them. Cars were arriving behind them—other chefs no doubt—and a sense of anticipation filled him with energy. They'd give it their best, and their best just might be enough. Then Anna could get back on her feet. Then he would feel a sense of redemption for hurting her all those years ago.

He could leave town a free man, open his new place with a clear conscience. When he came back to Briar Creek to visit, they might even grab a drink sometime. They could be friends.

If he could push aside that part of him that wanted to kiss her again, that was.

Anna came around to the front of the vehicle, keeping a healthy distance from him, he noted with disappointment. She shivered and rubbed her bare arms with her hands. Her top clung to her waist, and he felt his gaze drop to her curves.

He swallowed hard, forcing his mind back to the issue at hand. Of course he was attracted to Anna. And he liked her, too. Maybe...maybe even loved her. But that didn't mean they had a future. He should remember that. Especially now.

Still, his gaze lingered on the sway of her hips as he followed her through the revolving door and into the palatial lobby, its grandeur in stark contrast with the rustic environment.

Anna turned to him expectantly after she checked in, and then double-checked her key. "I'm in seven thirty-four. You?"

Mark couldn't resist the opportunity. "Seven thirty-four."

Her face blanched. "What? But...wait. What do you mean?"

"Hey, money's tight these days, right? I thought you'd be happy to share. Don't worry, they got us a king, and I'll stick to my side." He meant to keep going with it, to follow her to her room, maybe even make a grand show of unpacking his suitcases, or throwing himself down onto her bed—his groin tightened at the thought—but a sputter of laughter escaped from his lips, low and deep, until fire blazed in Anna's blue eyes and those pretty pink lips pinched tight.

"Very funny," she said, crossing her arms.

"Lighten up, Anna," he said, sobering himself. "Besides, would it have been so bad? You and me, alone in a room?"

Anna gave him a level stare, but surprise lit her eyes. "I think that would be a recipe for disaster."

He knew he should be grateful, relieved that she was sparing him a giant mistake. But the disappointment square in his chest unnerved him.

He wasn't thinking clearly. They'd spent too much time together. Everything could go back to normal soon. She'd go back to Fireside and he'd be back at Hastings.

His heart felt heavy at the thought of it. Anna was right. They *had* to win.

They walked to the elevator in silence. Mark pressed the button and turned to her, deciding to clear the air. "About last night—"

He felt her stiffen as the mirror-paneled doors drew closed. "Mark—we have a big day tomorrow. Do we really want to get into this now?"

Mark regarded her for a moment, deciding she had a point. "Fair enough." He paused outside the door of his room. "I'll see you at the cocktail party?"

Her face relaxed. "I'm looking forward to it."

"Hard to believe by this time tomorrow the competition will be nearly over," he said, thinking of his plans, of the money he'd stashed, and the recipes he'd collected for years. That dream was in his grasp, the contest could change everything. But in a way, it already had.

CHAPTER
23

The party was well under way when Mark stepped out of the elevator at ten past seven. People stood in groups, chatting and smiling and sipping drinks while hotel staff circled the room, passing hors d'oeuvres from silver trays. Mark snagged a mini egg roll and crammed it into his mouth, searching through the crowd for Anna.

Not seeing her, he made his way to the bar and ordered a Scotch. He took a sip, feeling the liquid burn down his throat, and then leaned against the polished wood surface, surveying the crowd. There had to have been over a hundred people, all chatting and lively, their voices nearly drowning out the music coming from the piano at the end of the room. Everyone looked happy and relaxed. He wished he could say the same for himself.

He should be thinking about the contest, of what he would do with the money if they won, but he couldn't stop thinking of Anna, and the way her ass looked in those jeans. The way her lips tasted last night. He chased back the rest of his drink and ordered another, vowing to go easy on this round. He needed a clear head. He needed to think this through. He couldn't make another mistake with Anna.

He narrowed his eyes to the crowd, looking for Frank Piccolino, sure to be here, puffed up and proud, believing himself, no doubt, capable of winning the grand prize, when a finger tapped him on the shoulder. He startled, turning in expectation to see Anna, and his face fell when he saw the woman standing before him instead.

"Cassie." He recognized her at once, even after all these years. Her rich black hair was swept off her neck, and her ice blue eyes were rimmed in dark, curly lashes. Reflexively, he glanced to the elevator in the distance, willing Anna not to come through its doors right now. "What a surprise." He leaned down and brushed her cheek with a kiss, catching a waft of that expensive perfume she'd always worn.

"Mark Hastings," she purred, leaving a hand on his arm. "Just as handsome as ever."

Mark stiffened and took another sip of his drink. "You're looking well, Cassie." He glanced back at the elevator and then subtly swept his eyes over the room, before turning back to the woman before him. Her black silk dress was cut low, and a diamond chain graced her neck. "Are you entering the contest?"

"Indeed I am." Her lips curved into a smile. "So tell me, what have you been up to all these years?"

Mark sucked in a breath. Such a simple question should not be so difficult to answer. "I'm running a place in my hometown. Nothing fancy, but the locals enjoy it. It's a family place, you could say."

She studied him with interest. "I've kept my eye out for you." She sipped her champagne, lifting an eyebrow.

"Here I thought the best chef at the academy would go on to run a four-star restaurant in a big city."

A bitter taste filled his mouth and he chased it back with another swig from his glass. "What have you been up to?" he asked, changing the subject.

"Oh, believe it or not, I've got a great little French bistro here in Cedar Valley."

"In the resort?" Mark couldn't help but be impressed.

"A few blocks down the road, in the village." Cassie smiled. "You should stop in some time."

Mark nodded. "Maybe I will."

She tipped her head, her gaze traveling over him with interest. "Call ahead and I'll set up a tasting menu for you." She opened her clutch and retrieved a business card. Pressing it into his hand, she said, "In case you're ever in the area again."

Mark glanced down at the card, noting the heavy cardstock, the elaborate scroll of the embossed lettering, the *Executive Chef* title next to her name, and felt his stomach knot. "Thanks."

Cassie gave a long sigh. "I should probably mingle, but I'll be in touch." She leaned in and whispered in his ear, "Good luck tomorrow. I'm curious to see if you've still got it."

Mark watched Cassie saunter off, her hips swaying in the form-fitting cocktail dress, her heels high. She looked like a woman who had made a success of herself, who knew the town and was confident in her place here.

That could be him this time next year: a chef people talked about, running a kitchen that sparked a buzz. This contest could open doors—but was he really ready to close one on the way out?

He gave the business card another hard look before slipping it into his pocket. Taking another swig of his drink, he turned, his breath catching when he saw Anna standing at the edge of the room. Her long blond hair was loose, falling in waves around her shoulders. She wore a navy dress that clung to every curve...and an expression that left no doubt that she'd been standing there just long enough to get the wrong idea.

Her jaw was set, her mouth a firm line, and before he could move, she turned on her heel and walked quickly in the other direction.

"Anna!" He set the drink on the bar, sloshing the remains, and elbowed through the crowd, weaving his path through the groups of people, his eye trained on her as she retreated from him. "Anna."

He caught up to her and reached for her elbow, but she stepped out of his way, pushing through a glass door that led to the veranda. Mark held up a hand, stopping the door before it hit him in the face, and hurried behind her. The night air was clean and cool, but the heat that coursed through his veins kept him warm.

"Anna, stop. You have the wrong idea."

She whipped around. Anger glittered in her eyes, stopping him in his tracks. In all the years since they'd broken up, she'd never shown a reaction; she'd simply fallen silent. She had never shed a tear, almost disappeared into the crowd, until she was out of his grasp. She'd never reached out for him. Never tried to get back what they'd once had.

Until these past few weeks.

"I didn't know Cassie would be here," he said firmly. "You have the wrong idea."

She snorted, giving a bitter laugh. "Oh, do I? The way I had the wrong idea that day I saw you with her? You didn't even wait a week before taking up with her, Mark. Not even a week!"

He reached out for her, but she pulled back. "Cassie and I never had anything. Not anything real. Not like you and I had."

"Then why'd you bother? With her...with me?"

Because he couldn't resist. He never could resist Anna. He opened his mouth to respond, and clamped it shut, rubbing the back of his neck.

A shadow passed over her expression, and the fury that sparked her blue gaze faded to something more tangible. He stared at her, hating the hurt he saw in her eyes, wishing he could take back the past five minutes, no longer—the past seven and a half years. He wanted to go back to that place they'd once been, safe and warm in each other's arms, with the entire future at their fingertips.

His hand dropped to his side. "I just ran into her tonight. She's entering the contest; I had no idea she'd be here. You have to believe me."

"Why?" She sighed, looking away. "What does it matter? You and I were over a long time ago. We just...got caught up in the past few weeks."

He wanted to tell her she was wrong, that she knew it. That there was so much more beneath the surface that had lingered over the years, buried by sheer will on both their parts. The tears that shone in her eyes unnerved him, made his gut twist and his mind spin.

She still cared. There was still a chance.

Just tell her. Tell her what she means to you. Tell her what you want. But the damn truth of the matter was that he didn't know what he wanted. Not then. Not now. He just knew how he felt when he was with her. And he knew he never wanted that feeling to go away.

Anna shook her head, brushing furiously at the hot tears. She could still feel the pain of that day, when she'd realized it was over, that she wasn't special to Mark, and he'd already moved on to another—Cassie—just as she'd seen him do with so many girls before her. She tried not to go there, tried not think about it, but now all that emotion she had tried to bury had come to the surface, and there was no turning it off.

She blinked and turned away from him, toward the mountain that loomed so large above them she almost felt she could reach out her fingers and touch it. She wanted him to go, to turn and leave; it was what he did best, after all. Why now, of all times, was he determined to stay?

"Say something." His voice was low and gruff, but there was something else there, too. Something vulnerable that prickled her senses and made her hesitate.

She rested her hands on the stone wall of the veranda. In the distance behind her she could hear the muffled sounds of the piano, the occasional burst of laughter. Strings of lights had been hung from metal poles anchoring either end of the space, but it was the darkness she was focused on. She wanted to run out there, into the wild, and escape this moment, the feelings that only Mark could stir within her.

"I used to think we had a future." The words slipped out, so softly, she wondered if he had even heard, or if the breeze had carried their sound away. It didn't matter. She'd kept her feelings—her deepest pain—bottled deep inside her for so long, she thought it might break her. Now, there was no holding back. All that effort, all that determination to keep her heartache at bay, to push the hurt into a place no one could access or touch, was gone.

She turned around to look at him. His dark eyes were hooded, and his shoulders rose and fell with each breath. Other than that, he didn't move. Didn't flinch. Didn't run.

"We had a plan, Mark. A plan for a life together." Her eyes burned, thinking of Cassie, elegant and beautiful, hanging on his arm, happy and carefree, while she fell into the shadows, replaced. She should have pressed when he brought her to the café that day—demanded to know if the flirting she'd seen meant something—but he'd already given her the best reason he had: *I can't give you what you need.*

And what did she need? A friend? A business partner? A father for her child?

"When did you realize you didn't want to open the restaurant together? Was that the reason you broke it off?" She had to ask. She had to know. How much was connected? How much was real? Had she been holding on to broken promises from the start, or had she been right to believe him at some point?

He dragged out a sigh and walked over to the wall, shifted his torso so he was facing her. His thigh brushed hers, sending a rush of desire up the length of her spine, and she tensed, stepping back.

A lock of hair spilled over his forehead and he pushed it back. "I thought I could do it. The restaurant. Us. I wanted everything you did. I just wasn't ready to make that kind of commitment."

It was the honest answer. Plain, really. She wasn't sure what more she'd been expecting. He'd told her the truth that day. She supposed that was better than lying to her.

"I don't know why I thought it would be different with us. I thought I was...special." She gave a small shrug, embarrassed at the admission.

"You were special," he said quietly, and her heart skipped a beat. He put a hand on her shoulder and she tried to look away, not wanting to meet that penetrating gaze, afraid of what it might reveal if she searched deep enough. "You know how much that friendship meant to me."

She met his eye. "Do I? If it meant so much, why didn't you just tell me how you were feeling? We didn't have to get carried away, or start planning for something that was never going to happen. We didn't have to be anything more than friends," she added, but she knew that part wasn't true. They couldn't resist each other. Even if deep down they knew they should have.

He pulled his hand away, raking it through his hair as he stared into the distance. "You don't know how it is, Anna. You don't know how it feels to have someone you care about, someone you trust, just disappear on you."

She stared at him. "Yes, I do. That's exactly what you did to me."

He didn't know the half of it. She had the sudden urge to tell him everything, to see how he would react, if he would even care. The only way he could ever understand how badly he had hurt her was to come clean and tell him about the baby. It was the only way she'd ever be able to move on from their past.

"I probably sound sensitive," she said, righting herself. This wasn't the time to tell him. Not when they were fighting. Not when Cassie, of all people, was standing just beyond that set of doors.

Mark shook his head. "Not sensitive. Honest."

Anna gripped the cool stone tighter. She wasn't honest. She was far from it. But how could she trust him with the truth? If he knew what happened, he might hate her for not telling him all those years ago, blame her...the way a part of her blamed herself.

"Anna. I'm sorry. I meant it when I said that I wished it had been different. Those other girls...Cassie...they never meant anything. I liked them because they never could, because they didn't want more than I could give."

"And I did?"

"You *deserved* more than I could give. I wanted to give you all those things. I just couldn't."

She willed herself to stay strong, to stare out into the night sky, to fight the emotions that waged a war in her chest and made her want to turn to him, take him into her arms, and apologize. He'd let her down, broken her heart, but somehow she'd failed him, too.

She'd lost their baby. Nothing could bring it back.

She stepped back. "It's late, and we have a big day tomorrow. I think we should end this conversation here."

He frowned. "If you think that's best."

"I do," she said firmly. She walked toward the door, refusing to look back.

She and Mark were long over. They shared a past, that was all. They could never share a future.

CHAPTER 24

Anna fastened the last button on her jacket and stared in the mirror. She hadn't worn chef's whites since she'd graduated from culinary school, but it was more than the uniform that made her feel like she'd stepped back in time.

Mark and Cassie, chatting and laughing, while she stood on the sidelines. Wasn't that a page straight out of her memory book? It hadn't even occurred to her that the other woman would be here, but now she was surprised she hadn't seen more of her classmates around the hotel.

They'd probably moved away, out of state. Something she probably should have done, too. Instead she'd come full circle. Pinning all her hopes on the man who had the ability to crush them.

Anna smoothed her ponytail and squared her shoulders. Time to get back on track. The competition was about to start, and here she was, getting all misty-eyed over a man who had already broken her heart once. She'd be damned if she let him do it again.

Too much was riding on this.

Glancing down at her crisp white jacket, Anna's mouth drooped into a frown. At the café, she wore regular clothes, aprons in cheerful colors or patterns. The last time she'd worn this, her father had been at her side, his arm tight around her shoulder, smiling for the camera on her graduation day. That picture in her kitchen at home was all she had left of that moment. Photographs were all she had left of her father. That and the bookstore.

I'm going to make you proud today, Dad.

She looked up to the sky, at the towering mountain above her, trying to imagine him up there somewhere, looking down on her, protecting her somehow. She clung to that thought as she turned away, feeling the first heat of the morning sun on her back, daring to believe it was her father's guiding hand, until she reached the double set of doors to the grand ballroom and stepped inside.

Mark was already at their station when she entered the ballroom reserved for the contest a few minutes later. Anna gave him a small smile and scanned the ingredients they'd ordered, making sure nothing was missing. All she had to do was focus. Keep it professional, not personal. Follow her own rules.

Judges paraded down the aisle, stopping at the platform at the end of the room where they took turns introducing themselves and welcoming the contestants. Fifty teams had entered, but only one would win. As if they needed to be reminded.

The timer was set for two hours. Anna pressed her minute-by-minute list flat on the table and waited for the clock to start. They'd prepared for this. They'd trained for this. This was it.

The first hour passed in a blur, but at the midway point, the room picked up. Sharp orders could be heard from neighboring stations; tension was high. The temperature in the room rose as ovens and burners were pushed to their full capacity, and smells wafted through the room, blending together, until it was hard to discern what stemmed from one station to the next.

Anna finished peeling the second butternut squash and glanced at the oversized digital timer that hung at the back of the room just above the judging tables, watching as it ticked off another second. "We're on track," she said to Mark.

"Good." He didn't look up as he diced purple beets into even cubes. "How's the dessert coming along?"

Anna bent down and peered through the oven window. The tarts' crusts were turning golden, and the sweet smell of apples could almost be detected. "Another five minutes and we should be ready to take it out," she informed him.

Mark nodded as he slid the beets off the cutting board and onto a metal baking sheet. He seasoned them with a drizzle of olive oil, salt, and pepper. "These are set to go."

Anna crossed the item off her list. Halfway there. She grabbed a knife and cut the squash in half, then quickly scooped out the seeds with a spoon.

"Here." Mark nudged her with his hip, sending a flare of heat over her skin. "Let me. You deal with the dessert."

Her eyes flashed on his. "That's not how we rehearsed it."

"Well, we're down to an hour,"

"I don't care," Anna said. "We agreed on a plan of action. Now's not the time to go off course." She began dicing the squash into orange cubes, careful to match the size with those of Mark's beets. The entire salad was dependent on making every mouthful a perfect mix of flavors and textures, without one overriding any others.

"I'm not trying to—"

"Mark." Her voice was firm, and she realized she was holding the knife at an alarming angle. Releasing a long, slow breath, she lowered it to the work station and began hastily transferring the butternut squash to Mark's baking dish. "Darn. We should have seasoned them together."

Mark cursed under his breath and grabbed some beets from the vegetable bowl. "I'll start over."

"There's no time now," Anna pressed, reaching for the olive oil. "We'll just have to make do." Anna balled two fists at her side, willing herself to stay quiet, to not light into him now. This wasn't the time or the place for any distractions, and she knew that the emotions building inside her had a heck of a lot more to do with the business card he'd accepted from Cassie than the fact that he had gone ahead and salted the beets.

"Let's just...stay focused," she ordered, hoping she was capable of following her own direction.

She bent down and pulled the tarts from the oven. The first, for the presentation score, had turned out better than she could have hoped, and she nearly wept with relief as she gingerly set it on the rack to cool. The second, which would be sliced for the tasting, went beside it, and Anna resisted the urge to take a bite. She had to learn to trust herself—something she used to be good at until Mark stumbled back into her life. She'd made this dish at least a dozen times over the past few weeks. She had perfected the recipe. She knew what it tasted like.

Besides, it was too late now.

Mark popped the baking dish into the oven and set

the time for the vegetables to roast. Anna scratched the item from her list. Her chest was beating steadily, at an accelerated speed like a drum in a marching band, but she couldn't stop now. They had a flow going, they were doing what they needed to do, and she had to admit it was all coming together easily.

But then, that was just the thing with she and Mark. They just fell into sync, into their old patterns, didn't they?

"Last chance to change your mind on the glaze." Mark cocked an eyebrow and held up the pink slab of salmon.

She gave him a hard stare. "We agreed on the maple and mustard."

"Just checking." Mark slipped her an easy grin and reached for the container of Sugar Maple syrup.

"I thought we agreed the soy was too much of a risk. Mustard went better with the salad."

Mark just shrugged. "Your call."

Anna felt her temper flare. "Please don't do this, Mark. We agreed on our plan. Don't yank it out from under us at the final hour." She blinked quickly. "You never change," she muttered under her breath.

"Hey," he said sharply. "Are we talking about the salmon or are we talking about something bigger?"

Her blood stirred. "You tell me. I'm the one staying the course. I'm the one who stuck to the plan. You're the one who just comes and goes as he pleases, changes his mind every five seconds, never sticking to one damn thing." Or one damn person.

He waited a beat. "I'm here, Anna. And I intend to see this out to the end."

Her breath had turned heavy, and she blinked, gritting her teeth against his words. "Good." She held the mustard container out to him. "Then let's finish what we came to do." She turned away, leaving him to the glaze, and began rinsing the baby spinach for the salad while the water for the gnocchi began to boil.

They fell back into their pattern, working quickly and confidently, each taking turns to move this way and that—stir a sauce, check the oven, adjust a temperature, as if in a well-choreographed ballet—and then the buzzer went off. Just like that, it was over.

Anna stepped back from the station, roaming her eyes over the three presentation plates and the tasting portions set just behind each course.

Out of the corner of her eye, she could see Mark standing less than a foot away, so tall and strong, so sure of himself in that white jacket and apron, and she felt a flicker of pride for all he had done. All *they* had done.

Perhaps feeling her gaze, he slid his eyes to hers, and her breath caught at the intensity in his eyes. "Couldn't have done it without you. We sure do make a great team."

All it took was one look, one murmur of kindness, and she was right back there again—wishing, hoping, for so much more than he could ever give her. More than they could have.

She gave a small smile. "We always did."

He nodded, and swallowed hard. "Anna..."

She stiffened, feeling him come near, and searched his face in alarm. He reached over and set his hand on the small of her back. The small gesture sent a ripple of pleasure up her spine, and her breath caught as her eyes widened in alarm. He slid his eyes to the left, and alarm prickled her skin, overriding the pleasure of his touch.

The judging panel stood before them. Three of Cedar

Valley's best chefs, all Michelin star winners, and two suited men who introduced themselves as senior staff at the tourism board.

The pleasantries stopped there.

Anna plastered on a smile she could only hope masked the sudden nerves that threatened to make her voice shake. She glanced to Mark, hoping he would take the lead, despite what they had planned, and realized it was no use. His naturally dark eyes had grown deeper, more unreadable in their intensity, and his attention was focused squarely on the men and women before him. He grinned, but there was a decided twitch in his jaw. He quickly pulled his hand from her back and folded his hands in front of him.

Anna let out a long breath and held her hand out to the first plate. "For our starter course we have a small plate of fresh butternut squash gnocchi in a maple sage brown butter."

From the smaller, sample-sized plates, the judges each took a small bite of the dish, chewing thoughtfully. Anna tried to intuit meaning from the slightest of gestures, but it was no use.

Mark waited until the judges moved to the next course to continue. "And for our main course, we have a maple- and mustard-glazed Atlantic salmon on a bed of baby spinach, roasted beets, butternut squash, and candied walnuts, with a maple dressing."

Anna stole a glance at Mark, wondering if they had made the right decision in going with the mustard over soy, and the butternut squash now sounded so redundant and unoriginal instead of consistent with the flavors.

She gritted her teeth. It was too late now.

"And for dessert," she smiled, gesturing to the final course, "we have a maple, apple, and cheddar tart."

The tart sat perfectly crimped and baked, its golden crust decorated with maple leaf cut-outs. The judges bit into their servings, and just as quickly finished.

All that work. All that anticipation. There was nothing more they could do but wait.

The judges nodded their goodbye, barely making eye contact, and Anna turned to Mark, sighing. "I don't think I've ever been so nervous in my life!" she admitted, watching with growing dread as the panel moved on to the next team. Her eyes fell to the food, to all their effort, and she felt a wave of sadness wash over her.

Next week Fireside's kitchen would be good enough to operate out of, and she could at least prep for the Annex while the rest of the space remained under construction. The contest was over, and there was nothing else linking her to Mark. Nothing but a handful of bittersweet memories and a secret she wasn't sure she could keep to herself much longer.

CHAPTER 25

Are your phones on, girls? Does Anna know who to call?" Rosemary darted her eyes from Grace to Jane. When neither reacted, she pressed, "Luke? Is your ringer on? Battery charged? You don't want to miss the call when Mark tries to reach you," she warned. "Oh, why doesn't anyone have a landline anymore?"

"My phone is right here," Jane said mildly, holding it up for everyone to see. "And we do have a landline. Between all of us, someone is bound to hear news soon."

Rosemary drew a shaky sigh and pressed her lips together, turning back to the television wedged into the corner of the Madisons' living room, where they had all been gathered for the past two hours. An old movie played in the background, but it would be ending soon, and it had done little to distract them. Jane exchanged a small smile with her mother, who sat on a club chair in the corner, reading a book to Sophie. The brass clock on the mantle ticked, and Jane could have sworn she saw Rosemary flinch at the subtle sound. The contest had ended at four, and Anna had said the judging round ended at five. It was nearly six now. How much longer could they deliberate?

"Well, I suppose we may as well eat," Sharon mused. No one stirred from their spots, though, and even Sharon seemed to have no interest in the pizza that had been delivered and was now growing cold on the kitchen island.

"I have to admit that I'm a little nervous." Grace twisted her engagement ring and let her hands fall in her lap. "I just hope Anna won't be too disappointed if they don't win."

Jane lowered her gaze. No one in this room knew the importance of Anna winning this contest other than her, and it was becoming increasingly difficult to pretend she wasn't worried. Main Street Books had been near closing in December when Grace came back to town; if she hadn't pushed to revive it—with Anna's help—there was no doubt it would have been cleared out by the end of last year. After everything they'd been through, it seemed a cruel twist of fate that their father's legacy was once again being threatened.

Luke would help, Jane reminded herself. He had the funds from his late father's inheritance. She knew Anna didn't want it to come to that, though. She was too proud.

Jane's phone buzzed in her hand and she jumped as the familiar song began to play. Her heart dropped into her stomach when she saw the caller display. "It's Anna," she said breathlessly.

Rosemary's eyes were sharp as she lunged across the room. Sharon, Kathleen, and even Sophie came to gather around the armchair where she sat. With a press of a button, Jane connected the call and brought her phone to her ear.

"Anna?" She listened with a thumping pulse, feeling her spirits fall as everyone stared at her, enraptured, waiting for the news. Smiling sadly, she murmured a few things to her sister and set the phone on the end table. "They didn't win."

A cry of disappointment went up in the room, but none could be more disappointed than she. Anna hadn't said if she planned to ask Luke for help with the loan, and Jane could only hope she would. There was no other choice now.

"All hope isn't lost," Rosemary said pointedly, a strange smile playing on her lips. "The night is still young after all."

Jane frowned at her. What did that mean?

"Does this mean we can't have balloons and cake tomorrow?" Sophie asked. Her chin began to quiver, and Jane had to laugh.

"Of course we can. Anna and Mark tried their best. That's what counts."

Sharon shook her head. "Working on this contest has been so good for Mark. It's almost like he's found his love of cooking again."

"That's not all he found," Rosemary added mysteriously, and Jane looked at her sharply. Rosemary tucked a strand of silvering hair into her bun and fiddled with her earring, humming a tune to herself. Jane narrowed her eyes, glancing to others for a reaction, but they were standing now, talking amongst each other, filing into the kitchen to eat.

"What did you mean by that, Rosemary?" Jane whispered, just before she crossed through the arched doorway. Luke was plating three slices of pepperoni, while Grace poured wine for the adults.

Rosemary appeared startled when she turned to her. "Mean by what, dear?"

Jane blinked. "Never mind." She stalked into the

kitchen, her heart feeling heavy. Sharon had made a good point: Working on this contest had been good for Mark and Anna. She'd seen that glow, the gleam in her sister's eyes return. It had been years since she felt a connection like that with her middle sister. Anna was usually so serious. So focused and driven. She was always pushing herself, always retreating into the kitchen. Hiding. She hated the thought of things going back to the way they were.

With a heavy heart, Jane fixed a plate for Sophie and started one for herself. She glanced at the table to make sure everyone had already taken what they needed. *Such a mom*, she could practically hear Grace tease.

Two chairs remained empty. "Rosemary?" Jane poked her head into the living room. Finding no one there, she ventured into the hall. She squinted, straining to make out what she was nearly sure was Rosemary's voice, hushed and urgent, from somewhere near the dining room.

She ventured closer to the half-open French doors, where Rosemary stood in the corner, shoulders hunched, her hand cupped over the receiver of the house phone. The hinges squeaked as Jane pushed the door open. Startled, Rosemary hurried a goodbye and ended the call, nailing Jane with a hundred-watt grin.

"I just came to tell you the pizza's almost gone, if you want to grab a slice or two." Jane studied Rosemary, who seemed to struggle with relaxing the smile that shone all the way to her eyes. "Is everything okay?"

"Never better!" Rosemary beamed and strode out of the room, back ramrod straight, feet angled ever so slightly out.

Jane lingered behind, trying to make sense of what she had overheard. She could have *sworn* she heard Rosemary saying something about rose petals and champagne...

• • •

Anna dropped her phone into her pocket and frowned. "I can't believe we didn't win."

It was the fourth time she had said it since the winner was announced—a team from Burlington, who had made an admittedly stunning maple-pecan cheesecake—but her tone was still laced with wonder at the turn of events.

Mark folded his apron loosely and set it on the work station. "Did you really think we would?"

She looked at him with big blue eyes that made his heart pull tight and gave him a half smile. "I actually thought we could."

"Me too," Mark admitted.

"Well." Anna sighed and looked around the room. The earlier undercurrent of expectation had been replaced with a weighty silence. Stations were being cleared out, and teams of weary chefs filed out of the room, posture slumped, smiles gone. "I guess there's no use sticking around."

Mark checked his watch. "It's after six. We could grab dinner in the village, if you—"

Anna's expression froze. "Oh. I'm pretty tired."

Mark nodded, trying not to let his disappointment show. It had been a long, intense day, and he should feel weary to the bone, but adrenaline still pumped hard. He felt restless and out of sorts, and it wasn't just because of the contest.

Anna smoothed her apron over her hips. Even in the flurry of the contest, she'd still managed to keep it pristine; not a drop had landed on the crisp white cotton. He watched as she slowly pulled the apron strings free, studying the pinch of her brow, the perfect slope of her profile, the full lips that he fought the urge to kiss.

"I forgot how cute you looked in that uniform."

Her eyes flashed on his. "Stop," she ordered, but the corner of her mouth twitched as she turned away.

He cleared his throat and fell into step beside her. She seemed smaller somehow, and there was an air of defeat about her he hadn't seen before. It occurred to him that winning this contest might have meant more to her than he'd suspected, more perhaps than it had meant to him.

He'd felt a strange sense of relief when the judges announced the final standing, but he knew it wouldn't last for long. A decision wasn't being forced on him—he hadn't reached the end of his excuses to strive for something beyond Hastings—but the past few weeks had only heightened his desire for something more. The idea of going back to the diner, to a sparsely furnished house and a revolving door of women, left him cold.

"You know I did promise Rosemary I'd show you a good time." He grinned.

She eyed him sidelong, her wary expression teased with a smile. "We wouldn't want to upset Rosemary..."

"Nope," he said quickly. He pushed the door open with one hand, letting her pass through, careful not to let her get too far. "Besides, this is the last day you're stuck with me. I sort of feel like you owe me a drink."

She stopped walking and arched a brow. "You did let me use your kitchen."

There was amusement in her eyes, but he'd suddenly lost the desire for banter. His gaze lingered on her face as he jammed his hands into his pockets. "I guess you could say I'm gonna miss having you around."

She looked skeptical, but dare he say, pleased. "Really."

"What's going to happen after tomorrow, Anna?" he asked.

"We're going to go back to Briar Creek," she replied. "Everything will resume like normal."

"See, that's what I'm afraid of. I don't want things to go back to the way they've been." She didn't blink as her eyes locked his. "One drink. For old time's sake. Give me one more chance to show you I'm not as bad as you think I am."

"Well." She paused and reached up to pull her hair free, shaking it out as it fell around her shoulders, and he swallowed hard, waiting for her response but knowing that regardless of what she said, he wasn't going to take no for an answer this time. He'd gotten used to her presence, to the way he felt when he was around her, and he didn't want to let that feeling go. "I guess one drink wouldn't hurt."

"Hey, you might just decide you like me again and stay for two." He winked, but her gaze turned steely.

"Don't push your luck. I'm still mad at you, you know."

"Come on, now. You can't stay mad at me forever," he countered.

She tipped her head. "I could try."

"But how much fun would that be?" he asked, and the smile that teased her mouth told him she knew the answer to that question as well as he.

"You're not going to back down, are you?"

He grinned. "Nope."

She sighed—a soft, sweet sound that made his blood heat. "One drink. Not two."

"Meet you in the lobby in half an hour then," Mark said, strolling to the elevator bank. "I'm going to show you a good time. Remember, Rosemary's counting on it."

And he was, too.

• • •

What would happen if tonight was another disaster? He couldn't think about going back to a life without Anna in it, knowing she hated him, knowing he had let her down. Refusing to think that way, he called Kara and checked in on the diner.

"It's a well-oiled machine," she informed him. "Vince knows the menu. The regulars know what they want. Don't hurry back on our account."

Oh, he didn't intend to. Disappointment lingered like a heavy stone in his chest when he thought of going back to Briar Creek in the morning, returning to the unsatisfying routine, while around him people were moving on with their lives, growing a future, planning for the next phase. He'd come back after culinary school to take care of his mother, then he'd stayed for Luke. He'd had a purpose, and now there was none. His mouth firmed when he pictured himself back behind the greasy counter, pouring coffee, chatting about town gossip. Slinging hash. Without the money from the contest, his hopes for something bigger remained on hold. It depressed the hell out of him. Anna had been a bright spot in his kitchen these past few weeks— a distraction from his surroundings. Now, there would be no silver lining. Unless he created one for himself.

A light rain had started to fall, spattering against the window of his room. The sun was still visible on its decent just between two craggy mountain peaks, but the clouds rolling in were thick and dark. Mark grabbed the sport coat he'd worn to the cocktail party last night and shrugged it on.

Minutes later, he entered the lobby, his blood pumping a little harder when he saw Anna standing near the windows, an umbrella in her hand. She was wearing a simple skirt that grazed her knees, revealing smooth, slender legs and a T-shirt that clung to her waist, defining the curve of her breasts. She was the most beautiful girl in the room— he didn't care to look around. When he was with Anna, he didn't need to search for a distraction, or someone to fill that empty space.

"Shall we?" he asked, crooking his arm. She hesitated, frowning slightly, then slipped her hand through.

They walked in silence under the umbrella, and he purposefully took the long way into the village, liking the feel of her warm body next to his, the soft, sweet smell of her shampoo that clung to her damp hair. They stopped to scan the menus of restaurants they passed, pointing out innovative dishes as they always had back in school. It was a little game of theirs when they went out to eat; they never ate the same meal twice, and they always chose the boldest item on the menu. "It's how you learn," Anna would say with that little smile. She'd challenged him—not just to learn, but to love. She'd opened his mind, made him want to experience everything, made him believe in the power of possibility. He hadn't just closed his heart to her that day he pushed her away. He'd closed himself off from everything.

"What about this French place?" Anna asked, stopping outside the restaurant whose name Mark remembered seeing on Cassie's card. The card that was still wedged deep inside his pocket.

"How about the bistro across the way?" he suggested instead, gesturing to a brick place with sidewalk tables and flower boxes.

Their meals arrived just as the rain stopped. The evening crowd began to fill the sidewalk; chefs Mark recognized from the contest strolled down the road, stopping to peruse menus, just as he and Anna had done. He watched as the French place across the street filled, and reached for his beer.

Anna took a small bite of food and gave him a knowing smile. "Not bad."

Mark bit into his burger. It was overcooked and lacking seasoning, and as much as he hated to admit it, Hastings scored better. Guess he was doing something right after all. Or maybe the credit went to Vince, the line cook.

"I don't have much of an appetite," she said, leaning back.

"Still disappointed over not winning?" he asked, dousing his fries with salt. "You never could eat when you were upset."

Anna's face paled. Her eyes went dark before she blinked quickly and shifted in her seat. "What do you mean by that?"

He crammed some fries into his mouth, watching as she rearranged the silverware on the table, shielding her face from him. "Oh, I just remember you saying before a big exam how you were too nervous to eat. I used to joke that it was ironic for a chef not to have an appetite. Don't you remember?"

She let out a long breath, seeming to withdraw into herself. "I guess I don't."

He took a swig of his beer, hating the disappointment that tugged at his chest. He'd hoped tonight would change things between them going forward. He'd clung to the good times, but maybe she was still thinking of the bad. "Is something wrong?"

The Anna he knew would shake her head, tell him of course not, hide behind that wall she'd built around herself. He knew, because he'd done the same.

"Something is wrong," he insisted, when she said nothing. He set down his glass, sighing heavily. "Is it last night? I told you, Anna, Cassie was just there—"

She shook her head firmly, squeezing her eyes shut. "It's not last night. It's . . . something else."

"What is it? The contest? The loan? You know Luke will help—"

"No. No, it's not that." She hesitated, and Mark set down his burger.

"Anna. What is it?"

Slowly, she turned to him, her blue eyes glistening with tears. She looked younger somehow, like the girl he had chased through the tide that summer on the Cape and later taken to bed in that little one-room apartment she'd rented through August. The girl who would curl against his chest and giggle into his ear, and make him believe that life could be oh so much more than it ever turned out to be. He reached and took her hand in his. Her fingers were cold, and he frowned, gripping them tighter. He sensed her stiffen, as if she were battling with herself over whether to pull back and push him away the way he had done to her all those years ago. He wouldn't blame her.

"I have something to tell you, Mark," she said softly, meeting his eye. "Something I've kept to myself for a very long time."

CHAPTER
26

"Mind if we go for a walk?"

Mark nodded and signaled for their waitress. He settled the bill quickly, brushing off Anna's attempts to pay for her share, and stood, understanding now what Anna meant when she said she couldn't eat when she was upset. Weeks, if not years, had built up to whatever she was about to say to him, and he had a bad feeling it went beyond the way he'd broken her heart. Anna walked slowly, her face pensive, carefully stepping over puddles. She motioned to a wrought iron bench tucked beneath the awning of a flower shop that had already closed for the day. "Let's sit here."

He noticed she was trembling as she brushed water from the seat and sat down. He sat beside her, tenting his elbows on his knees, watching as she pulled in a deep breath and let it out slowly.

"I've been thinking about last night," she started. "Seeing you with Cassie...it upset me, but not for the reasons you think. After you broke up with me, I was...crushed."

She glanced at him, her big blue eyes searching his, and shame tore through him, gripping him square in the chest. "I thought we had a plan. I thought you would graduate and work somewhere near the college, and then I would graduate a year later, and we'd finally open our restaurant. I pictured us in the kitchen, cooking side by side, just like—"

"Just like these past few weeks?" He tipped his head at her, catching her sad smile. "Yeah, I thought that, too." Then he had to go and ruin it.

"Something I thought I read more into than there ever was. It's not like you ever told me you loved me or anything."

He gritted his teeth. He had only said it when she couldn't hear, when he could take it all back and pretend the words had never slipped. He'd loved his father after all, and that hadn't stopped him from disappearing without so much as a glance back. They were just words. Three stupid words. But damn it if he didn't feel them every time he looked at her, every time he saw that smile, heard that laugh, saw those beautiful blue eyes light up.

"It was real."

"I think the hardest part for me about everything was losing your friendship. That feeling that I could always count on you and that it didn't matter which girl you were flirting with because you were always there for me." Her voice was so small, nearly lost in the breeze that tore down the street. "Then we dated and . . . I became one of them."

He looked at her sharply. "You were different."

Her hair rustled in the wind, and she tucked it behind her ear, gripping her hands in her lap. "I felt like I could tell you anything, you know? Like what we had was solid. Special."

Guilt stirred his stomach. She'd been honest with him, open and willing, while he'd had a wall up all along. She hadn't stood a chance. He hadn't given her one.

"After... after things ended, I didn't know who to turn to anymore. Who to share all those little parts of my day with. My sisters were busy with their own lives. You were the person I knew best at school. When you were gone, there was no one left, no one to tell..."

"Tell what?"

Tears shone in her eyes, and she blinked quickly. "I'm sorry, Mark." Her chin began to tremble as the tears fell down her cheeks, and she clasped her hand to her mouth to stifle a sob.

Mark's gut tightened. "What are you trying to tell me?"

Her eyes locked with his, big and bright and searching, and he felt the air stall in his lungs. He wanted to freeze this moment, capture it forever, because something told him that in the next second, everything between them was about to change.

"I was pregnant, Mark."

Was pregnant. *Was.* The word punched him in the gut, stealing his air. He almost didn't trust himself to speak. "What do you mean?"

She shook her head, running a shaking hand over her face. "I was pregnant with your—our—child."

He closed his eyes, waiting for his pulse to slow, but his mind wouldn't turn off. Anna had been pregnant. What had happened to the baby?

Anna dragged in a breath and shifted on the seat, hunching forward, eyes focused on the gravel under her feet. The tears continued to fall, steadily tracing their way down her cheeks, dripping off the edge of her nose.

His thoughts reeled. "When?"

"The day I saw you with Cassie. The day you dumped me." Mark winced on the word. It was appropriate, even if he didn't want to hear it. "I was coming to tell you."

"And you didn't get the chance." He ground his teeth, exhaling slowly, wishing he could turn back time and recapture that moment. She'd looked so eager as she'd come around the corner, a hesitant but hopeful smile curving her lips as they locked eyes. She'd raised her hand to wave, halting when she saw Cassie. He wanted to call out to her, but instead he'd planted himself to the ground, forcing his eyes back to Cassie, seeing his chance to get out, to put an end to anxiety that had been gnawing at him all summer, always there, a shadow on their time together. It was callous, cold, downright cruel in retrospect to flirt with Cassie in front of her like that, but it was the easiest way to ensure that Anna didn't fight for them, that she didn't give him a reason to continue on, even though he wished he could. God, he wished she could.

"You took me to that coffee shop, and I knew you were going to break up with me. It didn't make sense to tell you then, so . . . I just went home."

He remembered the tears in her eyes, the way he had to clench a fist under the table to keep from reaching out and wiping away the tears that fell. He'd tried to downplay it, tried to tell her she'd move on, find someone else, that he wasn't the guy for her, not in the long run. She'd barely said a word. From that day on, she fell silent.

And all this time, all these years, she had kept this to herself. Their child. He never knew.

"What happened?"

She turned over her palms. "I had a miscarriage."

Relief coursed through him, quickly replaced with a wash of sadness. "I didn't know if—"

She turned to him sharply. "I couldn't do that. I mean, I considered it, but no. I...loved that baby. Just like...I loved you."

Mark ran a hand over his mouth, hating himself.

"That night, I came home and took a second test, just to see if the first one had been an error. I waited, and I hoped and I prayed and I cried that it would negative. Some horrible mistake." She shook her head. "I knew I should tell you, but I didn't know how. You rejected me, Mark. I couldn't stand the thought of you rejecting the baby too."

That was the man she saw him as, and maybe it was even the kind of man he was, but it sure as hell wasn't the man he wanted to be. That was his father. Not him. "I would *never* turn my back on my child," Mark nearly spat.

Anna's eyes snapped in surprise and she shifted backward, flinching. "I was afraid of this. You're mad."

"Mad?" He knew anger. He knew disappointment. This was something altogether different. Grief, he realized, for a child he'd never known, for a life he'd thrown away. For a person he'd let down when she needed him the most.

An image of his mother, lying in that bed, with his father nowhere in sight, flashed bold and bright. He closed his eyes tight, just for a second. Just until it was gone.

He reached out and took her hand, giving her a reassuring smile when she gave him a hesitant glance. "I'm not mad."

She looked skeptical. "I should have told you. I kept thinking there was time. I'd figure out a way. Then it was too late."

He pictured her alone, leaving as she did that day from the coffee shop, her shoulders drooped, tears welling in her big blue eyes, knowing all the time that she was carrying his child.

"I wish you had told me," he said, and her frown deepened. He gave her fingers a squeeze, leaned in to brush a tear from her cheek. "I wish I could have been there for you. I'm here now, Anna."

Anna tried to blink back the tears but they flowed freely, down her cheeks, salting her lips and blinding her vision. She hadn't let herself cry since the night that she'd lost the baby.

"I wish I could have been there for you," Mark said. "I wish..."

I wish, I wish. How many times had she said the same thing to herself? How many times did she replay those two weeks after she discovered she was pregnant? The worry that plagued her as she went over it again and again, wondering what to do. So many times she thought to tell him, but all it took was another sighting of him with Cassie to send her running back to her dorm, putting it off for another day. She forced herself to eat, but she stopped sleeping. She started spending more and more time in the kitchen, working long into the night, testing recipes, honing her skills. She dropped off the food at the local soup kitchen; there was no way she could stomach it herself. She was sick nearly every morning, and it lingered into the afternoon. She knew she should call someone—one of her sisters, her parents, her friends—but they would tell Mark, and he was gone.

And just like that the baby was, too.

"I feel so guilty," she whispered, the words escaping her in a rush. There. It was out.

"*You* feel guilty?" Mark leaned in, brushing another tear from her cheek with the pad of his thumb, pushing the hair from her face, trying to get her to look him in the eye. She couldn't. Not after what she'd done. "Anna, I failed you—"

"*No.*" She turned to him sharply. "I failed. I failed our baby. I didn't take care of myself. I didn't eat or sleep..."

Understanding flattened his eyes. He jutted his lower lip, nodding sadly. "Because you were upset. Because of me."

She could neither confirm or deny it. She'd been upset, scared to the bone. They had a plan—a plan to graduate and open a restaurant. A breakup had never been part of that plan. Neither had a baby.

"I'm sorry, Mark."

"No." His voice was insistent, but gentle. She stiffened as he leaned in closer, clasping his other hand around hers. "I'm sorry, Anna. For everything. I ran; I shut you out. All my life, I've lived with what my father did to me. I thought I could prevent it, protect myself from that type of pain by never getting close and ending things before they could even begin. I was wrong."

He was telling her what she wanted to hear, but she knew he meant every word. Her chest ached for the two people they once were. For a friendship that had been made and lost. For laughter that had turned to years of silence.

"It wasn't your fault you lost the baby," he insisted, but she shook her head, unable to shed the weight she'd carried for so long. "I'm sorry, Anna. I'm so sorry."

Ever so lightly, his lips were on her cheeks, kissing the wet stains of her tears. He released her hands, wrapping his hands around her waist, pulling her close to the hard wall of his chest. She wanted to resist him, to push him, to beat on his chest for what he'd done to her, the horrible, awful position he'd left her in, but the fight was gone. The walls had come down, and everything she'd been holding inside her all this time was finally released.

She curled into his chest, letting the heat of his body envelop her. He stroked her hair, whispering into her ear, saying the words she'd longed to hear—words she hadn't thought she ever would. Not from him. Not after this.

His lips skimmed hers softly, and she parted her mouth, lacing her tongue with his, finding warmth in his touch. He kissed her slowly, stroking her face, and held her close when they finally broke free.

"You're cold. Let's go inside." He took his hand as they stood, leading her the short distance back to the hotel in silence. It was Saturday night, and Cedar Valley Village was alive and bustling; couples walked hand in hand in search of a romantic restaurant, and a few teams of chefs she recognized from the contest strolled down the path. The hotel was lit with glittering lights: a beacon against the stark, dark mountain range towering above them. Inside, the hotel lobby was quiet and relaxed, and they retraced their steps to the elevator. Anna pressed the button for her floor, and Mark made no signs of doing the same for his.

They'd learned to communicate without words, and she was grateful for the understanding. She wasn't ready to be alone right now. Too many thoughts and memories had come to the surface. She'd tried to distance herself from them, but now there was nowhere to hide. The only person who could understand, the only one who stood a chance at making any of it better, was at her side.

Anna slid her keycard in her door and flicked on the

light. An audible gasp released from her lips when she took in the sight.

The king-sized bed she'd slept in last night had been made, but covering its crisp white duvet were dozens upon dozens of red rose petals. On the table near the window, where the damask curtains had been drawn for privacy, was a silver-plated bucket containing what appeared to be a bottle of champagne. The expensive kind. Next to it was a platter of strawberries, and two crystal flutes, at the base of which sat a single long-stemmed rose.

Anna froze, her eyes darting from one object to the next. They were in the wrong room. But no—wait. They weren't. There was that silly bottle of massage oil on the nightstand— she could have sworn she'd set it on the bathroom counter after she'd fished it from her handbag yesterday...

Rosemary.

"It wasn't me!" she blurted, whirling around to Mark, who stood behind her, his hand still on the doorknob, his jaw slack.

Mark frowned and stepped deeper into the room. He picked up a rose petal, studying it with curiosity, and let it fall. It danced through the air before quietly drifting back in place.

Anna marched to the table, lifting the lid on a metal pot. Chocolate fondue. She thought she'd smelled something!

Her pulse began to hammer, and her face flamed with heat. She blinked, looking around the room in dismay, until she spotted Mark out of the corner of her eye. He was laughing.

"They must have made a mistake! They must have sent it to the wrong room."

"Or someone sent it up..." Mark grinned.

Her face fell. "You didn't—"

"No," he replied, and the heat in her cheeks rose a degree. "But since it's here . . . we may as well enjoy it."

"Oh." She looked at the champagne, wondering if she should uncork it or let him do the honors, but when she turned back to ask, the look in his eye told her he wasn't talking about the chocolate-covered strawberries. No, he was thinking of that ridiculous bowl of condoms basking in the glow of the bedside lamp.

He closed the distance between them, setting his hands on her waist, blinking as he leaned into her, pulling her close against the hard wall of his chest. She breathed in his scent, the familiar strength of his body, as he kissed her neck, circling his tongue on her earlobe, tracing his finger down the arch of her neck.

Her body warmed quickly with the heat of his, and she waited with growing need for his lips to move to her mouth. She craned her neck, inhaling the musk of his skin, until his lips again found her earlobe and he began nibbling, softly at first and then slightly harder, letting his teeth take hold of her soft flesh. His cheek brushed hers as his mouth moved to hers, and his hands slid over her hips, and lower. She sighed into him as his tongue probed deeper, sending a rush of heat coursing through her.

Without breaking their kiss, he moved her toward the bed, lowering himself on top of her. She arched her back as he slid her shirt over her head, bending to trace the curve of her neck with kisses, sending a ripple of pleasure down her spine. He breathed into her ear, nipping at her lobe, and she raked her hand through his hair, feeling the heavy weight of his body on hers, reaching under his shirt to feel the warmth of his smooth skin.

Mark slowly pulled the straps of her bra down her bare shoulders and unhooked the clasp, teasing her with his mouth, as his fingers skimmed the top of her panty line. He traced his mouth down her stomach, as he slid her skirt down her legs and shed his clothes.

She splayed her fingers over the span of his sculpted shoulders, down the curve of his biceps to the smooth plank of his chest. His skin was hot and smooth under her touch, and she held her breath as she waited for him to lower himself to her, needing to feel the strength of his body against her own.

Grazing his hands over her hips, Mark parted her legs, hovering close above her as he kissed her slowly, and then entered her with a slow thrust. She broke their kiss, gasping into his ear as he buried his face in her hair, and moved her hips to match his rhythm, enjoying the swell of him inside her.

As she reached her release, Mark muffled her cries with his mouth before lifting his head and emitting a long, low moan as he thrust once more deeply inside her. He fell heavily onto her chest and Anna lay on her back, enjoying the weight of his body on hers.

She smiled into his hair as he wrapped his arms tighter around her, feeling the burden of the past finally fade away. She stroked his back, marveling at how natural it felt to be with him again, and pushed aside the pain of their past. She'd clung to it for too many years, and for just one night, she would enjoy the present.

CHAPTER 27

The road into Briar Creek was wet, and the wipers were on high, but inside the car it was warm and dry. Anna wished it could stay like this for just a little while longer, sheltered from reality and all its implications. This weekend, like their time at school, had been just theirs—separate from their families and their regular lives.

She reached across the divider and stroked Mark's arm. It was hard to believe that less than two hours ago, they'd been curled up in bed together, his arm draped over her waist, holding her close. "Maybe you should turn the car around."

He grinned and cocked that devilish eyebrow. "You want me to? Because you know I will."

It was tempting to think of climbing back under the covers, with Mark's warm body beside hers, but she supposed she couldn't hide forever. Neither of them could. "Everyone's waiting for us. Besides, if we stay away much longer they might start to suspect something."

"Wouldn't my aunt just love that." Mark looked over at

her, chuckling. "Although, something tells me her plan for this weekend involved more than us winning."

Anna spared a wry grin, but the hard knot of dread grew tighter as they crossed the town line. "It would have been nice to win," she said wistfully.

"You had a lot riding on this," Mark commented, bringing his eyes back to the road.

"Too much." Anna felt her spirits fall. "I guess I have to come clean with Grace now."

"She's your sister; I'm sure she'll understand. The fire was a major setback."

"That doesn't matter. I told her I had everything covered. She'll know I wasn't being truthful." Anna set her head back on the seat. "That's not the only thing that I'm upset about, though. I had another plan for the money, too."

"Oh?"

"You know how Shea O'Riley moved her stationery store over to Chestnut Street?"

Mark nodded. "Yeah, my mom told me they broke the lease."

"I couldn't help thinking it would be great to expand into that space."

Mark's brow grew to a point, but he gave no other reaction. "That makes a lot of sense. Fireside has always been a success."

"The timing is bad. The same event that granted the opportunity to take over that space also made it impossible. The only way I could have expanded was if the loan was covered. Now I can't even pay it off..." Anna shrugged, looking down at her hands. There was no use dwelling on what might have been. She'd always lived by that motto.

"Maybe you can talk to my mom, see if she'll work something out—"

"No." Anna shook her head firmly, angry at herself for feeding into this pipe dream. Now wasn't the time to be thinking of growing her business. She had to get it up and running again first. "I wouldn't want to take advantage, and even if I worked something out with the lease, the construction costs would be too much. A bank isn't going to give me a second loan without any revenue coming in."

Mark ran a hand over his chin; Anna could hear the faint scratch of his stubble, and her pulse kicked with the reminder of how it felt to be close to him again last night, the way his cheek brushed with hers when he leaned down to kiss her ear, her neck... A tingle swept down her spine.

"True," Mark said. "If we'd won the contest, you could have freed yourself from the current loan."

"Even then, there's no guarantee I'd qualify for another. Your mom said the kitchen should be in partial working order by tomorrow, but the rest of the café won't be ready for at least another four weeks, and a bank wouldn't be able to overlook that revenue loss." She straightened in her seat as they approached Main Street. They'd been gone for only two days, but somehow it looked different now, driving back into town. The awnings on the shops popped with hues of blue, red, and pink. Cheerful tulips burst from planters at the base of lampposts, and the white gazebo in the town square was a crisp contrast to the vibrant green lawn.

"Home, sweet home," she mused, leaning forward to gaze out the window. "As nice as it was to get away, it's always nice to be back." She glanced at Mark, waiting for him to agree, but his eyes were fixed on the road, his jaw set.

He dropped her off at Main Street Books, as she asked,

and gave her a slow, lingering kiss before she finally tore herself away, hoping Grace wasn't seeing everything through the window.

Grace was behind the counter when she pushed through the door a few minutes later, seemingly unaware of the no doubt titillating event that had just occurred outside the shop. Anna had no doubt that her sister would have practically fallen over in shock if she had caught them. Instead, Grace gave a huge smile as she came around to greet her, arms wide.

Anna held up a hand, hating the way Grace's face fell. "Before you hug me or congratulate me, there's something I need to tell you."

Grace's green eyes searched hers. "Uh-oh. I don't like the sound of this." She motioned to a set of chenille armchairs in the back corner of the room, where they wouldn't be interrupted. The store was quiet for now, but a customer could enter at any time. Traffic was steady these days for both book sales and the café. It made this conversation ever harder to have. Their plans to transform the place had worked; now she had to go and ruin it.

Anna drew a shaky breath. Her heart was practically beating out of her chest from nerves. "After the fire you asked me about the loan."

Grace nodded. "You said you had savings."

Here it goes. "I said that because I didn't want to worry you. Any of you."

Silence stretched as the implication of her words fell over the room. Grace frowned in confusion. "You . . . you mean you don't have the savings?"

"No." Anna closed her eyes. There. It was out. "The loan covered most of the expansion, but I sunk in a fair share of my personal money, too. It all would have been fine if the fire hadn't happened."

"I can't believe you didn't tell me," Grace cried. The words were spoken more in disbelief than anger, but somehow the effect was worse. "You knew that Luke offered to help. This place meant a lot to him."

It did, and not just because of the bond between their father and Luke, but also because of Luke's late wife, Helen. He gave up her storefront next to the bookstore so that Grace and Anna could build the Annex.

Anna shrugged. Grace made it all sound simple. "I thought I could handle it. On my own."

"You're good at that," Grace commented with a rueful grin.

"You mean, you're not mad?"

Grace gave her a sad smile. "Not mad. I'm just... *disappointed* that you didn't think you could come to me. I'm your older sister. I know I was gone for a few years, but I'm here now. You can turn to me."

"I've been used to doing things on my own, to fighting my own battles." Anna gave her a pleading look. "I don't want to do that anymore."

Grace smiled. "Good, because it's a lot more fun when we can tell each other things. I was waiting until after the contest to share some news of my own, actually. I didn't want to overshadow the excitement, but you know that book I started over Christmas? I sold it."

"Grace! That's wonderful."

"And with the advance, I can cover the monthly loan payments until Fireside reopens."

Anna couldn't hide her relief, and for once, she was happy to accept some help. "You know I'll repay you once—"

Grace regarded her quizzically. "Repay me? We're a team in this. This is our family's shop. You know that bring-your-own-wine night you suggested? It's a hit. I have you to thank for that...and for everything. I couldn't have reopened the bookstore without your help. Now I'm just returning the favor." She smiled. "I guess I shouldn't have held off telling you about the book sale. I didn't want to look callous, with everything you've been going through these past few weeks, and I had just gotten engaged, too. Now I know it might have alleviated a big source of stress."

"From now on, we tell each other everything," Anna said, feeling her pulse skip when she thought of all that meant.

Grace's eyes lit up. "Luke and I set a date for the fall."

"You did!" Anna smiled her first real smile in days. The joy in Grace's face was contagious.

"I already have my eye on a dress, and we're discussing honeymoon locations. I was just wondering, if it isn't too much, if you would—"

"Cater? You know I will."

Grace's expression faltered. "Actually, I had something else in mind. I was hoping you'd be my maid of honor."

Anna couldn't hide her shock. "Me?" She'd thought for sure Grace would pick her friend Ivy, or Jane—though further apart in age, they'd always been so close.

"I know we've drifted in and out of each other's lives over the years, but rebuilding this shop with you has really made me feel like we've been given a second chance. This was Dad's dream, and mine, too, and you've made it come true." She smiled, and Anna swallowed the lump in her throat. "I may be the older sister, but...I really admire you,

Anna. I always have. You're so strong, so capable. Nothing knocks you down. You were there when I needed you the most. You have no idea how much that means to me."

"Oh, Grace," Anna sighed. "Of course I'll do it. I'm honored. Touched. But...there's something else. I need you, too, Grace."

Grace reached out and took her hand, and slowly, starting at the very beginning, that first, glorious day when Mark strode up to her in Chef Luciano's class, giving her that lopsided grin that made her heart flip-flop, Anna told her everything.

Mark took an ice-cold beer from the fridge and cracked the top. Taking a long swig, he caught Rosemary's disapproving frown across the room.

"It isn't five yet," she pointed out, pinching her lips tight.

Mark settled into a chair, grinning as Scout leapt onto his lap. He'd missed him these past two days, the way he hadn't dared to let himself miss anyone else since his dad left—except maybe Anna.

"That dog is too big to be jumping all over people. Do you have him in training?" Rosemary asked. "Of course not," she continued, under her breath, but audible enough for Sharon and Luke to exchange a glance.

"He's still a pup, Aunt Rosemary. He's only ten months old." He scratched Scout playfully behind the ears.

"Well," she huffed, shifting her eyes from Scout to the beer and then to her hands, which were folded tightly in her lap. "You haven't finished telling us about the weekend."

Mark shrugged. "Not much to tell. I've already told you about the winning recipe."

"Other than the contest, did anything...*special* happen?"

Mark stroked Scout's fur and took another sip of his drink, thinking back on this morning, waking up with Anna in his arms. "Nope. Not really."

Rosemary's brow flinched at his reply, and Mark felt his lip begin to twitch. *Aha.* He'd thought Rosemary was up to something the morning he picked Anna up for the drive to Cedar Valley, and last night's little honeymoon suite re-creation had only confirmed his hunch. Now, seeing Rosemary flustered and upset, shifting this way and that in her chair, trying to keep the exasperation out of her breath and the impatience out of each probing question, he wanted to burst out laughing.

"Although, come to think of it, something did happen last night...," he said slowly, taking the opportunity to run his hand over his mouth, fighting off a smile.

"Oh?" Rosemary perked up on her chair.

"It was the darndest thing. Someone mistook Anna's room for the honeymoon suite." Luke and Sharon laughed at this—a silly mistake, surely—but Rosemary's cheeks grew pink, and there was a decidedly pleased turn to her ruby-painted lips.

She darted her gaze to the left, taking sudden interest in the view out the window. "Is that so? How odd."

"Odd indeed," Mark mused. She glanced at him, and he held her eyes, waiting to see if she would let anything slip or ask what he was doing in Anna's room, but she simply stood and grabbed her handbag.

"Well, we should be going. Sharon. Luke? Mark's probably tired."

Luke looked lazily to his mother from his vantage point on the couch. "I think I'll stick around."

"We'll let you guys chat." Sharon gave Mark a warm

smile as he walked her to the door. Turning to him as she lifted her handbag from a hook, his mother said, "I know you didn't win, but I'm proud of you. You're an amazing chef, Mark. Don't lose sight of that again." She gave him a quick kiss and left, calling after Rosemary, who seemed hell-bent on fleeing the premises now that she sensed Mark was onto her.

Mark frowned as he closed the door. Was it so obvious that he wasn't living up to his potential? That he'd fallen into a rut, lost his passion? Just the thought of going back to Hastings tomorrow morning filled him with dread. Sure, it would be nice to see the familiar faces, chat about the weekend events, but by Tuesday or Wednesday the novelty of the gossip would fade, and he'd be right back where he had been for the past seven long years: standing behind that greasy counter. Alone.

"Thanks again for watching Scout," Mark said, dropping into his chair.

Luke looked fondly at the dog, now wedged between Mark's leg and the arm of the sofa. "He makes good company. Sure beats living alone."

Mark grew quiet. Sure did.

"Everything okay?" Luke asked.

"Of course," Mark said, reaching for the beer once more. He groaned, thinking of the day ahead. "I should probably swing by the diner, give Kara a much-needed break."

Luke nodded, standing. "I'll come with you if you don't mind. From what I know, though, she seems to be really enjoying working there."

Guess that makes one of us, Mark thought grimly. He set down his half-finished beer and grabbed his keys. The urge to call Anna burned deep, but he knew she was with her sister now, discussing the fate of their shop. He supposed he should feel grateful for the fact that he still had a family business, but right now, all he could think about was the stash of notes and recipes, left to collect dust.

Luke waited until they were in the car to say, "So... tell me to shut up if you want, but how exactly did you know that Anna's hotel room was given the honeymoon suite treatment?"

Mark glanced at his cousin. There was no getting out of this one. "You might find this hard to believe but... Anna and I have a bit of history."

Luke grinned. "Interesting."

"I'm glad you find this so funny," Mark commented.

"Not funny," Luke said. "Just... not surprising."

Mark frowned. "Not surprising?" He stared at his cousin, who could only shrug. "This is me we're talking about, Luke. You know I don't... commit."

"You date girls you know you would never have serious feelings for. You say over and over that you're a confirmed bachelor, like you're trying to convince yourself."

"So? What's your point?"

"My point is that there's only one girl in this whole damn town you've shown any sort of emotional reaction to and that's Anna."

"Yes, but before the fire we hadn't spoken to each other in years."

"You know what they say," Luke said with a shrug. "Silence speaks volumes."

CHAPTER 28

"Glad you're back, Mark!"

Wish I could say the same. Mark refilled Arnie's coffee mug and slid him a bowl of creamers. The Monday morning crowd was thin; people were back at work, and aside from the handful of retired widowers who lined the counter seven days a week, there was no one else to talk to.

Mark gazed out the window, looking for a hint of long legs and honey blond hair. He muttered to himself, shaking his head. Of course he wouldn't see her. She was at Fireside. In her own kitchen, prepping for the Annex. He should be happy for her.

Mark stripped off his apron and ducked into his office. He'd hated coming back here this morning, feeling that black hole of dread, the endless tunnel of more days spent like this. The notes he'd scribbled over the years were tucked in a folder in the top drawer of his desk. He took them out now, pausing just long enough to consider his folly, and slammed them in the trash. He cursed under his breath and flicked off the light. Coming back into the dining room, he settled Arnie's bill and waited for Kara to start her shift. She arrived five minutes early, fresh faced and perky. Last night she'd spent nearly an hour regaling them with stories from the weekend, chuckling about Arnie's insistence that the hash wasn't the same without him, even though he rarely cooked the stuff himself. Mark had tried not to curl his lip, tried not to think of the way it might have been if he hadn't come back here. If his mom hadn't gotten sick. If his dad hadn't left. If he'd never broken up with Anna.

But then what about Hastings? What would have happened to it if he'd been off with Anna and his mom had gotten sick? His gut twisted on the thought, reminding him of everything that could go wrong, all the reasons he had for ending things with her when he did. Doubt kept him awake last night, bringing him down that dark road he'd tried to forget. He had to tread carefully.

"Beautiful day today," Kara said brightly, tossing her dark brown ponytail off her shoulder.

Mark shrugged. He supposed. He poked his head through the service window to his cook, who was standing at the griddle. "Hey Vince, I'm heading out for the day."

"See ya," Kara grinned, stepping out onto the floor to take orders from a family that had just sat down near the window. Mark watched the family with passive interest— a young couple and a newborn baby, nestled in a carrier, the blanket pulled up to its chin, despite the warm spring sun.

He tore his eye from the scene, but his heart began to pound when he saw a woman standing hesitantly in the doorway.

"Cassie. What are you doing here?"

"You said you worked at a family place," Cassie replied, giving him a slow smile. "It was pretty easy to find the address for Hastings. The one and only."

Mark set his jaw, feeling exposed and tense, thinking of the hurt in Anna's eyes the night of the cocktail party. "Come back to my office," he said, leading her through the diner.

He wound Cassie through the kitchen, wincing as a basket of fries went into the oil, sizzling and filling the room with the smell of grease, and ushered her into his closet of an office. "It's not as fancy as what you're used to," he said, realizing the person he was apologizing to was himself.

"It's charming," Cassie said, sitting on the edge of the vinyl chair.

Mark sat opposite her, at the desk, and quickly began shoving papers to the side. He leaned forward, into his elbows. "So, to what do I owe the visit?"

"I'll get right to it. I'm opening my own restaurant, and I want you to be my executive chef."

Mark stared at her. "Me?"

"I saw your contest entry, and I was impressed. You know me...I was always more interested in managing the front of the house, interacting with customers and handling the business end. I loved those management courses."

"I couldn't stand those classes. I just wanted to get back to the kitchen."

It was in his blood. He couldn't deny it. No matter how much he tried to turn his back on cooking, on his dream—on Anna—he still wanted it, after all these years.

Cassie grinned. "Exactly my point. We'd make a pretty good team, Mark."

He frowned at that, breaking her stare. Was he really

considering this? Up until a few weeks ago, he was ready to get out of Briar Creek and focus on a new venture, but that was before Anna had come back into his life.

"You've caught me by surprise," he finally said.

Cassie held up a hand. "Of course. I should have called first, but I have a meeting with my business attorney in Forest Ridge in an hour so I thought I'd stop in." She tipped her head, sensing his hesitation. "Why don't we meet for dinner and discuss it further?"

From behind the door, he heard Vince calling out orders: "Cheeseburger and fries, hold the pickles. Eggs, scrambled. Hash browns, extra crispy." He winced. Could he really turn down this opportunity? But could he really stay in this dive? Up until now, he'd failed himself as much as his father had—he'd hidden behind his fear, turned his back on change and growth. Turned his back on the things he'd loved most.

"I'm staying in the area tonight," Cassie said. "How about seven thirty at that cute little place across the town square?"

Piccolino's, Mark thought bitterly. "Sure," he said, standing. It was just dinner. Just a meeting. He didn't have to say yes. He didn't have to say no, either.

He waited for her to go and then grabbed his keys, exiting out the back door, his chest pounding.

He gripped the steering wheel with both hands as he drove through town, slowing as he passed Fireside and then Main Street Books a few blocks down. His heart picked up speed when the door of the bookstore opened, but it was only Grace, popping out to water the flowers. Spotting him, she smiled, waving with the hand that wasn't holding the watering can.

Mark forced a smile in return and pushed down on the accelerator.

A real kitchen. Respect. A chance to do what he always wanted to do.

Making a detour at the light, he headed down the winding, tree-lined roads and pulled to a stop outside the gray Colonial where he had spent the first eighteen years of his life. He could still remember sitting on the floor near that front window, looking down the street for his dad's car, searching as night fell for the headlights, for the purr of the garage door being opened, and the sounds of that booming voice saying hello.

He slammed the door shut and jammed his hands in his pocket as he traced the brick path to the front door. He knocked twice before entering. "Mom?"

"Mark? Back here!"

He followed the sound of her voice to the kitchen, where Sharon was sitting at the old oak table, clipping coupons. For as long as he could remember after his dad left, she'd done this, and even when she eventually got back on her feet. It kept her busy, she said, but Mark had always suspected there was a deeper reason. They'd been broke, in debt, and taking handouts from Luke's father and, later, Rosemary. Their lifestyle had changed as abruptly as Mark's father's departure; once you struggled like that, you always worried. Worried that it could happen again, just as quickly.

Mark narrowed his eyes. He understood. When life turned upside down, you were always preparing for the worst.

Sharon folded the newspaper inserts and slid them to the edge of the table in a neat pile. Standing, she walked over to the counter and fetched a mug from a cabinet before filling it with coffee. The rich, strong brew perked Mark up and he accepted it with a grin. "Thanks."

"Everything okay?" Sharon topped off her own mug and slid back into her chair.

Mark leaned back, giving a small shrug. "A lot on my mind, that's all."

Sharon tipped her head. "Are you still disappointed about not winning?"

"Oh, yes and no."

Sharon's warm brown eyes were kind. "I'm just proud of you for entering." She hesitated, looking down into her mug. "If I may be candid, I've been worried about you, Mark. You used to have such a sense of passion, such a drive and ambition when it came to your career. It was nice to see you find that again these past few weeks."

Mark frowned at her words. The passion had always been there, dormant and suppressed, held at bay because it seemed the better way, the safer way. "You know I don't mind running the diner, Mom," he said, hating himself for the lack of truth in his words. He'd done it for her, and that was one thing he could never regret.

"Mark. I hope you know that I never expected you to take it over, not permanently. I certainly didn't want you to feel compelled to stick around."

"It's our family place—"

"No." Sharon shook her head. "Tavern on Main was our family place. Hastings was...a job. I worked there to get back on my feet, and I also enjoyed the company. It can get lonely sometimes, living alone..." Mark hated the thought of his mother, alone in this big house, one son off in Baltimore, and the other...

"Hastings is still a family place. You took it over. You bought it." His voice was gruff. Determined.

"It's not the same. I took it over because Gary Sullivan was retiring. He wanted to sell it and I didn't want to risk new ownership and be out of a job. It seemed like the sensible option at the time."

"It definitely has a loyal crowd," Mark agreed. He took a gulp of his coffee.

"I was happy enough with that. I needed that—security, stability. I had two growing sons to feed." She leaned forward. "But you aren't like me. Not deep down, Mark. You have your father's spirit. You always did."

"Don't say that," Mark snapped, and then, catching his tone, muttered, "Sorry."

His mother sat back. "You're still angry with him."

"Damn straight I'm angry." Mark stopped himself. "Sorry again."

"It's okay to feel hurt for the way he left, but don't let that ruin something else you love, Mark."

Mark's skin was on fire, and he clenched his teeth harder, unable to back down. "I was there for you. Dad—" He stopped himself before he said something he'd regret. "Working at Hastings all these years has been the best thing for all of us."

Sharon frowned at him. "I've been willing to go back for over a year, but if I'm honest, I wasn't sure what you would do if you weren't manning that counter."

This was news to him, and he tried to wrap his head around the information.

"You know, one of the things that made me fall in love with your father was his passion. The way he could visualize something beautiful and bring it to life. He really threw himself into everything. He was a perfectionist that way. He loved that restaurant. We all did."

"But he loved it too much," Mark said bitterly. "More than us."

Sharon frowned. "Is that what you think?"

"Well, it's true, isn't it?"

"Oh, I suppose it might have seemed that way," Sharon sighed. "The restaurant was a part of him. It's what made him happy. I don't think he would have been happy sitting back, doing something safe. He liked to run the kitchen. He liked to cook what he wanted to cook. He didn't take custom orders." She gave a wry grin.

"Then why did he leave?" It was the first time he had dared to ask, the first time he had confronted his mother on the reason their family had been torn apart. His father was gone. He wasn't coming back. He needed something to blame, damn it. "He left because Tavern failed, right?"

"You know we always argued about the business; I won't deny that. It was a source of stress, and a strain on us financially. But if you're asking if he left because the restaurant closed, no. He left because he was...in love with someone else. Someone he worked with—his sous chef, actually." Sharon held up her palms and let them drop back to the table.

Mark startled. "His sous chef?"

"They were close, working side by side every day. He left town with her."

"And he never came back," Mark nearly spat.

Sharon sighed. "He should have come, for you boys. But he wasn't the one who chose to leave. I was the one who kicked him out."

Mark stared at his mother for several, silent seconds. "But I heard you crying—"

"Oh, I was hurt," Sharon agreed. "I was also near bankruptcy. I was completely overwhelmed. But I know I did the right thing. I made my decision. I'm just sorry that your father made his own." She hesitated, glancing at him as if wondering whether she should continue. "Tavern had been struggling for years, long before Piccolino's opened. Your father kept it going because he loved it, and he believed in it. But he really kept it going for you."

Mark startled. "For me?"

"He saw how much you loved being in the kitchen. Even from an early age, you had an interest—and a talent." She grinned. "He hoped to pass it down to you someday."

Mark tried to make sense of this, how the man who had thought enough of him to pass down a restaurant would be capable of walking out of his life forever. "Is this why you always encouraged to me to go to culinary school?"

"I saw the way you resisted it, after your father left. It crushed me to see you so hurt, to think of you giving up that dream. When you stayed behind after high school to be with me, I wanted to think of a way to make it up to you. I wanted to encourage you to go for what I knew would make you happy, even if you didn't know it yourself yet. It's also why I held on to the property. It belongs with you, Mark."

An uneasy feeling took hold and rested square in his gut. "I don't want to be like him."

What would he have done years ago? If Anna had told him that she was pregnant, what kind of father would he have been?

She hadn't trusted him enough to find out.

"I don't want to be like him," he said again.

"Your father had his faults, but he had a lot of fine qualities, too. Don't resist the part of you he touched, Mark. Take it and learn from it."

Mark nodded, and reached for his mug. The coffee had gone cold, but he finished it in one gulp. All this time, he'd thought his father was incapable of love, but maybe that wasn't the case at all. He'd wanted him to have Tavern. It wasn't much. But for now, it would be enough.

Mark pushed back his chair and stood. No more indecision. No more waffling through life. It was time to move forward once and for all.

"I can't believe I'm doing this again," Jane groaned as she fanned her fingers, waiting for the polish to dry.

Anna gave her a nudge with her elbow. "You said yourself, the third time's the charm."

"Ha." Jane pursed her lips. "I guess I'm not holding out much hope. Even if this guy does turn out to be great, he could end up just like Adam in the end."

"I'd like to think there might be some good guys left," Anna mused.

Jane frowned at her sister's mysterious smile. "That's rather optimistic of you, Anna. I thought you didn't believe in happy endings."

Anna shrugged. "I didn't used to."

Jane flexed her fingers, hesitating on her next words. Anna was a private person; she kept her feelings close to her heart. Even the loss of their father had been her own, special struggle. Still, something in her words suggested an invitation for sharing, as if there were something on her mind she needed to talk through.

"Do you mind me asking what caused that?"

"I was in a relationship in culinary school." Anna didn't meet her eye. "With Mark."

Jane knew she made a poor show of masking her shock, despite her suspicions. Mark was a great guy—cute, Jane had to admit, and yes, a bit of a flirt. She could see where his smooth ways could rub Anna the wrong way, especially if there were lingering feelings, and it was becoming increasingly clear there were.

"You know," she said, grinning, "You've been a lot happier these past few weeks since you started spending time with Mark. Here I thought you were being brave, holding yourself together for Grace's sake, trying to put on a front because you were worried about Main Street Books and the loan. It was about Mark, though, wasn't it?"

Anna released a small breath. "It hasn't been easy being around him. Not at first, anyway."

"But now?"

Anna grew quiet. "Now I almost think there's a second chance for us."

Jane blinked. She had grown so accustomed to thinking of her middle sister as a career woman only, an independent force in the world, that the thought of her suddenly being involved with a man—Mark!—gave her pause.

"Maybe I'm getting ahead of myself," Anna muttered. "We all know how he is."

Yes, unfortunately, they did. Jane had seen Mark bounce from one woman to the next for years, seemingly only interested in each for a matter of weeks before his attention turned to the next. "I take it Nicole Johnson is out of the picture?"

Anna gave her a disapproving frown. "See, that's what

I mean." She shook her head. "Forget it. I'm getting ahead of myself. I know how he is."

"I didn't mean it like that," Jane sighed. "If you're telling me now, after all this time—after years of keeping this to yourself—that you think there's something between you and Mark then there probably is. You're a smart girl; you wouldn't waste your heart on the wrong man." *Unlike me*, she added quietly to herself. She understood all too well how it felt to want to trust in a man you knew deep down you shouldn't. Even when she knew that Adam was cheating on her, even when she'd witnessed him kissing another woman, she'd still held out hope that he could change, that it would never happen again, that he'd made a one-time mistake.

"I feel like this time, it will be different," Anna said. "I don't think he'd start something if he knew he was just going to hurt me again."

"Mark's a good guy, Anna," Jane added, reminding herself to stop comparing every man to Adam. "We all like him. We always have. I suppose that's why we've never understood your coldness to him."

"Well, now you know."

"Yes." Jane still marveled at the thought of it. Mark and Anna. Right under their noses! "I suppose Grace has no idea?"

Anna gave her a conspiratorial grin. "I told her yesterday. It came up and...it was time. I told her about the loan, too."

"Good." Jane felt her stomach uncoil with relief. She elbowed her sister. "It feels good to let people in, doesn't it?"

"It does, and I have you to thank for a lot of that."

"Me?"

"That morning in the bookstore when you told Rosemary you wanted her to set you up again, I thought you were just a glutton for punishment, but then I started to realize that maybe that was the reason you were blessed with so much. A child. A husband, even if only for a while. Even now, with your marriage over, your heart is still open."

Jane considered the words. She checked her watch, her pulse flickering at the time. She could have stayed and chatted with her sister all evening but she had somewhere else to be.

She said goodbye and walked to the car, calculating she had all of twenty minutes to dress. By the time she pulled into her driveway, she'd planned her outfit, deciding to shed her mom jeans for a cute pink pencil skirt she hadn't worn in years and a simple white T-shirt.

The problem was, the skirt was a little smaller than she remembered.

Jane held it up to her waist and regarded herself in the mirror with a frown. She didn't have time to sort through her clothes for something else, and she'd already returned that lace top to Grace, swearing her dating days were over.

A sundress seemed too casual, and her other skirts seemed too wintery.

Wait a minute...Jane crossed to her dresser, smiling in satisfaction when she pulled the flesh-colored shapewear from the top drawer. She'd bought this shortly after Sophie was born, when she was still trying to cling to her old life, her old clothes. Her old self.

Nearly five years later, she was right back there.

She slid one leg in and then the other, yanking and pulling and happy her daughter or heaven forbid her sisters weren't around to witness this struggle. Finally, she resorted to sliding her hand down the waist pant, shoving everything into place.

There. She smiled on a sigh, until panic quickened her pulse. It was so far out of her routine, she hadn't even considered...

Where just a matter of seconds ago her nails had been petal pink, evenly painted and glossed with just the right amount of sheen, they were now wrinkled and squished, like a contracted accordion.

"No, no, no!" she wailed, and ran to the bathroom to inspect the damage under better light. It was useless.

Blinking back tears of frustration, and forcing herself not to just call and cancel the whole damn thing, Jane found a cotton ball and soaked it with the nail polish remover, rubbing it deftly over each fingernail until the last trace of her earlier effort was gone.

She swept on some lipstick, ran a brush through her hair, and hurried out the door. So she was wearing a skirt that might not be at the height of fashion, and so her handbag contained a travel pack of tissues and a few princess bandages. She'd put her best foot forward tonight, but she'd do it by being herself. If there was another chance at love for her, then the next man in her life would have to love her just as she was.

Twenty minutes later, she marched straight up to the hostess stand in Piccolino's and inquired about the reservation instead of shifting her eyes this way or that, wondering if one of the few men in the waiting area was her date.

A finger tapped her on the shoulder, and she whipped around, coming face-to-face with a perfectly pleasant-looking man with wire-framed glasses and kind green eyes.

"Jane? I'm Brian." He smiled at her, and held out a

hand, giving it a firm shake, as his head tipped with interest. He motioned to the dining room, where the hostess
was waiting, two menus clutched to her chest. "Shall we?"

Jane nodded, and let him lead her into the bustling
room. Perhaps Adam was here, or maybe he was at home
with Kristy, curled up on the couch, laughing and talking,
having the time of his life. She didn't care.

Brian held out her chair and then came around the
table, giving her a bashful grin as he dropped into his
chair. Jane bit back a smile and reached for her menu, but
her hand froze as she looked across the room.

There he was, with that disheveled brown hair and
easy grin, smiling and laughing and looking at his date
with unsurpassed intensity.

It was Mark. And the woman he was with was most
definitely not her sister.

Anna set the timer on the oven for the last batch of scones and gave a sigh of contentment. She hadn't thought it possible, but Fireside's kitchen had never looked better. The six-burner range was now replaced with an eight-burner, all shiny and ready to be put to use. The marble counters were so new, she could catch her reflection in them, and each station was fully stocked with stainless steel pots and pans, waiting to be filled with her favorite ingredients.

If only the dining room were ready, they'd be able to open the doors today. The contractors were scheduled to start on that next week, once the last of the cabinet doors were affixed in the kitchen. Anna was impatient for things to get under way, but at least the sense of dread was lifted. She'd land on her feet. In many ways, she already had.

"Anna?"

Startled at the sound of her youngest sister's voice, Anna set down her oven mitt and came out of the kitchen.

Jane stood in the cleared-out dining room, almost hesitant to come farther into the space.

Anna couldn't resist letting her gaze linger on the singed wall that had once separated Fireside from the stationery shop. Soon, her café would be up and running again and a new tenant would move in next door. Maybe someday she'd have the chance to expand. For now, this would have to be enough.

"The rubble has been cleared out and you're safe without a hard hat," Anna joked. She waved her sister into the kitchen. "I'm just finishing with the last of this morning's batch. Did Grace send you over to pick them up?"

"Not exactly." Jane frowned and hitched her handbag higher on her shoulder before almost reluctantly following Anna into the kitchen. Her slumped posture lifted along with her expression when she saw the kitchen. "Oh, Anna! It looks beautiful! You'd never even know it had been damaged."

"I know!" Anna beamed. It was a sunny day, and warm, natural light filtered in through the windows. The back wall had been destroyed in the fire, and when they'd reconstructed it, Sharon had made a point of adding this touch; Anna had plans to grow her own herbs on the sill. "Sharon really did a great job with the renovation. Even though this place holds such bad memories for Mark, his mother really cherishes it."

"Hmm." Jane walked over to the sink and then glanced out the window, seeming distracted.

Anna fell silent and transferred the oatmeal cranberry cookies to a box. "So... anything new?"

Jane turned around, giving a shy smile. "I had my date last night."

"Oh my goodness, that's right!" No wonder Jane seemed far away. Anna pushed the pastry box to the side. "How was it?"

Jane bit the corner of her lip thoughtfully. "He was... a really *nice* guy."

Anna regarded her quizzically. "You don't seem all that excited about it."

Jane shrugged. "He seemed like more a friend type. I don't think I'm ready to date right now, not seriously at least. When Adam moved out right before Christmas, and then moved in with Kristy, I just felt like I needed to get back out there right away, move on to the next phase of my life."

It was the opposite of what Anna had done when Mark had broken up with her, but she understood. "Sometimes the best way to avoid the hurt is to bury yourself in something new." Like Fireside.

"I don't think I've really been dealing with the implications of this divorce," Jane said. "I've tried to run from it instead. My husband cheated on me and then he left me. I need to process that, and more than anything, I need to learn who I am again. Without him."

Anna nodded. "You were only nineteen when you married him. Now you're coming up on twenty-six. That's a big age difference." *A lot could happen in that amount of time.* "So this guy, Brian? You think you'll go out with him again?"

"Probably not," Jane sighed. "He was a nice guy, though, and... it's nice to be reminded that good guys are out there."

"It is," Anna agreed, but her grin fell when she caught the tightness in Jane's expression.

"I didn't actually come by here to talk about my date," Jane said slowly. "I came here to tell you about something I saw last night. I...wasn't sure if I should say anything, but I know if the situation were reversed, I'd want to know."

A wash of ice fell over Anna's stomach. "What is it?"

Jane gave a reluctant sigh. "It's Mark. He was at the restaurant. With another woman."

He'd told her he had work to do. "Nicole Johnson?"

Jane shook her head. "Someone else. I've never seen her before."

"What did she look like?" Anna inquired, trying to will herself to stay calm, to not jump to any conclusions. He'd sounded so honest on the phone...

"Dark hair, almost black. Pale skin."

She gritted her teeth. "Tall, pretty, blue eyes?"

Jane gave an apologetic smile. "I didn't see her eyes," she offered weakly.

Cassie. Anna gripped the counter, trying to steady herself from the emotions that tore through her body, leaving her shaky. Her mind whirred with possibilities, replaying the past few days with Mark. She'd told him everything—how much she'd cared about him, how deeply he'd hurt her. The horror of seeing him with Cassie that day. And he'd taken her to bed after promising her that woman had never meant anything, that the little flirtation she'd witnessed at the cocktail party had been nothing but two former classmates making pleasantries. He'd kissed her, long and deep, explored every inch of her body with his mouth, told her everything she needed to hear, and taken away years worth of pain and regret and fear with his touch.

"I just can't believe it," she murmured.

"Do you know this woman?" Jane set a hand on Anna's shoulder, her face lined with concern.

Anna nodded, swallowing hard, trying to process what this meant. There was only one conclusion: "He hasn't changed."

"I shouldn't have said anything," Jane burst out, but Anna shook her head firmly.

"You're my sister. You were looking out for me. If you don't, who will?" Not Mark. Certainly not Mark.

"I'm so sorry, Anna," Jane said softly.

"That makes two of us," Anna replied. She wiped away a tear before it could fall, gritting her teeth against the pain. She'd shed enough tears for that man. Those emotions had cost her enough already.

"I can stay if you'd like," Jane offered. "Why don't I call to have a friend pick Sophie up from preschool?"

Anna shook her head, hating the concern in Jane's voice as much as she appreciated it. This wasn't like her—not anymore. She straightened her back and sniffed. "I'm fine. Really," she added, sensing the hesitation in Jane's eyes.

"Well…" Jane picked up her handbag and tipped her head. "I can stop by in half an hour after I get Sophie and take you to lunch. Sophie would like that."

"Thank you, but…not today." Anna smoothed her hands and began boxing the last of the scones. "Besides," she said with false cheer. "I have a lot to do today. Account books to go over, meetings with contractors…"

Just stay busy.

Jane gave her a sad smile and reluctantly turned. Anna waited until she heard the front door close before burying her face into her hands. She allowed herself five minutes—five final minutes—and then rinsed her face in the shiny new sink, patted it dry, and slid the flour canister across the counter.

She had cookies to bake.

It was nearly nightfall by the time Anna closed the door on Fireside and turned the key. It had been a long day, but she could have worked through the night, going over the plans the contractor had emailed, restocking her pantry, and prepping for tomorrow. In some ways, it was almost depressingly easy to fall back into her quiet, lonesome routine. This was her life. This was reality.

The headache that had started shortly after Jane left still raged, and Anna knew it was time to rest. She'd pop an aspirin, maybe watch some television, and wake up tomorrow to start all over again.

She drove home in silence, the radio off, the window rolled partly down. Crickets chirped in the distance, and children played on lawns. She smiled at a little girl struggling to pedal her pink bike on her driveway, the gentle, patient way her father guided her along, purple streamers skimming his strong hands. Sometimes, during those scary, lonely two weeks after they'd parted, she imagined telling Mark about the baby, imagined what their life might have been together, the kind of father he would be. Recently, almost subconsciously, she'd watched him with Scout, seen the warmth in his eyes and the joy in his smile and dared to go back to that time and place and wonder what might have been.

Her mouth thinned and she jerked her eyes away. As much as she wished it, that never could have been them. He might have stuck by her, but it wouldn't have been for the right reasons. He'd already strayed. Maybe he would have strayed again. Maybe she would have ended up just like Jane. In the end, it always came back to a broken heart. There was no escaping that outcome when it came to Mark.

Her mind was as heavy as her heart, tugging and pulling and taking her in directions that she shouldn't entertain, but all thinking ceased when she pulled up in front of her apartment and saw Mark sitting on the front steps.

Damn it. They were supposed to go out tonight. The one time he had to stick to something.

"Hey," he said, giving her a lopsided grin as she slammed her car door shut.

She strode purposefully up the brick path, glaring at him. "I'm surprised you're here," she said, hating the emotion that shook her voice.

He frowned in confusion. "I've been waiting for twenty minutes. I figured you got busy with something."

Anna nodded. "Just like you were busy with Cassie last night?"

The flash in his eyes confirmed everything, and Anna cursed under her breath, pushing past him. He grabbed her by the arm, just tightly enough to make her turn and face him. God, she hated looking at him, hated the impact of those eyes, the way they penetrated her, made her question her own judgment, made her want things she shouldn't, things she could never have. Not with him.

"Jane was at the restaurant last night, Mark." Her voice was steely. "She saw you. I know you were with Cassie."

His brow knit. "It's not what you think, Anna."

"Oh, no? Enlighten me."

He released her arm, letting out a long breath. "Cassie and I are friends. Not even friends, really. We never were."

"No, of course not. Because you don't sleep with your friends. Well, unless the friend is me, of course."

A shadow fell over his face. "Don't be like that."

"Like what? I'm just stating the facts, Mark. I'm sorry if the truth hurts." She looked at him hard.

Mark seemed to hesitate. "You asked me the other day what I would do with the money if I won."

"Yeah. You didn't have a good answer for me."

Mark ran a hand over his jaw. "I've been wanting to do something different. A little more in line with what I set out to do."

She blinked. "And what is that?"

"You know the kind of restaurant I've always wanted to run."

Oh, she knew. Her heart panged when she remembered the way they'd talk for hours about their plan, even doodling designs, jotting down recipes, squabbling over stupid things like the color of the walls. "I don't see what this has to do with Cassie," she insisted.

"I was meeting with Cassie because she's opening a new restaurant and she asked me to be her executive chef."

Anna froze. "What?"

"She's opening a new place in Cedar Valley. That's what the meeting was about, Anna. There was nothing personal about it at all."

"Oh, yes there was, Mark. It's damn personal." The magnitude of what he was telling her hit her in waves. Would he really go into business Cassie when he wouldn't with her? "Are you going to accept her offer?"

Mark waited a beat. "I haven't decided yet."

"You haven't decided yet?" She choked on a laugh, even though there was nothing amusing about any of this.

"Cedar Valley isn't that far from here. Did you honestly think I was going to run that diner for the rest of my life?"

"Considering it has your name on it, I suppose I did." She knew deep down that wasn't true. "I knew you were capable of more, though."

"And I know it, too," he insisted.

"You said you've been thinking about this for a while."

"That's right. I want a restaurant, Anna. A restaurant of my own."

Her heart began to race as understanding took hold. "Those recipes, all those notes I found in your kitchen. They weren't plans for the diner, were they?"

"No."

"What were they for?"

He shrugged. "Plans. Ideas. For what, I don't know. I just know I needed more than I had here. More than Briar Creek could give me."

"So why didn't you do something about it?" Suddenly she knew. She shook her head, feeling the bitter sting of tears.

"I needed to win that contest just as much as you, Anna."

She laughed again, even as the tears started to fall. "So after this weekend, after I told you how I felt. After we..." She swallowed hard. "You had one foot out the door, just like you always did."

"Anna—"

She took a step back, holding up a hand. Her mind was spinning, and despite the tears blurring her vision, she'd never seen him more clearly.

"You were willing to go into business with Cassie, but

you weren't willing to open that restaurant with me. Why?"
She hated the way her voice broke on the end of her question. Too much hurt had been buried for too long. It didn't
matter that she'd come out strong—better, possibly—what
mattered was that he'd let her down. Again.

"It's different—"

She folded her arms across her chest and glared at
him. "How?"

He pulled in a sigh but when he met her eye, she knew
she was about to get a straight answer from him. For a
split second, she wasn't sure she wanted to hear it.

"Because it could never be just business with you,
Anna. It had to be personal, too."

"And you didn't want that," she finished for him.

He closed his eyes briefly, wincing as he shook his
head, and something deep within her, the last bit of herself she'd protected from him, broke. "Not then."

"How long would you have stuck around if you'd
known about the baby?" She was trembling, her entire
body shaking like a leaf in the wind as she stared at him.

"Don't do this—"

"Answer me." She bit down on her teeth, willing herself not to cry.

"I told you I would have been there for that child. I
would never, ever turn my back on my own child."

"And me?" She folded her arms across her chest,
hooking her eyes on his.

Mark stared at her, his lids slightly drooping. "I don't
know what would have become of us. All I know is that
the restaurant destroyed my family, and I sure as hell
didn't want the same outcome with you and me."

She stared up at the house, at the dark window at the

front, imagining the dread of stepping inside, hearing nothing but the echo of her own shoes against the floorboards. That day she'd read the test and gone to tell him, only to find him with Cassie, she'd come back to her room, knowing with certainty that he would never return. His T-shirt was tossed on the bed where he'd left it that morning, and his spare toothbrush was propped in the holder on her bathroom sink. She'd closed the door behind her and leaned back against it, sinking down onto the ground, wracked with sadness, and loss, and fear. She'd let it consume her. Well, never again.

"You know that little bird you won for me at the carnival," she said, glancing at him.

He frowned, seeming confused by the sudden change of topic. "You have it in your bedroom. You still kept it."

"That day you ended our relationship, I came home and cleared out all your stuff. Everything that reminded me of you. I wanted it gone. But that bird...I wanted something to remember the happy times. I really loved you, Mark."

Mark closed his eyes briefly. "You never told me."

"Would it have mattered?" She knew the answer to that. "It wouldn't have changed the inevitable."

Mark's brow pinched. "What's that supposed to mean?"

"It means we never stood a chance. You never gave us one." She shook her head, stepping backward. "I have to go."

"Anna." His voice was husky. Insistent. "Stop fixating on the past. I'm here now. I'm trying, Anna. I'm...trying to make this work. Can't you see that? Don't walk away."

Her pulse missed a beat. For a second, he was her friend again. Just Mark. The same old Mark who had teased her in class and then followed her all the way back to her dorm, and who walked her back every day after that. The Mark who had kissed her on the beach under the orange glow of the summer sun, and who had stroked her hair as she fell asleep in his arms. The same old Mark who had stolen her heart... and then stomped all over it.

Mark reached out and grabbed her arm, his dark gaze was hooded, locked with hers. "Cedar Valley isn't even far from here. It doesn't have to be one or the other, Anna. I can do both."

For a moment she wavered, feeling the heat of his breath, the way his shoulders rose and fell with emotion. Maybe he was right. Maybe they could make it work this time. But if they didn't? How many more times would he let her down, remind her of the way he'd crushed her all those years ago? Their past was too deep. There was no way out of it.

"I have to go," she said, tearing her arm from his. He stepped forward, calling out her name, and she could feel his tread behind her as she ran up the stairs, her key already in her hand. She pulled open the door and walked into the hall, quickly shutting herself in her dark apartment. She didn't cry, or dare to look out the window. Instead, she marched to her kitchen, tied on her apron, and plucked the lid off the flour canister.

Mark splashed cool water over his face and looked up into the mirror, hating the man he saw staring back. He gripped the counter tighter, putting his weight into it, and then grabbed a towel from the rack.

Scout began to whine and paw at his leg. Mark looked down into his big brown eyes and grinned. He needed to get out of this house, take a walk and clear his head. As soon as he grabbed the leash from the hook, Scout began to jump, his big, bushy tail waving with excitement. If only he could please everyone so easily, he thought wryly.

Mark opened the door, and Scout released a loud bark at the sight of Luke, standing on the porch. His grin faded as the dog jumped up on its hind legs and set his paws on his chest. "Someone's happy to see me," he remarked, gently coaxing Scout down.

Mark frowned and let Scout off his lead, guiding him down the porch steps and around the side of the house to the fence gate. "Go on, have a good run." He picked up a ball from the ground and chucked it far. Scout bounded across the lawn for it, and then became distracted by the trail of a scent. Deciding he was good on his own for a while, Mark circled back to the front of the house, where Luke was sitting in an Adirondack chair.

"Beer?"

Luke shook his head. "Nah, I'm good. I'm meeting Grace in an hour. I was passing by on my way home from work; just thought I'd drop in."

"Long day?" Mark lifted an eyebrow as he settled into the next chair. Across the gravel driveway, the forest was deep and lush. A branch rustled, and a squirrel zipped up a trunk. High above, birds circled and swooped, chirping loudly. It was peaceful here, and remote. He'd chosen this house for those reasons precisely, but more and more, it made him lonely, reminding him of his place in the world—the position he'd so carefully chosen. It was fun to banter with the locals and chat with a date, but at the end of the day, he was alone. He was tired of being alone.

"I had two kids in my office today," Luke said. "Recess fight. I gave them detention for a week and called their parents."

Mark stared at him in wonder. "I still can't picture it. You. School principal." He chuckled under his breath.

Luke gave a quizzical smile. "What's so funny about it?"

"I mean, it's just... so serious. So adult of you."

Luke tipped his chin. "I'm thirty-one years old, Mark. Hell, I'm old enough to be the father of most of the kids at the school. We both are."

Mark's gut knotted and he grew silent, choosing to focus on the forest again. "Think you and Grace will have kids soon?" he asked, even though he knew the answer.

"Hopefully," Luke said. "I'm counting on you to be the

fun uncle, so to speak. Between my sisters and Grace's sisters, any child of ours will most likely be spoiled rotten." He pretended to be annoyed by this, but Mark could see it pleased him to no end.

"You can count on me," Mark said. He frowned, considering the implications of his words. He'd never said that to the one person who needed to hear it the most. When she needed to hear it.

Luke would make a great father, a loyal, invested father. The kind of father a kid deserved. He gritted his teeth, wondering if the same could be true of himself. If he would have been the man that Anna needed him to be in the end—if he would have been the man their child deserved.

Anna had worried he'd run, just as he had with her. It was his father who ran—not him. Not anymore.

"Did Grace decide on her maid of honor yet?" Mark asked, shifting the conversation.

Luke shot him a glance, his mouth twitching. "Anna."

Arm in arm down the aisle with Anna. Wasn't there some kind of formal dance required of them, too? "She's not going to be happy about putting up with me all night," Mark grunted.

Luke arched a brow in interest. "What did you do?"

Mark shrugged. "I blew it."

Luke narrowed his eyes. "Then or now?"

"Both," Mark said grimly.

Luke leaned in. "You love her?"

"What?" Mark pulled back in his chair. "You know I don't believe in that crap."

Luke chuckled, shaking his head. "Then why'd you push me to get back together with Grace?"

"Well, that's different. That's you." Mark let out a long breath, wishing Luke would drop it.

"You knew I'd be happier once I gave my relationship a second chance."

Mark drummed his fingers against the arm of his deck chair. "Are you telling me I'll be happier if I do the same?" His gut knew the answer, but he needed confirmation.

Luke shrugged. "Unless living in this house all by yourself is more fun."

"Hey, I have Scout," Mark pointed out, only half serious.

"The day you got that dog, I gave you one year."

"What's that supposed to mean?" Mark demanded.

His cousin looked at him squarely. "Face it, Mark. You don't want to be alone."

Mark felt his lips thin. No. He didn't.

He shifted in his chair, not knowing how to answer that. Of course he had feelings for Anna. He always had. But it didn't mean he should act on them. He never should have acted on them. He'd done exactly what he'd hoped to avoid. He'd gone and hurt her again. "I have an opportunity to leave town. Executive chef."

Luke frowned. "What? Would you really go?"

"A week ago I would have said no." Mark shrugged, but hearing the words from his cousin's mouth sent a sharp pang through his chest. "Even yesterday I would have said no," he said, recalling Anna's reaction, the hurt in her eyes. No restaurant was worth that. He just hadn't been able to prove that to her. She hadn't given him the chance.

He scratched at the stubble on his chin, thinking of the way she'd recoiled last night, cringing at his touch, looking every bit as confused and betrayed as she had that day he'd broken up with her. "There doesn't seem much reason to stay."

"Maybe you haven't given yourself one," Luke said.

"Maybe I don't know what I want anymore," Mark said, but he knew that wasn't true. He wanted picture frames and memories, and even floral throw pillows, damn it. He wanted a wreath on a door, welcoming him home every night. He wanted laughter and companionship. He wanted to be the father he never had.

He wanted a restaurant of his own. But more than anything, he wanted Anna. He wanted it all. And with nothing left to lose, it was time to go for it.

"Is your mom still playing matchmaker?" he asked, and Luke groaned.

"Yes. Why?" His eyes widened. "No, Mark. Don't tell me you're looking for her to set you up—"

"As a matter of fact, that's exactly what I'm hoping she'll do."

Luke's expression turned wary. "All this bouncing from one casual date to the next. Is this really what you want?"

"No," Mark said, standing. "It's not."

Before Luke could reply, he let himself into the house and quickly dialed his aunt's number. She answered on the second ring, her tone uncertain. No doubt worried he'd mention those rose petals, Mark thought, grinning.

He leaned against the doorjamb. "Aunt Rosemary, do you have a minute?"

"For my favorite nephew?" she purred. "Of course."

"I was wondering...Are you still matching Anna up on dates?"

Her heard the smile in her voice when she said, "I certainly am."

His pulse skipped. "Good. Do you think you could arrange something for tomorrow night, say eight o'clock?"

A squeal pealed down the line. "My boy, I thought you'd never ask."

When his aunt Rosemary set her mind to something, she found a way of making it happen. Mark sucked in a breath and pulled the handle of Piccolino's, hoping this was a family trait, even if Rosemary wasn't technically a blood relative.

He checked his watch; he'd purposefully arrived ten minutes late to make sure Anna was already seated. A quick scan of the dining room caused his heart to drum. She was in the corner, her chin cupped in her palm, her long blond hair falling around her shoulders.

He stepped out from behind the plant that blocked her view of the lobby and began walking toward her, his stride in beat with the pounding in his chest. Her eyes narrowed as they met his, and her pretty pink mouth fell open. Quickly, she reached for her menu, but it was too late.

"Hello," he said lightly, stopping at her table.

She lowered the menu and lifted her chin. Without looking up, she reached for her water, lips pinched.

Mark inhaled sharply. This was going to be more difficult than he'd expected. He set a hand on the back of the chair opposite her, forcing her attention from the paper in her hands.

"What do you think you're doing?"

He gave a small shrug. "Joining you."

A mirthless chuckle escaped from her lips, and her icy smile lingered. "I'm actually meeting someone, Mark. A date."

"Ah, but you see," he said, slipping into the chair. "I am your date."

Her carefully arranged smile slipped. "Excuse me?"

"I'm your date for this evening," he replied evenly. Ignoring her wide-eyed stare, he unfolded his napkin and set it in his lap.

"No," Anna said, giving a low, nervous laugh. "I'm sorry, Mark, but you're not. I'm waiting for someone, so please, just go."

His chest tightened at the plea in her tone, at her insistence that he leave, that he was unwanted. Refusing to back down now, he took a sip from his water glass. Anna's face flared.

"I'm fully aware that you're waiting for someone. Brown hair, six feet tall, loves fine dining?"

Now her face blanched. "I don't understand."

"I asked Aunt Rosemary to arrange this, Anna." He held her gaze, watching as awareness took hold.

Her lips pinched on a huff. "You shouldn't have bothered. I have nothing to say to you."

"Maybe not," he said. "But I have a lot to say to you."

"Mark. Please. We've said everything that needs to be said." She pressed her mouth tight and set her menu on the table. "Just . . . go."

Go. It was what he did best. He could practically hear her thinking the sentiment. "Not until you've heard what I've come to say."

Her lashes fluttered, but her gaze remained lowered. Mark clenched the napkin in his lap, hating the slight drop of her shoulders, the rise and fall of her breath. He'd done this to her—not once, but twice now—and he never wanted to see her like this again.

"I told you," she said through gritted teeth. "There's nothing left to say, Mark."

Mark cast a fleeting look around the room, noticing the other diners, who laughed over the table, sipped wine, and chatted happily. He dragged his attention back to Anna, at the frown on her pretty face, and he suddenly felt like the biggest jerk on the planet. She fidgeted with an earring, blinking rapidly at the tablecloth, her cheekbones stained with pink dots.

She'd gotten dressed up in a simple black dress with thin straps—she'd put time into her evening, into the hope of moving on, putting distance between them.

He shook his head. "I didn't mean to upset you. I thought this would be the only way...that you'd be forced to hear me out." He set the napkin on the table. "I'll go if that's what you really want. I won't bother you again. But just so you know, I don't regret the past few weeks. Even if you hate me, and even if you go back to ignoring me for the next six years, I'm glad we had a little more time together. I love you, Anna. I always did. Hell, maybe I always will. And if it will make it easier on you for me to walk away right now, that's what I'll do. I only want the best for you. That's all I ever wanted."

He pushed back his chair and stood, allowing himself one last look at the only girl he'd ever dared to love, and then he closed his eyes, on their past, on any chance of a future, and turned to go.

His breath caught as her fingers laced around his wrist. Her voice was so low; he almost believed he'd imagined it.

"Wait," she said.

Anna's heart was doing jumping jacks. The napkin in her lap was twisted and squeezed, and for a fleeting moment she wished they were at the pub, so she could shred and rip the paper in her hands instead of anxiously tugging at the square of cloth.

He was watching her over the table, his eyes dark, his mouth a thin, grim line, and everything she'd told herself these past few days, every emotion she'd tried to banish came tumbling back. After everything they'd been through, he still had a way of looking at her that made her knees go weak and her heart start to flutter.

She took a sip of her water, checking herself. This was Mark. Typical Mark. Mark flitted. Mark flirted. Mark ran.

But Mark never came back. Until today. And Mark never said I love you.

"I'm not leaving town," he said, and she hated the part of her that perked up at this bit of information. So he wasn't leaving; it didn't change a thing. She and Mark were not meant to be.

She nodded slowly. "So you're going to continue running the diner?" Why did she ask, why did she care? This was awkward at best. People surrounded them, a waitress stopped to offer a bread basket. He'd cornered her, damn it, and Rosemary had allowed it!

She knew she shouldn't have agreed to this, but then Rosemary had to go and guilt trip her about all the help she'd given Jane, and how nice Brian had turned out to be, and a part of Anna—a small, secret part of her—thought that if she just went out tonight, she would be one step closer to getting over Mark for good.

Instead, she was face-to-face with the one man who had stolen her heart, and who unfortunately still had it.

"My mom's going to come back to Hastings," Mark volunteered. "I'm still working on my next plan."

Of course. Typical.

Mark slid a piece of paper across the table. Anna frowned. "What's this?"

"Open it."

Reluctantly, she took the letter, telling herself she should just hand it back, not feed into this a second longer. Curiosity got the better of her, though, and she slid her finger under the seal and removed the single sheet of paper tucked inside. She scanned it quickly, her brow furrowing. "What is this?"

"It's the lease to the old stationery store. It's yours."

Anna's pulse skipped, and she did a miserable job of hiding her shock. Mark stared at her hopefully from across the table, but Anna just shook her head. It didn't change a damn thing.

She handed the letter back to him, but he didn't reach for it. "Take it. Please."

"No. I want you to have it."

She set the envelope on the table between them. "I appreciate what you're trying to do." She sighed, feeling weary. "Let's just... be civil, Mark. I can't bear to live like we have for the past few years."

"Neither can I." Mark reached across the table and grabbed her hand, holding it tighter in his grip when she tried to pull away. "I don't want to walk by you and pretend I don't see you. I don't want to act like we never meant anything to each other. Like we still don't."

"Mark—"

"Hear me out," he whispered. "I don't want to live like we have all these years either. I... don't want to live another day without you."

She was aware that she was holding her breath, and she released it now, in a small puff, and snatched her hand back, bringing it to the other, safe in her lap. She blinked quickly, trying to compose herself, trying not to see the sincerity in his eyes. Trying not to believe a word he was saying.

Pushing him away was the only way to protect herself from him, from those painful memories, from the disappointment only he could bring. But oh, she didn't want to push him away anymore.

"I wasn't ready back then, Anna. I won't try to deny it. You were the real deal, the girl I saw an entire future with. And I was scared of how that made me feel. I was scared that I wouldn't live up to it somehow. That we'd let each other down." He paused. "Instead, I let you down."

"How do I know it won't be the same this time around?"

Mark shrugged. "I know you're scared. I am, too. You gave me your heart, Anna, and you trusted me with it. And now...I'm giving you mine. I love you, Anna. I always did. Nothing can change that."

"Nothing could," she said. No matter what had happened, one thing was constant over time. Her feelings for him had never faded, even when she'd hoped they would.

"I want you to have your dream restaurant, Anna. I want you to have all the dreams I stole from you."

She glanced down at the envelope. "It doesn't matter. I don't even have the money for the renovation. I'd never get a loan for it in time."

"No, but I could," Mark replied evenly, and Anna darted her eyes to his. A smile twitched at the corner of his mouth. "What do you say, Anna? Do you think it's too late for our plan?"

A hot tear rolled down her cheek and she didn't bother brushing it away. "But the location. Your father's old restaurant. It's—"

He gave her a reassuring smile. "It's where I was meant to be, Anna. It just took me a long time to figure that out."

"I guess we both needed time," she admitted.

"That," Mark grinned. "And Rosemary."

She was smiling, laughing through her tears, and she didn't care who saw. Let them know, let all of Briar Creek know that there was a reason for their silence, and a reason for it to be finally, permanently, forever broken.

EPILOGUE

Are you sure you're okay with changing the name?" Mark asked, staring up at the bronze patinaed hanging sign. "You know I'd be happy staying with Fireside Café."

Anna stopped watering the yellow and blue pansies that burst from the window boxes and came over to wrap an arm around his waist. "We never came up with a name for our restaurant all those years ago. I'd like to think this one was worth waiting for."

And some things are, she thought, looking up to give Mark a slow kiss before picking up her watering can. She drained the contents into the rest of the flower beds while Mark straightened the sidewalk tables lining the extending storefront down Main Street. A crisp white awning lent them shade, and a sunflower was tucked into a vase on each table.

Weeks of hurried construction and long nights of menu planning had all led to this day. In a matter of minutes, all their friends and family and hopefully dozens of locals would come through the forest green painted doors, hungry and curious, eager to see Briar Creek's newest establishment.

Anna pushed through the door now, her heart swelling with pride at what she saw. The wall separating the old stationery store had been scaled down to waist height, and polished walnut-stained tables stretched along a wall of paned windows, draped in burnt orange velvet curtains hanging from black iron rods. The bakery counter had been rebuilt, and the smell of fresh breads and cakes drifted over the lobby area, where casual chairs and tables still nestled around the fireplace; no doubt the morning traffic would be heavy tomorrow.

Kara stood at the hostess stand, her rich brown hair bouncing at her shoulders, studying the list of specials. It had been Mark's idea to include at least one item from their ill-fated contest entry, and Anna had agreed. They might not have won the grand prize, but they'd ended up with so much more.

Mark came through the kitchen door, calling her name, and Anna hurried to the back. It was nearly time.

"How does it feel to be back here?" she asked as she tied the apron around her waist, noticing the way Mark seemed lost in thought, his eyes trained on the workstations, prepped and ready.

"It feels right," he said firmly. He offered her a smile. "It feels like it was meant to be."

He came forward and set his hand on her hip, bringing her in for a kiss that was quickly interrupted by one of the new waitstaff, who cleared his throat in embarrassment.

"Remember," Anna teased. "When we're in the kitchen, it's professional. Not personal."

Mark grinned suggestively. "I'm already counting the hours until we close."

Anna smiled, but a ripple of butterflies took hold

when she glanced at the clock—three minutes to go—and quickly counted out the baskets of French bread, even though she'd already done that twice. They'd planned for this, prepared this. Not just for hours or days. For years. It was time to enjoy it.

Squaring her shoulders, she passed through the kitchen door, where Mark was waiting near the gleaming windows.

"Look." He gestured to the line forming on the sidewalk.

A flutter of nerves zipped through Anna's stomach, and she reached for Mark's hand, wanting to savor this moment for just a second longer, before they dared to share it.

Mark slanted her a glance, arching an eyebrow on a grin. "Ready?"

Her breath caught on that smile—the same as he'd given her all those years ago, when he'd quickened his pace to meet up with her after class. The leaves were rustling then, turning brown and floating from branches, crunching under their feet. The air was crisp with the chill of autumn, and life felt full of so many wonderful possibilities. His deep brown eyes danced with suggestion, and now, just as she had then, she couldn't help but fall, long and hard, and permanently.

She nodded once. "Ready."

Mark turned the lock on the door and stepped back, waiting with her as the crowd hesitantly pushed forward, their wide eyes sweeping the room, their mouths lifted in wonder.

"Welcome!" Anna said at the same time as Mark. They glanced at each other, laughing at their mutual excitement, and turned back to their guests. "Welcome to Rosemary and Thyme."

When she needs help with her struggling dance studio on Main Street, the only person single mom Jane Madison can turn to is Henry Birch—the best friend of her cheating ex-husband...

See the next page for a preview of

Hope Springs on Main Street.

CHAPTER 1

I have something to tell you, Mommy." The words were whispered, almost shyly. "I'm in love."

The light ahead turned yellow, and Jane Madison hit the brakes a little harder than she'd intended. Looking up, she caught her five-year-old daughter's reflection in the rear view mirror and tried not to show her amusement. "Oh really? What's his name?"

"I don't know," Sophie replied simply. "But we're in love."

"I see." Was it already starting? Trading in dolls for boys? Jane glanced into the mirror once more, noticing the multiple strands of pink princess jewelry roped around her neck and the clip-on plastic earrings that had been part of a set from her birthday last month. She was still her sweet little girl, albeit a slightly boy crazy one. They watched too many cartoon movies where the prince swept the peasant girl off her feet, whisking her away to the castle where they would live happily ever after...

Jane hated to rob her child of such a beautiful fantasy, but it might be time to introduce a new message, one where the girl goes to college, finds a career, and doesn't pin her entire life on one man. A man who could just leave her in the end.

Jane waited for the light to switch and then eased down the winding roads, slick from three days of rain. The leaves had started to turn, and the strong winds from the past week had blown many in her path, dotting the pavement with bursts of orange and gold. It was a gray day, a dreary day some might say, but not for Jane. It was the perfect night to curl up with a bowl of homemade soup and catch up with her daughter. Though Sophie had been at her father's house for only one night in the last week, the house had been too quiet, the evening without purpose, and Jane had spent all of last night counting the hours until the house was again filled with endless chatter and peals of laughter.

"So tell me, Sophie. How do you know you're in love?"

"He pushed me on the swings at recess today," Sophie explained. "That's called true love."

If only it were that simple, Jane mused, finding herself frowning at the innocence of her daughter's conviction. She pulled onto their street, waved at the neighbors she'd come to know in the six years she'd lived on the block, and felt the same sense of calm she always did when her house came into view. The orange and white berry wreath she and Sophie had picked out last weekend hung from the hunter green front door, secured by a twine ribbon, and the colorful red, purple, and orange mums they'd sprinkled throughout the landscaping were downright cheerful, there was no denying that. But just as she began to perk up at how nice the fall decorations looked, she felt the familiar dull heaviness settle over her chest—it was still happening, nine months after her husband had moved out.

"Well, he sounds like a very special young man," Jane said with a grin, and then stopped as she considered something. The new music teacher at Briar Creek Elementary was pretty cute, and Sophie had developed a fierce crush on her seventeen-year-old camp counselor over the summer. "Is he ... as tall as you?"

Sophie nodded eagerly as Jane released her from the booster seat and grabbed her sparkly unicorn backpack. "Although, actually." Sophie froze and put a finger to her mouth. "He might be just a little bit shorter."

Jane laughed. "Come on," she said, pulling the overnight bag from the trunk. "I made you some chocolate chip cookies last night. Your favorite!"

"Oh, yummy! Kristy made me some, too."

Jane flinched, but said nothing. She took her time opening the door, trying not to think of the woman her husband had left her for as she turned the lock and flicked on the light. The soup she'd left simmering in the slow cooker all afternoon filled the house with warmth and spices, but it did little to touch the emptiness that lingered in her heart.

Sophie made a mad dash for the kitchen, ignoring Jane's cries to take off her rain boots first. Jane sighed as she hung her coat on the hook in the mudroom. She could already hear Sophie peeling the foil off the plate of cookies. Next she'd be telling her how much better Kristy's cookies were. It wasn't enough for the woman to steal her husband. Now she was trying to win over her daughter's affections, too.

Sophie looked up as Jane entered the kitchen. "These

are a lot better than Kristy's cookies. Hers are all burned around the edges, and they stick to the inside of your mouth. She uses applesauce instead of butter. Aunt Anna made a face when I told her that."

Jane turned to her daughter with interest, a slow smile creeping over her face. "You don't say," she murmured as she pulled a gallon of milk from the fridge, her spirits all at once lifted. She knew she was Sophie's mother and that nothing could break or sever that bond, but it hurt her more than she could bear to know another woman was tucking Sophie into bed these days.

"I told her I liked them but when she wasn't looking, I fed my cookie to the cat. You're not mad, are you, Mommy?"

Joyful might be a better word. Jane pressed her lips firmly shut as she handed the glass of milk to her daughter. "You did the polite thing, Sophie, but as for feeding the cat, it's probably better to stuff the cookie in your pocket next time. Chocolate isn't good for animals. You don't want to make the poor thing sick. Now, why don't you go upstairs and unpack your bag while I finish getting dinner ready?"

"Can we have a pajama party tonight?" Sophie asked excitedly as she hopped off the counter stool.

Jane glanced at the clock to see it was only ten past five. On the days she didn't work, the party sometimes started as early as four. "That sounds like a *great* idea." She sighed at the mere thought of removing the ballet tights that clung to her waist under the yoga pants she wore, leaving an unflattering imprint on her skin. Fall session had started today after a three-week break since summer boot camp—in less than a month she had forgotten how confining and itchy a leotard could be.

She patted her hips. Maybe she should be baking her cookies with applesauce, too.

Taking her daughter's hand, they raced up the stairs, quickly changing into their comfy cozies, as Sophie called them. While Sophie busied herself with a coloring book at the art table in her bedroom, Jane started a load of laundry, humming under her breath, until the doorbell rang and everything stopped.

Her heart began to pound. Who the heck would drop by at this hour? But right, it wasn't even five thirty. And she was robed in pink and purple plaid pants, a long-sleeved T-shirt, and—God help her—no bra. Hot faced with shame, Jane ran through her mental list of possible visitors. A Girl Scout selling cookies perhaps? Or a door-to-door salesman? She could claim she was under the weather; that would explain her choice of late afternoon attire, though not Sophie's nightgown... She bit on her nail. The worst scenario would be her ex-husband—actually, no, the worst would his girlfriend—dropping off something that Sophie had forgotten. The bell rang again, and Jane began frantically rifling through the laundry basket, looking for something that wasn't stained or wrinkled or didn't smell, anything that was more appropriate than what she was wearing. The bell rang a third time. Jane stepped away from the laundry pile. She was a mess either way, but at least this way she was clean.

Anxiety tightened its grip as she rounded the corner, and she chastised herself for not holding out for at least another hour—six was a far more acceptable time for pajamas, sort of... She edged to the door, holding her breath, and then sighed in relief when she saw her oldest sister through the glass panel.

"Grace! Come on in!" She smiled, ignoring the way Grace's expression folded in confusion as she swept her eyes down to Jane's feet, cozily covered in oversized bunny slippers. Jane felt the heat in her cheeks rise. She'd forgotten about those.

"Off to bed already?" Grace laughed, but the insinuation stung, and Jane told herself that this particular part of her weekday routine really needed to stop. And it would. Soon. Sure, it was more comfortable to live in pajamas, but the day was still young enough for people to stop by— people who were fully clothed and, unlike her, willing to go out in public.

"It's a dreary day," she explained good-naturedly, taking Grace's umbrella from her hand. "I have homemade minestrone soup if you'd like to stay for dinner."

Grace nodded and followed her into the kitchen. "Luke has a Board of Education meeting tonight," she explained as she set her bag on the floor and slid onto a counter stool. From above them there was a thump and a scamper of feet. Grace laughed and pointed to the ceiling. "Is she dancing?"

"I love my daughter, but I don't think the Moscow Ballet is in her future," Jane said with a rueful grin.

"How was class today?"

"Good," Jane said pensively. It had actually been very quiet compared to previous sessions. She should probably view that as a good thing, considering how rambunctious the girls in one of her summer classes had been. Between the squealing and jumping, she'd had to start carrying a bottle of ibuprofen in her dance bag.

Grace raised an eyebrow. "You don't seem very sure about that. Has Rosemary been trying to set you up on more dates?"

"Jeez, no." Jane laughed. She'd allowed her boss to set her up on a series of eye-opening dates last spring, all of which confirmed her belief that she was better off alone. One of her dates hadn't like children, and had consumed so much booze she'd had to tell the hostess to take his keys. Then there had been Brian. She had pinned so much hope on the man pitched as a bespectacled doctor. He *was* sweet, even if he had turned out to be a male nurse instead of a surgeon, but he didn't make her heart flutter, and besides, he had now been in a long-term relationship since about a week after their dinner date. She'd tried to tell herself that was for the best, that she hadn't felt that spark, but she couldn't deny the part of her that felt the sting of rejection. The lack of attraction had clearly been mutual.

So, yes, she was alone. Not by choice, but she would embrace it. What other choice did she have?

"Rosemary thankfully hung up her matchmaking hat after she finally got Anna and Mark back together," Jane said, smiling at the thought of her sister and Rosemary's nephew living so happily together after years of stubborn silence. "If my little string of dates taught me anything, it's that dating is no fun at all."

"You just haven't found the right guy yet," Grace encouraged.

"Show me someone who is uncomplicated, committed, emotionally available, and crazy in love with me and my daughter, and then I'll reconsider. Until then, I'm happy right here."

"At home in your pajamas." Grace held her gaze.

"That's right." Jane nodded. "I've had enough dating for one lifetime, thank you very much."

Grace gave her a stern look. "You know how I feel about that."

Yes, Jane did, and she wasn't about to continue this conversation. Now that Grace was getting married and Anna was equally in love, it seemed both sisters were more focused than ever on seeing their youngest sister settled down and happy.

"Yes, well, my classes were fine today," Jane said briskly. She paused, wondering why she felt so bothered by the day. Enrollment capped at ten students per class, but her three forty-five Intro to Pointe class had just four students, and Rosemary had been unusually quiet when she'd left for the day.

Oh, well, the session was just beginning, and seasonal colds were already going around. Perhaps a few of the girls had been sick, or would be late joiners. Surely they'd want to audition for *The Nutcracker*, after all.

"It was very calm. Very . . . stress-free."

"With Rosemary?" Grace didn't look convinced, and Jane had to laugh at that. Her boss could be demanding, but Jane was too grateful for the work to complain. If Rosemary hadn't stepped in and offered her a teaching position at the studio last winter, she wasn't sure she would have had the nerve to confront Adam on the affair. It was just the ray of hope she needed to prove to herself that she could stand on her own two feet. She'd given up any hope of a ballet career to marry when she was just nineteen, not to mention a college education. Her husband had been her life, and now she had to live one without him in it.

Jane took a loaf of sourdough bread from a bag and set the oven to preheat. "So, to what do I owe the honor of your visit?"

Grace's eyes twinkled as she gave a slow smile. "I found Sophie's flower girl dress."

"For real this time?" Grace had already changed her mind on her own wedding gown six times, and she was yet to commit to the flower arrangements, even with the big event only a few weeks away.

"I just want it to be perfect."

"I know." Jane felt bad for giving her sister a hard time. She'd been a bride herself once, caught up in all the little details that seemed so trivial now. She should have spent less time worried about flowers and more time worried about her future husband and the little voice that kept warning her to walk away. "Let me see what you picked out."

Jane hurried to the island and leaned in as Grace rummaged through a glossy bridal magazine, stopping at a picture of a little girl wearing a deep crimson ball gown in raw silk, with a thick ivory bow at the waist. After the chocolate brown option Grace had proposed last week, Jane knew that Sophie would be thrilled with the idea of wearing this dress.

"Should we get Sophie?" she asked, grinning.

"She had better like it," Grace said. "These dresses take at least three weeks to arrive. I'm really cutting it close."

Jane grinned. "Sophie! Sophie, come on downstairs. Aunt Grace has something to show you!"

Soon there was a thump, heavy enough to make the sisters wince and then giggle, followed by a pounding of small feet down the wooden stairs.

"What is it, what is it?" Sophie announced breathlessly as she scampered into the kitchen.

"You're in your pajamas, too, I see," Grace remarked, taking in the pink nightgown with the ruffle trim. She gave Jane a pointed look, and Jane pulled in a deep breath, telling herself not to let it get to her. So, yes, she had become a bit of a hermit in the months since Adam had moved in with his girlfriend, but could anyone blame her? Her husband had cheated on her, lied to her, and then proceeded to move in with his mistress just three miles across town. Briar Creek was small and word traveled fast—even if she was the wronged party, and even if she did have the support of many, she didn't need the sympathy. Or the reminder. She just wanted...She popped the bread into the oven and set the timer. She just wanted to feel safe, she supposed. And what better way to feel that way than to stay home, surrounded only by those you let in?

"Sophie, look at this dress," Jane said. "Do you want to wear that when you're a flower girl?"

Sophie jutted her chin at the picture Grace held up and shook her head. "I'm going to wear a blue flower girl dress."

Jane and Grace exchanged a look of alarm. This was at least the eleventh dress Grace had fallen in love with, usually before finding one she loved even more the next day or, in the case of the chocolate brown gown, to have it be boycotted by the flower girl herself. Time was running out for further indecision. This dress was going to have to work.

"But honey, Grace and Luke are having fall colors for their wedding. Remember how we looked at those pretty red and orange flowers?" *And the green ones, and the purple ones...*

"But my flower girl dress is blue! Blue velvet! Kristy said so."

Jane slid her eyes to Grace, who stared at her, not blinking.

"What do you mean Kristy said so?" Grace pressed gently, when it became clear Jane was unable to ask.

"Kristy showed me my dress. It's blue velvet with flowers around the neck."

Jane was having trouble breathing. Her chest felt tight, and her heart was pounding. She stared at Grace, willing her oldest sister to make this right, to clear this up. Grace bit down on her lip, studying her niece, confusion knitting her brow.

"Kristy said you're going to wear a blue dress for my wedding?"

"No! For *her* wedding!" Sophie cried, frustration causing her plump little cheeks to grow pink. "When she marries Daddy!"

Jane felt the blood rush from her face, and for a moment she thought she might be sick. Or faint. She slumped into a chair, listening to Grace make cheerful conversation with Sophie in a blatant attempt to smooth over the situation, but her mind was spinning. Adam was getting married—to the woman he had left her for! He had strayed from their marriage, ripped apart their family, and yet he was ready to settle down with a new wife, live the life they should have shared and could have—if he'd loved her.

Tears prickled the back of her eyes, but she blinked quickly, refusing to let them fall in front of Sophie. There would be plenty of time to cry tonight—God knew she wouldn't get any sleep now, ultra-soft flannel pajama pants or not.

It was so easy for Adam. He'd gotten bored of one wife

and quickly found another. He didn't have to live with an emptiness in his heart, or think of something funny that had happened that day and find there was no one in the bedroom to tell it to—and that it was too late to pick up the phone and call someone. He didn't have to stand at the playground on a Saturday afternoon and watch other smiling couples push their child on the swings, feeling like his heart was twisting with each breath—because Adam was actually one of those happy couples!

He'd moved on. He'd found someone. He didn't have to go on dates, try on new people, see if they fit. While she...she was still trying—in vain, it would seem—to make sense of her new life, the life she hadn't chosen, and to forget the one that had been taken from her.

"Jane?" Grace's voice was overly bright, her smile bared, her green eyes electric. "Why don't we have some of that delicious soup?"

"I'll set the table!" Sophie volunteered. She took three placemats from the basket on the counter and began arranging them on the pedestal table. "Daddy said it's important for me to help, so I can show a good example."

What was she talking about? Jane moved slowly to the slow cooker and lifted the lid, feeling her stomach stir from the aroma. She couldn't eat if she tried. Adam was living the easy life, wasn't he? No harm done, on he went. No regard for her, or the damage he had caused. No glance back. Must be nice. Must be nice indeed.

"Daddy said I'll have lots of responsibility when the new baby comes."

The glass lid fell from Jane's hand, shattering in the ceramic sink. Grace's hands were on hers instantly, but she wasn't cut. Not physically at least.

"What did you just say, Sophie?" she managed, even though she didn't want to know, she didn't want to know anything.

"There's going to be a baby, Mommy!" Sophie's eyes danced with excitement. "I get to be a flower girl! *And* a big sister!"

Jane swallowed the lump in her throat, trying to process everything, waiting for the wounds to seal shut again. She'd told herself she was better alone, that she preferred it that way. If she didn't give her heart away, it couldn't be broken. This was a fresh reminder.

Grace's hand was still tight on hers. "You sure you don't want to give dating another try?" she asked half-heartedly, but concern darkened her eyes.

Jane nodded firmly, but the tug in her heart said otherwise.

Fall in Love with Forever Romance

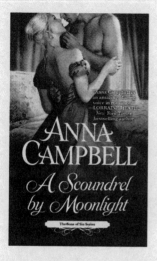

A SCOUNDREL BY MOONLIGHT
by Anna Campbell

Justice. That's all Nell Trim wants—for the countless young women the Marquess of Leath has ruined with his wildly seductive ways. But can she can resist the scoundrel's temptations herself? Check out this fourth sensual historical romance in the Sons of Sin Regency series from bestselling author Anna Campbell!

SINFULLY YOURS
by Cara Elliott

Secret passions are wont to lead a lady into trouble... The second rebellious Sloane sister gets her chance at true love in the next Hellions of High Street Regency romance from bestselling author Cara Elliott.

Fall in Love with Forever Romance

A GOOD ROGUE IS HARD TO FIND
by Kelly Bowen

The rogue's life has been good to William Somerhall, until he moves in with his mother and her paid companion, Miss Jenna Hughes. To keep the eccentric dowager duchess from ruin, he'll have to keep his friends close—and the tempting Miss Hughes closer still. Fans of Sarah MacLean and Tessa Dare will fall in love with the newest book in Kelly Bowen's Lords of Worth series!

WILD HEAT
by Lucy Monroe

The days may be cold, but the nights are red-hot in *USA Today* bestselling author Lucy Monroe's new Northern Fire contemporary romance series. Kitty Grant decides that the best way to heal her broken heart is to come back home. But she gets a shock when she sees how sexy her childhood friend Tack has become. Before she knows it, they're reigniting sparks that could set the whole state of Alaska on fire.

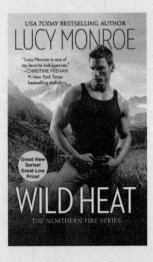

Fall in Love with Forever Romance

SUGAR ON TOP
by Marina Adair

It's about to get even sweeter in Sugar! When scandal forces Glory Mann to co-chair the Miss Sugar Peach Pageant with sexy single dad Cal MacGraw, sparks fly. Fans of Carly Phillips, Rachel Gibson, and Jill Shalvis will love the latest in the Sugar, Georgia series!

A MATCH MADE
ON MAIN STREET
by Olivia Miles

When Anna Madison's high-end restaurant is damaged by a fire, there's only one place she can cook: her sexy ex's diner kitchen. But can they both handle the heat? The second book of the Briar Creek series is "sure to warm any reader's heart" (*RT Book Reviews* on *Mistletoe on Main Street*).

Fall in Love with Forever Romance

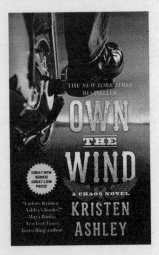

OWN THE WIND
by Kristen Ashley

Only $5.00 for a limited time! Tabitha Allen is everything Shy Cage has ever wanted, but everything he thinks he can't have. When Tabby indicates she wants more—*much* more—than friendship, he feels like the luckiest man alive. But even lucky men can crash and burn...The first book in the Chaos series from *New York Times* bestselling author Kristen Ashley!

FIRE INSIDE
by Kristen Ashley

Only $5.00 for a limited time! When Lanie Heron propositions Hop Kincaid, all she wants is one wild night with the hot-as-hell biker. She gets more than she bargained for, and it's up to Hop to convince Lanie that he's the best thing that's ever happened to her...Fans of Lori Foster and Julie Ann Walker will love this book!

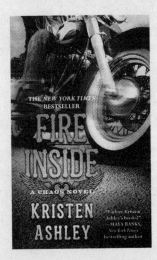